The Prodigal Prince's Seduction

Olivia Gates

He shouldn't have been so smug.

He should have known that she'd had more cards to play. And she'd played them. Played *him*. And how.

She was the woman he'd spent the most revitalising, enthralling time of his life with. The woman who'd made him forget exhaustion and every preconception about himself and what he could feel.

She whimpered at his sudden withdrawal. It had only been moments since their lips had met, before he'd learned her real name and plunged from the heights of delight to the depths of disillusion.

So what if she wasn't the woman he'd thought her to be? It should change nothing. His body was reaching critical mass. And she was offering… everything. He should drag her inside, throw her to the ground and take it all. *Then* walk away.

The Heir's Scandalous Affair
by Jennifer Lewis

"I came to New Orleans to find my late husband's son, his heir," Samantha explained. **"His name is Louis Dulac."**

"I'm Louis DuLac," said the handsome mystery man with whom she'd just shared a night of incredible passion. His features grew hard and he gazed at her through narrowed eyes.

Sam's knees almost gave out. If he hadn't been holding her wrist she might have plunged backwards down the stairs.

"But you can't be." The words fell from her lips, dazed and barely coherent. "It's impossible."

"Come in," he said. This time, it was a command rather than an invitation. He still held a firm grip on her wrist.

She felt herself struggling for breath. He tugged her towards him. "You're my late husband's…oh no." She tried to free herself.

He pulled her closer. "You're not going anywhere."

Available in May 2010
from Mills & Boon® Desire™

THE PRODIGAL PRINCE'S SEDUCTION

BY

OLIVIA GATES

THE HEIR'S SCANDALOUS AFFAIR

BY

JENNIFER LEWIS

🌹 MILLS & BOON®

First published in Great Britain 2010
Harlequin Mills & Boon Limited,
Eton House, 18-24 Paradise Road, Richmond, Surrey TW9 1SR

The publisher acknowledges the copyright holders of the
individual works as follows:

The Prodigal Prince's Seduction © Olivia Gates 2009
The Heir's Scandalous Affair © Jennifer Lewis 2009

ISBN: 978 0 263 88168 4

51-0510

Harlequin Mills & Boon policy is to use papers that are natural, renewable
and recyclable products and made from wood grown in sustainable forests.
The logging and manufacturing processes conform to the legal environmental
regulations of the country of origin.

Printed and bound in Spain
by Litografia Rosés S.A., Barcelona

THE PRODIGAL PRINCE'S SEDUCTION

BY
OLIVIA GATES

Dear Reader,

Being a romance author has got to be one of the best jobs there is. For in what other job can one experience the rush of falling in love over and over again?

And it happened again in the second instalment of THE CASTALDINI CROWN trilogy, where I fell in love with my hero, Prince Durante D'Agostino. Each hero I write is another fantastic specimen of manhood and humanity, but Prince Durante has characteristics that surprised even me as I wrote his story. Contrary to all the über alpha males I've written about, he was so open to the notion of falling in love, so wholehearted about it. He was like that massive source of romanticism and sensuality that had gone unplumbed until he laid eyes on Gabrielle Williamson and it all came pouring out.

I mean, who could resist a hero who wants to savour the torment of not touching the woman who has him on fire until he gets to know more of the "real" her, who serenades her, who actually offers the other cheek, and who eventually gives up everything to atone for the sin of not trusting her, for hurting her?

I was certainly not immune, and I hope no reader will be, either.

I hope Durante and Gabrielle's story gives you as much pleasure as it gave me while writing it.

I would love to hear your thoughts at oliviagates@oliviagates.com.

Also please visit me at www.oliviagates.com.

Thank you for reading.

Olivia Gates

Olivia Gates has always pursued creative passions – painting, singing and many handicrafts. She still does, but only one of her passions grew gratifying enough, consuming enough, to become an ongoing career: writing.

She is most fulfilled when she is creating worlds and conflicts for her characters, then exploring and untangling them bit by bit, sharing her protagonists' every heart-wrenching heartache and hope, their every heart-pounding doubt and trial, until she leads them to an indisputably earned and gloriously satisfying happy ending.

When she's not writing, she is a doctor, a wife to her own alpha male and a mother to one brilliant girl and one demanding angora cat. Visit Olivia at www.oliviagates.com.

To my husband. To my daughter.
Both of you, my one and only.
More and more, I wouldn't be doing all this
without you. Thank you for being who you are.

One

"I want one hour with you."

Prince Durante D'Agostino froze at the foyer's threshold.

That voice. Coming out of nowhere. So low he shouldn't have heard it over the live jazz music blaring its infectious energy from the ballroom where the charity function was in full swing.

He heard nothing but its softness. As if faders had been hit, boosting it, dousing every other sound. More. As if it had been generated inside his head, a caress of a thought, making all else recede from his awareness. An awareness that bristled with responses so tactile that every hair on his body rose as if he were caught in a field of static electricity.

He frowned. What was all this, over hearing a woman's voice? Over yet another blatant invitation?

A scowl seized his face as he swung around to the offending entity. And everything receded farther. Disappeared. He felt as if his blood stopped in his arteries even as everything else hurtled through him. Heat, sensations. Urges.

Eyes. From the shadows behind the foyer's door, they transfixed him. Pieces of heaven. Staring up at him from a face that was what the offspring of an angel and a siren must look like.

Then the impossible creature spoke again. "One hour. I'll pay one hundred grand for it."

His eyes dragged away from the clear skies of hers to the lips spilling that offer. Dimpled, dewy and flushed as if she'd been sucking on bloodred cherries. They were still again, slightly parted. But he could see them as they'd wrapped around each syllable of her spell, could imagine them nibbling and suckling their way down his body...

He shifted, stunned to feel himself hardening, zero to one hundred in two seconds.

Aroused? Here? From just a look and a few words?

He expanded his chest in an effort to draw in more oxygen, to drive blood to his head instead of his loins. He managed only to suck in her scent—clean, with a tinge of jasmine and a deluge of pheromones. Every cell in his body twitched, revved.

Then she stepped out of the shadows and he forgot any intentions or delusions of subduing his body.

This might not be happening anyway. He might still be in the back of his limo, dreaming this apparition as he dozed off on the way to the charity event he was sponsoring. Thirty-six sleepless hours must have taken their toll on his nervous system. It would explain *her*, the epitome of his every far-fetched fantasy. From hair the shade of fire he'd once seen in a painting and wondered if it truly existed in nature, a waterfall of silk his fingers itched to twist through, to a complexion of such clear olive that it offset the vividness of her hair and the lightness of her eyes, to features sculpted and aligned in such an unusual way that they screamed character and whispered sensuality, to curves and swells in the abundance and the distribution to answer his every specification.

But she was no figment of his overworked mind. She was real.

What was unreal was her effect on him. Women had been throwing themselves at him since he'd turned seventeen, and even then he hadn't operated on hormones. Then had come this woman.

She'd aroused everything in him just by breathing those words, by being near. Now, by just looking at him, she had his imagination flooding with images and sounds and sensations and scents, of drenched silk sheets and hot velvet limbs, of cries rising in the dark along with the aromas of arousal and satisfaction.

Was this it? The overtures of the breakdown Eduardo and Jade claimed he was teetering on? Was this surreal reaction the first crack before a chasm tore his psyche wide open? Not that he cared. If this was a breakdown, maybe it was exactly what he needed.

"I have a check right here." She fumbled inside her evening purse. "Make it out to the charity or cause of your choice."

He watched her supple hands, with those neat, short, unadorned fingernails, found himself imagining grabbing them, sucking each finger until she was begging for his lips and teeth and tongue elsewhere…everywhere.

He took a step toward her, maybe not to translate fantasy into action, but to feel her—any part of her—against him, to confirm that she—and what she evoked in him—was real.

She stumbled back. He surged forward to stop her, only to become trapped in the swarm of people who'd materialized between them.

Maledizione. He hadn't even heard them approach. Now there was nothing but the cacophony of their intrusion, the encroachment of their self-interest.

"Prince Durante! You're finally here!"

"Prince Durante, this way."

"You must come this way first, Prince Durante."

"I have someone who's dying to meet you."

"Me, too, and you'll definitely want to meet him first."

He was suddenly sorry that he'd left his bodyguards outside.

He fought the urge to signal them to disperse the throng who'd so rudely fractured the pristine intensity that had cocooned him with *her.* But they might rush to deal with the situation with inappropriate force. They'd been jumpy ever since Jeremiah Langley had stabbed him a month ago.

Apart from bellowing for everyone to get the hell away from him, he had no recourse but to let them sweep him along, watch her recede as she remained standing where she'd first intercepted him in that evening gown that could have been spun from the hues and radiance of her eyes. The last thing he saw of her before the ballroom doors closed was her arm falling to her side, the check held limply in her hand.

He buzzed his head bodyguard, muttered an order to keep track of her if she left. He couldn't risk losing her.

Only then did he start playing the evening's sponsor, burning to wrap everything up so he could do what he really wanted to do. The first thing in years that he couldn't *wait* to do. Seek her out, give her whatever she wanted and experience that eagerness and exhilaration she'd inspired in him, something he hadn't felt in…ever.

Gabrielle Williamson's eyes clung to one thing among the ebbing wave of people. The man they'd swept along, the one who towered above them all.

So *that* was Prince Durante D'Agostino.

She'd thought she knew what he looked like from endless photos in newspapers and magazines, including her own publications. She'd known nothing. Every photo had downgraded him to the man who deserved every letter of his reputation as the world's most notorious, eligible and panted-after royalty.

In reality he was a…a god.

And she'd approached him—okay, ambushed him more like—with her pathetic offer. A hundred grand felt ridiculous now. But what would an hour with a god rate?

The ballroom door closed, severing the mesmerism of those azure twin stars he had for eyes.

A tremor hit her. A second hit harder. Then a deluge broke out, until she was shaking like a rag in a storm.

What was wrong with her? She was the one who was supposed to surprise him into agreeing to give her that hour. To make a solid pitch *before* he asked questions. Especially about who she was. She'd wanted to eliminate—or at least postpone—the prejudice her name had already elicited from him. She'd wanted a fair hearing.

But seeing him in the flesh, even from the back, had almost blanked her mind. Then he'd turned, and everything had vanished.

She'd forgotten where she was, what she was supposed to say, could only stare at him. She'd moved only when the tractor beam of his will had forced her forward for his inspection. And boy, had he inspected. She'd felt…inspected down to her cellular level.

Then, those people had charged him, saved her from doing that rag-in-the-storm impression in his presence. They'd also taken him away before he'd said yes. And he'd been about to. Or she could have been imagining that, along with his surreal impact on her.

Imagining shimagining. She was a thirty-year-old divorcée who hadn't had fantasies even as a young girl. Being the only child of parents whose marriage had sunk daily into the dark realities of bankruptcy and depression hadn't been conducive to flights of fancy.

That was part of the convoluted journey that had brought her here today, on a mission to save her own company from bankruptcy, while repaying the man who'd supported her family during those desperate years. King Benedetto of Castaldini—Prince Durante's father.

After her father went bankrupt, the king, a friend and former business associate, had convinced him to move his family closer, to Sardinia, so that the king could be of more help. And he had more than helped, had continued to do so after her father's death six years later. He'd supported her and her mother and financed her education until she'd graduated from journalism school.

She'd since insisted on repaying her family's debts with interest. But while she'd needed to settle the financial debt, she'd always cling to the emotional one.

It had been because of that bond, along with what had been solid financial advice at the time, that she'd invested heavily in stocks and assets in Castaldini. It was partly why Le Roi Enterprises, her publishing company, was in trouble now. The kingdom had been hit by a steep recession after the king's stroke six months ago.

His condition had been hushed up until his recovery hadn't conformed to his doctors' optimism. His grim prognosis had leaked out, and Castaldini's stock market had crashed like a meteor.

He'd called her a couple of weeks ago, requesting a video meeting. He'd said he had a solution to all her problems. She remembered that call…

She'd waited for the meeting to start, contemplating how to turn down his offer of more help. It was one thing to settle her father's debts and see to their household upkeep, but another to float a company with multinational subsidiaries. She didn't think he could afford anything of this magnitude now. And she couldn't be so deeply indebted again, even to him. She'd been so driven to repay her family's debt that she'd done something as crazy as marry Ed. But…could she afford to turn down help, when hundreds of people depended on her for their jobs?

Then a stranger came onto the screen. It was several dropped heartbeats before she realized it was the king. The incredibly fit and virile seventy-four-year-old man she'd last seen seven months ago at her mother's funeral had metamorphosed into an emaciated, hundred-year-old version of himself.

Tears surged behind her eyes, at seeing him like that, at the acrid thankfulness that her mother's illness had been quick and merciless so that she hadn't suffered his fate, hadn't lasted long enough to see her beauty almost mummified.

"It's good to see you, *figlia mia*."

The wan rasp that used to be the surest baritone forced a tear to escape her control. She wiped it away, pretending to sweep her hair back. "I-it's good to see you, too, King Benedetto."

His smile was resigned, conciliatory. "No need to tiptoe around me, Gaby. I know that seeing me must be a shock for you. But I had to speak to you face-to-face as I ask you this incalculable favor."

He was asking, not offering, a favor? She didn't see how that could solve her problems, but the very idea of being of service to him infused her with energy and purpose.

"Anything, King Benedetto. Ask me anything."

"You once wanted to approach Durante with a book offer."

She frowned, nodded. She'd asked him how best to approach his elusive son with an offer for a motivational biography, when the enigmatic media-magnet had turned down every offer to publish anything about his life. The king had told her to forget it.

That had been before her mother's death and she'd since forgotten about it, along with every plan she'd had, lacking the drive to pursue anything new that required focus and determination. Her grief was dulling to a pervasive, crippling coldness, and there was nothing and no one to ameliorate it.

She'd made no friends since she'd returned to New York, seemed to have made only enemies. She had colleagues and employees, was on good terms with most, but she hadn't forged a real closeness to any of them. Her uncles and their families lived states or continents away and she'd never been close to them anyway. From the men who hunted her for the fortune they thought she'd inherited and the one she'd acquired, to the disaster of her marriage, to the disappointment of her attempts to wash away its ugliness in other men's arms, to the women who treated her like a succubus who'd drain their men of life, it felt as if she'd lost one bond to the world after another. Her mother's death had cracked the last link. *Why bother?* was the one thought left echoing inside her.

Only the employees who'd lose their jobs and the causes she'd be unable to contribute to if she threw in the towel had kept her going, just enough to keep her head above water.

"I feel responsible for your company's problems."

The king's rasp dragged her back to the moment. She blinked.

"Please, don't, King Benedetto. It's not your fault."

She bit her lip on much more. Her company's decline had started with the discovery of her mother's terminal illness, and its slow death had begun when a part of her had died with her mother, a part she didn't know how to resuscitate, didn't feel like trying. Castaldini's recession had just been the last straw.

But she could see how he'd think that, because she wasn't alone in her decline. Many smaller corporations heavily invested in Castaldinian stock were floundering. Even though the new regent, Prince Leandro D'Agostino, had stepped in and floated the economy, the original hit had been bad. She'd heard that Leandro would work his way down to companies at the level of hers, but doubted her company could last until he did. And then, even with his power and financial clout, as regent only, he didn't promise the market the long-term stability a king would. Advisors had urged her not to await rescue, said Leando might even let lesser interests go under to stabilize the big picture.

The king went on. "Durante could revive your company, either with a bestseller or in other ways if he so wished."

That was what her advisors had said. That only a guaranteed bestseller or a merger with any major player would buoy her company. Prince Durante would have answered both criteria. But previously, the king had said Durante wasn't an option. Which meant… "So he'd be amenable to an offer now?"

"I'm not saying he would be."

That stymied her. "Then what has changed?"

"Your situation. And mine."

She didn't understand what her situation had to do with h_
only that he thought a positive result might be obtained now. She
should jump at the opening. Yet she wanted to do nothing but
say goodbye and sit staring into space. It seemed that her lethargy
wasn't about to let her challenge-tackling abilities escape its
somnolent grip. She sighed. "I'll give it some more thought—"

"I'm *asking* you to do it, Gaby." The king interrupted her.
"And I don't just want you to sign a contract with him. I want
you to insist on being his editor or ghostwriter or however you
get such books written. I want you to work as closely as
possible with him so that you can convince him to come back
to Castaldini." Gabrielle adjusted the screen, as if that would
help his words make sense. He elaborated, ending her confusion. "He left five years ago, saying he'll never return as long
as I live. And he's kept his promise. He didn't even call when
I had my stroke."

Something trickled through the clotted mass of indifference
inside her. Emotions. Surprise, indignation…anger.

What kind of monster would do that to his father, and a great
man like King Benedetto, too? And to think Durante had been
the one she'd admired most among all Castaldinian princes, his
self-made success intriguing her far more because it didn't
have the crown as its goal. As the king's son, Durante was the
one prince who was ineligible for the crown. And then, *success*
didn't describe what he'd achieved. He'd become one of the
world's richest, most powerful men, starting with investment
banking, then branching into just about everything, garnering
a worldwide reputation for being unstoppable, as well as inaccessible. But it was one thing to reject intimacy as evidenced
by his misanthrope/heartbreaker reputation, another to reject
the man who was his father and king.

"Why all this…antipathy?" she asked.

"Durante blames me for terrible things, things I haven't been able to prove I wasn't responsible for." Okay. So it was more complicated than she could imagine. She really couldn't form an opinion here. She shouldn't. It had nothing to do with her. And she wanted it to stay that way. "But it doesn't matter what he believes. He must come back, Gaby. It's not only that I need my son—Castaldini needs his power and influence."

Scratch the no-opinion status. No matter Durante's reasons, he was a callous creep if he not only didn't care about his father's incapacitation but also about Castaldini's troubles. And *she* was supposed to make him care?

She asked that, and the king nodded. "I know you can. You'll come in with a fresh slate and views, with legitimate business offers and concerns. But give me your word that you'll never tell him of our connection. That would make him send you straight to hell. And none of us can afford that. The situation is grave, and I must be clear. I want you to do *anything* to make him come back."

His words had echoed long after their goodbyes. What he'd meant by *anything* was so glaringly clear, it was blinding. Seduction.

She was resigned to her femme fatale reputation. But it hurt that even the king thought seduction was one of her weapons, her only one, even. Still, she excused him. He was old and sick and desperate to resolve his problems, to secure his kingdom's future.

And then, what he'd proposed *was* a worthy cause. If she succeeded—seduction certainly *not* on the menu of maneuvers she'd use—everyone would come out a winner. The king would have his son back—a reconciliation that was bound to make said son happier, too—Castaldini would get a heavy-hitter to help its regent pull its fat out of the fire, and she'd stabilize her company.

But the damned prince hadn't even acknowledged her messages. She could think of only one reason. His initial background check on anyone who approached him must have accessed the usual slander. Seemed he'd thought such unsubstantiated filth enough to condemn her.

Furious, she'd called in a favor with one of his insiders and gotten his schedule for the next week. Besides being impossible to get hold of, he was also known for badgering the privileged into doing more for the world. This function was one of his traps where he wrung what he could get out of them for his favorite causes. She'd intended to intercept him, make him an offer he couldn't refuse. At least, that had been the plan.

So far, all she'd done was stammer three sentences and got nothing out of him but that disconcerting stare.

She needed results, but she had to restart her own volition first. Or at least the autopilot that had steered her for months now.

One or the other must have kicked in, because she moved at last.

She leaned on the door as she opened it. The exuberance of jazz and the forced gaiety in the overcrowded ballroom slammed into her. But what almost knocked her off her feet was the power of his gaze. He'd been watching for her, as if certain she'd follow him.

Not that she could. Those people who had the same idea as her—of ambushing him here—left her no chink to get through.

He left her no air to breathe as his gaze drilled into her across the ballroom. She began to think it might not be a bad thing after all if she didn't get a chance to talk to him alone.

She was a seasoned businesswoman who'd been through a battlefield of a marriage and divorce, who'd before and since been pursued by men, had thought she'd seen and tried all kinds, to her crushing dissatisfaction. But Prince D'Agostino fell far outside what she'd thought to be her inclusive experience. To lump him under "man" with those she'd had experience with was as accurate as lumping a top-of-the-food-chain predator with a jellyfish. Something very sure of itself told her she shouldn't get closer. For any reason.

She should leave. Now.

She had to pry her gaze—her will—from his first.

Somehow she did, was at the door when a rough velvet whisper hit her between the shoulder blades. "Don't run off yet."

Logic said that omnidirectional/internal sound effect was the surround system's doing. But there was no logic here. There was only the influence the voice exercised, the reactions it ignited. The certainty that it was talking to her.

She swayed around, found him on the dais in front of the mic, his gaze still cast on her like a stasis field.

"Ladies and gentlemen," he said. "Thank you for paying the ten-grand admission fee. But because you're getting…restless, I'll fast-forward to prying some *real* contributions out of you. You have the auction list, but in light of a certain…development, I have made some changes. Now the first item on auction is… myself."

Two

If Prince Durante D'Agostino had announced he was Superman and launched into the air to circle overhead, there wouldn't have been a more drastic reaction to his announcement.

Not that it would have shocked her. He did look like some superhuman being as he dominated the scene just by standing there, the rugged nobleness of his features and his leonine forehead accentuated by the swept-back mane of raven satin, the jacket of his sculpted designer charcoal suit casually pushed back by the hand resting on his hip, his white shirt stretching across his torso, detailing the daunting power beneath. He looked like a modern god swathed in the trappings of the times that equalized other men but that didn't begin to contain the influence he exuded, to disguise his in-his-own-league nature.

His gaze panned the ballroom yet somehow managed not to release hers. That alone kept her heart practically dropping to the polished Carrara marble floor. But what restarted her tremors was what she saw in those eyes—an intensity untouched by the cynical amusement with which he watched the mayhem he'd kicked up.

"Before you get too excited," he finally said. "I'm not auctioning off all of me, just my ear. Considering how in demand it is, with so many of you attempting to talk it off, I'm offering one hour of its exclusive use." His lips tugged into what had to be the most arrhythmia-inducing weapon ever deployed on susceptible females. And it had her in its crosshairs. "I already have an opening bid. One hundred grand."

Now she knew how *mamma mia* had been coined. It had to have been a woman who'd first exclaimed it, as a brutally gorgeous male plucked her strings.

And she did feel like a marionette, compelled to obey his every tug, any reluctance or misgiving evaporating in the excitement his mischief sent through her. She walked back under the pull of his challenge.

When she stopped at the fringe of the bidding crowd, he put his lips to the mic, implanted hot, wild images and sensations straight inside her, pitched his voice an octave lower. "Do I hear one hundred ten?"

Over three-dozen people, mostly women, raised their hands. She'd beaten them all in speed of response.

His lips spread in satisfaction, his pose grew more languid, a conqueror certain of his victory, indulgent in his triumph. "Thank you. Do I hear one hundred twenty?"

Her hand was up in the air before she could will it to be there. Seemed he'd jumpstarted her competitiveness. More. He'd sparked the first sign of life in her since she'd witnessed her mother's being extinguished.

He kept raising the bid, and her competition dwindled. Soon suspense was fast reaching the point of overload.

When a dozen hands still shot up in the air when he reached the four hundred fifty grand mark, her stamina snapped and recoiled like an overextended string.

She blurted out, "I bid one million."

A hush fell. Everyone turned to gape at her.

He straightened, his eyes losing all lightness, singeing hers through the charge that filled the space between them. "Now that's a nice round figure. Anyone willing to top that? No? Fine, then. I have one million from the lady in blue. Going once, going twice—"

"I bid *ten* million."

Durante saw shock seize his mystery woman's face before he registered the words that had caused it. Only then did he drag his eyes and senses from her and search out the new speaker.

His every muscle tensed. How had *he* gotten past security? How had Durante not noticed him before?

His security had messed up. As for him, all his faculties had been converged on *her,* everything else skimming his consciousness without leaving an imprint.

And there was the now-gaunt, wild-eyed Jeremiah Langley. Staring at him like a drowning man would at a lifeboat. A month ago he'd looked at Durante as if at his own killer, before attempting to stab him. Durante couldn't imagine how Langley had ended up blaming him—and not the investments he'd made against his advice—for his bankruptcy, but he'd hushed everything up, not wishing to add criminal charges to the distraught man's troubles. He'd also postponed announcing Langley's bankruptcy until he sold shares that would leave the man with minimal debt. But he'd made it clear to Langley, and to his security—he didn't want to see the man again. Not in this lifetime.

No one knew how things stood between them, or that Jeremiah didn't have the ten million he'd bid for Durante's leniency. He couldn't call Langley on it without outing him. Langley had cornered him into accepting his so-called bid as the winning one.

And *that* was his worst crime.

She had already accepted defeat. This time, she *was* walking away. He might not have more of her. Not tonight. Unacceptable.

He would have more of her. And if he had his way, as he always did, he would have all of her.

Gabrielle felt all animation drain from her system.

The moment her bid had burst from her incontinent mouth, she'd launched into feverish calculations to determine how she could part with that much cash in one lump sum in her current situation. Then that ten-million-dollar sledgehammer had fallen, pulverizing both worry and hope.

So that was it. She'd bid and lost. And he was no longer looking at her. Ten million dollars would distract even him.

So what was that tightening behind her ribs? Disappointment?

How stupid was that? This scheme wouldn't have worked anyway. She didn't know how she or King Benedetto could have thought it might. All her moronic endeavor would achieve was to give the scandal sheets fuel for the coming decade. She had to leave before the paparazzi he'd banned from the event got wind of this and ambushed her. *Leave. Now. And don't look back.*

She managed that, but still felt as if she were wading through quicksand. His gaze had latched on to her again, robbed her of dominion over her own body. Desperation to get away kicked in.

In minutes she was in the parking lot, running to her car.

She remote-opened her door, was reaching for its handle when a boom cracked the silence of the night.

"Stay."

She dropped her keys. Her purse. Probably a few months' to a couple of years' life expectancy, too.

She slumped against the warm metal and glass as if pressed there by the presence closing in on her. She heard nothing but the blood thundering in her head. The presence expanded at her back, pinning her to her support, squeezing her heart.

She fumbled for the door handle. She'd managed to open the door when that voice hit her again, a quiet rumble this time.

"Stay."

She clenched her eyes shut, pitched forward, her nerveless weight closing the door with a muffled thud. That one word.

An invocation. Deeper and darker than the moonless night.

She turned around, leaning on the car. And there he was.

The good news was that he kept a dozen feet between them. The bad news was that it made no difference. And why should it? He'd been dozens of feet away in that ballroom and had still overwhelmed her.

"*Stay?*" Where was her voice? She'd addressed him before in a breathless whisper. This time it was a husky rasp. Both were nothing like her usual crisp tones. "What am I? Your poodle? What's next? Roll over? Beg…?" She winced, stopped. Where were her brakes?

"How about 'stop,'" he drawled. "Before you inflame my already-raging imagination beyond control."

His voice wasn't the same as what had flowed from the sound system earlier. It was so much more layered and modulated and hard-hitting, the prominent r's of his accent far more intoxicating. Hearing it without distortion delayed her comprehension of his words. Then it hit her and she almost went up in a puff of mortification.

She couldn't *believe* she'd said something so provocative, just begging for misinterpretation. He'd never believe she hadn't meant anything beyond sarcasm.

But wonder of wonders, his eyes weren't stained with that knowing derision she was used to from men. His emitted only pure excitement. "Would 'stop' be less open to unfavorable interpretation? How about 'don't leave'?"

His voice sluiced another rush of heat over her. She quivered. "Still orders, both of them."

He tilted his head. Light ignited the azure depths of his eyes and carved dimples in his sculpted cheeks. "At least they don't have canine connotations, if my idiomatic English serves."

And she did something she'd thought was beyond her, now and forever. She giggled. *Giggled.*

His eyes widened as if she'd electrified him. He retaliated with something far more debilitating than electricity. He chuckled.

She struggled not to melt into the ground. "You're pleading less-than-perfect English skills to explain the inappropriateness of barking 'stay' at me across the parking lot like that?"

"Barking? Still going with the dog motif, eh?"

"You did bark," she mumbled in embarrassment. "You frightened me out of my skin. I think it's still pooled on the ground."

His eyes swept down her body, until she felt it was her dress that lay at her feet. "From where I'm standing, your skin is still enveloping you like a glove and, propriety notwithstanding, you can see what the sight does to me."

More heat splashed through her as she fixed her gaze on his so it wouldn't stray to "see" anything. "See? Perfect English skills."

"I'm sure my English tutor would love to hear that the ulcer he swore I gave him has ultimately been validated."

"You gave your teacher hell? You're pulling my leg."

"Again, do watch what you say to me, or I might succumb and tell you exactly how and where I want to pull both your legs."

Images slammed into her. Vivid, tangible. Those large, perfectly formed hands dragging her by the thighs, opening her around his bulk as he bore down on her…

"I've changed my verdict," she choked. "Your English skills are not perfect. They're horrible. Evil. *Sietto un uomo cattivo.*"

Suddenly the sounds of the night were amplified in the stillness that echoed between them. Whoever had said one could drown in another's eyes must have been describing Prince Durante's endless azure seas and the submersion of their focus.

Just as she felt her lungs using up the last tendril of oxygen, he exhaled. *"Mia bella misteriosa…parlate italiano?"*

She realized she'd said he was a wicked man in Italian. It had once come to her as unconsciously as English did. She used to talk and think in an inextricable mix, a habit that had faded since she'd returned to the States. This was the first time in many years that she'd reverted to the second-nature practice. It felt as if a missing part of her had clicked back into place.

Then more registered. He'd called her his mysterious beauty, asked if she spoke Italian.

"I lived in Sardinia and Italy from age five until I returned to the States to enter college at seventeen."

These revelations were way beyond the simple *yes* his question warranted. But he made her want to do unknown things. Flirt, tease. Confide. It had to be the premium royal testosterone overexposure.

After a long moment when he looked at her as if at a gem with a thousand facets, he breathed, "*Dio Santo,* what are you?"

"What…? Uh, yeah, I haven't exactly introduced myself yet."

"No, you haven't. Exactly or otherwise."

"Umm…yeah, there's sort of a reason I haven't. You see, I'm—"

"You are *mia bella misteriosa,* who's done what no woman has ever done—offered money to spend time with me."

"Now *that* I find impossible to believe. I bet women offer anything and everything for time with you. I bet most wouldn't mind if it wasn't even one-on-one."

"You think so? Because of who I am?" Her gaze wavered with uncertainty. He elaborated. "Rich and royal?"

Her laugh morphed into a snort that would have made a sailor proud. "Are you kidding? Or are you fishing? Women would throw themselves at you if you were a penniless nobody."

His eyes flared. "Coming from anybody else, I'd think that a worthless exaggeration, but from you, I know it's how you see me. For it's how I see you, too. As for the one-on-one basis, that is the only way I would accept to have time with you."

A moan of stimulation stumbled over her croak of embarrassment.

Hell, the man was reducing her to a pubescent state. But he was doing something even worse.

He was obliterating the distance between them.

Mesmerized, she took in the control and power that permeated his every move, the breadth of shoulders and chest that owed nothing to padding, the sparseness of waist and hips, the hardness of thighs rippling beneath exquisite fabric as he prowled toward her, a majestic creature by birthright and by merit. Now *this* was a man to make her revise her stance on swearing off men forever, a pledge she'd made happily years ago.

Which was a crazy thing to think.

Crazier would be to act on such insanity.

She stood there waiting for him to reach her with the same fatalism she'd watch a collision in progress, could think only that no man had ever looked at her like this. As if she was something incredibly unexpected, and unexpectedly incredible. The wonder in his eyes drowned out the urgent voices that yelled that his damage potential would far surpass the devastation caused by any such collision.

Every step closer to his mystery woman solidified into fact what Durante had sensed from the first moment he saw her.

This was new. Surprising and stimulating. When he'd been certain nothing and no one would ever surprise or stimulate him. She did both, and far more, with every breath.

Her effect on him was so unprecedented that he'd done the unprecedented. He'd delegated running the rest of the charity function to his deputy. And he'd sent his bodyguards away, forbade them to follow him. He wanted to be alone with her at any price.

Her face tilted up as he approached. Beams from the nearest streetlight embraced it in a swathe of highlights and shadows. Her tresses billowed in the night breeze like undulating flames.

Contradictory compulsions wrenched at each other inside him. The need to capture, conquer, and the urge to savor, slow down.

The second impulse won out, forced his feet to stop before they took him all the way pressing her against her car.

He was close enough to reach out and run his fingers through that blazing cascade of hair. He didn't. Somehow. He drew deep of her scent instead, let it permeate him, before he let it escape on a grudging exhalation. "So…you bid one million dollars for an hour with me."

Her shoulders jerked on a dejected shrug. "Yeah. And for the record, I would have doubled the winning bid if I could have."

He inhaled sharply. "You think I'm worth that much?"

"I think you're worth every dollar of your billions."

He bit into his lip. It was either that or drag her to him and bite into hers. As he would. Just not yet. What flowed between them deserved the reward of leisure and thoroughness. But holding back was a punishment, too. One her every word made harder to take. He was used to flattery, could sense falseness and self-interest even in trace quantities. He detected only sincerity from her. Alien urges swamped him, to punch the air, to thump his chest.

He shoved his hands into his pockets so they wouldn't find their way around her. "I do have more hours available apart from the one that other bidder won, you know?"

"Oh. *Oh.* You mean…?"

The surge of hope on her face made him fist his hands in his pockets, emphasizing his—problem. It was either that or snatch them out and pounce on her. "I mean, if you're still interested, I'll take that million-dollar check."

"If?" She coughed. Her eyes tore from his, slammed around, the dazed excitement in them tingling through him on a path that connected his fingertips to his scalp, his loins to his toes. Her gaze settled at her feet. "*There* it is." She dropped down in a crouch, pooling her flowing taffeta skirt on the ground, making her look like a gigantic flower as she retrieved the matching evening bag. She jerked back up, not lingering to look up at him from that position, to milk it for all the sensual promise it could yield.

She didn't need any of that. She needed only to breathe— to be—to exercise maximum effect on him. But it pleased him beyond measure that she didn't operate that way.

She fumbled with her bag, produced her checkbook. He watched as she scribbled furiously with even, beautiful print. Then she tore out the check, extended it to him. "Fill in the beneficiary."

He took it, folded and placed it in his outer pocket before he reached into his inner one, produced his own checkbook and pen.

In a minute he tore a check out, handed it to her. "*I'm* bidding *two* million. Add to that whatever amount you see fit, fill in the total and make it out to whomever you like."

Her movement to take the check felt like a reflex. She didn't look at it, remained gaping at him. "What's this for?"

"The two million is my bid for the time we've had together so far. The amount you'll specify is for the rest of the evening."

"The *whole* evening?"

"And the night."

"The *night?*"

Durante's lips twitched. Her squeaks would have amused him if they weren't pouring fuel on his inflamed senses. She really hadn't thought it a possibility he'd offer this. "If you wish it."

Her blush intensified until she seemed to smolder in the night. And he saw it in his mind's eye in high-definition clarity, himself carrying her to the nearest flat surface to ravish her for that hour she'd bid on, before sweeping her away from the world to do so again for several nights on end.

It was all so surreal he felt he was dreaming it. Yet it was so real it abraded him with its intensity and immediacy. He'd never experienced such a state of distressed arousal. And for him to be in this condition just by looking, imagining… Unbelievable.

At last she spluttered, "Uh…isn't this a bit…you know…?"

He inclined his head. "Too fast? Too soon? You think so?"

A moan-giggle escaped her, another blow to his restraint. "If you think I can think right now, think again."

"Exactly. This isn't about thinking. This is about feeling. About knowing. I know what you make me feel. You made me feel it from the first moment. I wanted more than an hour with you. I want this night, *bellissima,* and as many more as you'll give me."

"That's assuming you'll want more nights after the first…" Her face scrunched into a wince. "Okay, excuse me as I give swallowing my tongue a serious shot."

"With me around to do it? What a waste that would be. And why would you even want to try?"

"Because it sounded as if I was agreeing to share this night with you and was trying to make sure it wouldn't be the one and only."

Every word out of her mouth… He pressed the heel of his palm to his breastbone, as if that would quell the itching behind it. "And you didn't mean that?"

"God, no, I-I…" She threw both hands over her face, before looking up at him, helplessness and accusation filling her expression. "It's your fault. Exposure to you is turning my gray matter into day-old milkshake."

A laugh tore out of him, drove his head back with the force of its unexpectedness and power. "Turnabout is fair play. Although you turn mine into the boiling version." He reduced the distance between them another step, testing his stamina, thrilling to the torture of balancing on the edge of loss of control. "And I will want more nights. As many as I can have. I hope you won't hold back to observe an 'appropriate' period before indulging in intimacy. I want nothing more than to end this night with you in my arms, in my bed."

She melted back against her car. "And I want nothing more than to end this night in both."

Gabrielle watched Durante's eyes flare at her admission, knew he'd reach for her. She had to say the rest now. *Now.*

"But I can't."

The flare subsided, ice putting out the blue-hot flames.

Something twisted beneath her ribs. She couldn't bear to see disappointment replacing exhilaration in his eyes.

She hurtled on. "Believe it or not, I did approach you with business and only business in mind."

Relief swamped her when his eyes simmered again. "I believe you. But it ceased to be business the moment you laid eyes on me."

She didn't even think of denying the fact. "Yes." She still had to qualify it. "But I can't afford to let it be that way—"

He cut across her unsteady words. "You can't afford to let it be any other way. Business will be taken care of in due time. But I'm not postponing this for anything else's sake."

"But what *is* this?"

"Something unknown to either of us, something unprecedented. And you know it as well as I do."

Gabrielle stared at him. He kept stunning her. But what most amazed her was that she picked up no malice from him, that malignant triumph most men transmitted when women made the mistake of not only falling for them, but admitting it, too.

Not him. She felt he was above pettiness and double standards. This was also no line that he gave every desirable woman he met. In fact, his ruthlessness likely originated from his never instigating the pursuit. He was renowned for his detachment.

There was nothing detached about him now. She just knew he was being swept along the same unstoppable current as she was.

That didn't mean she could let herself be swept. There was far more at stake than the elapsing of "an appropriate period before indulging in intimacies." And not only couldn't she tell him what, but that this was happening at all made her feel she'd fallen flat on her face into someone else's life. Men like him—and there *were* no men like him—didn't appear in hers.

She looked up at him, at once pleading for him to understand her chaos and afraid he'd shimmer and disappear. "Whatever this unknown and unprecedented thing is, and no matter how I feel about it or how right it feels to feel this way, I'm still totally weirded out by the detour everything has taken. Hours ago I didn't dream…"

"…you'd see me and the world would cease to matter."

His confidence sent her explanations scattering. "Oh, quit making it harder for me to make sense. The world might have ceased to matter, but it didn't cease to exist. I had this proposal memorized and now I barely remember what it was all about."

"I barely remember why I came here tonight, too. I don't care about anything now beyond you."

"Maybe if you hear my proposal, you'll change your mind."

"I won't. Not even if you're coming to me with the patent for an eternal-youth or super-power serum."

"Actually, I was thinking along opposite lines. That you'd be so opposed to my offer, you'd drop *me*."

"So it's something you think I'm liable to turn down flat? Is that why you were trying to sweeten me with the hundred grand? Is there something dark and controversial about you, *mia ragazzaccia?*"

The way he said *"my bad girl"* quickened her melting rate. "Oh, I wish. Okay, really, I don't. I'm pretty grateful there's nothing so…interesting about me. I'm just—"

"The woman I want to know everything about. And to that end, I want to conduct an experiment."

She blinked. "An experiment?" She stopped. "God, I keep repeating things. I might start asking for crackers next." His smile widened, blinding her with a flash of charisma. She groaned. "So, what's this experiment? What are you out to prove?"

"That you were onto something great when you approached me without revealing your identity and purpose. The labels might have interfered with our impact on each other. I don't think your name or your business will shed any light on who you really are. I want to know *you*. What you are, what makes you tick, what shaped you, what you want and why and how you want it. I want to revel in what we have blazing between us, to enjoy us, man to woman. For tonight."

Another breaker of reaction shuddered through her. "Are you for real, or am I dreaming you up?"

The heat of his smile became almost unbearable. "I take it you agree to participate in my experiment."

She shook her head. "That experiment is skewed and the results are bound to be unreliable. *I* know exactly who *you* are."

"You only think you do. But what do you know? My statistics? My reputation, status and estimated fortune? Sterile facts mixed with conjectures and financial data. Did knowing any of the above prepare you for the effect I have on you in the flesh?"

She raised her hands begging for respite. "Okay. I admit the 'labels' conjured up a man who, while impressive, has nothing to do with the flesh-and-blood reality of you. In fact, I'm having a tough time connecting you at all to that man."

"You see? If you can't access your preconceived ideas about me, we're on a level playing field. Say yes, *bellissima*."

"Now I know why you've soared so high. You're relentless."

"That's your expert opinion as a fellow unstoppable force?"

"Hah, I wish. Or again, not really. Okay. On one condition."

"Anything."

She exhaled a tremulous chuckle. "Not very businessman-like of you, all these carte-blanche concessions."

"I'm not a businessman now. I'm just a man who knows

you're the woman to whom only carte-blanche concessions will do justice."

"God, stop with the impossible-to-live-up-to stuff."

"You've already lived up to all of it by making me feel this way, think this way. So, what's your condition?"

"That you give me back my check."

He didn't hesitate, not in expression, not in action. He produced her check as the words left her lips. Delight fizzed in her blood. He hadn't paused to ponder her intention, trusted that whatever it was, there was nothing underhanded about it.

Her hand trembled as she extended his back to him. "Here's yours. Now I don't owe you untold millions."

He didn't reach for it. "Keep it, *bellissima*. You wouldn't owe me a cent. That's for the causes of your choice."

"Oh, I would owe you. I wanted to make a donation through you, while gaining something for myself. But if I take your check, I would be 'donating' *your* money. So, you donate what you wish and I'll do the same and let's take money out of the equation, start this on a real equal footing."

He took the check. "I'll just keep it until you wish to donate something you can't afford. Now, shall we?"

Her heart began to race her. "Shall we…what exactly?"

"Spend the rest of the evening together. As for the night…I won't push for anything you can't wait to…donate."

Three

Durante leaned back against the railing of his yacht, almost tasting the beauty of his *bellissima* an arm's reach away.

She stood on the first rung, holding on to the railing, arching into the wind, framed against the lit-up Manhattan skyline they were sailing parallel to.

They'd just left port. There was no moon, but stars hung like tiny beacons above her, and beams of light from the yacht's interior stroked her back in gold, flaring fire through the tresses that billowed behind her as if they were powered by her vitality.

Up until a moment ago, he'd kept catching himself bating his breath. He realized why.

Subconsciously, he'd been waiting for something to kick in, that cynicism that had always been an integral part of him. On some level, he expected to be slammed back to a reality that had nothing to do with this state of affinity. Experience—his and others'—kept trying to intrude with warnings that interaction always doused the testosterone-generated spark.

But then, his pleasure in being near her wasn't just about anticipating the pleasures of bedding her, being inside her. He thrilled to her every gesture and glance. Her every word engaged his demanding sense of the absurd, fueled his eagerness for repartee. He'd wondered if the uncontainable drive to possess her painted his reactions to the rest of her in such intensity, or if it was the other way around.

Now he knew. The amalgam that was her was inextricable to his senses, his mind. Physically and mentally, she was a woman the likes of which he'd never dreamed of encountering.

The thrill of their encounter had been escalating, and he'd gladly succumbed to that unprecedented rapport, reveled in the overpowering attraction. And he hadn't even touched her yet.

"This is magic."

He hardened more at her huskily voiced wonder just as he softened, too, inside. "*Si, ciò è magica, bellissima.* You are."

She swung toward him, a smile frolicking across her lips, her eyes glittering with awareness and delight. There was also a touch of mischief. But the emotion that made him struggle not to crush her in his arms was the hint of hesitation—trepidation, even.

Could it be she was wary of him?

No. He knew she trusted him just as instinctively as he did her. So why was she uneasy? Did she suspect that this couldn't be real? That it would end? He didn't share that worry. Not anymore. He couldn't tell her not to worry, but he would show her she had no need to.

She took one hand off the rail, swept her arm in a graceful arc, eloquently encompassing their surroundings. "I meant this. This perfect night, on this enchanting yacht as it sails through the placid ink of the river."

"But take your magic—ours—out of the equation and it would be just another yacht cruise on another pleasant evening."

She sighed, a sound of contentment. "You must be right.

I've been on night cruises before, in great weather. Felt nothing like this."

Before he could revel in her admission, Giancarlo, his all-around right-hand man, caught his eye in the distance.

Durante inclined his head at her. "Are you ready to eat?"

She jumped down from the railing. "I'm ready to dive into the river and catch fish in my teeth."

"Why didn't you say you were hungry?"

She seemed taken aback. "I didn't realize I was."

"I didn't, either. Other hungers overshadowed it."

Delight swelled in his chest at the guilelessness, the unhesitating consent of her gaze and nod.

He wanted to forget his resolve to delay their gratification, knew she wouldn't stop him if he did. But holding back, while chafing, was more gratifying than anything he'd ever done. He gestured for her to precede him, exhilaration shooting through him. She gave a choked laugh and almost skipped ahead.

As they traversed the massive deck to the dining hall, she exclaimed, "Is that *another* swimming pool, under that plexi roof? There was a huge one on the second-level deck."

"Yes, that's the covered one. I'll take you around after I've fed you. You can take a dip in either. I can't offer you something to wear, but you'll be draped in night and wrapped in water, their silk caressing yours unhindered by barriers."

She sped ahead as if to escape his suggestion, muttering, "I'll take a dip-check, thanks."

He chuckled, pointed out another section. "This is where the whirlpools, saunas and Turkish bath are." He pointed to another area. "And *there* are the only modern additions to the yacht's outfitting—a fitness room and comprehensive water sports equipment storage. We can windsurf, water-ski, jet-ski, scuba dive and sail, if you're into any of those."

"I'm into them *all*. I was raised on a Mediterranean island, too, remember? In my opinion, water sports are the ultimate freedom a human being can enjoy. It's been too long since I've had the pleasure."

"You'll never again be deprived of your freedoms and pleasures, *bellissima*. This yacht and all its facilities are at your disposal to enjoy whenever and however you please."

Her eyes glowed up at him with that light that seemed to shine from inside her. "That's too generous, but I can't—"

"It isn't, and you can and will accept. Say, 'Yes, Durante. I'll do you the honor of considering your yacht my own.'"

Her grimace was at once teasing and moved. "You have the rest of your life to wait? That's how long it will be before I say something like that." He opened his mouth to override her and she rushed to add, "But if your offer stands after tonight, I will take advantage of one or two weekends' windsurfing or jet-skiing."

She still didn't believe this was going to last beyond tonight. He'd have to convince her by action, not words. So he said nothing for now, just smiled down at her.

They were crossing the foyer of the uppermost deck when she turned to him. "When you said 'yacht,' I thought, 'yacht.' Then, when I became certain this floating fortress is where we were headed, I wanted to ask just how you define the word."

His lips twisted. "Yacht-obsessed magazines define this one as the ninth largest private boat in the world. From my specs, it's four hundred feet long with twelve suites of more than six hundred square feet each, not counting the thousand-square-foot master suite. There is also more than eighty thousand square feet of covered and open space."

"Whoa. It's beyond anything I've ever seen and I've been to some exorbitant places. Just this staircase is mind-boggling. I tried to count the steps and got lost."

"Now I feel guilty that I had you climb all one hundred and twenty steps. I should have carried you."

"When I run up to my tenth-floor apartment for exercise? I pick my teeth with a hundred steps." His admiring gaze devoured the results of her hard work. Her constant blush deepened. "This endless balustrade looks like it's made of one piece of solid brass. Which it can't be. Care to explain how it came into being?"

He grinned at her attempt to swerve to safer topics. "It *was* hand-beaten from solid brass by twenty top metal craftsmen who re-created it from remnants of the original balustrade."

She whistled as he seated her at the table that had been set for them. He signaled for Giancarlo to serve dinner right away.

Her eyes panned the huge chamber, lingering on the heavily gilded and embossed wall paneling and the intricately carved and adorned Baroque- and Ottoman-style furniture.

"Everything is so…ornate." She turned to him, her eyes reflecting the flickering candles, that intelligence simmering in her ponderous look. "I somehow didn't think you'd go for something so humongous and elaborate."

"You mean pretentious and gaudy, don't you?"

She didn't seem to give denial a moment's thought. "It is mighty pretentious, though I guess it stops a step shy of gaudy."

He guffawed, loving this. "Everyone I bring on board bursts into raptures extolling my extreme taste. Not you, though."

The look of absolute horror on her face was priceless. "*Maledizione…spiacente…*I'm sorry…" She groaned. "God… I'm so rude."

"You're *candid*. And it goes straight to my head. You're also right. There's nothing here that appeals to me, either. But this yacht was my mother's. It was her father's gift to her on her marriage. He was flaunting his wealth, wanting to prove he was on par with the king his daughter married. He named the boat *La Regina del Mare,* to underline my mother's new royal status. He also wished her to keep the Boccanegra family name and old-world nobility in the minds and envies of the jet-set, the new world's aristocracy. But she had no interest in that and sent the boat to languish at the docks of Napoli, where it fell into disrepair.

"After her death I renamed it *Angelica* for her, commissioned its restoration to its exact former glory, which I didn't have the vaguest recollection of. I regretted my act the moment I stepped on board the finished product. But even with its…excessive size and interiors, I discovered I loved living on board and roving the seas. I thought to re-outfit it to my needs and tastes, but I decided to leave it as is. Eventually I will donate it as a museum in my mother's memory, one that can be rented for huge sums that will go to the charities I founded in her name. I'm in the process of buying another yacht that doesn't scream 'party animal.'"

She sighed with the satisfaction of someone who'd been listening to a poignant tale. "Which is just about the last thing you are."

"*Sì.* The sporadic sponsored charity event is the limit of my social mingling." He only then noticed that Giancarlo must have served their entrées. "Which must be why the etiquette my mother struggled to infuse me with as a small child has rusted from disuse. *Andare avanti*…go ahead, please. I'll talk and you eat."

She immediately pounced on her plate, snatched up one of the golden, crisp lobster puffs. "I thought you'd never ask."

He chuckled, shaking his head at his all-out reaction, started to eat himself. "So tell me…what made you move to Sardinia and/or Italy when you were five?"

She chewed, moaned in enjoyment, beamed at him. "I thought it was you talk and I eat. Lucky for you *my* mother never succeeded in teaching me not to eat and talk at the same time." She reached for a second puff. "About the move—gotta say outside influences helped me make that decision. Like my parents hauling me there."

"*Ragazza difettosa.*" His no-touching-yet rule was growing difficult. His hands ached to smooth those glowing cheeks, cup them and dip his tongue in those tormenting dimples and smile grooves. "You must know where I want to haul you." Her eyes all but groaned *Yes, please.* He inhaled, reminded himself of his resolve. "So why did *they* haul you there?"

She reached for her champagne flute, her eyes losing heat and brightness. "It's a convoluted story. I think it started with my father's business in the States having many outlets in Italy and the surrounding Mediterranean islands. He went bankrupt around the time I was five. He also suffered from depression. In the years following his death, I've often asked my mother if she thought that influenced the decisions that led to his bankruptcy, or if it was the other way around. Not that I expected an answer, or thought it would make a difference."

"When did he die?" He watched her put down the puff. It was clear her appetite was gone. He groaned. "Don't answer that."

The surprise in her eyes seemed directed at her own reaction, not his words. "No, I-I want to tell you. He died when I was eleven."

He gritted his teeth, hating to see her suffer echoes of the anguish the child she'd been must have felt. "You were old enough to be aware of all the problems going on around you then."

She nodded. "I was."

"It still haunts you."

She put down her glass unsteadily. "It's not fun remembering nothing of my father but a man buried under so much gloom and despair. I try to cling to memories of the man he was beneath all that, but they're rare. During those times he was wonderful, which makes it all more painful, knowing how much of him was wasted. Remembering how angry I was at him doesn't help, either. I've since realized that he couldn't help his condition, but try to convince a kid of that. I blamed him for his moods, his inaccessibility. And later on, I blamed myself for that blame."

Everything she said struck chords inside him. He'd suffered something very similar. "Where was your mother during all that?"

She started to eat again, an adorably determined look on her face. "Struggling to protect me from the torment festering within Dad as it spread out to engulf us, and to keep him from disintegrating while not succumbing herself under the burdens thrown on the so-called 'healthy adult' in this setup."

"You have a good relationship with her."

She swallowed her mouthful convulsively, her eyes tearing up. "I had the best relationship a girl could hope for with her mother. She died seven months ago."

He ached to stop this, to spare her reliving her anguish. But he felt she'd refuse to abandon the subject. She more than wanted to tell him. It felt as if she needed to. He wanted to give her anything she needed. He asked quietly, "How?"

"Sh-she had rheumatoid arthritis. A severe condition. Then, during a regular checkup, she was diagnosed with stage-four pancreatic cancer. She was dead within two months."

"You were with her when she passed away?"

She nodded. "She didn't live here with me, because her condition deteriorated whenever she left the Mediterranean climate. I went to her every minute I could. When we knew there was no hope of remission, she wanted to live at home. I wanted to be the one to take care of her, so I moved into her villa. I'd taken paramedic courses and administered the palliative measures that were all that could be done until…until the end."

"You had medical supervision during that time?"

She bit her lip, hard. "Her doctor was on call and two nurses came twice a day to check on my measures."

"And they found everything to their satisfaction."

"It was easy to get it right. There wasn't much to be done."

"Yet you're still afraid you messed up those simple measures, didn't give the mother you loved—who trusted you to take care of her during her last days—the best care."

He saw shock rip through her, as if he'd reached inside and yanked out her heart. Then, to his horror, her face crumpled, her teary eyes spilling over. "Sometimes I wake at night crying, terrified I gave her a wrong painkiller dose, that she was in agony and bearing it as usual, that I made her make the wrong decision in going home. That she died suffering because of me."

Battling their physical need was one thing. But *this* need, for solace, he was powerless against. He hadn't offered or sought comfort since childhood. He had to offer it now, seek it. To and from her.

He exploded to his feet, came around to her, pulled her up.

The moment she filled his arms, it was as if things were uprooted inside him. Separateness. Seclusion.

This. He'd been waiting for this. This woman. This connection. And he'd never known he'd been waiting.

She lay her head against his heart and trembled. He stroked her hair as he'd longed to from the first moment. It was beyond anything his imagination had spun. And so was what he felt for her. He wanted her to let go, give him all her resurrected misery to bear. He wanted her to pour out the rest. He was certain she'd never unburdened herself.

He prodded her to give him all. "Why did your father take you to Sardinia when his business collapsed? Was he going home?"

"No." She sniffed, stirred, her eyes beseeching him to resume normalcy. He complied, let her go, somehow, seated her, went back to his chair, signaled for Giancarlo to serve the main course.

She stalled, tasting her lobster in lime butter sauce, asking Giancarlo about the recipe. When she ran out of delaying tactics, was in control again, she began talking. "Dad had a friend who asked him to relocate us there so he could help, which he couldn't do effectively if we lived thousands of miles away."

"And did he? Help?"

"Above and beyond. He paid off Dad's debts, tried endlessly to put him back on his feet. But no matter what he did, Dad kept spiraling downward. This friend even took care of us after he died, financed my education until I graduated."

"And you didn't like that. Even though you liked the man."

"God, how do you keep working out how I feel? Do you read minds?" She groaned. "But of *course* you do. You wouldn't be you if you didn't." Before he could tell her it was only her he was so attuned to, she went on. "Yeah, I love him. But I hated feeling so helpless, so indebted. I worked, paid my rent and expenses, but he was adamant about not letting me get a tuition loan. I only accepted when he promised he'd let me pay him back."

"But he was only humoring you so you'd accept."

"Your insight is uncanny, isn't it? You realized at once what I only realized when I got a great paying job and demanded to repay him only for him to—surprise—refuse to take a cent."

"But you drilled your way into making him take it, *giusto?*"

"*Assolutamente giusto*…dead right. I bet he finally took the money so he'd hear the end of it. Not that that was the end of it. When my mom finally gave me a real idea of the magnitude of our family's debt to him, I became consumed with the need to repay it all, so I'd feel free, and she would, too."

"And I bet you managed to pay it all back."

Her lashes fluttered down again. "Eventually, yes."

"And that cost you. What did it cost you, *bellissima?*"

Her lips twisted in something too much like self-loathing. "Marrying the worst possible man."

The world stopped. His heart followed. "You're *married?*"

Her eyes slammed back to his, enormous with alarm and agitation. "*No.* I'm divorced. Six years ago now. *Grazie a Dio.*"

His heart attempted to restart, lurched and clanged against the insides of a chest that felt lined with thorns. "Was he rich?"

She winced. "Filthy."

"Like me?"

"Uh, no. Your wealth transcends filthiness into obscenity."

He couldn't reciprocate her tremulous attempt to lighten things up. "You married him so he'd repay your family's debts?"

"Actually, it was his idea. I was his PA and he heard me on the phone with my mom and used it as another pressure tactic."

"He needed to? You weren't attracted to him?"

"I felt nothing beyond unease that I couldn't reciprocate his interest. But the job was great, so I kept hoping he'd find someone else. He didn't, kept pointing out that I didn't, either, that maybe I can't feel…passion, which was okay because love stories never end well, anyway. I began to think he was right, as I knew nothing of what makes a relationship work or what a man who'd make a good husband was like. Compared to my father, he seemed like the essence of stability. And he made a solid case for a marriage between us built on mutual respect and realistic expectations."

He barely stopped himself from snarling. "He conned you."

"Oh, no. I decided to disregard my reservations, my lack of feelings for him, followed the lure of paying off my family's debts in one chunk. I dug my own grave by being so mercenary."

He snarled now. "You were nothing of the sort. *He* was the conniving bastard. If he felt *anything* for you, he would have freed you from debt and left it up to you to take him or not."

"That would have only transferred my debt to him, and I would have felt honor-bound to marry him anyway."

"He could have made it clear that there would have been no debt, or offered that you repay it in installments."

"I did insist on including the condition in the prenups that our funds be separate and whatever he loaned me I'd return."

"And he pounced on those terms," he bit off. "You were what? Twenty? Twenty-one? And how old was he?"

"I was twenty-three. He was thirty-nine. And a widower."

"He *did* con you. He convinced you to consider it a business deal in which pros outweigh cons, pretended he was satisfied with that. Until he got his hands on you." Her shrug was loud with concession. He wanted to slam his fists down on the table. "And he didn't pay off your debts."

"How did you…? Oh, OK. I did say I married the worst man."

"Actually, you said paying your debt cost you marrying said man. Most would assume that he did pay it. But I'd bet my fortune he didn't. I know that because I know users, and that man was beyond that. He kept after you to break your resistance, but instead of building anticipation as he pursued you, he built up antipathy, planned to wreak vengeance on you as soon as he had you in his power." He caught her hand, pressed it. "I only wish to God the extent of his aggression was the passive breaking of the pact he never meant to keep. But he didn't stop there, did he?" She shook her head. "He abused you. Verbally, mentally." The last word seemed to cut him as it came out. "Sexually."

She stared at him again as if he'd torn her open and looked inside, distress brimming with the shock of exposure, with the misplaced shame of the victim.

At last she gave a choking gulp. A mortified nod admitted his insight. "I bought his excuses, his blame, for four months. I didn't love him, he was frustrated, yadda yadda. Then he…he…"

"He hit you."

She lurched. Her chest heaved. With a sharp inhalation, she muttered, "He put me in the hospital."

Four

Durante had never considered himself a violent man.

Now, as he stared down at her bent head, murderous aggression took hold of his every nervous transmission. Need boiled his blood—to defend her in retrospect, to avenge her, to torture and cripple that vermin who'd hurt her.

Words left his lips in a vicious staccato. "Tell me you reported him and he's now serving time."

"Uh, no…actually, I didn't." He heard something rumbling, vaguely realized the sound was issuing from him. She rushed in to add, "But he didn't get the chance to come near me again. I started divorce proceedings before I even reached the hospital."

He glared at her, his brain seeming to expand in the confines of his skull with the brutal buildup of anger, the inability to vent it. At least not yet. He *would* pay that man back.

She suddenly shut her eyes. "Okay, let's rewind and replay before I dig a hole to Malaysia. I made it all sound so pathetic and self-pitying, and that isn't how I see my life. I've had it way better than most people. Despite my father's problems, so many things, starting with my mother and our benefactor, provided me with a secure and reasonably happy childhood. I had a great time at boarding school and college, and my marriage, ugliness and all, lasted only four months and I own up to my role in it. I've established my own company and I loved every second of exploring and achieving so much on the way. My mother died, but I'm thankful she didn't suffer long and that I had such an incredible friend and parent for so long. So…I hope I haven't caused you to reach your whining tolerance level."

She was making light of her ordeals, and, *maledizione,* meaning it. The expectedness of her last words awoke his humor, which he thought an insult to the suffering she'd related. But her come-on, laugh-with-me expression forced him to submit.

He coughed a distressed laugh. "You sent my sense of perspective levels through the roof, after they'd dwindled to trace elements. You forced me to revise how I perceive my own life. Seems I've been guilty of letting my…issues rule my mind-set."

She shook her head, teasing radiating from her heavenly eyes. "I thought higher beings like you had global obstacles and dilemmas and crises, but nothing so petty as 'issues.'"

He gave a grunt laden with self-disgust. "Leave it to you to underline how oblivious and tiny and self-indulgent it all is."

She chuckled. "Anytime."

He reached out across the table, took her hand. He needed to be connected to her as he made his own confessions. "My experience with my mother reflects yours with your father. She died five years ago, but I too was eleven when I started to realize I was losing her. It was then that I set out to detach myself, that I learned that no one is guaranteed to be there for me. I've become so comfortable being disconnected, so driven and distracted, that I no longer notice all the good that fills my life."

Her other hand descended to his, imbuing him with a calm

that was previously unknown to him, a restfulness to mirror the compassion that filled her eyes. "She suffered depression, too?"

He'd never discussed this, never given what his mother had suffered a name, not even with his siblings. He needed to talk about it now, with her, needed to name what had taken his mother away a piece every day, look it full in the face instead of evading it and having it invade far more of him instead.

"I think she was bipolar. Severely so."

"So it's true. No one is exempt. My father, a man who had everything, your mother, a queen with the world at her feet, both prisoners to something so dark and inescapable inside them."

Pressure built behind his eyes as cold outrage at the injustice of it all gave way to the empathy flowing between them in sweeping currents. He surrendered to the release of sharing, of having another fully appreciate and understand.

Suddenly, urgency stained her gaze. Everything inside him became primed to defend, to contain. He had no tolerance for her distress, he was discovering. "What is it, *bellissima?* Tell me."

She grimaced. "It's nothing. It's…" She stopped, closed her eyes, exhaled. "What the hell. I've put my foot in it too much already to get delicate at this late stage. I was just wondering if… if you've ever wondered if you have that seed of sourceless desperation and instability inside you?"

He stiffened with yet another jolt at how in tune she was with him, sensing fears that never came into focus, but cast their darkness over his existence nevertheless.

He let his counter-question acknowledge her insight just as it expressed his concern for her. "Do you?"

"Only since my mother died. I finally wondered if I've never been able to be close to others because I had something lurking inside me, because I subconsciously felt that emotional involvement would raise the chances that it would manifest."

"And what's your verdict?"

"I don't know. What complicates matters and stops me from

coming up with anything conclusive is the fact that it wasn't a struggle not to be close. I wasn't even tempted until…"

She stopped. He couldn't anymore. He cupped her cheek as he'd been aching to. "Until tonight."

Warmth surged from his gut when she acquiesced, to the truth of his statement, to his hold, letting her flesh mold to his palm.

And he had to ask. "Did you ever wonder if whatever consumed your father wasn't sourceless, after all?"

She nuzzled into his caress. "I guess *sourceless* is the wrong word to use, what with all the physiological and social factors involved in the development of such a major disorder. I guess it's the out-of-proportion, ever-compounding emotional response that becomes so far removed from whatever triggered it, making it seem as if there were no origin." She sighed, singeing his flesh with the heat of her breath. "As I said, I'll never know what started my father down that spiral."

"I know what started my mother down hers. It was my father."

Such shock, such pain flooded her eyes at his muttered bitterness that he groaned, cupped her head, needing to alleviate her distress.

She reached out to his face, her hand trembling in a caress that assuaged some of the darkness festering inside him.

She finally said, "I'm so sorry you believe that. I can't imagine how painful it is to think one of your parents was responsible for the other's deterioration. It's the only thing that holds me together, that I believe that there was no one to blame."

He rose, bent across the table. He gazed into her misty eyes for a heart-thudding moment, then descended, pressed his lips to hers in a brief, barely leashed kiss. *"Grazie, bellissima."*

Her moan reverberated inside him. His fingers fisted in her tresses, spilling another moan from her lips, detonating charges of sensation across his skin. He withdrew before temptation overwhelmed him, sat down. His gaze pored over her, the image of her beauty burned onto his retinas.

Such beauty. Totally her own, following no one else's ideas or rules, including his own before he'd set eyes on her. Beyond physical, with so many levels to it—levels he kept discovering with no end in sight. She was short-circuiting the civilized man he'd been certain he was, unleashing a primal male who wanted to possess, plunder. But it also made that same male want to protect, to pamper.

She inclined her head at him. "You can sing, can't you?"

He blinked at the question—the statement, really. He didn't even think to inquire about such a detour's origin and intent. He just flowed with her along the wave of unpredictability, of freedom from rules and expectations.

"Can't everyone," he said. "to some degree or another?"

"Uh, no. Not according to my singing teacher, another suffering soul who told me she had nightmares of waking up in a world where everyone had my same singing ability, making her profession obsolete and putting her permanently out of a job."

He frowned. "*My* teacher criticized my intentional truancy. He wouldn't have disparaged my performance or made me feel responsible for it had it been a limitation on my part. That inconsiderate wretch who taught you had no business telling a child something like that, just because your talents didn't meet her standards and your progress didn't conform to her timetable."

She beamed him such a look, full of mischief and embarrassment, that he wondered where he found the will to remain where he was. "Uh, I wasn't exactly a child when the brilliant idea of taking singing lessons sprouted in my mind three years ago. And I did test her last tune-sensitive nerve by insisting on singing along with Whitney Houston and Maria Callas. The comparison was agonizing even to my own self-forgiving ears. But I have a feeling you can hold your own with the Elvises and Pavarottis of the world."

He raised one eyebrow, goading her into telling him more. "Hmm, I wonder how you came by that conviction."

Her grin grew impish and indulgent at once. "In your case, fishing will get you whales. You reaffirm that conviction every time you open your mouth and unleash that honed weapon you have for a voice. *Uomo cattivo* that you are, you unrepentantly use it to its full destructive effect. It's very easy for me to imagine you taking your mastery over it to its highest conclusion."

Stimulation revved higher. He let himself revel in the gratification of their repartee, challenged, fishing for even bigger whales. "I've heard many superlative singers who don't sound special when they talk."

"Sure, but I bet that's not the case with you."

"So what are you after? An admission? An audition?"

Her dimples flashed at him. "The first would be great, so I can gloat over my uncanny acumen. The second, alas, would be so much better even than having your ear for an hour—or a week—that I think it would warrant something larger than a ten-million-dollar bid."

He reached for her hand and placed it on her fork. "I have a third option. Let's finish this meal, and I'll offer you something better than either at no cost but your willingness to accept it." She sat forward, anticipation ablaze on her face. And he offered something he'd never imagined offering to anyone, ever. "A serenade."

Darkness was melting under dawn's advance, the horizon starting to simmer with colors, the rest of the sky's blackness bleaching to indigo, the stars blinking out one by one.

Durante had taken his *bellissima* to the bow, initiating a match of quips around the *Titanic* movie parallel. Merriment had dissolved with the night into a silence filled with serenity and companionship. Soon it seemed as natural and needed as breathing for her to fill his embrace, just as she seemed to need to be contained there.

For the next hour, as the magic of the night segued into the new spell of dawn, he encompassed her, her back to his front, his arms crisscrossed around her midriff, his legs parted to accommodate her, imbuing her with his heat, protecting her from the chill of the breeze. She accepted him as her shield, surrendered to his cosseting and to that of the wind on her face as the yacht sailed toward the sun.

In this proximity, there was no disguising the extent of his arousal. Not that he tried to. He'd admitted his reaction to her minutes into their first conversation. His body had made its own admissions to her the moment he gathered her to him, his erection obvious through the confines of clothes and control.

Her own state must be as acute. The only movements she seemed capable of were the spasmodic pressing of her hands on the railing, and trembling. Was she trying not to press back into him as hard as he wanted to grind into her?

But he wouldn't fracture this intensity, this purity of feeling for anything. This was too rare to rush, too precious to squander even for the ecstasy they were certain to find in each other. Not yet. They had to have this first.

It was magnificent, sharing this with her, experiencing each other without words after the liveliness of their verbal communication. Now the only sounds that permeated the whispers and whistles of the wind and the splash of the water were his groans as he pressed his lips into her neck, against her cheeks, the corner of her mouth, her moans as her tremors spiked with every press and glide. He felt as if every inch of her was made to click into every inch of him, that the eight or nine inches he had on her five foot six or seven had been bestowed on him so he'd envelop her like this.

Then she turned her head, turned up eyes glittering with the wonder of what they'd shared since they'd met twelve hours or a forever ago, whispered, *"Ora, per favore."*

Now, please. Indeed. So this was it. The moment of truth.

He'd never sung in another's presence. Not since primary

school, anyway. And he was about to sing to this enchanted creature who'd appeared out of nowhere and made him forget everything, his exhaustion, his wariness. The world.

He let his arms tighten around her for a moment before he stepped away. Then he went down on one knee.

A sharp gasp tore from her. Then, with another distressed sound, she swooped down, tried to pull him up.

He tangled his hands into her hair, tugged gently, brought her down for another of those fleeting, tormenting kisses.

Then, as his lips clung to hers, he breathed the first line of Caruso. *"Qui dove il mare luccica, e tira forte il vento…"*

Here where the sea sparkles and the wind is blowing…

She bolted up, severing the last clinging touch between their lips, and staggered back to lean limply against the railing, her eyes stricken, her lips parting on choppy puffs.

He remained kneeling at her feet, giving his voice full rein as he continued to sing the song he'd only ever memorized because he felt like he was soaring when he let his voice ride the beauty and power of the melody, never giving a moment's thought to the lyrics. Now the lyrics seemed to have been written so that he could describe these moments with her. They took on meanings their writer hadn't intended, poured into the mold of the moment.

Then he came to the refrain, and that, most of all, resonated with the exact expressions that crowded inside him, let the passion she'd aroused in him take shape and sound and flow with the fervor of the timeless words.

"Te voglio bene assai, ma tanto tanto bene sai. È una catena ormai, che scioglie il sangue dint' e vene sai…"

I want you so much, I truly want you so much it's now like a shackle that melts the blood inside the veins, you know…

Tears gushed from her eyes, and her face shuddered with too many emotions to follow, let alone fathom. She seemed in pain.

Alarm and suspicion crashed inside his head. What if this

song provoked raw memories, if he'd managed, not to please her, woo her, but to upset her? He surged to his feet. He couldn't stop his arms from gathering her to him until he had her off the ground and in his safekeeping.

"Durante...please..." The quivering of her voice augmented his alarm, made him hold her away so he could ascertain her state, apologize, divert her agitation. His gut clenched, now he grimaced as he saw her lips working before he realized they were forming a tremulous smile. "Please...don't stop."

His whole body slackened with relief.

She swayed when he set her back on her feet, gripped his arms, eagerness blazing on her face. "Please, please keep singing. I thought I could imagine how incredible you'd sound, but it seems even my imagination is tone-deaf."

He guffawed. There was no way he could ever predict what she'd say next. "If so, how do you know if I sound incredible or not?"

"Oh, my 'difficulties' lie in tone reproduction, not recognition. And then this..." She waved both hands at him, before taking them both to her chest to press her heart in a gesture so moved and moving he groaned. "...transcends hearing. *Please*—sing."

He plastered her against him, no longer restraining his urgency, one hand dipping below her corset-like top to bask in her firm softness and heat, the other digging into her mane, turning her face up for his worshipping. And he sang.

The liberation, the exhilaration was indescribable. To cut the tethers of separateness and wariness and propriety, to let himself go, let his voice boom with passion, break with poignancy. The storm of emotions and expressions that raged on her face with every note, the tears of acute enjoyment that streamed, were the purest form of adulation he'd ever had, the only he craved having.

When the last vibrato died away, she was panting, then she

flung herself at him, pressed her wet face into his chest, until he felt her fervor practically eating through it, her essence permeating it. "*Grazie,* Durante. *Molto, molto grazie.*"

It was a long time before either of them stirred. It was she who moved, casting stunned looks around, before looking up at him sheepishly. "It's morning."

"*Sì,* that's what usually follows dawn, I hear," he teased.

Something warm danced in her eyes. "I wouldn't know. I'm no expert on dawn or how long it takes to break. I'm always in a coma from one until seven a.m."

"So this is your first time staying up all night?"

"It's my first time…for just about everything."

There was no doubt in his mind that was the truth. There was no thought of hiding how he felt in return. "*Sì.* For me, too."

The blast of delight in her clear-again eyes made him feel limitless, swathed everything in new meanings and depths. He basked in it all until contrition entered her expression. "I kept you up all night on a work day."

He waved it off. "Why did I strive so hard to be where I am if not for the flexibility of forging my own timetable?"

"Who're you kidding? You crack the whip over your own head harder than you do over anybody else's."

He guffawed again, loving this. "Very subtle way of saying I'm a slave driver. One with a fetish for self-flagellation."

"I bet you didn't become who you are by being flexible with your time and taking days off."

"To put your mind to rest on the sacrifice of my taking a day off, I can afford to in this instance, because before we met I put in thirty-six hours of work, more than covering for it in advance."

"Oh, God…that means you've been awake for forty-eight hours now. And I kept you up all night yakking and singing and…and…"

"And being tormented within an inch of my sanity? Laughing my head off? Confessing my darkest secrets? Being fully alive?"

"Yeah...uh...all that," she croaked. "But I bet you were longing to hit the sheets."

"The only sheets I want to hit are those with you spread out on them. Being with you has been the most worthwhile reason to forgo sleep that I've ever had. I never realized there was anything to want as fiercely as I want a steady supply of sleepless nights with you."

She stared up at him, motionless, breathless. Then the first tremor broke through the stillness. The second merged into a stream that shook her. Gratification swelled, that he affected her to that extent. He might not be exhibiting the same outward manifestation, but she shook him, too, to the core.

He embraced her again, absorbed her tremors. They were her response to him made tangible. They belonged to him. He wanted them, along with everything that made her herself.

He'd given Giancarlo orders to keep sailing until he told him otherwise. He wanted to keep on sailing, never to return her to her life, never to return to his.

He was thinking she'd say yes if he proposed that radical plan when she raised an agitated face, whispered, "Take me home, please, Durante."

Five

Durante raised an eyebrow at Gabrielle's TriBeCa apartment building's concierge in response to his open surprise and curiosity. Very strange reaction coming from someone whose job description was headed by discretion and diplomacy.

Did the man recognize him? Or was it his tenant's return dressed in an evening gown in broad daylight, escorted by a strange man?

He did see recognition in the man's eyes. Which *wasn't* strange. Royalty was an endless source of public fascination and romanticizing anywhere in the world. But it was far more so in the States, especially in New York, his adopted home for the last five years. It seemed New Yorkers clamored for anything that would transport them from their hectic lives. Being a prince of an exotic kingdom, combined with his vast wealth, was the stuff of fairy tales to them. That this view did not match the reality of his life had nothing to do with their perception of it. The perception was there to stay.

So the man recognized him. But Durante was still convinced his second interpretation of his reaction was the correct one. Which led to another conviction. The incident had so surprised the man because he hadn't seen her coming home with a man before. She'd told the truth about first times. As he knew she had.

Not that he was "coming home" with her. He was taking her to her door, had no idea if she'd invite him in.

She'd asked him to take her home after he'd again stressed his open-ended desire, had barely spoken during the ride there. Considering how fluent she'd been up until then, her fraught silence had disturbed him more by the minute. He'd tried to tell himself she was exhausted, that not everyone was an insomniac able to function on sporadic half hours of sleep. But what if this night hadn't meant as much to her as it had to him? What if she'd decided that it wasn't prudent to let things develop further?

The sharp *ping* of the elevator as they reached her tenth-floor apartment cut through his oppressive thoughts. He let her precede him, fell into step with her through the dimly lit corridor leading to her corner apartment, his hand gripping hers as if he were afraid she'd dematerialize. Then they reached her door.

It was the same as all the others. It was also the gateway to the one place on earth he wanted to be.

Behind this door lay the stage of her unseen existence. Where she walked barefoot, dressed and undressed, reflected, shed tears. Where she sang in out-of-tune abandon as she cooked her meals, danced in front of mirrors to snippets of music that blipped inside her head, washed away exhausting days under the spray of hot water, drowned her angers and anxieties in steaming baths and surrendered to oblivion after a book dropped from her hand at the strike of 1 a.m.... or after she'd pleasured herself.

Crossing this door into that microcosm became his highest goal. To be allowed into her sanctuary, to be given the privilege to witness her secrets, see to her safety, cater to her needs.

She turned, her eyes overflowing with so much emotion that his mind seized. Then her whisper floated in the silence, impeded, unsteady.

"I wanted to be on my turf when I said this. I-I…"

She was going to say goodbye. *No.* He couldn't let her. "Don't say anything now, *bellissima.* Just get some sleep. When you've taken it all in, let me see you again. We'll take it from there."

Her gaze wavered, then she groaned. "God, I'm so stupid. You must be exhausted. Oh, just go please…"

He caught her arm, stopped her babbling. "The last thing I need now is sleep. What did you want to say? If it's anything other than 'I don't think this should go any farther,' please say it."

Her flush rose. His whole body bunched as her lips parted on a hectic inhalation and she burst out, "I want this night, Durante. Or this day. Or whenever we are. And I want as many nights and days as I can ha—"

Durante couldn't wait for her confession to finish exiting her lips before he devoured it along with them. The way she met his ardor halfway with as much ferocity told him everything he needed to know. This time there was no hesitation on her part, as there was no intention of holding back on his.

He stilled the tremors invading the fullness of her lower lip in a bite that made her cry out, arch into him, all lushness and surrender. The taste and feel and scent of her eddied in his arteries, pounded through his system. Her urgency spilled into his mouth in moans and gasps that blanked his mind. He gathered her thighs through the layers of cloth, raised her, opened her for his bulk, pinned her to her door with the force of his hunger. His tongue drove inside her as his erection thrust against her heat through layers of barriers, losing rhythm in the wildness.

Her tongue slid against his, rubbed, tangled, her lips suckled at his, her teeth matching him nip for nip until he slammed against her, rattling the door, the wall that housed it.

This—as she called it—was everything. It couldn't be

spoiled, could only deepen and widen and intensify. This wasn't rushing things, wasn't too soon. This was how it should be. They didn't need time to know this was right. It was. Time would only provide the leisure to explore and savor all the ways of how right it was.

But this totality of response was also frightening. His grip on control was softening, the need to ram inside her, here, now, ride her until she convulsed around him, drenched his flesh with her pleasure and he pumped her full of his, was replacing his mental faculties. And that was after just a kiss.

But it wasn't a kiss. It was a rehearsal for their mating, enough to portray what that would be like. Something so outside the realm of his experience he couldn't even begin to imagine it.

He knew that on a fundamental level. He had to know the rest.

He tore his lips from the lock of her passion, shuddered with her cry, her lurch, her demand that he resume their fusion.

He molded her features with his mouth as if mapping them into tactile memory. "Tell me your name, *bellissima*. I need to know it now, to whisper it into your lips and against your every pleasure point. I need to think it, have it fill my mind as I look on your beauty. I want to roar it as I fill you."

"Gabrielle…" Her moan penetrated his brain, lodged in his erection. Gabrielle. *Yes.* Laced with femininity and strength and complexity. It fit her. But then she'd make any name exceptional, magical. "Gabrielle Williamson."

Everything decelerated as her full name sank into his mind. Then it hit bottom, detonated like a depth mine.

Gabrielle Williamson. The woman who'd recently approached him with an offer he'd refused, as he had dozens of similar ones.

She hadn't accepted "not interested" for an answer, had contacted just about everyone who had an in with him to secure face time with him. He'd heard from many on her behalf, but it was one of his associates who'd finally roused his curiosity. Gerald Whittaker, as shrewd a businessman as they came, had said she was confident her offer was one he couldn't refuse. When he'd said that he'd heard the Don Corleone line too many times for it to work, Gerald had had every confidence himself that she must be on to something Durante would want to know about, that he should at least give her a chance.

Out of respect for Gerald's opinion, he almost had. He'd also wondered what kind of woman had such a rock so taken with her.

But he hadn't agreed to meet her. Because he'd found out exactly what kind of woman she was. The most casual background check had returned a screaming verdict. *Don't let her within a mile of you.*

So he hadn't. Not because he'd believed himself in any danger from the femme fatale whose favorite snack was billionaires. He'd been disgusted by the picture he'd put together. Of her stringing Gerald around, using him to get to an even bigger prey. *Him.* The offer he couldn't refuse would have been the pleasure of having her, no doubt. She'd have been confident that he, like dozens before him, would succumb once she had him in range of her charms. He'd fleetingly entertained agreeing to her panted-after meeting, just to get the message across that *he* could snack on women like her. If he was into junk food.

He shouldn't have been so smug. He should have known that she'd have more cards to play. And she'd played them. Played him. And how. She'd reinvented her approach, hit from another angle. And she'd struck the bull's-eye. He hadn't only proved himself susceptible to her wiles, but he also must have been her easiest quarry ever.

Gabrielle Williamson. *She* was the woman with whom he'd spent the most revitalizing, enthralling time of his life, a time he'd planned never to end. The woman who'd made him forget exhaustion and every preconception about himself and what he could feel. The woman who was wrapped around him, her flesh feeling as if it were as vital to him as his own.

She dragged his face back down to hers, whimpering at his momentary withdrawal. It *had* been only a moment since the lips claiming his had formed the name that had sent reality crashing into him. It had taken only a moment to plunge him from the heights of delight to the depths of disillusion.

His whole being in revolt, he tried to pull back, but she wouldn't let him. She tightened her vise around his body, his will, her ragged whispers of desire impaling his brain, causing another geyser of response to erupt inside him.

So what if she wasn't the unique woman for whom he'd broken all his rules, was instead a siren who came with a warning ignored at the price of defamation and destruction? It should change nothing. His body was reaching critical mass, demanding hers. And she was offering…everything. He should drag her inside, throw her to the ground and take it all. *Then* walk away.

Disillusionment bellowed its bitterness over the flames of desire. It wasn't powerful enough to douse them. Only agony might be.

It tore him apart to think of it all reduced to…this. Rutting. Sexual release. He wanted the unprecedented passion, the sublime emotions along with the all-consuming lust.

But those had all been an illusion. She was everything he abhorred and despised. Nothing like what she'd projected so seamlessly all night. How had she done it? How had she misled his senses to this extent? How had she imbued herself with a vibe that had been so attuned to his? How had she been able to assume a nature so alien to her own? To project characteristics she couldn't begin to understand, let alone have?

The answer to all that was obvious. She was a chameleon. A black widow. A cold-blooded predator.

"Durante, *te voglio bene assai…*"

Her words echoed the ones he'd sung—*sung*—to her. They ripped into him, made him go rigid with the spike of arousal.

For a suspended moment, he let her overwhelm his reason, let himself surrender to the need to forget caution, to deny his realizations. But the very loss of the control finally hurt enough to ignite the deep freeze of rage.

He was just another quarry to her. One she'd gambled she could capture if she got close enough. And he wouldn't let her win. Not even if he was dying to let her. Especially because he was.

He tore her arms off his body, feeling as if they'd taken off strips of his own skin.

Still oblivious to his awakening, she cupped his face, her own etched with her *coup de grâce,* an expression that would have brought him to his knees if he hadn't realized the truth. Total trust, full surrender. Temptation thundered through him.

He staggered away in self-disgust.

This time when he recoiled, he broke free from the prison of her thighs, dropped her back on her own feet. She stumbled, crashed back against the door.

Panic flashed in her eyes. His heart stampeded. Had his involuntary force frightened her, brought back memories of when another man had used his superior strength to hurt her?

Dio, what was he *thinking?* This was an *act.* Her sob story about the husband who'd abused her—the husband she'd used and destroyed instead—had been a string of masterfully composed lies.

Sure enough, the panic was turning to an uncanny emulation of pained confusion, then dread. "Durante...what's wrong?"

Everything, he wanted to roar. *You, the woman, the treasure I thought I found, doesn't exist.*

He glared at her, everything he wanted to yell frothing inside him. His body quaked as if on the verge of explosion.

Then, after a long moment filled with labored-breathing,

without another word or glance, he turned on his heel and walked away.

He wouldn't look back. Ever again. The dream was over.

Gabrielle stood plastered to her door, watching Durante walk away.

She couldn't breathe. Something sharp and burning had lodged in her gut, twisting her to shreds, coagulating into a mass of pain.

A wave of darkness swamped her.

She stumbled around, pressed her clammy face to her door, fumbled inside her purse. Key. Get inside. Damned if she would faint out here. She'd given the tabloids enough fodder for a decade. This would see her to her grave.

Then she was inside. Alone. As she should have remained, as she would from now on. She'd never let anyone close again, never…

All her nerves seemed to snap. She went down in a heap on the ground, her dress swirling around her like a suffocating vortex.

She tore at it. Couldn't bear the oppression. Had to breathe.

It took forever. Then she was in her panties, staggering up and to her bedroom. She fell onto her bed, folded into a ball of anguish. Her body was still throbbing, demanding him… *Stop it.*

Misery engulfed her, wrung her, first with dry heaves, then with tears so violent she thought she might dissolve, dissipate.

She'd thought she'd braced herself for the worst when she'd sought him out, preparing for anything from cold dismissal to ireful rejection. But how could she have predicted the events that had dominoed since she'd laid eyes on him, knocking sense and good intentions out of reach until she'd found herself wrapped around him, unaware and uncaring if the world was watching, begging for him to possess her, all but offering him carte blanche with her life?

She'd been certain of what he felt. She'd thought they'd

shared something that transcended time and explanations, something real on the most fundamental level.

It had all been an illusion. He'd lied when he'd said he didn't care about labels. He must have been trying to stimulate his glutted senses by leading on yet another desperate female to see how far she'd go, how much of herself she'd offer.

She'd offered him everything. Her pain and shame and trust. She'd left herself wide open, and the blow had crushed her.

In her mind, the feverish moments played again, filled with the cherishment and pleasure his every word and touch had bestowed. Then he'd demanded her name and she'd given it, delighted to complete his knowledge of her, unable to wait to hear it on his lips in all the ways he'd promised.

More images and sensations rose until she felt she was drowning in black ink. Durante, his body losing its gentle ferocity, stiffening, withdrawing, pushing her away.

For one moment, panic had flashed, fear that he, too, got his kicks abusing women. Worse, that something was wrong with her, like Ed had told her, something that drove otherwise normal men to abuse her.

The fear had passed as soon as it had flared. Not Durante. She wouldn't let Ed's vicious psychological sabotage fester again, not for a second. The only one who had something wrong with him was Ed.

But then, something worse than physical abuse had filled Durante's eyes, twisted his face. The rage and revulsion he'd transmitted would leave a deeper scar than anything Ed had done.

After all they'd shared, she hadn't warranted the benefit of a moment's hesitation before he believed the labels she'd been stuck with rather than the reality of her. His decision had been instantaneous, the change in him clearly irreversible. It was the final proof that there was no use. That Ed had won.

He'd been winning for years now, he and his lackeys painting her so black that no one would believe her even if she broke her pact of silence and told the world what a sick bastard he was. And she hadn't cared. She hadn't cared for anyone enough to care what they thought of her. Until Durante…

Was this how despair took root in someone's psyche? Would it now blossom into a monstrous growth that would suffocate everything in its path? Had an injury like this been the origin of her father's suffering? His mother's? Would she react the same way, follow in their footsteps down that bottomless spiral…?

She came to no conclusion before the blackness of exhaustion and heartache dragged her under.

Six

Durante was standing in the distance. His eyes were heavy with disparagement, accusation, his fists clenched at his sides.

She began to walk toward him, her steps gaining speed until she was running. She had to beg him to hear her out. She wasn't what the rumors made her out to be. He of all people knew that. He was the only one she'd shown her real self.

But as she approached him, he turned around and strode away. And she went mad.

She felt her feet lifting off the ground as she caught up with him, sank her fingers in his arm, wrenched. He turned on her with a snarl. And she punched him. In the face. Felt the crunch of cartilage and bones in her hand and his nose, the pain explode through her joints.

She stared up at him in horror as his eyes brimmed with icy rage, and she knew he wouldn't hit back. She almost wished he would, to show her some reaction besides that chilling disdain.

He gave her nothing, stared down at her as if at a maggot.

*Her thoughts were swerving from insisting on paying for the reconstructive surgery that would repair the nose she'd pulverized, to deciding to give him a matching broken jaw to go with it...*when she lurched awake.

Her eyes wouldn't open. She'd cried them shut.

Damn. Damn, damn, damn. Damn him and damn everyone else in this damn stupid world. But the biggest damns were reserved for herself and her stupidity.

She was done being stupid. She'd start by never again shedding a tear. Certainly not over Prince Durante D'Agostino.

She spilled from the bed, barely saw herself in the mirror through her turgid lids as she plodded to her bathroom.

She came out an hour later feeling as if the hot bath had homogenized the pain clamping her chest and melted it to seep through her. She now ached down to her toenails.

She called Megan, her PA, and told her she was taking a few days off. She was sick.

She wasn't lying. She was. Sick of the whole world. Heartache should be at the forefront of ailments one should take sick leave for. And she was taking it.

She needed time to rearrange her mental and emotional papers, invent some priorities, locate her vanished purpose. First on the agenda was purging her memory of Prince Durante D'Agostino.

To do that, she had to admit she owed him a debt of gratitude. He'd made all the slander she'd ever suffered come crashing down on her. She could now face her fury and bitterness, deal with it, put it in perspective and move on.

She should also thank him for curing her of a delusion she'd been suffering from without even realizing it—that miracles happened sometimes and Prince Charming existed somewhere.

Now that she knew for certain that was a load of crap, she could at last have her mind functioning at capacity, unhindered by the insidious virus of such self-sabotaging illusions.

Maybe now she could get rid of all the shackles that had been holding her back. Maybe now she would start to live for real.

Gabrielle looked at her cell phone.

Come on. Do it.

She'd put it off long enough. It had been ten days. She had to call him now. He wouldn't be happy. But he, too, had to face facts. Like she had.

Facts said she'd back down if she waited another moment.

Do. It. Now. She hit the speed dial button, flinching as if she'd hit a remote for a nearby bomb.

The ringing blared on speaker mode until the line disconnected. Relief that he hadn't answered and reluctance to try again sent nausea bubbling in her stomach. *Coward. Do it. Get it over with.*

She pressed the button just as the phone came alive.

She almost dropped it in fright. Then she remembered. She had it on vibration-mode. The caller ID blazed on the screen. The king.

She gulped and hit the answer button.

His voice flowed into her ear, sounding worse than she'd last heard it. *"Figlia mia,* apologies for the delay in answering."

"I should have called much sooner. I-I…" The words congealed into a lump, choked her. *Just spit them out.* "I-it's about your son. I-I tried and failed. He wouldn't talk to me."

That last bit wasn't exactly the truth, but it was true. All the talking Durante had done had been with his *"bella misteriosa."* He hadn't given *her* the consideration of one word.

Not that the king who'd told her to do "anything" would take her failure lying down. She braced herself for his arguments, for the brunt of his desperation, the distress of having to disappoint it. Just as she thought she was ready for anything, his exhalation almost deflated her with its dejection.

"It was a desperate gamble, Gaby. I was deluded to hope that Durante would relent. Castaldini and I will have to face our fate without his intervention. Forgive me if I caused you any discomfort by involving you in this."

A long time later, she didn't remember what she'd stammered in answer to King Benedetto's apology and acceptance of defeat.

She knew only that her temperature was rising geometrically. *Durante.* That cruel, intractable, holier-than-thou bastard.

So he'd condemned her and walked away without a glance back. Fine. She was no one to him. But she was damned if she'd let him get away with doing the same to his father and live happily ever after with his sanctimonious "disconnection."

She didn't care that he thought his position validated. It was still indefensible. And besides, she'd bet he had as much proof of his father's so-called crimes against his mother as he had of *her* alleged ones against male-kind.

She didn't care about the level of demeaning disdain with which he'd no doubt smear her. She was not letting this end without stripping off a few layers of his rhino hide. Maybe she'd even find something beneath to shame into coming through for his father and his kingdom.

She unclasped her death grip on her phone, hit another speed dial button. Megan answered on the first ring.

She fired away. "Megan, I want you to get me every shred of info on Prince Durante D'Agostino of Castaldini. And I don't mean financial and personal profiles. At least, nothing reported in 'reliable' or 'respected' sources. Dig me up all the dirt. Make it thick, and make it quick. I need it…ten days ago."

Durante stared at the wall across his extensive bedroom.

It looked so…tempting. All walls did. He wanted to bang his head against each and every one.

It was the conviction that some explosive pain and serious self-abuse might dampen the volcano seething inside him that tempted him.

How? How had he found himself in this position?

He trusted his instincts, which had steered him through his meteoric rise. But he'd always deferred acting on them until he'd deliberated all ramifications. Instinct didn't equate with impulse to him. He'd believed that he was without urges, did nothing with spontaneity. His closest people told him he took premeditation to uncharted and aggravating heights. That was, until Gabrielle Williamson. *Her.*

His instincts hadn't just totally misled him about her nature. He hadn't thought *once* before accepting their verdict, hadn't found ramifications to ponder as he let himself be swept away in the tide of what he'd thought mutual perfection. She'd satisfied his every demanding taste, his merciless critical eye finding only things to appreciate in her. Even the qualities that she'd put forward as her shortcomings, her hang-ups, had charmed him, secured his unquestioning empathy. And it had all been the practiced routine of a hardened seductress who got ahead in the world by seducing powerful fools like him.

If that night had been her first approach, if he hadn't researched her in advance, if he'd found out her truth after he'd tasted her for real, he wouldn't have been able to walk away, would have blinded himself to wallow in the pleasures she offered. He would have signed that contract, and maybe, like her previous victims, would have ended up signing over half his fortune. Or all of it.

And the worst part? His condition seemed hopeless.

He'd known how hopeless it was when his cousin Eduardo had passed by to check on him with that outspoken bride of his, Jade.

Durante hadn't exited his penthouse for five days, spending that time prowling the cage of his mind. He'd thought it might save his sanity to have a distraction, especially that of people whose show of caring wasn't a setup. So he'd invited them in.

It hadn't played out that way. He'd bristled at their alarm at the sight of him. But when their solicitude had taken the form of questions, prodding, advice, with Giancarlo joining in the chorus of concern, he'd gone off like a landmine.

They'd exchanged the same look that he'd seen on employees faces during the last and most aggressive of his uncharacteristic blowups at his offices. Eduardo and Jade had given Giancarlo—the keeper of the beast—sympathetic murmurs, before they'd left, telling Durante he needed to seek one of two things. A radical lifestyle change. Or psychiatric help. He'd faced it then.

The one thing he needed to seek was her. Gabrielle.

No matter how much he'd told himself to forget her, to move on, he couldn't.

He still couldn't bring himself to seek her out. He missed the persona she'd projected as much as he missed his mother, with the same hopelessness of ever seeing her again. To him, that persona had also disintegrated before it died. The night he'd shared with Gabrielle was entrenched in his memories and senses. He couldn't bear to see her wear another face.

But he'd reached the point where he no longer cared. He had to see her, with any face, at any cost.

He grimaced at his reflection in the full-length mirror then exited his bedroom. At least he no longer looked like the missing link between primates and Neanderthals.

He'd go to her now. This time, he knew what he was getting into, who he was dealing with. He'd walk into the situation with all the brutal clarity of disenchantment, take from her what he needed to get her off his mind and out of his system before walking away...

"I hope this won't get me tossed from the veranda."

Durante rounded on Giancarlo. "If you're worried, as you should be, wear a parachute first. We're high up enough that there's a fifty-fifty chance you'd land with only minor fractures."

Giancarlo grinned. He was Durante's deceased valet's youngest son and was eight years Durante's junior. But for the past seven years, since he'd taken over his father's position, he'd become even more invaluable than his father had been. He was an irreplaceable assistant who observed their situations impeccably in public and in private became a friend as trusted as Durante's younger cousin Eduardo and younger brother Paolo, if less intrusive than either. Not that that said much, because those two were incorrigible. Each had married the "love of his life," and things had gone from bad to dismal.

But Durante wasn't in any condition to humor even Giancarlo. Now that he'd decided to see Gabrielle, he felt as if there were burning coals beneath his feet.

"I know you forbade me to interrupt you unless there was a lot of blood involved—"

"And you're not bleeding," Durante growled. "Yet."

Giancarlo went on as if he hadn't spoken, unperturbed. "—but there's a lady downstairs asking to speak with you. She's—"

"Gabrielle." Her name blared in his mind. He growled it, not wanting Giancarlo to utter it as if he had to be told she was here. When he knew. *Knew.* "Gabrielle Williamson."

Giancarlo nodded. "That's her name, yes. I took the liberty of admitting her to the foyer. I judged she warranted the courtesy, because she was the first woman you ever took to *Angelica,* and the first—and I trust, the last—creature you'll ever sing to. But because you've been like a tiger with a half-ripped-out claw since you stormed down from her residence, I assume you don't want to see her? Shall I tell her you're busy having a breakdown?"

Durante's hiss could have scraped steel. "Bring her up."

Giancarlo gave him an opaque glance. *"Molto bene, principe."*

Durante paced on those coals, feeling the burn spreading through his system. Gabrielle. Here. She'd sought him out. At the exact moment he'd been about to seek her. How did she know that he was ripe for another incursion? How could she be so attuned to thoughts and decisions that seemed random even to him?

Giancarlo returned within two minutes. He wasn't doing a

good job of hiding his smile. Durante would bet he wasn't even trying.

The man cleared his throat as if he were going to sing. "*Signora* Williamson insisted I deliver her message word for word. She said, quote, 'I'm not coming up. You're the one who's coming the hell down here and facing me like a man. If you are one, that is'…unquote."

Durante came the hell down.

After a moment of being unable to believe anyone could not only talk to him that way, but have the temerity to deliver a slap through his right-hand man, to even win said man to her side so that Giancarlo had felt justified and satisfied to transmit it full force.

So he came the hell down. He hurtled, streaked, zoomed and tore his way the hell down. He forced himself to slow once he exited his private elevator. She might have thrown down the gauntlet, but damn if he would give her proof of how she had seeped into his blood, had taken hold of his reactions.

He came to a stop just outside the foyer, depleting reserves of control that he saved for navigating crises of global scope. He yelled inwardly at his instincts, wrestled some rhythm into his heartbeat and breathing. He should make her wait.

He couldn't wait. Her challenge, his eagerness to see her again, was boiling in his blood.

He started walking again, his gait a study in subterfuge, radiating the opposite of what roiled inside him.

He turned the corner and…there she was. Standing at the reception desk, part of her profile visible to him.

She was wearing a skirt suit in another shade of blue, a cross between royal and navy, the richness and depth of the color setting off the clarity of her complexion, the vivid gloss of her hair. The getup was impossibly more flattering than that evening outfit he'd thought the best showcase of her lushness. It molded to her lithe frame, emphasizing her height, the perfection of her proportions, detailing each curve and dip, showing off the symmetry and sculpted creaminess of her legs. Those *legs*. Her flowing skirt had deprived him of seeing them before. He'd had them wrapped around him when he'd been stupid enough to walk away from the promise of fulfillment they'd been offering, almost dealing his potency an irreparable blow.

She was carrying a briefcase. Navy blue to go with her outfit. She looked all business today. And there was this…royal assurance to her bearing, a bring-it-on air to her stance, befitting the potent woman that she was and the mission that had brought her here. To conquer him? He'd bet that was it.

She turned, as if she'd sensed his entrance. She couldn't have possibly seen him, not at the periphery of her vision, not in any reflection. He was still too far for his footsteps to be heard. She had *sensed* him.

And he sensed *her*. Her emanations were unchanged. How did she do that? How did she mess with his perception so that he felt only what she wanted him to feel?

He didn't care. He had to get closer, get more.

He struggled to keep his stride tranquil, as if reaching her was low on his priorities.

When he was finally within arm's reach, he stopped. Her face was a mask captured in blankness, her vibe transmitting nothing of her mood or intentions.

A crack exploded by his ear, on the side of his face, slashing the tranquility of the exclusive foyer's silent occupants and sourceless music.

Seven

Durante blinked, gaped. Beyond stunned. Paralyzed.

He would later swear that she hadn't even moved. But the evidence that she had would resound inside his head forever. Echoes ricocheted off every sound-reflecting surface in the all-marble, chrome and quartz massive space. He barely heard the gasps that went off in a chain reaction of incredulity around him, the quickening footsteps of the guards whose perpetual orders were to stay out of sight.

He made an adamant gesture, banishing them back where they came from. He couldn't bear for others to exist in this moment. Only Gabrielle. Gabrielle, whose eyes were panning away from his with the same void filling them as if she didn't even see him.

Then she brushed past him, walked away with all the grace and serenity of a fairy creature.

It was only when she exited the door the stunned bellman held open for her that Durante registered the burn spreading through his flesh. His hand went instinctively to the pain from the imprint of her fingers, as if to investigate the damage. He moved his mouth from side to side. His jaw felt almost loose.

It excited the hell out of him.

Which made him even more of a colossal fool than he'd realized.

She was pulling his strings. He knew it. But he could sooner resist the pull of a black hole. He rushed out after her.

He caught up with her in less than a minute, her head start and brisk stride no match for his longer legs and urgency.

She suddenly stopped. He overshot her by six strides and retraced them at once.

"Here's the other cheek." He presented her with it. "Go ahead, I know you want to."

She gave no indication that she heard him or even felt him there. She put her briefcase on the ground, opened it, produced a dossier, took papers out, straightened, started reading.

"Prince Durante Benedetto D'Agostino. Eldest son of the King of Castaldini, and therefore, according to the ancient laws of succession, the only member of the extensive D'Agostino royal family ineligible for the crown."

She was reading him a report? On him?

"To prove to the world that his inability to run for the crown meant nothing to him, Prince Durante decided to be king of his own kingdom, emperor of his own empire."

Would there be a point to this somewhere? Knowing what he did about her, she was bound to have a whopper. But what could it be?

"During his meteoric ascent from age twenty, the prince masterminded takeovers that redefined the word *hostile*. Those he took an ax to say that they would have preferred it if he'd taken a contract on their lives and been done with it. Two of those he destroyed *did* end up taking their own lives. Then, at thirty-five, he engineered a market crash that sent thousands into bankruptcy while catapulting himself from mere billionaire status to that of financial god. Ever since, he's been shearing his way through the pantheon, cutting down fellow deities in his climb to the absolute and solitary top."

He'd heard all that before. Not that articulate or concentrated, and certainly not to his face.

She wasn't finished. "On a personal level, it is said that Prince Durante is as cold-blooded and unrepentant a lady-killer as he is a rival-slayer. He is known to pick beauties from those who crowd around his feet, use them and discard them. On one notable occasion, one of his fleeting indulgences tried to commit suicide and is still undergoing intensive psychiatric treatment. Her family reports that Prince Durante systematically destroyed her self-esteem, and she ended up despising herself. A second woman—a married one—said that Prince Durante's influence rivals that of the Prince of Darkness himself. After her husband divorced her and gained custody of their two toddlers, denying her even visitation rights, the spellbound and discarded woman still said that, even knowing where it would lead, she'd do it again. She only wished Prince Durante would take her back."

And he got her point. Right through the heart.

Something else skewered him there. Shame.

He of all people, who suffered slander, shouldn't have been party to perpetuating it, to judging her and carrying out his judgment based on secondhand information.

But beyond shame, which was self-indulgent and worthless, something harsher tore at him. The hurt he felt emanating from her.

He could no longer deny it. His instincts hadn't been tampered with. They'd told him the truth all along. Everything *else* had lied. Everything he'd heard about her had been as false as the reports propagated against him by his enemies.

The fair reports were also out there, as abundant, but they

weren't as interesting as the defamatory ones, weren't sensational enough to be bandied around. His friends didn't feel the need to defend him and he'd never wanted them to, leaving the field wide open to the foes who spoke loudest, were most persistent.

She stopped sifting through the pages. "All reports of Prince Durante's atrocities remain unsubstantiated allegations, because he manages to remain beyond reproach, faultlessly covering his amoral and immoral tracks. As such, he is considered to be our era's only Machiavellian prince. Some even claim that he used Machiavelli's most famous work, *Il Principe—The Prince*—the immortal guide to acquiring and maintaining power, as the template from which he forged his persona and kingdom. What he added of his own heartlessness and intelligence has created a modern hybrid even the philosopher couldn't have imagined being spawned."

He raised his hands, surrendering. "*Abbastanza,* Gabrielle. Enough. You can stop now. I get it."

Without a glance at him, she rearranged the papers back into the dossier, bent to pick up her briefcase. He caught her arm.

"We need to talk." Her blank stare deepened his desperation. He gritted his teeth. "*I* need to talk."

"That you do, now, is of no consequence. I am not here to talk. I am here to tell you something. You're a paranoid bastard who's so full of your own convictions and hang-ups, you can't see how your actions injure and maim people around you. If you have one shred of humanity—and according to your lofty opinion of yourself, you're full of…it—I'm giving you an assignment to find out how much you *do* possess. Write down a list of all the people in your life. Be honest about their condition today, emotionally, psychologically, financially, and calculate the role your condemning, unforgiving nature has played in it."

Her accusation slid right off him. Not because it didn't shame him that it might be true, but because his only concern was for undoing the injury he'd caused *her.*

Pedestrians and even drivers were slowing down to watch the scene unfolding between their city's most famous resident royal and the stunning woman who was clearly telling him off. Some were openly gawking. Some were clicking away on their cell phones.

Not that he cared. But he was beginning to realize the role speculation and the media must have played in smearing her reputation.

He had to take her away from prying eyes and wagging tongues. "Come up with me, Gabrielle. Please."

"No." She extricated her arm from his urgent grip. "If there's one thing I've learned from my…vast experience, it's what to avoid in the interest of self-preservation. I thought being punched black and blue was the worst thing that had happened to me, but now I know how hard *you* hit, I'd be crazy if I came near you again. Goodbye, Prince Durante."

He blocked her path. "*Per favore,* Gabrielle, you must listen to me."

Her disdain would have annihilated a lesser man. At least a less determined one. "As you listened to me? Oh, wait, you didn't give me the chance to say anything to listen to. You heard my name, recalled the report some bored assistant collated on me and disregarded everything you learned about me during that night you kept calling magical and unprecedented—the line you handed me when you wanted to score another one-night stand. Funny part is, although your criteria for one-nighters are reportedly pretty flexible, it seems you draw the line somewhere. At my level."

He surged forward as if to stem the flow of her bitterness. She took two steps back to his every step forward in a wretched parody of a waltz.

He stopped, clenched his fists so he wouldn't haul her over his shoulder and take her someplace where he could make her listen. "You think I leave functions I sponsor, dedicate whole nights and ignore work—for days on end—for anything, let alone what you make sound like scratching an itch? It *was* all real and magical to me."

Something terrible flared in her eyes, which turned the color of turbulent smoke. "Yet as soon as you heard my name, you looked at me as if I were something vile. You made me feel soiled, worthless, like no one has ever made me feel—not the sick jerk I married, not the paparazzi who scoop up his poison to mix with their own and peddle it to the rumor addicts of the world."

Suddenly a man with a cell phone held up toward them came too close. The bastard wanted to get sound with his footage.

"Gabrielle, let's stop this sideshow. Come inside with me."

"This *sideshow* will stop when you move out of my way so I can get on mine. So move. Just don't forget to make that list. Start with your father and work your way down."

"I will. I promise. But I'll start with you."

"Don't bother. I'm sure you felt validated as you walked away from me. Enjoy the company of your prejudice, Prince Durante."

"*Maledizione,* Gabrielle, I wasn't feeling validated when I walked away, I was feeling violated. I've been incapacitated ever since. All the vile things I had heard about you overwhelmed me until all I could see was another trap like those that have been laid for me ever since I became old enough for women to consider me a ticket to wealth and social status. But I'm used to those traps. I watch them being laid in bored amusement. When I thought I'd failed to see yours, I was enraged. But what really hurt was when I started negotiating with myself to let you have whatever you want, so that I could have you, too. That was the lowest place I've ever been. So I walked away."

Her eyes darkened to the color of cumulus about to hurtle down a deluge. Then she gave a slow nod. "Okay. It must be tough being you. It must be almost impossible for you to trust people's motivations enough to indulge in even healthy casual contact. I can relate to that, because the would-be exploiters in my own life make it tough for me to trust anyone. In your case, that must be multiplied by a factor of thousands. I just hope you remember it wasn't my idea to hide my identity that long, that I only delayed introducing myself until you gave me a fair hearing, fearing the reaction you ended up so predictably having anyway."

"You don't have to remind me how things went, or that it was I who steered the situation. I remember every second of that night."

"I'm sure you had fun superimposing your version of my 'trap laying' on every second."

"Fun? I said I was paralyzed for the past few days. I've been going mad wondering how you fooled my instincts so totally, yet wanting you so fiercely still, I was willing to risk anything to have you."

"Sure. You were so out of your mind you would have never seen me again if I hadn't insulted you into confronting me."

"I wasn't in the least insulted. I was stunned, then thrilled. And I was on my way to find you when you arrived."

That startled her. But not for long. She clearly discounted his claim, huffed. "What a coincidence, huh?"

"I don't believe it's a coincidence. I think we're attuned to one another on a very basic level. We reached the same decision, reached our limit for staying apart at the same time."

"Not exactly the same time. I arrived here when the idea of coming after me was still in the embryonic stage with you."

His lips twitched. "Actually, it was in the last stage of labor."

Her lips almost gave in to the humor tugging at them. Almost. He knew part of her was reveling in their volley match, but she wasn't about to let him get off that easy. As she shouldn't.

"Still, according to your theory, because I acted first on that transmission between us, either my receptors are keener, or signals take longer to penetrate that thick skull of yours."

This was a serious situation. As serious as when she'd been relating her life story. She'd poked fun then, too, if at herself.

He shouldn't. He couldn't help it.

He threw back his thick skull and laughed.

No one else had or would ever talk to him like that. Only her.

He stopped laughing abruptly when her gaze strayed behind him. He turned. His bodyguards had closed in and were trying and failing to look as if they were not on full alert.

"So even your bodyguards are terrified I might suck you dry or swallow you whole, huh?" She smirked.

"Should you really be saying things like 'suck you dry' and 'swallow you whole' to me, out here, where I can't do much about it? Now that's a spectacularly effective method of punishment."

Divine color cascaded from her sculpted cheekbones to flood her face and neck. His mouth tingled to latch onto every inch until *he* swallowed *her* whole.

"You turn everything into a sexual innuendo," she muttered.

"Believe it or not—and you're not in the mood to believe anything I say—I never did before. I never saw the attraction in the practice. Now I can't see anything but."

She fidgeted, as if her skin were suddenly too tight. No matter how affronted, how hurt she was, her body still yearned for his. That was the one thing he hadn't doubted. He'd thought she'd been playing him, but enjoying him with every fiber of her voluptuous body while at it.

She stole a self-conscious look at his bodyguards. "They're almost reaching for their guns. Do you have an APB out on imminent redheaded danger?"

"They're jumpy because the last time I stopped in the street to talk to someone I know, he stabbed me." Horror burst into her eyes. After a frozen moment, they wrenched from his, careened down his body, as if she could see the injury through his clothes. "Then he bid ten million for a chance to say he was sorry."

"He was the…? Oh, God…was it…? Are you…?" She seemed unable to go on, her throat working as if swallowing tears.

After what he'd done to her, seeing her so disturbed to think of him hurt was too much.

He interrupted her agitation. "I moved out of the direct path of his thrust. He only penetrated skin and muscles in my left flank."

Her hand jerked up, trembled as it reached halfway to where his injury was, before she fisted it, pulled it back.

The unwilling gesture of concern closed his throat. "And you know what? I'll add him to my list. I was adamant about not giving him a second chance, but now I'll seek him out to talk this through. I find I have a new wealth of empathy for him and his need for forgiveness now that I'm in the same position."

She gaped. "You're equating a physical wound with a moral one?"

"I think the moral one is far worse in this situation. I didn't lose any sleep over the flesh wound. And there are no lingering ill effects. But even though I don't expect you to forgive me any more easily than I chose to forgive him, I demand that you give me another chance, so that I can earn your forgiveness."

"Demand? My, is that a royal edict, Your Highness?"

His lips twisted. "I'm a bit out of my jurisdiction, royally speaking. But then, this is my new kingdom, as your report put it. My demands here *are* considered edicts."

She coughed a furious chuckle. "You've just shot through the barrier of unbelievability into the realm of what's-he-on." She thrust her dossier at him. "Here, keep this. Read it through for laughs if you want to see how creative people can get in their vindictiveness, in case you don't fully know yet. I only read you the highlights, which amounted to three pages out of sixty-two."

She walked away then. He knew she wasn't going to stop.

He had to get her back anyway he could. He called after her.

"You wanted me to write a book baring the details of my life and journey to success, the workings of my mind and methods. I'm interested."

She whirled around, a magnificent lioness with a mane of fire, her eyes iridescent with ire. "Oh, no, you're not."

Lust corkscrewed in his loins. He savored the twisting ache, cocked his head. "You've changed your mind about your offer?"

Her eyes narrowed at him. "You know I haven't."

"How do I know that when you didn't bring it up again?"

"I didn't bring it up at all. First you wouldn't hear of business, then you wouldn't hear anything I had to say."

"I want to hear everything you have to say now."

"*Sei serio?* You're serious? This isn't just pretext for…for…"

"For taking you to bed? No. Although I am suffering permanent damage here as we speak, because I haven't taken you to bed and kept you there for the last ten days, because I'm standing in the middle of smog-infested, ground-level downtown New York instead of lying inside you in a bed eighty floors up in serenity and seclusion, I *am* interested in hearing about your book offer."

Suspicion flared higher in her eyes. "And why are you?"

"Because I believe that anything you propose will have a lot to recommend it. I didn't say I'd accept, though."

She pursed her lips. "Fair enough. I want you to accept only if I convince you, not because you want me in your bed. In fact, I won't sign a thing if that's your motive. Contrary to 'common knowledge,' I don't barter my body for business deals."

"I don't either." She narrowed her eyes. He held out his hand, inviting, placating, coaxing, barely holding back the need to reestablish the connection, to drag her into his arms. "I owe you one hour of the exclusive use of my ear. Then, if you wish, you can have the exclusive use of the rest of my body."

Eight

Gabrielle looked up at Durante from his kitchen table.

He was handing her a hot chocolate he'd prepared himself.

She took the very masculine, clean-cut, but clearly expensive and possibly specially made fine China mug from him. He brought his own and sat across from her, dominating his stainless steel and obsidian marble spaceship of a kitchen.

This was surreal. To be in his kitchen of all places, with him waiting on her. In fact, she didn't know if she'd actually walked back to his building, crossed the extensive foyer littered with still-gaping denizens, entered his private elevator and ended up in his floor-wide penthouse, or if he'd levitated her there.

She wouldn't put it past him. Those reports hadn't exaggerated his influence at all.

He leaned across the table, enveloped her hand in his—the one that had slapped him—smoothed his thumb over her knuckles, before turning it over and doing the same to her palm.

"Can you please stop that?"

"Why? You like it. From your breathing, I'd say too much. Is that the problem?"

"I didn't come here with slapping you in mind, Durante…"

"But you saw me and emotion overwhelmed your judgment?"

"Quite the reverse actually. I held myself back at the last moment." She told him what she'd done in her dream.

He bellowed with laughter. "So I owe it to your self-mastery that I'm not now undergoing rhinoplasty and a jaw reset." He wiped tears of hilarity with one hand, the other taking hers to his lips. He planted tiny kisses on knuckle after another, zapping her with enough voltage to power a block. "Ah, *Gabriella mia, grazie a Dio* you held back, or these works of divine art would be bruised and swollen now. But let me assure you, your slap almost achieved one of your wishes. My jaw may never resume its former position."

"If the way you're using your mouth is any indication, I'd say I made it extra efficient."

He lunged across the table. Before she even blinked, he twisted hair at her nape, tilted up her face and claimed her lips in a compulsive kiss. He inhaled as he took and took of her until she felt he'd drawn her essence inside him. The warm, moist firmness of his lips, the way they plucked at hers, massaged, kneaded, shot tremors from her lips to her core. Then he exhaled and thrust deep, flooding her with his taste and scent.

Each kiss he gave her was new, different, giving her more and more. It was as if, through every press and glide and thrust, he was fathoming her preferences, many she didn't know herself, deciphering the code of her responses, the combination to unlock the pleasure her body had the potential to feel and never had.

She'd become addicted from the first exposure, had felt hollow knowing she'd never have more.

She did now. Could have far more if she dared. Again.

His rejection still reverberated in her marrow.

She recoiled from the echo of anguish just as he released her, sat down heavily in his chair, threw his head back and closed his eyes, veins standing out in his corded neck.

He let out a slow, ragged breath and opened his eyes. Streaks of brilliant blue radiation seemed to sweep over her and through her with unbridled carnality. "In the interest of self-preservation, let's drink our concoction and discuss your offer." He sat forward, linked his hands. "So, what makes your offer different? You advertized your certainty that I couldn't refuse it."

She blinked. "I only said that to Gerald Whittacker as he wanted to champion my request but wanted to make sure I was on to something that wouldn't be a waste of your time. I didn't think he'd relay it to you."

"How do you know Gerald?"

She set her teeth. "How do you think?"

He sighed. "I admit, I thought…the worst. At first." She bristled, and his eyes gentled. "Now I'm just curious, not suspicious."

She searched his face. There was no trace of the distrust and condemnation that had destroyed her the day he'd walked away.

Something inside her broke down in relieved sobs.

She bit her lip on the surge of moronic elation. "He used to be Dad's golf instructor before my dad's condition worsened, and before Gerald made his fortune. I earned myself a soft spot in his heart by running my own heart out retrieving balls for him."

He closed his eyes, tipped his head and smiled, as if he were watching something funny and endearing across his lids. When he opened his eyes, they were filled with something far more dangerous than passion, suspicion or anger. Tenderness.

"You must have been younger than five. I can just imagine you, strong limbs and boundless energy, streaking after errant balls, in pursuit of approval and smiles."

That was how it had been exactly. Gerald had given her a glimpse of what paternal indulgence could be like, when her father hadn't been able to provide it. And somehow Durante had looked back in time and knew. She wanted him to know the rest.

"While I'm debunking the myths about my being a gold-digging man-eater, I want you to know where they came from."

His wave was dismissing, adamant. "I don't need explanations."

"*I* need to tell you. The details, anyway. I already told you the basics…about my ex. I've never told anybody the truth. In fact, that secrecy is the reason behind my negative reputation. You see, I didn't bring up my hospital stay and the charges I pressed during divorce proceedings. My lawyers insisted that if I exposed him, he'd be harmed, but I'd gain nothing but more lawsuits and having him in my life endlessly. They got me a huge settlement in return for silence. It wasn't enough punishment for what he did to me, but I figured I was cutting that monster in half. But then, he took advantage of my silence to defame me. He gets more vicious as time goes by, knowing that if I speak up now, I'll be known as the bitch who's slandering the poor ex she robbed of half his fortune. That final day in court, he swore he'd make my life hell. And he sure is trying his worst. I guess the few men I rejected afterward make a good chorus for his venom."

His look had darkened as she spoke, was almost black now.

She groaned. "What are you thinking?"

Something chilling slithered in the depths of his eyes. His lips spread in a frightening parody of a smile. He looked like some malevolent deity. She already knew he was formidable, but she could now see how deadly he could be.

"I'm thinking it's time Edward Jamieson lost the other half of his fortune. And for the truth about him to become public. A man like him would be a serial abuser. There are bound to be other women he's hurt and paid off into silence. I'm also thinking it's time for his first wife's death to be fully investigated."

She gaped at him. "Remind me never to become your enemy."

His switch from ferocity to fondness was dizzying. "Not only is there no danger of that, but I'm only an effective enemy to those who've been their own worst enemies. All I need to do to crush him is expose the crimes he committed."

"So that's how you decimate your rivals, huh? Through their own wrongdoing?"

"And by doing nothing wrong myself, so no one can retaliate. Except with allegations such as what you came armed with today."

She chewed her lip. "I would have told you to leave him alone, that he and his lies don't matter, if you hadn't reminded me that he could be abusing other women—women who may not be able to defend themselves like I did. So, as long as the investigations are honest, by all means, crush away."

He crooked her a whimsical smile. "As long as? You think there's a chance I'd fabricate evidence? Frame him?"

"No! I know from your history—and from personal experience—that you retaliate with disproportionate force when crossed, but I've come to believe that you do so when you think you're justified, not out of malice. I believe you're unforgiving, but not unscrupulous. You're an avenger—you might act before you get your facts straight, but you're never a villain."

He sat forward, placed both elbows on the quartz table, cupped his face in his palms, his eyes heavy with exhilaration and indulgence. "That's quite a testimony. I think." He winked at her. "If I ever run for public office anywhere, my slogan will be An avenger, never a villain."

She was struggling to convince her heart to restart when he drawled, "So…sell me on your proposal."

Thankful for the detour away from personal landmines, she breathed deep, struggled to access the pitch she'd prepared.

"Okay." She sat forward. "The book I envision is not like any you've received offers to write. I'm not after the sensational angles in your life, real or fabricated. In fact, I don't want you to expose anything about your personal life beyond your health, exercise and relaxation habits. You know, anything that kept you functioning to capacity for the past twenty years, soaring from one pinnacle to the next. I want you to explore your drive, your discipline. I want this to be the work-ethic motivation book of all time, a book any young person would read and be inspired to jump up and tackle the world."

His eyes had grown serious as she talked. He suddenly huffed. "It's ironic to hear you saying 'soaring' when those closest to me are insisting I'm perilously close to crashing and burning."

Her heart skipped another beat. "What's *your* opinion?"

"I think they're on to something. At least, they *were.*"

The meaning simmering in his eyes quivered in her heart. She almost shouted for him to stop. Keep it strictly sexual. She might know how to handle it if he did. But he didn't, and she couldn't hope he meant what she hoped he meant. Therein lay certain annihilation.

But there was something far stronger than fear for her fate. Concern for him. "Do you have any complaints, any symptoms?"

He started to dismiss her question, then changed his mind, leveled his eyes on her. "The main symptom is that I 'retaliate with disproportionate force when crossed.' I never had a temper and it's maddening that I seem to have developed one."

"So what's loosening your screws?"

"Public opinion says I've been chronically fatigued and sleep deprived for years. All I know is that I'm working more and more and sleeping less and less. When I do sleep, I don't remember any of my dreams, to the point that I think I don't dream."

"Do you need to work that hard?"

"That's what my friends keep asking."

Her eyebrows shot up. "You have friends?"

His laugh boomed. "Wonders will never cease, will they? I, for one, sometimes wonder how I do. There are two in particular I want you to meet, my cousin and his bride. I think you'll really get along with Jade. She hones her tongue at the same rapier maker that you do." She made a face at him and he laughed again. "No, I don't have to work a fraction as hard to 'maintain my power.' But I've become unable to slow down, like a train without brakes. It's become self-perpetuating, sort of an addiction. I guess I am too much like my father. He slowed down when he was in his fifties. And he still streaked past everyone else."

It shook her. Again. The enormity of feeling that radiated from him when he mentioned his father. The first time there'd been so much anger it had thrown her. This time there was no doubt. He *loved* him.

It was probably the magnitude of his love that caused his feelings of betrayal to be so vast, made what he believed to be the breach of his trust so irredeemable.

She wanted to protest that he had it all wrong, as he had with her, that he didn't have to live with disillusionment eating away at him, that he had to give his father the benefit of the doubt, even if the king couldn't provide evidence to exonerate himself.

But she couldn't. She'd given King Benedetto her word. And if she started that argument, Durante would notice she wasn't just drawing parallels between his treatment of her and his father, would see her emotional investment in his father's cause. He'd ask. And if he asked, she'd tell him. And she *couldn't*.

But maybe there was some way around this, other than breaking her word. Durante was starting to talk, as she was convinced he hadn't before. Maybe he'd purge his angst, give his father a chance, like he was willing to give one to the man who'd stabbed him. Maybe things would go where the king hoped.

Not that it made her situation any better. When she'd given her word, she'd thought there'd be nothing but business contact with Durante, that she'd be the voice of reason before she exited his life at the conclusion of the deal. Now everything had changed and she felt as if she was lying to him when she—

"Any number of millions for your thoughts."

Durante's deep purr short-circuited her turmoil. She breathed a nervous laugh. "You always toss around carte blanche like that?"

He sipped his drink, his gaze caressing her over his mug's rim. "Never even in jest. Only for you. So where did you go?"

She reached for her mug, gulped the rich sweetness as if it would fortify her. "I was musing if your case is genetic."

He took another sip, looking thoughtful. "Maybe. Probably. Still think I'd make a good example for the youths of the world?"

"I think this glitch in your system…humanizes you, makes your experience more accessible, can make young people aspire to walk in your footsteps while learning how to recognize bad habits before they take hold of their lives."

He gave her a bedeviling smile. "As they did of mine?"

She groaned. "Believe it or not, I used to be a very suave negotiator. But don't hold my big mouth against the project, okay? I do believe your story can change lives, and although I know there is no advance that wouldn't make you yawn, if this is a bestseller—and I can't imagine it won't be—Le Roi will only keep what would float us and the rest goes to charity. All returns will be distributed for free wherever you choose."

He frowned. "You company is in trouble?"

"You didn't know?"

"I ran a personal background check on you. If I'd decided to talk business, I would have run the business check."

So that was why he hadn't brought up her company's Castaldinian connections. He didn't know of them. She might not be able to tell him of her connection with his father, but she had to inform him of those, before he ran that check.

He ran a tender finger down her cheek. "Tell me."

And she told him. Everything. Everything she could.

He'd stilled when she'd mentioned Castaldini, his expression going opaque. When she fell silent, he lowered his eyes, lost in thought. Then he finally looked back at her. His eyes were glittering with wonder.

"So this is why you were interested in me originally."

She gave a difficult nod. It was the truth, but not the whole truth. And she was not at liberty to share the rest.

"This *is* fate, for you to be connected to my homeland, to seek me out, to let me find you through this connection." He rose, came around, pulled her to her feet, his hands filled with such gentleness. Thoughts scattered on his kitchen's porcelain floor as he put a loose arm low around her waist. "But don't worry, about anything. Everything is going to be fine, I promise."

She blinked up at him in confusion as he walked her back through his hangar-sized penthouse. "What do you mean?"

They passed through a twenty-foot-wide arch into a sitting room with one wall made of floor-to-ceiling glass overlooking the most spectacular view of Manhattan and the ocean that she'd ever seen.

"Just what I said." He took her to the wall window, his smile the essence of reassurance. She looked down the eighty-floor sheer drop and pressed back into him. He tugged her a couple of steps back where she could get the full impact of the view without activating any twinges of acrophobia. "Everything will work out."

And that was clearly all she'd get from him on the subject.

She stood there, unable to fracture the moment, break the meld, her body a battleground of desire and dread. Then he whispered against her temple, "I never wrote anything, let alone a book. I was the worst essay writer in my class, in any language. My essays, to borrow an Americanism, sucked. A few dry-as-tinder lines with a sledgehammer of a conclusion along the lines of 'Own your mistakes or you're screwed.'"

She pushed away at last, put much-needed air between them, raised an eyebrow. "As you always do?"

He took her ridicule with a grin. "I try. I'm trying now."

She gave him a considering look. "Hmm. It's clear you owned far more mistakes than not. In your professional life. That's why *that* isn't screwed." He grimaced at her allusion that his personal one was. "Anyway, that sledgehammer would be perfect for the heading of a chapter. That's the kind of succinct conclusion I want you to fill the book with. Coming from you, the epitome of phenomenal success, you have the platform and the credibility to make self-help gurus of the known universe look like they're spouting unsupported nonsense."

"I might have the platform and the credibility, but I also have a handicap to negate them both. I write like you sing."

She burst out giggling. "Trust me, you can't be that bad."

He grinned back at her, riddling her sight with blind spots. "See, another handicap. No subtlety. I was trying and failing to hint that I'll need help." He pulled her to him, his hands filled with careful power as he contained her. "Lots and lots of it."

She moaned. "Durante…"

He lowered his head. "*Sì, Gabriella.* Say my name like that."

She averted her face before his lips connected with hers. It was like leaping over one volcano to plunge into another. His lips scorched down her face instead, her neck, his whispers of her name an invocation, a supplication, tampering with all electrical activity powering her. Her brain waves blipped, her heart rhythm plunged into arrhythmia.

She gasped, pushed at him. He let her go at once, his gaze heavy with desire and regret. "Still punishing me?"

"I don't indulge in pointless posturing. Life's too short."

"Exactly. And this, along with the past ten days, is time we won't get back."

"Philosophy is great, when one can afford it. I can't. Life is also too short to spend any of it feeling as miserable as I did during those ten days."

He reached for her again. "And you won't. I promise."

She scrambled away as if from the ledge of this skyscraper. "I-I came up here for two reasons, Durante. Because I believed you were interested in my offer. And because I couldn't take one more would-be paparazzi covering our little sideshow."

He grunted. "Forget them. They don't matter."

"Really? Strange. You condemned me based on 'facts' people like them perpetuated."

"*Ero uno sciocco,* I was a fool. A moron."

"*And* a senseless jerk. Oh, wait, am I allowed to say 'jerk' to Your Highness? No? Bummer. I'll say it anyway."

"You're allowed to say anything to My Highness as long as you deem to talk to me at all. But senseless jerk that I am, I came to my senses. Don't I get points toward a second chance for that?"

"You would have, if you *had* come to your senses. Which you didn't. I slapped some sense into you. You were wallowing in your senselessness and decided to seek me in spite of what you believed, not because you no longer believed it. You thought I was a succubus but were risking being drained of life to satisfy your curiosity and lust. Or was danger what fueled your desire, sort of like the rush of sticking your hand in a snake pit?"

"I was doing it in spite of the danger I thought you represented, not because of it. I don't get my kicks that way."

"You get them by thinking the worst of people. By never giving them the chance to defend themselves, condemning them and carrying out the sentence. And if one of your victims is your own father, I guess I was in great company."

"*Maledizione,* Gabrielle...*sì, bene?* It's true, only those who matter can make me react emotionally. I've only ever had those crippling feelings in relation to two people in my life. My mother and my father. Now you."

"That's supposed to make me feel special? I got the full, mutilating effect of your anger because of how much I mattered?"

"Hard to believe but...*sì.*"

"What's freaking impossible to believe is you. I live with a lot of casual cruelty, but now I know how it can hurt when someone who *matters* doles it out. I have no support system and the only one who'll defend me is me. The only way I know how to do that is to stay away from you. So if you're not interested in my offer if it doesn't come attached with me in your bed, say so and let me go."

"You said you understood why I reacted the way I did. If you do, then you realize it will never happen again."

"All I know is that you judged me based on unsubstantiated evidence. The evidence against you was as damning, yet I believed my own senses, my own mind, my own experience of you."

He raked his fingers through his hair, linked them at the back of his head in a gesture of a man at a total loss. He closed his eyes, rumbling the unmistakable fury of self-abuse. Then he opened them, all previous lightness and cajoling gone.

"I've broken your trust in my basic fairness, in my ability to always treat you with consideration and respect."

Every muscle in her face trembled. He'd put her biggest fear in words. She nodded. A tear splashed on her lip.

He winced as if the tear had hit his flesh, burned it. "I would offer amends, anything at all, but it seems I hurt you too much and it won't matter what I do, not now." He rubbed a hand over his eyes. "I *was* interested to hear your offer. And you've convinced me. I agree to the basic concept, but we'll work out the specifics. Send me the draft of the contract at your convenience. I'll inform you of any amendments at the earliest."

When he said no more, she stuck her hands at her waist. "So what are you saying? 'You don't want my amends so I won't bother to make them'? And then what? 'Would have been fun knowing you'?"

His eyes probed her. "What are *you* saying, Gabrielle?"

"That it's surely heartening to see how long you thought 'making amends' warranted. It's been—" she flicked a look at her watch "—forty-eight minutes. That must be an all-time record for you. Bet you don't even consider apologizing to anyone. Guess that's another thing that makes me mighty special. Yay me."

"Are you being a contrary female, *Gabriella mia?* Saying you want something, then getting disappointed when you get it? Or are you saying no when you mean yes, to make me grovel?"

"Are you being a condescending chauvinist, Your Highness? I was commenting on the limits of your perseverance. When I didn't collapse under your charm after a few nudges…poof. Suddenly it's "I would do anything, but you don't want me to, so I'll save myself the trouble.' Talk about staying power. Lack of, that is."

"Do watch what you say to me right now, *Gabriella mia.* I am in a very critical condition. I'm a breath away from an all-day-and-night campaign to prove my…staying power to you." Desire forked from every point his eyes touched to her womb. He trickled a phantom touch down her cheek. "I was letting you go because I thought you were still raw, that I was causing you more distress. I was giving you a couple of days to cool down—*maledizione,* I probably wouldn't have lasted a couple of hours. Then I was coming after you and never stopping until you gave me a second chance."

"Great. And because *never* has forever scope, you won't mind if I go now. Plenty of time for 'we'll see, won't we' in forever…"

And she was in his arms, singed in the inferno of his ardor. "Don't walk away, *bellissima.* I'm the knee-jerk jerk here."

"Let me go and no one will get hurt, Your Royal Jerkness."

"It's too late. I would have gotten hurt if I'd let you go before I laughed with you, caused your tears, tasted your hunger."

"Durante…" Her voice broke as she put her fear into words. "You're way out of my league."

"You're the only one I want in mine. Say you want me, too."

She squeezed her eyes, shuddered. "You *know* I do."

"Then forgive me, *Gabriella mia.* And don't be afraid, I won't consider this license to forgive myself." She succumbed, nodded, buried her face in his neck. He groaned in relief, branded her forehead in a convulsive kiss. *"Grazie molto, bellissima."*

She burrowed deeper into his neck. This was inevitable. He was inexorable. She craved him with such intensity that she no longer cared if it all ended horribly tomorrow. She had to have now.

"Now tell me…" He swept her up in his arms. "Would you mind if I took you fast and ferocious the first couple of times?"

Nine

"The first couple of times?"

Durante lips spread at the squeak in Gabrielle's voice, the disbelief in her eyes. At having her precious weight and surrender filling his arms after almost losing her, in so many ways.

And he had almost lost her. In the one way he wouldn't have been able to live with. Through his own actions.

She was everything he'd felt she was from the first moment, everything that captured his imagination and commanded his appreciation, roused his soul and aroused his senses. Proud and fierce, sharp and quick, pure of heart, rich in soul, as vulnerable as she was indomitable. He'd read her as accurately as she'd read him. He was certain now. No more doubts. He'd never let the outside world come between them again.

This time, and from now on, there would be no holding back. There'd be only holding on. He'd never let her go.

He gathered her tighter in his arms, filled his eyes and senses with her beauty as she clung to him, answered her incredulity.

"Maybe after the second time I'll be able to slow down a bit. I can guarantee slow, though, so slow until you beg, until you faint with pleasure, after the third time."

"The *third* time?"

"Do you hear an echo?" He smiled into the eyes he could swear were emitting silver heat and hunger and…anxiety?

He wanted to kick himself. With what she'd suffered at a man's hand, she could be totally misinterpreting his words.

He stopped in the massive vestibule separating reception and living quarters. Even though everything in him screamed not to lose contact with her, he gently put her down. She swayed, clung to him, her eyes a mixture of drugged arousal, confusion and alarm.

"What are you thinking, *bellissima?*"

She blinked at him. "Thinking? You think I can think now?"

"You look…anxious." She bit a lip that trembled her confession. He cupped her face, freed that lip with a caressing thumb. "Is there anything you want me to know? Anything you don't want me to do? Anything that might trigger distasteful memories?"

Understanding crept over her face, followed by urgency. "No! No, Durante, don't think that, please. If I'm anxious it's because I don't know if I can…you see, I-I've never…you know…"

Suspicion rose in him at her embarrassment, became certainty in a heartbeat. "You never enjoyed sex."

"I-I know I can, since I-I…"

"You pleasure yourself. But you never climax with a partner."

Her color became dangerous. "Do you know everything? Or are you reading my mind?" She shut her eyes in mortification.

He brushed her eyes open with both thumbs. "And I told you I'll take you fast and ferocious and you thought I'd take my pleasure and leave you feeling used and frustrated."

"No, no…I know you wouldn't…it's me…I'm having…"

His lips twisted. "Performance anxiety."

"You *do* know everything!" She buried her face in her hands, before dropping them, exhaling, eyes downcast. "Way to go, huh? Telling you that now, ruining everything."

"You told someone before, probably your ex, and he used it to blame you for his shortcomings," he growled. Giving that piece of trash a taste of his own medicine was fast becoming an emergency. "And of course he told you how he never failed to please other women, women who miraculously attain orgasm through their own feminine normalcy, even with a fumbling, re-pulsive, self-seeking, two-minute scumbag who thinks all he has to do to be a great lover is get an erection, insert and ejaculate."

She coughed a distressed laugh. "Basically…yeah. Apart from that description of him, which he of course didn't say, but was and did. This is uncanny. How do you know that? Do you know men like that?"

"There *are* no men like that. He's not a man, he's one of a breed of inferiority-ridden, ugliness-infested bastards who feel nothing but the urge to relieve their pathetic itches, who know no higher motivation than to grab, use, and when confronted with their own deficiencies, abuse."

She nodded, averted her eyes. "I agree."

He frowned. She didn't look as if she did, not fully. "But?"

She looked as if she hoped the parquet floor would become an ocean she could plunge into and never resurface. "But in this case, it wasn't his fault alone. I-I tried with others…many others…"

Images charred imprints on his mind. Of her, in other men's beds, her body open to their exploitation, at their mercy…

A wave of nausea rose until it tinged his sight with yellowed bile, something monstrous, grotesque ripping him open from the gut outward, fang and talon.

Jealousy. Something he'd never imagined feeling before.

Next moment, it subsided. It had no soil to take root in. The past meant nothing, not hers, not his. Or hers did only in terms that he must adjust his approach, from the freedom of taking by storm the woman he'd thought experienced, holding nothing back in his certainty that she could match his ferocity, know her preferences and demand them from him, to the care of taking the woman who'd experienced nothing but abuse and dissatisfaction.

"You were a virgin when you married him?" She nodded, her unease bordering on pain. "And we know how you felt about him. And those others—how did you feel about them?"

"I felt nothing, really. It wasn't about feelings. It should have been about physical gratification."

"Did you feel a fire inside you that could only be extinguished by physical union with any of them?"

"Uh, no, nothing like that. But I didn't hate the sight of them. They didn't fire me up, but they didn't repulse me, either."

"So you were trying to force yourself to eat when you weren't hungry, things which from the scent and look of them, weren't appetizing at all. Is it any wonder you didn't enjoy your meal?"

She stared at him before hooting with laughter. "That's priceless. And perfect. I was trying to eat limp, taste-free, homogenous-looking veggies because I was told they were good for me."

"Limp, eh?" He watched her wipe tears away, stopped himself from gathering her up again. She needed to sort this out in her mind before he took it to the realm of the flesh, where even he had no experience. Not with what would happen between them. "And how did I make you feel when you first saw me? How am I making you feel now?"

Her eyes widened, wonder seeping in, inching away agitation. "I saw you, and everything around me…vanished. Everything inside me started…tingling. I ached every time you moved and spoke. It got so bad, I wanted to scream. But it was also so good. Incredible. Like everything was enhanced, like there was this super charge of…*life* powering me. You made me feel with parts of me I was unaware of. And it hasn't stopped since, not even when you weren't there. I have only to think of you for you to affect me. Even when something else forces itself into my focus, you exist here now…"

Her hands flew to her head, pressed convulsively, before cascading over her face, her neck, her breasts, her abdomen and then lower, where they crossed and stroked their way from her hips upward until she was hugging her own arms.

He felt as if she had taken him inside every part of her, had him wrapped around her now.

"You're everywhere, a burn my blood carries to every inch of skin, a pressure building inside me. And then you look at me, talk to me, and it all becomes overwhelming. Flames burst out wherever your gaze lands. Currents bolt through me at the sound of your voice, at your touch. But it's your desire that…that…" She stopped, consternation clenching her face. "I'm doing a lousy job here. I can't describe it. And that was the easy part, the physical one."

He did have superhuman powers. He bit back at the urges sinking their fangs in him, didn't devour her in one go per his original impulse. Even though he was almost certain he'd give her as explosive a pleasure as he'd get.

The "almost" part stopped him. That and the need to show her the truth. About herself. About what he felt for her. There'd be endless time later for all levels of unrestrained mating.

He moved until his thigh brushed hers. Her chest heaved, her nipples conquering the thickness of her blouse through her open jacket. The creaminess of her skin had long disappeared in a tide of pink. Her lips were glazed with the flush of blood, skin taut over swelling flesh. His mental possession was doing this to her. He had the power to make her feel he was ravaging her for real just by imagining it so fiercely.

His forefinger skimmed her nose, her lips, down, until it rested at the edge of a now-visible cleavage, tormented them both with gossamer glimpses of what would be. "So when you feel all that, what do you expect it would be like with me?"

She moaned. "I-I don't know, okay? I just need to feel you, be with you."

He held her at arm's length. He couldn't just grab her. He had to prove to her that she was a sensual being of the highest order, attuned to such a level of sensitivity only a specific vibe—his—would release her potential, that any other's had been bound to grate, to even injure.

Yet he couldn't just claim that she'd been made for him, as he was now certain. He could only show her. And how he would.

But she was looking at him as if he'd stuck a knife in her gut. She wrenched herself from his detaining hands, almost ran away. He was so surprised that she was in his reception area, scooping up her briefcase when he caught up with her.

He put himself between her and the elevator. He had to be careful here. He didn't know what was upsetting her now.

"Any hope you'll explain where you think you're going?"

"Away. Before I mutilate the mood I just murdered."

That was the one thing he hadn't extrapolated as a reason for her sudden flight. Her surprises would never cease.

"I bet when you spent all this time cajoling me, you thought you were in for hot sex, not a sex therapy session with a thirty-year-old frigid divorcée." She took a step back, preparing to circumvent him. "No harm done, though. I hope. So—"

He dragged her to him, slammed her length against his, the collision a need, a must. Her briefcase slapped the floor as she arched into him, a carnal sound keening from her, her hands clawing an anchor in his flesh.

He wanted her to sink in all the way, penetrate him to the bone. His growl sounded feral as he snatched her off her feet, aching at how totally she distrusted her influence, how she'd been sought out only by men who had dealt her self-esteem and expectations of others one blow after another. It only made her trust in him that much more precious.

He captured her hands, withdrew enough to take one to his

heart, the other to the erection that hadn't subsided since he'd seen her. "So…which part of me seems not in the mood, *bellissima?*"

"This-this isn't just a typical male reaction? All my pathetic confessions didn't turn you off, here?" She freed the hand on his erection, pressed it to his head.

He pressed back, showing her he needed her assuagement. "I don't have male reactions if 'here' doesn't sanction them. And none of what you told me was pathetic. It ranged from criminal to inept on the men's side, and tragic to futile on yours. But I am honored beyond expression that when it came to me, you knew, like I did, that nothing that happened before applies to us. And it doesn't. This *is* us, and you have nothing to worry about. Not now, not ever." He turned his lips into her palm, planted his pledge. "You'll find only pampering and pleasure in my bed, support and protection everywhere else. I promise."

She surged forward, tears brimming over, and hugged breath out of him. "Oh, Durante, just take me. Take me before I wake up."

He threw his head back in exultation and relief. "This is one dream we're not waking up from. This I promise, too."

And she did something that made his whole being quiver as if it were about to explode.

She curled up against his heart and subsided. The extent of trust in the gesture almost brought him to his knees with emotions he'd never experienced. Gratitude, humility.

He crushed her to him, drank her down to her last moan. She only gave more, rubbed against him, opened her lips over any part she could reach of him and her legs as far as her pencil-slim skirt would allow, offering all the exquisiteness and passion that was her. He wanted to probe her, go berserk on finding her soaking, burning, crazy for everything he'd do to her. Then he wanted to do it all.

But something niggled at him. Something vital. He couldn't remember what. His mind had shut down, her arousal hitting him like a full-body blow. He'd better put the plan he'd just come up with into action, keep her with him until he remembered. He held her off, cupped her face. "Tell me, *Gabriella mia,* how do you feel about flying?"

Gabrielle had said she felt fine. About flying. And Durante had kissed more of her sanity away before walking out.

He now returned, a force of nature enveloping her as he led her out to his soccer field of a veranda.

She squinted into the sun as it glowed red on its descent into the ocean. Flying, huh? Literally or figuratively?

She wouldn't put anything past him.

Then they turned a corner against the high-rise wind, and it all made sense. As much sense as finding herself staring back at the gleaming black vicious beauty crouching in the middle of a large yellow circle on the ground.

He had his own freaking copter and helipad right outside his veranda door! With seventy-foot rotors, a passenger compartment big enough for half a dozen people and an outer body right out of some sci-fi flick.

Which really figured. When you had a fleet of jets, why not a multimillion-dollar toy to avoid the hassle of traffic jams?

Durante strapped her with utmost care on board the futuristic vehicle, taking the pilot seat, performing all safety measures then launching them in the air. She felt she'd left her stomach on the ground, along with a few nerves that snapped as she had her first personal encounter with seeing land recede almost beneath her feet.

He touched her gently, as if he knew, as he always seemed to know what she felt. Then he seemed to remember something major.

He'd cleared the city and veered out over the endlessness of the ocean, when he looked at her with that tenderness she'd never seen in another man's eyes and murmured, so quietly that she was stunned to hear him over the drone of the rotors, "Are you safe?"

She nodded before she realized what he was talking about. *Then* she contemplated jumping out. She couldn't have this conversation. Yeah, right. And this reluctance had to be some new standard for stupidity.

She was willing to have sex with him, but not to discuss protection from its risks?

She forced herself to spill all she had to say on the subject in one go. "I am. In every way. Checked and rechecked, although I *never* neglected protection. I also protected myself just in case. Measures still in place. I'm also at a safe time. I'm certain."

He made her breathing difficulties worse when he murmured, "I'm safe, too. I never neglect protection. But I can't even think of using it with you. I want to feel you without barriers and scorch you with my pleasure as you scorch me with yours." When she gurgled something he turned to her, serious, placating. "Don't feel under any pressure to agree. I'm just telling you how I feel. I'll arrange for protection to be delivered—"

"I don't want you to use it, either," she blurted out.

His eyes flared his satisfaction. It was all she could do to draw in enough air to keep from passing out.

In less than fifteen minutes she saw their destination. His yacht, moored miles offshore.

He landed on the uppermost deck where they'd had their first conversation on board. He turned off the motor, jumped out and was at her side in what felt like a flash, undid her belt and carried her down. She let him. She couldn't have walked if she tried.

He put his lips to her forehead as the sun dipped into the water, setting in a conflagration of color.

Suddenly the languorous spell of the moment fractured. He was putting her down, tenderly, languidly, but still letting her go. He took a few steps backward, the crimson rays of the departing sun striking turquoise lasers off his eyes.

Then he slowly, oh so slowly undid his tie.

She watched every movement of his large, beautiful hands, his corded neck as he flexed it and pulled the tie from around it, then his sculpted fingers as they finally held the tie away from his body, like a magician showing his audience the setup of his trick before he executed it. He let the tie go.

It plummeted, the silk sighing as it hit the deck.

He licked his lips, made her feel as if he'd licked hers then continued down the trail his eyes traveled down her middle. "Your turn."

Ten

Gabrielle shot a panicked look around, the warmth of the June day seeming to rise into raging heat instead of cooling with the sunset.

"Here?" she gulped.

"We have the place and the ocean to ourselves, *bellissima*."

So this was what he'd arranged during those minutes away.

It thrilled her that he gave her this freedom from scrutiny. It also terrified her, how much she wanted to take advantage of it, lose every inhibition. She wanted to attack him with kisses, but…

What if it *was* her? What if even wanting him this…terribly, she still felt nothing? Where would she be then?

Where she'd be anyway, eventually. Out of his life. So she just had to take what she could. Whatever the outcome.

As for what to take off, the logical thing was her jacket.

She was done doing things logically. Her logic had messed up her life so far. It was obviously essentially flawed. And logic said this couldn't be happening. But it was. And how. So to hell with it.

Elation simmered from her bones outward as she slowly, oh so slowly took off…her watch.

His face blazed in wicked delight when she let it fall to the deck, simulating his actions to the last move.

"Tormentress," he rumbled, took off his cufflinks.

She raised him her earrings. He surrendered his phone. She reciprocated with her hair clip. He threw down his checkbook.

The challenge arced between them in currents of elation and stimulation. She'd never laughed so freely with anyone. Or at all. And to be laughing even as longing melted her insides— *that* was unreal. And yet it felt like the only real thing she'd ever experienced.

Then she was out of nongarment things. He wasn't. The man *was* a magician. He had to be pulling all that stuff out of thin air. Her shoes went, then her jacket. When it was her blouse's turn, he moved closer. He took one step forward and something new off for each button she undid. Then all the buttons were undone and he was a breath away. The blouse hung open, still revealing nothing. She quivered. "Your turn."

"It's still your turn. With the last button, it comes off."

Her hands trembled uncontrollably as she pushed her blouse off. Then she was in her skirt and bra, unable to look at him, afraid to document his reaction, cringing inside.

What if he thought her breasts too big? Ed had said they were grotesque, unbalanced for her body. What if he preferred slimmer women? Different proportions? What if…?

A shockwave swept through her. Her eyes flew to his face.

She might have been alarmed at the eruption of testosterone blasting off him, the carnal ferocity in his features, if it hadn't gratified her, aroused her to the point of near-frenzy.

He tore off his jacket, muscles rippling, his whole body expanding. Then he hissed, "Next."

She expended the remnants of her coordination undoing her skirt.

Durante's nostrils flared, his gaze pouring heat over her, his chest rising and falling as if with exertion. He flicked open the first button of his shirt, hissed again, "Next."

She fumbled her bra open, instinctively held it in place.

"Let it drop, *bellissima.*"

She did, whimpered. With the relief of releasing her swollen breasts from the imprisonment of the bra that had grown stifling. His jaw muscles worked as he undid another button then dropped to his knees, hands spanning her hips in a girdle of fire, his fingers hooking into her panties. "And last."

By the time the torturous sweep of lace and steel fingers skimmed her toes, she was panting. His hands reversed their path, inflaming her flesh with raw need. Then they stilled, an inch from her core.

He raised eyes like incendiary precious stones. *"Divina, preciosa mia…divina."*

He bent his awesome head to her flesh, suckled and nibbled her thighs and abdomen, moving higher like a starving man who didn't know where to start his feast. Her fingers convulsed in the wealth of his silky hair, pressed his face to her flesh in an ecstasy of torment, unable to take the stimulation, unable to get enough.

He took her breasts in hands that trembled, pressed them, weighed them, kneaded and nuzzled them as if they were the most amazing things he'd ever felt. Tears broke through her fugue of arousal. "You said fast and ferocious…*please*…"

"There's been a change in plan. The first two times will be torturously slow. We'll get to fast and ferocious the third time. Or maybe the fourth. Definitely the fifth."

She watched his head move against her breasts, heard her pleas thicken as his tongue and teeth turned the flesh she'd always thought sensitive to discomfort or pain into an instrument of unbearable pleasure. He tasted and nipped and murmured wonder and hunger, circled the center of her distress. If it wasn't for the ocean air cooling as the sun disappeared, she might have spontaneously combusted. Then his hands moved away and his tongue and teeth strayed over her...

This was nothing like she'd expected or imagined. Every squeeze had the exact force, each rub and nip and dig the exact roughness to extract maximum pleasure from her every nerve ending. He layered sensations with each press and bite, until she felt devoured, until she was overloading. Something was burning inside her. She undulated against him feverishly, pressing her clamoring flesh against any part of him in mindless pursuit of assuagement. Only then did he drag a rough, elec-trocuting hand between her thighs, teasing and tormenting his way to her core. The heel of his thumb found her outer lips at the same moment the damp furnace of his mouth clamped over a throbbing nipple. Sensation slashed her nerves.

He supported her collapsing weight, carried her to rest against the railing where they'd stood that night, one knee beneath her buttock, one between her thighs.

"I wanted to do this to you that first night..." He slid two fingers between her molten inner lips, stilled at her entrance. "I wanted to see you like this, on fire, open, hunger shaking you apart. Then I wanted to do this..."

He again dropped to his knees, spread her legs, placed one after the other over his shoulders, opening her to his eyes and touch. He inhaled her, rumbled like a lion maddened at the scent of his female in heat, then blew a gust of acute sensation over her quivering flesh. Her hips bucked, her last "please" morphing into a squeal. It became a shriek when he pumped two fingers into her, in a slow, slow glide. The sunset turned into darkest night as she convulsed, pleasure slamming through her in desperate surges.

Her sight burst back to an image from a fantasy. Him,

clothed, kneeling between her legs, her, naked, splayed open over his shoulders, in the midst of an ocean that did feel as if it were their own.

Then, among the mass of aftershocks she'd become, she felt it. His fingers still filling her, pumping her, beckoning inside her.

Her gasping mouth widened as his tongue joined in, licked from where his fingers were buried inside her upward, circling her bud until she heard her voice sobbing pleas again. His lips locked on her core. She bucked, pressed her burning flesh to his mouth, opening herself fully to his double sensual assault, bewilderment shooting through her as each glide and graze and pull and thrust sent hotter lances skewering through her, as if she hadn't just had the most intense orgasm of her life. And before she could draw a full breath, she was in the throes again, quaking and screaming with an even more violent release.

She tumbled from the explosive peak, drained, sated. Stupefied. What had just happened?

Her drugged eyes sought his, as if for answers. Even in the twilight they glowed azure, heavy with hunger and satisfaction.

"You are the most magnificent thing I have ever touched or tasted. I will never get enough of you."

Suddenly she was hungrier, the emptiness where she needed him gnawing at her. She writhed, her hands running over his lush hair. "Can we skip to fast and ferocious now...*please?*"

He chuckled against her inner thighs, cupping her, desensitizing her. "But those two times don't count. The ones I promised will be with me inside you, riding you to ecstasy."

Her mouth dropped open.

Before she could respond, he swept her up in his arms, headed inside the yacht, taking a route she hadn't seen before.

In minutes he entered a huge, elaborately furnished suite with marble floors, Persian carpets and soaring ceilings that traversed two decks. Must be the master suite he'd mentioned. A gigantic, circular bed draped in royal blue satin crouched beneath a domed skylight that glowed with the last tendrils of twilight. Oil lamps blazed everywhere, swathing everything in golden mystery and intimacy.

Sinking deeper in the sensory overload realm, she tried to drag him on top of her as he put her on the bed. He sowed kisses over her clinging arms, withdrew, stood back looking down at her.

"Meravigliosa," he breathed. "Do you realize how amazing you are?" Elation, embarrassment and disbelief gurgled in the back of her throat. "Do you want to *see* how amazing I think you are?"

That got her voice working. "Yes, please."

And he started to strip. And if their stripping game had had her begging, his as he exposed each sculpted inch almost had her passing out with the pressure of anticipation. She'd been right the night of the ball. He did have the body of a higher being.

He was down to his boxers when he turned into the light... and she saw it. The scar. A two-inch, puckered line across the smooth perfection of his skin. Negligible, really.

A wave of nausea hit her. She scrambled up on hands and knees, hugged him convulsively around the waist, pressed her trembling lips to where he'd been hurt. A few inches to the right, where its perpetrator had aimed, and the knife could have caused untold damage. Could have snuffed out all this uniqueness and vitality.

He smoothed his hands over her hair. "Don't think what-ifs, *amore*. I'm fine and that's what matters, *sì?*"

He understood, as he always seemed to. She hugged him harder, opened her mouth over his wound, as if she could drain away the pain of the memory. He groaned, pressed her against his flesh, surrendering to her need to heal him. She couldn't *bear* it if something happened to him. She moaned the dread out loud.

"Nothing will happen to me." His eyes were serious, pledging. Then they suddenly melted in sensuality and teasing as he rubbed her breasts with the silk-roughened steel of his thighs. "Except maybe a heart attack from this display of beauty."

She gazed up at him, her insides trembling. How she *wanted* him. In every way.

He stepped back and dropped his boxers, released the proof of how much *he* wanted *her.* In that way, at least.

She'd felt that he was big. But this…she'd never seen anything half as huge. Or anywhere near as beautiful.

Her senses swam. The spike of desire combined with shock of intimidation almost dragged her under.

One thing brought her back to full focus. The need to feel his manhood, touch it, smell it, taste it. She'd never wanted to do that, had even been repulsed when she'd imagined doing it, to other men. She shook with wanting to do it to him.

He let her hold him, shuddered at her touch, groaned at the flick of her tongue, growled when she overcame the last shred of inhibition and opened her mouth wide over the satin crown. She moaned around his hot hardness, lost in the pleasure of him. Then she leaned back to look up at him.

"Oh, Durante," she whispered. "You're the most magnificent thing I've ever touched or tasted, too."

His fingers dug into her scalp, shooting pleasure to every hair root. "Take your every pleasure from me, always. But I need to pleasure you now, with my body."

She relinquished him as if all her strings had been cut, melted onto her back awash with the enormity of craving and anxiety.

She'd know now. Her body was weeping in an agony of need for him. If she didn't feel pleasure with him, it was hopeless.

But he'd already given her pleasure like she'd never known. She truly didn't care if she couldn't feel anymore. She just needed to feel him inside her before she disintegrated.

He prowled over her, kissed his way from her toes to her center to her breasts to her lips until his bulk pressed between her trembling thighs. He cupped her buttocks, touched the head of his erection to her entrance, nudged her, bathing himself in her wetness. Her hands pressed his biceps convulsively, her intimate flesh fluttering around him, begging him to enter. His eyes roiled with a dizzying mixture of lust and tenderness as he finally pumped his hips, breached her tightness with persistent yet restrained pressure. Then he was there, where she needed him, penetrating her in a long, languorous thrust.

The expansion of her tissues around his erection went on and on. The fullness sharpened into an ache that became almost a pain. Darkness danced at the periphery of her vision.

She gasped, thrashed. He stilled, started to withdraw. She felt she'd implode if he left her body, grabbed him, arms and legs and core. "No…don't…stay inside me…please."

"You took half of me and started shaking. Let me move *bellissima,* we'll take it easier."

Half of him? She slackened her muscles inside and out, and he pushed up on extended arms. She looked down, open-mouthed. He *was* only halfway inside her. Would she be able to take all of him? But she needed to. She wanted him to shatter her with his full invasion.

She fell back, shuddering, panting. "No, do it, please. I need you inside me all the way, hard, *please…*"

With a pained groan, he bent, suckled her nipples, sending a million arrows of pleasure to her core with every pull, squeezing more fiery arousal from her depths. He had her mindlessly pumping her hips up at him, begging for impalement with fevered sobs before he succumbed, slid back into her.

This time he didn't stop, kept invading her, stretching her, the head of his shaft pressing against her internal flesh, setting off a string of charges that buried her under layers of sensations she'd never felt before, a buildup that seemed to originate from her every cell and radiate from his flesh all at once, a pressure that distilled desperation into a physical symptom. He stopped his onslaught only when he reached her cervix, and everything

in her seemed to compact into a pinpoint of gravity for an un-
endurable moment before detonating outward. She shattered.

Her hips heaved, so hard that she almost lifted him in the air,
the sensations exploding from her depths so fierce that she
couldn't scream, couldn't breathe, not for the first dozen clenches
of release as the excruciating pleasure ripped through her.

Then she screamed and screamed as it went on and on. He
withdrew then plunged, then again and again, riding her ecstasy,
not letting it subside, building the pressure inside her again as
he took her lips, thrust inside her mouth with his tongue, simulating the powerful thrusts of his manhood until another
tsunami built, hovered, then crashed over her.

This time she screamed with the first crashing chord of the
climax, her muscles squeezing the hardness and girth piston-
ing satisfaction into her, convulsing around it, drenching it with
wave after wave of pleasure.

He rose above her, muscles taught, eyes tempestuous, face
seizing with the pleasure of possessing her, pleasuring her, his
beauty supernatural in the extreme. Then he threw his head back
and roared as every muscle in his body locked, his erection
pressing to her womb, gushing his own release to mingle with hers,
long, hard jets that ignited her nerves into one more conflagration.

The last thing she knew was that aftershocks could hit a level
of excitement all their own, that they were more draining than
the peaks of pleasure…

Gabrielle stirred in cottony bliss, opened her eyes.

The gibbous moon came into focus. It hung in the piece of
sky framed in the skylight above. She was being stroked like a
cat from face to thigh. She was purring.

Durante purred, too, the deep rumbles of the sated, tri-
umphant lion that he was. He had a right to be. She'd thought
he'd given her the orgasms of her life, that she'd never recharge
enough to want sex ever again. But he'd aroused her to weeping

again, before showing her that, a) she had buttons that only he knew how to push to give her shattering orgasms in succession, b) she recharged in record time and c) so did he.

"You were saying? This thing about being frigid?" he rumbled against her neck, his smile tickling her.

"Uh…it was clearly a case of misdiagnosis." She sounded like what she was. A woman who'd been savagely pleasured, had screamed herself hoarse in appreciation.

"One of vast proportions. You're the most sensuous, responsive creature imaginable, and your capacity for pleasure is limitless. But then, capacity is just a potential. It means nothing without the right touch to release it. Your body is a complex, extremely selective instrument of sensual delights. It responds only when everything satisfies you. As I do."

As only you will ever do, she almost blurted out. She bit it back.

It felt as if he were the first and only man she'd ever been with. Really been with. No man had ever taken her like that. She'd never accepted a man inside her like that. Beside his phenomenal size, stamina and rebound time, the things he'd done to her had been undreamed of. The way she'd responded, the way she'd opened herself to whatever he wished to do, had been something she hadn't imagined herself capable of.

But that was probably more info than he'd want to know. She'd better keep it light.

"You're in a league of your own, *bellissima.*"

"Look who's talking. You weren't kidding. Or bragging."

He chuckled, consumed her in a leisurely mating of mouths, smiling into the warmth and intimacy of the meld, soothing the soreness he'd inflicted, before moving down her body and performing the same healing ritual to the nipples she'd begged him to devour in the throes of ecstasy.

"Far from kidding or bragging, I actually downplayed things. I didn't want you to think you'd fallen into the clutches of a sex maniac and run off screaming."

"So you misled me about the nature of what awaited me, conned me onto my back, uh—among other positions—and made me scream there instead?"

"And how you scream. Every scream was like an intravenous shot of aphrodisiac, shooting through my system to deluge my brain. I almost blew an artery."

"Good thing you have a safety valve."

"And it's going to come to my rescue constantly. Like now."

He pressed between the thighs that trembled apart for him, unable to bear those last moments as desire became pain before his hardness and heat filled her again, stretching her into mindlessness, thrusting her to oblivion.

Pangs started to throb, dragging Gabrielle back from the void. She didn't want to float up from the realm of bliss, wanted to remain suspended there forever.

But the ache mounted, pushed against the lethargy, advancing awareness through her body, until she realized.

Durante. She was wrapped up in him, virility made solid gold muscles, power and hunger and satisfaction made man. Her head was resting on his biceps; her lips were buried in his chiseled chest. Every inch of her was imprinted with his sleek, slightly hair-roughened silk-over-steel body.

The ache rose, changed texture to something she hadn't felt the many times she'd woken up to more lovemaking. This time it was different. This was the morning after the transfiguring night.

She had nothing to compare to what she'd shared with him. She hadn't even had morning-afters with her disappointments.

She couldn't leave this time. And it wasn't because she was in the middle of the ocean with no way to go home unless he took her. She wanted to stay, for as long as it was possible to stay, wanted to experience everything again, and more, with him.

He rumbled something deep and unbearably sexy as he threw one leg over both of hers, his arms sliding into the deep curve of her waist to her buttocks, hauling her against him, his erection, intact as ever. She was so ready again, or rather, still, it was embarrassing.

He took her mouth, took her breath and will away.

When he relinquished her lips to nibble his way down her face, her neck, she gasped, "*Buon giorno* to you, too."

His fingers probed her, slipped into her, circled her bud. She thrust her hips into his pleasuring, needing, desperate, just like that.

"It isn't a good morning, *Gabriella mia.* It's a *magnifico giorno,* the most magnificent morning in history." He turned her onto her back, looked at her as if he couldn't decide which part of her to ravish first. "And do you know what your magnificence did to me, besides the loud and obvious? I dreamed all night. And I remember each second of every dream." He quickened his fondling. "Now I'm going to reenact each and every one."

She gasped as he drove her over the edge. And she knew. Her anxiety had no root in reality. There could never be a letdown with Durante. Only soaring.

And if a voice rasped that a fall from such heights could be far more devastating, she stifled it as she gave all of herself up to the wonder of him, of what they'd found together.

Eleven

Gabrielle watched Giancarlo close the door behind him, a smile hovering on her lips.

For the past two weeks it had become a ritual. She'd arrive at Durante's penthouse, he'd open the door for her and disappear.

She'd torn through her work like she'd been doing every day, the work for which she'd found her passion and enthusiasm miraculously resurrected, to hurtle back to Durante.

The day after they'd returned from his yacht, she'd left the next morning, returned eight hours later. She hadn't stayed the night since. Durante hadn't asked her to. But they spent their afternoons and evenings together, making love and every other thing under the sun before he escorted her to her apartment.

She couldn't believe she'd thought herself frigid. Evidence said she was bordering on nymphomania. A condition with a specific activator by the name of Durante D'Agostino.

Now she had only to think of him for her body to gnaw at her with the need for him. He had only to touch her, sometimes just suckle or caress or blow his breath on any of her triggers, and those were many and increasing, to unleash her first release. But the shattering climaxes he gave her when he took her boggled her mind.

Not that it was all about or even mainly about sex between them. They reveled in each other in every other way. Every day brought ever-expanding harmony and deepening involvement in each other's lives. This evening was another milestone. He was introducing her to his friends. Or as he'd said, "producing them for her inspection and approval."

"Stay."

Durante's gruff whisper forked through her.

Not from surprise. She'd felt his approach. She'd probably felt it when it was still an intention forming in his mind. She'd waited for him to initiate the reconnection, set the pace and tone of this encounter as he had every other so far.

She had no idea what this one word could mean. She'd just come in.

Could he…? She didn't dare think what he meant. So she quipped, "Again with the canine references. But then you already got me to roll over and beg."

His eyes crinkled as he pulled her to him, tenderness mixing with rough sensuality and possession into a mind-melting concoction. "You got me to beg, too. I can even do back flips and walk on my hands, at your order."

He bent, opened his mouth over the pulse in her neck, suckled her in long pulls as if he were drinking her. Fireworks exploded inside her, followed by a gush of readiness and the need for him to fill her again.

But his friends were coming in minutes.

That was logic's voice. Her body's said *take all you can, while you can.*

She obeyed it, moaned, "Take me, Durante *bello,* take me…"

He raised his head, instant ferocity taking over his face,

thinning his lips. He snatched her skirt up to her waist, took her by the buttocks and spread her around his hips. He staggered with her to the nearest erect surface as she clung to him, disintegrating with the firebomb of hunger he'd detonated inside her. He set her against something that rattled as he freed himself, tore her panties out of the way, slid her up her support to scale his length. She felt the head of his erection at her moist entrance, keened. He let her crash down on him, just as he thrust up, piercing her. It took no more than feeling him forging through her to shatter her. She shrieked with the sledgehammer of orgasm, convulsing around his shaft as if she were imploding.

He growled into her mouth. "*Sì, Gabriella, sì,* take all of me, take your pleasure of me, come all over me."

The orgasm raged on and on until he roared and slammed her against the rattling support, his release so powerful that she writhed, trembled, sobbed with the sensations. She went nerveless and he tightened his hold around her, still hard and twitching inside her. Her flesh quivered around him with the aftershocks of the profound release.

He took her slack mouth in carnal possession, blowing air into her breathless lungs, growling all the while, rocking gently again and again inside her, satisfying her to her last tremor. *"Siete magici, mi' bellezza…magici…"*

Her head flopped on his shoulder as she tried to get her nerves to spark. She needed to hold him, to revel in his existence, his magic. "It's you…you who are, *bello mio*…"

The bell rang.

Durante jerked. *"Maledizione.* I should have told Giancarlo to entertain them somewhere else until…" He swore again. "I should have known I wouldn't be able to last until they left to make love to you. I yearned for you all day, *Gabriella mia."*

She moaned. "And I for you."

He took her lips, strode with her wrapped around him to his bathroom. He put her down gently on the huge platform of marble flanking the sink. Then he reluctantly, and so slowly, withdrew from her depths. She moaned at the ache of separation.

She groaned again at the sight of herself in the mirror behind him, at his brutal beauty and caring as he kneeled in front of her, intimately taking care of the evidence of their lovemaking, so her skirt wouldn't be stained. Then he rose to his feet and towered over her, his muscles rippling under his shirt as he struggled to straighten and smooth his pants.

"Take your time getting ready." He took her face in his hands, urgency rippling in the passion in his grip, his eyes. "But answer me first. Will you stay, *bellissima?*"

"Tonight, you mean?"

"I mean every night."

Gabrielle gazed across the room at Durante. He was putting on some music, laughing with his younger cousin, Eduardo. Her heart quivered. She'd said yes.

But…he'd said stay. Not live. Was there a difference?

"So how long have you known Durante, Gabrielle?"

She turned to the mahogany-haired, green-eyed woman so aptly named Jade. A few years younger than her, she judged, Jade glowed with that special vitality healthy pregnant women had. She and Eduardo were both floating on air. Their love for each other was almost visible, tangible.

Jade was also curious in the most innocuous way Gabrielle had ever experienced.

"Not long. We met three weeks ago."

"Bet it feels like three years."

Now, how did she know that?

Jade answered her unvoiced question, "It was like that with me and Eduardo. Did you have a tempestuous beginning, too?"

Gabrielle laughed. "So there *is* a pattern with the D'Agostino princes."

As she laughed, she felt rather than saw Durante stiffen. Her eyes flew to his, locked, mingled, mated across the huge space until the room flooded with tension so carnal, so predatory and proprietary, she felt as if he were inside her again, occupying her, dominating her, dissolving her in satiation.

The volcanic exchange lasted only a couple of seconds before Eduardo drew his focus away again as Jade caught hers.

Jade sighed. "But they're worth every heartache. At least I know Eduardo is literally worth dying for. How's your Durante?"

Gabrielle spluttered with laughter. "You say that as if you're asking me 'How's your steak.'"

Jade grinned, her beauty blazing a few notches higher with the unbridled expression. "They are far more edible than the juiciest steak, aren't they? Not that I think Durante could be anywhere near Eduardo in tastiness. Eduardo is pure ambrosia."

Gabrielle laughed again. "Fair enough. To me Durante is on a celestial menu of his own."

"You love him."

The statement hit Gabrielle between the eyes.

She struggled not to lurch with its power, its certainty, murmured, "It's too early for anything like that."

"Uh-uh, it isn't. Not with these men."

And "these men" were heading toward them now. Eduardo was a gorgeous male, Gabrielle acknowledged, but in her eyes, Durante was far beyond that. He was above comparison.

"Durante seems…younger," Jade said as the men progressed slowly across the room, still talking but with their eyes on the women. "I haven't seen him laughing—hell, I haven't even seen him smile—since I first met him six months ago. And because of Eduardo's friendship and business with him, I've seen him a lot. I didn't know he *could* laugh. I thought he came without the laughter software." She turned to Gabrielle. "But you reformatted him."

Gabrielle chuckled again. Almost everything Jade said tickled her. "Ah, Jade, isn't reformatting reserved for the hard drive?"

"What's this about reformatting and hard drives?" Durante came to Gabrielle's side, sat on the couch's armrest, pulled her to him, kissed the top of her head, her temple, her jaw. Then he murmured in her ear so softly he almost didn't produce sound. "Look at me like that and I'll haul you to bed and hard drive your software and to hell with them."

She looked up at him. Yes, like *that*. She pulled him down, whispered in his mouth. "You didn't need a bed, or much time, for that in extremely fresh memory. I'm sure you can manage with them here and not in hell."

He bit down on one of her tormenting lips. "When we serve dessert, you'll skip it. You're having me."

Eduardo had mirrored Durante's actions with Jade, as if they'd agreed to. After he let her up from a clinging kiss he belatedly answered Durante's question. "That's *mia bella Giada,* always talking computers. Watch that you don't get her started on programming, though."

"You're the only one who makes me blurt out code, *amore.*" She beamed at him, then turned to Durante. "We were talking about you."

Gabrielle held her breath. Jade was clearly even more outspoken than Durante had complained. Would she blurt out that she believed Gabrielle loved him?

She almost deflated to the floor when Jade related only the part about his missing laughter software and the subsequent comments.

Durante laughed, demonstrating his newly restored sense of humor. "That's one of many things Gabrielle reformatted about me."

Jade's grin grew devilish. "I saw her reformatting your arrogance, in public. On YouTube."

Eduardo grinned at his bride conspiratorially. "*Sì,* and from the marks on your cheek, I'd say that in a previous scene, she reformatted it, too."

Durante looked at Gabrielle. After a moment of stunned silence, they burst into howls of laughter.

Raucous ribbing was exchanged in the aftermath of their fit, and from then on, the evening flowed with the harmony of the men's deep friendship and the women's instant rapport.

All through, each man pampered his woman with every gesture and word and touch. Jade reciprocated her demonstrative husband's affection with gusto. Gabrielle, feeling the odd man out, the one who didn't share the same status as them, reciprocated Durante's doting but wasn't as spontaneous. Not as she longed to be.

For Jade had been right.

She might not have let herself say the words, even to herself, but she'd fallen flat on her face in love with him from that first night. She'd been stumbling deeper with each breath ever since. She didn't see an end to her plummet.

But she'd effectively been lying to him.

She didn't know how to come clean about how this had started without implicating his father per her promise.

It was so unfair. Why should she risk spoiling what they had now, when it had never been her fault, this inadvertent deception? It didn't matter how it had all started, as he'd said. It had ceased to be a mission on his father's behalf, or on her company's, the moment she'd laid eyes on him.

At the evening's end, something disturbing nagged at her.

The difference. Between "stay" and "live."

"Stay" might mean that he didn't feel the same about her as she did for him. That he'd sooner or later have enough of her. And there would be no point in confessing anything, anyway.

She tried not to hear the voices that said if he ended it, she'd be far worse off than she'd been before she'd met him. That this time, there would be no hope of finding a point to anything ever again.

Twelve

Gabrielle was balancing on the edge of the springboard.

She flashed Durante a grin that turned the night into day, one all but yelling "Look, look."

As if he could do anything else. His gaze clung to her every move, as it always did, his heart in a state of constant expansion.

Once she was certain she had his full attention, she looked ahead, concentration settling over her face, showing him another side of her, the determined woman who could and did succeed in anything she endeavored. She tensed her body so that every muscle in her toned firmness was on alert, stood on her tiptoes, raised her arms. Then she dipped her weight, jumped once, twice, launching higher in the air with the elastic recoil of the board, then on the third launch, she catapulted into a backward somersault, tucking her whole body in a ball, revolving in two full turns before unfolding fully, her whole body stretched and straight like a human missile, entered the water fingertips first, cutting the surface like a laser beam. She didn't splash a drop.

He sprang to his feet the second she was submerged, ran to the edge of the pool, clapping and hooting, elation tumbling in his blood. She broke the surface with a smile as huge as his, swept around and around in the water like a giddy mermaid, reveling in his adulation, taking her bows.

Unable to wait, he plunged after her, surfaced with her wrapped around him. He squeezed her, ravaged her with clinging, smiling kisses, which she reciprocated with ardor enough to make him steam the pool. He slid his lips up to her ear. "So you're an Olympic diver and you never told me."

She giggled. "Nothing so exalted. I used to be my school's diving champion, got so far as the regional competitions. Won me some gold medals in those. But the last time I saw a springboard was seven years ago. I wanted to show you one of the few things that made me feel alive. I practiced while you took care of your business so I wouldn't disgrace myself. And it's true. It is like riding a bike. My body will curse me tomorrow, but it was worth it." She yelped with the excess adrenaline still coursing in her blood. "It felt *great!* I thought I'd grown old and creaky."

"You will never be that. And you will never again neglect your passions and your talents, *Gabriella mia.* Promise me."

She nodded, her eyes blasting him with unadulterated appreciation, for his solicitude, for everything that he was. She made him feel treasured to his last cell. Just as he treasured her.

He swept her into his arms, swam on his back in leisurely strokes with her nestled at his side, the largest part of his soul. His gaze swept through the now-open plexi roof at another moonless, star-blazing night. Exotic plants teemed at the pool's periphery forming an oasis in the middle of the ocean. Their oasis. He'd changed his mind about donating this boat. He was going to re-outfit it for them. He reveled in being with her in the freedom of such a setting, such a huge personal space.

He luxuriated in feeling her this way, through the silk medium of perfect-temperature water, her satin resilience and strength tapping into and feeding his own in a closed circuit of harmony. This had long surpassed any heaven he'd ever heard about.

What they shared was something he'd never imagined there was to be shared. He'd witnessed family and friends finding their soulmates, but he'd never believed he'd find his own. Now, he hadn't just found his in her, he'd also been given a second chance when he'd wasted the first that fate had handed him. He still woke up in cold sweat thinking he'd forever alienated her only to subside, nerve-wracked and kissing-the-floor thankful at finding her curled up next to him.

Only one thing disturbed him. Every now and then he felt some reticence from her. He could think of only one reason for that unease. The speed with which everything had happened.

He didn't feel that they'd gone too fast. He felt everything had unfolded in total leisure. Time stretched, widened, deepened when they were together. The month since they'd met felt like a year. More. He couldn't remember a time when he didn't know her. Didn't want to remember. For what was there to remember before her?

But he forced himself to let her set the pace. It might look like he'd rushed her to move in with him in ten days. But in his view, he'd *waited* ten days. He'd wanted her to stay from that first night. He didn't have the least doubt. He knew. She was the one he'd thought he'd never find. The one he'd been made for.

He kissed her again. "Thank you for sharing your dive with me, *bellissima*. Share everything with me, always."

She enveloped him in the contentment, the serenity and certainty only her embrace had ever imbued him with. Then she suddenly wriggled, broke his hold, kicked away.

She giggled as he gave pursuit. She was such a strong swimmer he almost didn't need to slow down for her to beat him to the other end of the pool. She pulled herself out in one agile move, stood there in her flame-colored, one-piece torture device of a swimsuit, grinning down at him, before she ran to the dinner table he'd had set for them before he'd sent everyone off the yacht. He never wanted anyone around when he was with her.

Tonight of all nights, it had to be just them.

He followed, taking his time to get his fill of watching her as she dried herself in brisk movements that grew languid, sensuous as he neared. He kept walking until he imprinted her from breast to calf, gathered her to him, cherished her with caresses and kisses as she stroked him dry.

"About sharing…" she purred against his neck, rubbing against him, stoking the fire perpetually raging for her. "I keep realizing I told you my life's sob stories in embarrassing detail. Whereas you told me outlines. Very unbalanced, if you ask me. I feel fully naked, with you with only your tie undone."

"But you love it that way."

"That is a supreme truth only equaled by the fact that I am just as addicted to watching your mind-blowing stripteases."

He raised an eyebrow, pseudo-suspicious. "You want to get everything out of me so you can help me sort through my issues, don't you?"

Her eyes melted with tenderness. "Got me. Is it so bad to want to do for you a fraction of what you did for me?"

He stared at her. Would she ever cease to surprise him? To do and say exactly the right thing, at the right moment?

He sat down in one of the chaise longues where they sunbathed in seclusion, brought her down straddling him, wrapped her in his arms, rested his forehead on her bosom.

Sì, it was the right moment to share all of him with her.

Durante nuzzled her like a lion would his mate before resting his ear on her heart. The poignancy of the revealing gesture swamped her, the so freely demonstrated admission that he needed the solace of her.

He stroked her back rhythmically, making her insides quiver with bliss. Then he started talking.

"Everything was perfect, or so I thought, until I was eleven. Looking back, things were never anywhere near perfect between my parents. Or with my mother. She had this…irrepressible energy. It was sometimes painful to watch her, like…looking at the sun. But she always dimmed around my father. I didn't give it much thought until she dimmed all the time, during her pregnancy with my sister. After Clarissa was born it was like she forgot she had other children. I was hurt by her neglect, more on my brother Paolo's behalf. She explained that I was a big boy, could take care of my brother, and I needed to be with my father more, while her baby girl needed her. I conceded that, thought it the natural order of things. And for years I got involved in my own life. But by age eighteen I could no longer overlook it. My mother had become unbalanced, one day manic, the next in a stupor. I thought my father was not doing enough—or anything—to stop her decline.

"Then I walked into her apartments unannounced one day and saw her…hitting Clarissa. Really hitting her. Clarissa had curled up in a ball on the ground as my mother beat her. But what really horrified me was that Clarissa's cowering felt habitual. This wasn't the first time. I charged in, overpowered my mother, and she kicked and writhed in my hold like a madwoman. I could no longer find my mother in her eyes. She spat in my face, told me I was so like my father she couldn't bear to look at me. I was… devastated. I…hated her at that moment."

A gasp tore through her. He pressed her closer, lost in the past. "But what I felt didn't matter. Only Clarissa did. I faced my father. I didn't care what was going on between him and my mother, but I wouldn't see Clarissa hurt. He swore he'd been ignorant of this, that he'd never let my mother lay a hand on Clarissa again. I left Castaldini the day Father took Clarissa to his apartments. I returned periodically to check that she remained safe from our mother's mood swings.

"She was. For those moods stopped swinging, became a

steady downward descent. Until the day she died. I came home for her funeral, almost didn't recognize the woman in the coffin.

"After the funeral I had a long conversation with my father. He said he'd tried his utmost to help her over the years, but she'd been unapproachable about undergoing therapy, had accused him of trying to make her admit that she was crazy.

"I went to her apartments looking for jewelry and personal items that I thought Clarissa should have and would never think of taking for herself. After the abusive period passed, Clarissa had become closer to our mother, sort of her keeper, and I wanted her to have some reminders of better times before mental illness took our mother away from us, to equalize the anguish and sadness that had taken over Clarissa's memories of her. And I found my mother's diary.

"The entries started with her discovery of her pregnancy with Clarissa. Some were written in…blood." Gabrielle gasped, squeezed him as hard as her heart contracted. "Page after page, year after year of agony, of obsession, of unbearable feelings of betrayal. I could almost hear her laments blast me from the pages. How she'd given him her life, her soul, her heart, given birth to the flesh of his flesh, and he'd told her she'd always been a convenience, a means to an end, that his true love was a woman who might not be a queen but was the queen of his heart, a woman she wasn't fit to be a servant to. The last entry made it clear that my mother intended to end her life."

Gabrielle panted, her heart threatening to punch a hole in her chest.

"I stormed to my father, hurled the diary at him. It *had* been him all the time. He *had* systematically destroyed my mother while he earned our sympathy for suffering such a wife. I demanded to know who the woman was whose comparison he'd used to dismantle my mother's soul. He said it had been her delusions talking. But I saw the lie in his eyes. And I told him he'd taken my mother from me, from all of us, pushed her until she'd killed herself, that I'd leave Castaldini and I'd return only when he was dead."

She crushed him to her as if she'd take him into her, hide him from hurt, and sobbed. Until she felt she'd come apart.

"Shh, don't cry, *preziosa mia,* it's all right."

She hiccupped a syncopation of incredulity before bursting into even more hacking sobs. *He* was soothing *her?*

He was, kept gentling her, murmuring to her as if she were a frightened child, until his caring and consideration became too much to bear.

She pushed away, wiping angrily at the tears blinding her, winced when her vision cleared. She'd soaked his hair and face.

She blotted them frantically. He caught and kissed her hands. She surged to him, raining kisses all over his face, quavered, "You've got this wrong. *I'm* supposed to comfort *you.*"

"And you did, *amore mio.* With every beat of your heart as I recounted the story, as it pounded, tripped, held its breath then burst with empathy and compassion."

"But what good is that when you have all this pain inside you? This way you've lost both your parents in ways worse than death…"

She stopped, couldn't breathe. King Benedetto *couldn't* be guilty of such cold-blooded abuse at all, let alone to the woman who had loved him to the point of self-destruction, his queen and mother of his children, could he? If he had, then he wasn't the man she'd believed him to be, didn't deserve to get Durante back. Worse, if that was how he treated those who loved him, what if he did the same to Durante? And he'd wanted *her* to convince him…

Sobs wracked her. "I can't *bear* it."

He took her face in his hands, stroked both thumbs over her cheeks, wiped away her tears and anguish. Then he began to sing.

"Vorrei che i tuoi occhi siano la mia prima luce al risveglio…"

I want your eyes to be the first light I see when I wake up every morning.

Everything stilled. The air filled with the magic that emanated from his lips, potent, unstoppable, the sound of power and virility and wonder. Of love.

Quakes started again, different in origin but just as devastating, as consuming. He continued his spell, deepening its destruction, spreading its restoration.

"E il profumo della tua pelle accompagni ogni mio passo... per sempre."

And the perfume of your skin to accompany my every step... forever.

"Vuoi percorrere il sentiero della vita insieme a me, amore?"

Will you walk your life's path with me, my love?

Then he fell silent. And she wept. Her first tears of wonder, of being moved by beauty to an extreme surpassing any pain.

Suddenly trepidation pushed aside the tenderness in his eyes.

She couldn't let him think her reaction wasn't one of extreme joy and enjoyment. She blurted out, "That's the most unbelievably, almost painfully beautiful thing I've ever heard. How did something like that not become an immortal hit?"

"Maybe because its writer wanted only one woman to hear it."

"You...?" Shock hurtled through her. *"Dio...Durante..."*

"Sposami, anima mia."

Marry me, my soul.

"Gabriella mia, mi vuoi sposare?"

Durante asked again. *Will you marry me?*

And nothing. Gabrielle was staring at him as if she'd suddenly stopped understanding Italian.

His certainty wavered. This didn't look like surprise. Not the pleasant kind. But...why? What could be so...shocking? Surely she'd known where all this was leading? But if she was...unpleasantly surprised, did that mean she didn't...?

No. He wouldn't speculate. Never again. No doubts. He'd ask, and she'd tell him the truth. She always told the truth.

"Gabrielle? Don't you have anything to say, *bellissima?*"

"Say? I-I can't think of anything...can't think..."

"Then tell me the first thing that jumped into your mind."

Her eyes were enormous, shock still expanding. "I-I thought I heard wrong, then I thought, it's only been a month. Three weeks, if you take away your famous Ten Days of Tantrum."

He stared at her for a moment. Then he hooted with laughter. "Ah, *preziosa mia,* I never laughed for real before you."

Her eyebrows shot up, her shock receding, her effort to match his teasing evident. "You want to marry me and make me your jester?"

"I want to marry you and make you my *everything.* My lover, my confidante, my friend, my ally, my psychoanalyst, my conscience, my perspective. As for how long we've known each other, you've known many people for years. Did that make you need them? Even like or tolerate them? Time isn't a factor here and you know it."

She nodded, shook her head, looking lost. "So time doesn't promote involvement, but lack of it makes said involvement's validity iffy. If...if in a few months' time, a year's, you still feel the same..."

"I will feel the same in sixty years' time. This is only going to deepen, as it has every second of the past month."

"You don't know that."

"You mean because no one knows what will happen in the future? But anything the future brings is irrelevant, because I am positive of one thing. Myself. In my thirty-eight years I have never even fancied myself in lust with any woman. I was waiting for you. From the first moment, it was like finding the missing parts of *m'anima e corpo*—my soul and body. You think I can go back to living without what makes me whole?"

Pain streaked across her face. His heart compressed, the world going lightless. He groaned the unbearable fear. "Don't you feel the same, Gabrielle? Are the doubts yours?"

His heart almost ruptured in the moments before she gulped the breath she needed to cry out what made him breathe again. "No! God, no! I love you so much I have panic attacks with it sometimes. I-I just can't imagine having this, you, for always. I never thought happiness like this could be anything but tempo- rary. I was waiting for you to…to have enough of me and…and…"

"Can I have enough of bliss? Of sustenance? Of air?"

"Durante…this is too much…too much…"

"Nothing is too much for you. My life, the whole world, they're yours, if only you'll take them. Will you, *alma mia?*"

She looked as if something was tearing her apart. Before he could blurt out his demand that she reveal whatever burden she had for him to bear, she surged into his body. "Yes, please, please, Durante. I want to never be without you again. I want to live my whole life enriching yours, if only you'll let me."

He groaned as if his soul had been dragged out and suddenly left to return to its sanctuary deep within him. He crushed her in his arms, moaned the ache of relief. "You have already enriched it beyond imagining, *mia cuore.* You healed me, purged my anguish. Now I owe you, us, myself without bitter- ness or shadows anywhere inside me. I owe you the best man I can be. And you were right, as you always are. This can only happen if I let go of my anger. I also need to give you the wedding that you deserve, and all of that can only happen one way. By going back. To make whatever peace I can with my father, to marry you on Castaldinian soil."

Thirteen

With every mile deeper into Castaldinian soil, it rose.

The suffocating feeling of being dragged into the worst days of her life, of feeling that they would start again, and this time, they would never end.

Gabrielle had spent what she remembered of her childhood on a Mediterranean island. Although that childhood had been turbulent, the sheer beauty and brightness of the backdrop it had played against had ameliorated much of its anxieties and heartaches. That had been reversed during her last stay in Cagliari.

Witnessing her mother fade away in that sun-drenched, olive grove-ensconced villa, watching her eyes empty of life on that veranda overlooking her beloved white-gold beaches and azure bay, burying her in the embrace of the land she'd called home, had forever linked this magnificence of nature, this balminess of weather, with irretrievable loss and bottomless grief.

Now similar scenes unfolded before her eyes, the influence of another ancient, blessed-by-the-gods land permeating her senses.

She took what comfort she could in the differences she'd been discovering since they'd started their drive to the capital, Jawara, from the private airfield Durante's jet had landed in.

Castaldini's landscape was wilder, more varied, segueing from mountain chains with rivers traversing them to plains with lakes and ponds that softened the harshness of the craggy terrain they rolled from. Then, at the very edge of the island, the land gave way to dense maquis followed by miles-deep expanses of powdered gold lapped by what seemed to be liquid turquoise.

Durante embraced her, as if feeling her turmoil. "This is your first trip here, isn't it, *bellissima?*"

Tell him. Tell him now.

The urge almost burst her heart. It had been doing so ever since he'd asked her to marry him two days ago.

Dread had won out then. It won out again now. Weakness, too. She'd snatched at his offer without coming clean, and she still couldn't do that now. And in an hour's time they'd meet the man who could reveal the secret he'd made her keep. She dreaded Durante's reaction, but at least she'd finally breathe easy that it was out.

For now she was powerless to do anything but let him clasp her to him. "It is strange that I never came here."

Stranger than she could let on, with her lifelong relationship to King Benedetto.

"But it was your connections to this land that led you to find me. And this convinces me. Someone out there must really want to reward me. I wonder what I ever did to deserve that much? I must have done something huge. Why else did I find you? Why else do you love me? But even if I didn't deserve you before, I'll do everything I can, for the rest of my days, to deserve the gift of you."

Awe and gratitude deluged her. She clung harder, until she felt as if she were submerged in his flesh, his love. "Don't start me on correcting you about who's the gift here." After an endless moment of supercharged communion, he looked away as if compelled, watched the scenes going by. "You miss it. It's been five years?"

"Months," he muttered. "I came back after *Padre's* stroke."

"But you said…"

"I couldn't stay away. I stayed until he was out of danger. Paolo and Clarissa have been supplying me with constant reports of his condition ever since. But I swore them to secrecy. Needing to make sure he is all right has nothing to do with forgiving him, as *they* both seem to have done."

"But you're willing to give him a chance now."

He seemed to struggle for an answer. He had pledged it to her, but it was tearing him up. King Benedetto had better have something solid to put Durante's mind to rest, or she would be the first one to tell Durante that the king didn't deserve his turmoil.

She stroked his hair until he moaned his enjoyment. "Don't say anything, *amore mio*. Whatever happens, I just want you to be at peace."

"I am, now that I have you. And I want you to be at peace, too. Remember when I told you not to worry about… anything?"

She nodded slowly. She'd almost forgotten. She'd been pulling her company back into the black just by working to full capacity the past three weeks. The news of Durante's book was also restoring stockholders' faith with a vengeance.

"The moment I realized that the recession in Castaldini wasn't temporary, I started making plans to put an end to it. I slowed down their implementation when Leandro came into the picture, giving me time to perfect them instead of rushing in without every long-term outcome accounted for. Then I met you, and I felt I owed it to our love to consider nothing else but us for those short weeks. Now everything is in place, so you have nothing to worry about, but my plans have to wait a bit longer while I give you a wedding and a honeymoon like no bride has ever had."

She turned in his arms. "But the simplest wedding is all I want, and every day with you is like a hundred honeymoons. Don't you worry about my company. You've done way more than enough and we're going to be fine. It's Castaldini that needs you now, and I can't have you putting off any work because of me or I would have failed in my most basic function as your lover and wife—to give you the peace of mind that will make you even more productive and effective."

He let out a shuddering sigh. "It's hopeless. I'll never find words or deeds enough to express how much I love you." Suddenly his lips crooked. "Now have mercy and let me give you what I need to give you without exhausting me. I need all my stamina for all that work ahead of me."

She melted into him, deluged by another wave of love and wonder. "I called it right the first time I saw you. *Sietto un uomo cattivo.*"

Jawara was very much what its Moorish name said it was. A jewel of a city, glittering bright and unique under the perfect heat and illumination of the Mediterranean sun. It nestled between the banks of a river, which Durante informed her was the Boriana, and an imposing, vegetation-covered mountain, the Montalbo. The rolling plains to its north and south looked like a carpet.

Durante had warned her that the past decade had taken its toll on the city's former flawlessness. But Gabrielle couldn't see the deterioration that he as a native discerned. The place looked pretty incredible to her. She'd been to almost every European and North African capital in the last few years, and Jawara was the only one that didn't have one building younger than the seventeen hundreds. It looked like an ancient city transplanted into the twenty-first century, a mixture of Gothic, Moorish and Baroque architecture and influences that she'd never imagined could mingle in homogeneity, but that here was simply breathtaking.

As they came to the first cobblestone street, the royal palace came into view, crouching like a gigantic, ancient creature on a hill that dominated the oldest part of the city.

On entering the palace grounds, a complex of enormous buildings surrounding the central palace, Durante pointed out the National Library, the Royal Museum, the ceremony halls and government offices. He said it would take some time to get to the Royal Apartments, because they were at the end of ten miles of grounds and he wasn't asking Giancarlo to drive faster over the cobblestones and risk giving her a headache. When they drove past the central palace itself, she gaped, comparing it to a twilight zone episode in which someone passed a never-ending building. Durante laughed, said it was just another of his family's pretentiously sized places. It did lie over four-hundred-thousand square feet.

Then the car stopped. In seconds she was smiling up at Durante as he opened her door even as her heart stampeded.

In a few minutes they'd see King Benedetto. And her horrible burden would be lifted. And then…?

"If it isn't the prodigal prince returning."

The deep drawl had Durante relinquishing his smile and turning on his heel. She followed his gaze and did a triple take.

Strolling toward them was a man who, while looking nothing like Durante in features or coloring, made almost his same impact, in size and height and in sheer radiation of power and charisma. It took her a moment to realize who he was. Prince Leandro D'Agostino, the one-time rebel, once-exiled prince, now regent of Castaldini.

"Leandro! My regent!" Durante exclaimed as he strode toward him with open arms.

Durante pulled his cousin into a rough embrace, one Leandro reciprocated, adding thumps on his back before drawing back to grin widely. "You're looking absolutely radiant."

Durante guffawed. "I thought the term was reserved for

brides. Preferably our brides." He looked back at her, elation turning his beauty from breathtaking to heartbreaking, before he looked at the woman Gabrielle noticed coming up behind Leandro with tranquil steps. He turned to Leandro with a quirked eyebrow. "But then, *you're* absolutely glowing."

"Indeed, I am. Any wonder with such a power source?" Leandro put his arm around the woman's shoulders, gathered her to him in a gesture so eloquent with tenderness, possessiveness and dependence that it sent a frisson of emotion through Gabrielle, at how much it mirrored what Durante blessed her with. The woman—who must be Phoebe Alexander, the sister of Durante's sister-in-law and Leandro's brand-new bride—smoldered reciprocation into her husband's adoring eyes.

Phoebe was the first truly silver-eyed person Gabrielle had ever seen. She was gorgeous, with all that glossy black hair and creamy skin. She looked blissful. And pregnant. The fact that she was showing meant she'd been already pregnant before the wedding.

Something hot and overwhelming stormed through Gabrielle, lodging into her womb. She'd never thought of having a baby. Until Durante. How she yearned to have his. She prayed to God she could.

"So miracles do happen." Phoebe was looking at her in candid and benign interest. "I never thought the day would come when anyone softened the inflexible Durante."

Gabrielle took her hand, grinned conspiringly at her. "So you're a power source, and I'm some sort of softener. We must put our disparate abilities together in an unstoppable collaboration."

Leandro sighed, winking at Durante. "We're doomed."

Durante looked heavenward. "From your lips."

They all laughed as they started walking into the palace, the men falling into step with each other, as she did with Phoebe.

The conversation flowed with bantering ease, to her immense relief. Phoebe was going to be a constant presence in her life and it would have been a source of unneeded strife if they hadn't hit it off. But she felt they'd only like each other better on deepening exposure. It felt so good, looking forward to this unexpected bonus. A woman her age, in her same unusual situation, becoming an ally, a friend. Something she sorely needed.

Suddenly they both fell silent. It seemed Phoebe's ears had pricked like hers on hearing the turn in conversation their men had taken.

"He isn't in good shape, Durante. Take it easy on him."

"I *am* taking it easy on him. I came back, didn't I?"

"Not enough, *amico mio*. Give him a chance. Let him talk this time. Maybe he has something to say."

"If he did, he would have said it years ago."

"You already tried thinking the worst and it ate up five years of both of your lives. Why not try giving other possibilities a chance? I would have thought you incapable of relenting on this one, but because you are here, I am hopeful that miracles indeed do happen."

After a moment's silence, Durante turned, caught her eyes in a searing look of passion and tenderness and whispered, "They do."

Gabrielle almost cried out with the slam of emotion.

And she prayed. For this miracle of his love to overpower whatever ugliness there was, even if there was no hope of erasing it. To overlook the unwilling deceit she'd perpetrated.

"Durante. You came back."

Durante looked at the man who'd once been his hero. The father he'd idolized. He almost didn't recognize him.

Pain seared his heart. He refused to give in to it. "*Sì*. But not for you. For Gabrielle."

He held out his hand to her. Her gaze was frozen on his father's face as she unsteadily came to his side. "Gabrielle Williamson, my bride-to-be. We're getting married here in a week's time. It's for love of her, for needing to give her a future untainted by the shadows of the past that I'm here, *Padre.* But I've also met you halfway. Now it's your turn. Tell me the truth."

"The only truth, Durante…" His father's weakened voice revved sickness and regret behind his sternum. He gritted down on the weakness. "…is that there was no villain or victim."

"So you didn't have a mistress?"

"No, I did have a mistress." Gabrielle lurched at his side. He barely stopped himself from exhibiting his own shock at having all his doubts validated. "And she was the only woman I ever loved. She was the one, Durante. Like your Gabrielle is to you."

The lava of betrayal and hatred and anger rose in him, obliterating all his intentions to give peace a chance. "And of course you discovered this after you married a woman who gave you her heart and life and children."

"I loved that woman before I ever met your mother. I banished her over insane and wrong suspicions and married your mother on the rebound."

Every word was prodding skewers deeper into his wounds. "So not only was my mother your victim, but the other woman, too."

"Your mother was my queen. But I was not in love with her. Neither was she with me. She married me to become queen. I thought she was what the crown needed. When I renewed my relationship with the woman I loved, I kept it a secret for many reasons, your mother's feelings not being among them. She wouldn't have cared."

"Why did she write all that, then? If she wasn't going literally insane with jealousy over your loving another?"

His father seemed to shrivel back into his bed. "I…I don't know. But there's nothing to be gained from digging up skeletons."

Accumulated heartache and confusion and disappointment erupted through him like a geyser. He lunged forward, wanting to shake his father and roar for him to put him out of his misery. He was hiding things. Things that would make every-thing make sense.

Then he felt it. Gabrielle's hand trembling on his arm.

He cursed himself. He'd sworn he'd never distress her again, and here he was, forcing her to witness him resurrecting his family tragedy.

He pulled her into him, looked his entreaty for forgiveness into her reddened, teary eyes, his heart compressing at having caused her such anguish.

Then he turned and almost wept himself at seeing the dev-astation on the face of a man he'd thought indomitable. He had to believe at that moment that his father might also prove to be not as heartless as Durante believed him to be.

"We'll leave skeletons in the past, *Padre,* even if they come out of the closet sooner or later. Now, the future and all I am belong to Gabrielle."

As he supported the almost-collapsing Gabrielle and turned to lead her out, his father's thick, tear-filled rasp stopped him. *"Gabrielle."*

Gabrielle lurched in his hold as if she'd been shot. Durante almost had to support her full weight as he turned them around.

His father was smiling, a smile distorted by the devastation his stroke had left in its wake. It twisted Durante's heart. And that was before his father rasped, "Thank you for bringing my son home…*figlia mia.*"

Fourteen

The wedding was tomorrow.

And Gabrielle was going insane.

King Benedetto had pretended he didn't know her. She'd been so shocked that she'd gone mute.

Then Durante had taken her to his apartments, drowned her in his passion until she'd forgotten that a world outside him existed. Before she could remember, he'd swept her into the whirlwind of preparations and one chance to tell him after another slipped by.

She needed to see King Benedetto before she could reveal the truth to Durante. This was the first day he'd been allowed visitors since they'd seen him. His health had taken a turn for the worse after his confrontation with Durante.

She waited until the king's valet had left them alone before she blurted out her agitation and fear. "Why didn't you tell Durante of our relationship? It's been killing me, keeping my word, but I believed you finally would. He might…*would* have understood then, that it was never my intention or idea to hide facts from him. Now, after that stunt you pulled, I'm dreading the worst."

The king struggled to sit up in bed, reached a trembling hand to her. "No, Gaby. He loves you so much he'd give his life for you. He wouldn't blame you for abiding by the promise I made you give me. But I can't tell him of our relationship and neither can you."

"But this is ridiculous. It's bound to come out sooner or later, and then what would you have me say? Oops, I forgot to tell you, your father was my family's benefactor?"

"It's imperative that Durante never find out."

"Why?" she cried out in confusion.

The king seemed to age another twenty years before her eyes. Then he finally slumped back in bed and whispered, "Because if he finds out, he'll put two and two together and realize that my mistress, the only woman I ever loved, was your mother."

The world receded, her vision narrowed. Cold flooded in on her from all sides. Her heart lost momentum, stuttered, stalled.

The king's voice became distorted. "I wanted to take our secret to my grave as she did. We never wanted you of all people to find out. But I have to tell you now."

She felt her heart bleeding. "Not true…Mom loved Dad…"

"She did, but it was nothing like the love she had for me or I for her. She met him in my court, married him years after I left her in heartache and misery. It was almost as soon as she had you that your father's depression began to manifest. Then I found proof that my suspicions—which had led me to break both of our hearts—had been unfounded. I sought her out, begged her forgiveness for the way I'd treated her. When I offered them my support, it felt as if your father suddenly let go with me around to carry the burden. She'd suffered so much,

I had to offer her solace and then it was beyond us not to succumb to our love. Your father wasn't there by then, either mentally or emotionally, to notice let alone care.

"We kept our relationship a secret so that we wouldn't hurt our children, but we were deeply in love and perfectly happy. Then she started to suffer from her rheumatoid arthritis and I started to let go of my own life and duties as I suffered her suffering. She chose to die without me around to witness it. Getting the news of her death, knowing that I wasn't there for her in her last days, was almost a deathblow. I held on until I attended her funeral, made sure that everything was in order with her legacy and with you before I broke down. The only reason I'm still hanging on now is, I need to hand over Castaldini to a new king.

"I always wished Durante would be that king. But the laws were against it. Then he came to despise me so much he wouldn't have accepted becoming my crown prince even if the laws changed. Then everything changed after your mother died, after I almost did. After Leandro turned down the crown, I had my chance to finally change the laws, to make Durante eligible despite his being my son. But the hard part was getting Durante himself back here. That's when it finally came to me—the one thing that could bring him back, to me, to himself. *You.*"

"How did you *know* that?" she wailed. "God…*why me?*"

"Because, although I risked exposing everything by bringing you together, I had to try to give you what I and your mother could have had if I hadn't spoiled it for us. I sent you to him because you're so like your mother and he's so like me, I was certain you'd fall as madly in love as we had. And you did."

Durante stared down at the report in his hand.

He'd been trying to put the past into its inaccessible corner, never to touch the present or future again.

He hadn't expected to end his own world.

His knees gave way under the enormity of the conspiracy the cold data spun.

"Durante!"

Durante heard the booming voice, the powerful footsteps' escalating tempo as if through a separate consciousness. It felt as if it were another's body that was dragged to its feet, that stumbled backward to hit something soft and yielding that broke its falling momentum.

"Durante, what's wrong?"

He stared up out of eyes that felt alien, at a stranger with concern and anxiety blazing on his face. Somewhere in the black cascade that eclipsed everything, he knew this was Leandro, his cousin. But was he really? Did he know who anybody was anymore? Hadn't it all turned into one big, convoluted lie?

"Did something happen? Is Gabrielle all right? The king?"

"Something happened. Gabrielle. The king." Durante heard the stifled echo droning in a monstrous parody of his voice.

"What *is* it, Durante? *Tell* me."

Durante wanted to tell him. He felt sure that uttering the words would finish him. And he wanted it all to be over. But his mind and tongue had lost their connection.

Leandro sat down slowly, as if afraid any sudden movement would make him crumble. He pried free something Durante was crushing in his fist. The report. The end of his world.

Every nerve in his body snapped. He fell back like a skyscraper coming apart in an earthquake.

Numbness crept over him like an army of spiders as Leandro looked at the papers. Nothingness expanded in his skull until he thought he felt the lines connecting its bones separate, widen, as if in preparation for explosion.

He pushed back against the inexorable pressure. "Read it. Out loud. From the beginning."

Leandro gave a grudging nod and began to read.

"Investigations reveal that when King Benedetto was newly crowned, he had a secret lover, Clarisse LeFevre, a French-Canadian ballerina in an Italian ballet company that frequently performed in Castaldini. He broke off the affair over reports that she was cheating on him with a business rival, and almost immediately married Countess Angelica Boccanegra. Ten years later, the king, after investigating and proving the falseness of the allegations that had caused him to cast away his lover, finally located her. She was now married, but he became a constant presence in her family's life, supporting them all after her husband, Andrew Williamson, suffered bankruptcy and depression. He had them all relocated to Cagliari, where he also kept a private home, where it was revealed after intensive investigation that he met with her regularly and in utmost secrecy a few months before her death seven months ago."

"And a month later he had his stroke." Durante heard the whisper, didn't recognize it as his voice. "He weathered my mother's death without a tear, but almost died when his lover did. The lover he named his own daughter after. The daughter of the woman he was betraying, the woman he broke in mind and spirit. And that lover's daughter is now my bride-to-be. The love of my life."

Leandro fixed him with a blank stare. Durante knew his lightning-swift mind was calculating all possible outcomes of every comment he could make.

Leandro finally exhaled. "I admit, this is totally unexpected. I can imagine how shocked you feel."

"Can you, Leandro?" Tendrils of fury began to rise among the ashes of deadness. "Can you imagine what it feels like to surrender your heart only to find out you've fallen for your enemy?"

Leandro's jaw hardened. "That is shock talking, Durante. Gabrielle has nothing to do with your parents' affair."

And the fury ignited. "*She lied.* She pretended she didn't know my father—*Dio,* she blinded me so completely I never suspected a thing. And all the time she's been lying...about *everything*."

"Don't start jumping to conclusions," Leandro said, like a father chastising sense into an overemotional son. "There could be a perfectly good reason why she couldn't reveal their connection."

"There *is* a perfectly good reason. Gabrielle's reputation includes a warning not to let her within a mile of you. She knew I would never have met with her had I known. She played me so seamlessly, she had me groveling for believing the rumors about her instead. *Dio!* The hurt she poured out, the act I bought to the last tremulous treacherous gasp. I trusted her so much I didn't even *think* of investigating her. And she's been deceiving me all along. She's—"

"Durante, *stop*." Leandro's growl was like a pressure bandage slammed on the hemorrhage of his rage and agony. "I once jumped to conclusions, listened to my fears and prejudices about Phoebe, and I ended up wasting eight years of our lives. Eight endless, miserable years of our living apart and in emotional exile. Don't make the same mistake. The price is incalculable."

And the torrent of pain gushed again. "Did Phoebe turn out to be the daughter of the woman your mother died of a broken mind and heart over? Did she keep lying to you until she had you depending on her for your every breath so that you wouldn't be able to break free once you learned the truth? Is she a cold-blooded, manipulative cheat?"

Leandro's gaze hardened to flint around the core of burning empathy. "All I can say is that this is circumstantial evidence, and I've learned the hardest way possible how misleading that can be. But as impossible as it may be for you to think right now, there are more important things at stake than your heart. Castaldini is in danger. The financial dangers are the least of our problems and the easiest to deal with. Political and ethnic conflicts are brewing, and as regent I don't have the influence of a king. Everyone believes they can wait for my proxy to be over—they don't feel the necessity to bow to my power. Castaldini needs a king."

"What does that have to do with this?"

"It has everything to do with it. The king has forbidden anyone to reveal to you his intention to approach you with his demand before he judged the time right to do so himself, but I believe none of us can afford to wait anymore. I can see that your personal situation is about to blow to kingdom come, and you *cannot* let that interfere with your decision."

"What decision? What the devil are you talking about?"

Leandro looked as if he were about to stab him, hating to do it but knowing there was no escape. "After I declined to become crown prince, the king had the Council make an exigency amendment to the laws of succession. By this new amendment, he can now make you his crown prince. If you agree." Leandro took him by the shoulders, shook him. "As you should, Durante. As you *must*."

And it all made sense. Sick, macabre sense.

His father had set out to *make* him agree.

He'd known nothing would bring Durante back—nothing except an irresistible woman armed with thorough knowledge of him so she could project the image of his soulmate.

And she'd manipulated him to the point where they would achieve their objectives. At his expense. His father would get back the son who'd rejected him, would pass the crown to his line through Durante, while Gabrielle, the king's partner in crime, the daughter of the woman he'd loved above all else, would be that son's worshipped wife and queen, as his father had failed to make her mother.

His father was going to make his demand today. He knew it. And if he'd still been blind and fathoms-deep in love and trust, he would have agreed to anything to keep peace and harmony.

He exploded to his feet, rage and agony boiling his blood.

Leandro shot up, caught him. "Don't do anything in this state, or you'll regret it for the rest of your life."

"*What* life?" Durante roared as he pushed his cousin away with all the violence tearing apart his insides before staggering away, a mortally wounded beast bent on slashing apart the two people who'd killed him before he surrendered to oblivion.

Gabrielle stared at herself in the bathroom mirror, whimpered as she brought the ice cube again to her swollen eyelids, trying to ameliorate the swelling.

She'd been back in her quarters for an hour now. She'd run there to get a hold of herself, but she'd failed miserably.

Shock and misery still wracked her. It felt as if acid were gushing through the gaping cracks of her shattered world.

How *could* they? Her mother, and King Benedetto? All these years, lying to her, to everyone?

Now everything made sense. Why her mother had always had that look of apology, why she'd sent her to a boarding school in Napoli when she was old enough to suspect what was going on.

Betrayal ate at her. But it was nothing compared to the dread that tore at the tethers of her mind. If she felt this way, what would Durante feel when he found out?

The king had said he should never find out. But this couldn't be hidden. Not anymore. And she had to be the one to tell Durante the terrible truth.

She had to do it now. Before their meeting with the king. Come what may. Even if it was something she might not survive.

The icy feeling had reduced the telltale signs of weeping, but she still looked like she had on the day she'd lost her mother. She felt as if she had lost her all over again. She might lose her life now. She would, if she lost Durante.

No. No, she wouldn't. Durante believed in her now. He'd know she had nothing to do with any of it. He trusted her.

She staggered out of her suite…and was almost knocked off her feet by the wall that materialized in her doorway.

Durante! God…here…no, she needed a few more minutes…

Stop it. This had gone on long enough. It ended now.

"Durante…I need to tell you something."

"What a coincidence. I have something to tell you, too."

His voice. She'd never heard his voice like that. Emotionless. Lifeless. He looked as if he'd been crying, too, his eyes shards of brilliant blue simmering in angry redness.

She clutched at him, her heart bucking its tethers. "Durante, what is it? God…are you okay?"

"I will be."

Then he turned and walked away. She rushed in his wake, a fireball of fear and confusion exploding in her mind.

The king was waiting for them at his reading table, the first time she'd seen him out of bed. His face started to tug into that skewed smile. It fell back into bleakness at the sight of Durante.

Silence settled over the scene. Something terrible radiated from Durante. She stumbled sideways as if out of the path of a lethal ray.

He couldn't already know. She had to be the one to tell him. But he looked…rabid. He…he *did* know. Was incensed. But not at her. It couldn't be at her.

"You wish me to become your crown prince." The hiss that emanated from him sounded inhuman. Shudders started to creep over her. "What do they say about being careful what you wish for? You manipulated me to get me back here only for me to find out your secrets, crimes that I will expose. I'll tell the world what a sadistic, adulterous husband you were. And I will take the crown now, not after you die."

Gabrielle's heart had stopped with the first salvo out of Durante's lips. Now it beat like the wings of a hummingbird, yet pushed no blood to her brain. The world constricted into a pinpoint of darkness.

Something wrenched her from the edge of oblivion. Durante was dragging her away.

He was so angry at his father. She had to defuse his shock and agony. Had to mend this horrific breach.

"Durante…don't do this to yourself…it's not like you think…" His abrupt stop had her crashing into him. She leaned on him, for support, for both of them, her lips trembling into his heaving back, with love, with desperation to explain before one more minute passed. "Your father's only crime was loving my mother, hiding their affair, from everyone, starting with me, but he did it so that he wouldn't hurt anyone…he loves you…but was so afraid you hated him, made me promise…"

He wrenched away, turned on her. "You were congratulating yourself, weren't you? As each phase of your seduction worked on me like a spell?"

Seduction? Spell? What did he…?

"Now you've reached the point where you believe your hold on me is unbreakable, that I'd sooner let go of all my pride and fortune, of my very life, than let you go, don't you?"

He-he believed…the worst? *Again?* He didn't trust her? Didn't think she deserved a chance to defend herself?

"And you were right."

Wha…? She'd misunderstood? He wasn't saying that he doubted her?

"I would give my life for you, the woman, the treasure who shares my soul and mind, the owner of my body and heart."

He wasn't! He didn't doubt her. Her churning world stilled, quaked with relief. "Oh, God, Durante, oh, my love…"

"But that's not you." His hiss froze her jubilation. "That woman was a role you played to seduce me, reading the lines my father taught you. That woman doesn't exist. So now, my bride-to-be—you're no longer my bride-to-be. I cancelled the wedding. I'll tell the whole world why. I'll show anyone who had any doubt about you how the worst so-called rumors were only the tip of the iceberg. I'm cancelling the book deal, too, and if you try to play any of the penalty clauses, I'll crush you and your precious company under my foot." He gave a hideous laugh. "Oh, wait, I'll crush you and everything you hold dear, anyway."

A stranger. She was looking at a vicious stranger. One who'd played an elaborate game of make-believe, of knowing her down to her last thought, caring for her with his every breath, respecting and trusting her with his every fiber. It had all been empty. All the proclamations, the promises of forever.

The world started spinning again, swinging her away with it. He receded as everything drowned in a sea of distorted images.

"Gabrielle."

That growl, a predator enraged to find his prey about to escape his talons. She turned back, no survival instinct left.

And he delivered the killing blow. "If you have any shred of self-preservation left, you will make sure I never see you again."

She stared into his cruel eyes, and everything came to an end.

Fifteen

Leandro had been right.

He'd warned him. Durante hadn't listened. He'd been deaf. Blind. And totally out of his mind.

Madmen didn't realize the depth of their insanity. Didn't see it at all. Saw it as justified action, inescapable reaction.

He'd foamed and fermented in the delusion, thrashed and plummeted down a spiral of intensifying agony. Then he'd hit bottom. And he'd remembered them. Gabrielle's eyes. In the blood-red haze of his fevered memories. The shock of letdown there, the horror of loss. The realization that the one who'd pledged to protect her from all harm, the only one she'd trusted with her true self, was the one dealing the deathblow. And he'd known.

She had nothing to do with any of this. Hadn't known most of it. What she'd hidden had been the burden, the pain he'd seen in her eyes. That she couldn't tell him what wasn't hers to tell. She'd tried to tell him that.

He believed her. Without question. Now. When it was too late.

No. He couldn't let it be. He wouldn't. He would do anything to turn back the clock. Erase the hurt he'd inflicted on her.

But he'd resurfaced from his madness to find her gone. Two days ago. He'd learned that she'd left within an hour of his throwing her out of his life with a threat he wouldn't have hurled at his worst enemy. But he'd thought her far worse than that then. He'd thought her his murderer. When he'd been the one who'd stuck a knife in her heart. And twisted.

He didn't deserve her forgiveness.

But he would. Whatever and however long it took, he would.

Gabrielle counted her steps, her breaths. The seconds.

It was the one way she could go on from one to the next. She had this conviction that if she stopped counting, she'd stop moving, stop breathing. Stop moving forward in time. Be trapped forever in a second of pure agony.

She wished she would. But couldn't. Not before she made sure her employees were safe from Durante's wrath.

She cared nothing for what he would do to her.

She opened her office door, stepped inside, the plush wall-to-wall carpeting absorbing the sound of her steps, amplifying the feeling that she'd ceased to exist.

But it wasn't insubstantiality that engulfed her now. It was something else. Something overwhelming and all-encompassing.

Him. Durante. *Here.*

She dropped the count. She'd been right. Her breath stopped. Time. The second held her in its grasp—and crushed her.

"Gabrielle. Perdonami."

Forgive him?

The second fractured. Breath tore into her lungs. She spun around. And there he stood.

A god come down to earth, in an immaculate suit the color of the night of his hair, he made the crisp blues and grays of her space—made *existence*—pale into colorless nothingness.

His scent, his eyes on her. They made her forget everything. Every muscle in her body quivered like a bound bird's, the blinding urge to fly to him tearing her apart.

Weak, self-destructive moron. She might never truly live again, but it was his doing. He'd crushed her.

What more did he want?

Anguish almost ripped her chest open. "You didn't cut me into small enough pieces to satisfy your self-righteous rage? You want to see me a bloody mass on the ground before you're satisfied?"

"Gabrielle, *no.*"

His urgency exploded into strides that obliterated what remained of the flimsy safety of distance, brought him against her, around her, hard and hungry. Then he was taking of her, taking her into him again, spreading her against him, pressing her between the persistence of his passion and something as unyielding, drinking in her moans, absorbing her shudders, draining her of will and memory and pain.

He was the air that would make her breathe again. But he was also the poison that would asphyxiate her if she did.

She tore herself away, stumbled against the wall at her back, pressed against its coolness. "So is this it? You…invested too much time and effort in…training me, and even though you despise and abhor me, you want your sex-marathon-on-demand nympho back?"

"No, Gabrielle, don't… Don't say anything like that."

"You mean you *don't* want to have sex with me? That wasn't why you almost took me against the wall just now?"

"No, Gabrielle—yes, I desire you, now and always, but that isn't why I'm here. I now know the truth, and…"

She cut him off. "So you deigned to talk to your father? Oh, wait, you think his word is as worthless as mine. So you must have done more investigations. And they…what? Cleared me? No, thanks. I'm not doing this again. I'm guilty of not telling you how it all started, when it wasn't my secret. But you accused me of *crimes*. You found such comfort in believing the worst without even trying to hear me out."

He neared her as if approaching a wounded, terrified animal, his voice a hypnotic croon. "I was in shock, in agony, over finding out you're the daughter of the woman I spent years hating without knowing if she even existed. I went mad thinking you knew all along and had been leading me on. But I didn't need you to slap sense into me this time, Gabrielle. What we shared, what I feel for you, what I *know* you feel for me, made me overcome the pain and madness. I did no investigations. And I didn't talk to my father." Hesitation entered his beseeching eyes. "What would he have told me?"

His words swirled inside her brain, making no sense. She refused to let them. They'd be lethal if they did. She'd succumb to their influence. Sink. All the way this time. And next time he gutted her and tossed her out to drown, she wouldn't resurface.

But among all the things she couldn't hear, there was one thing she could. A question. About his father.

She owed him no answers. Not after he'd judged and executed her. But he wasn't just the man she'd loved beyond self-preservation, would love against all reason, for the rest of her days. He wasn't just the one being who held the power of destruction over her, who'd used it again and, she swore, for the last time. He was also the man who held the fate of a kingdom— and that of his father—in his hands. She knew her mother would have wanted her to do anything she could to defend the one man Clarisse LeFevre had lived and died loving. Gabrielle's answer might exonerate King Benedetto in his all-powerful son's eyes. Or at least ameliorate his guilt. Durante might not exact his revenge on his father to the full.

She told him everything she knew.

Durante listened to Gabrielle, his heart twisting in his chest. She seemed sentient but not alive, aware but unfeeling, held together with the glue of automations and obligations, which was bound to come undone at any point. Even if it didn't, and it stuck her together, fractures traversed her psyche and soul, fault lines that would splinter her again at the least pressure.

He'd done that to her. And he had to restore her, at any price. Starting with his own life.

He'd hoped that begging her forgiveness would garner him a hearing. Why had he hoped she'd grant him what he'd denied her?

He knew why. He'd counted on her being more forgiving than he was. But even her mercy had limits. He'd pushed her beyond them.

One hope remained. That something in what she'd said would give him insight into how to repair the devastation he'd wreaked.

He replayed every word, looking for clues. He got only blows, every one battering him with more shame at how he'd lashed out at the two people who'd put their pride and hearts on the line to save him from his bitter loneliness, to help him find contentment and joy, to learn what living truly meant at last. The one thing to redeem him was that his heart had already believed in her without proof, against all damning evidence.

It *had* all been his father's orchestration, as he'd thought when he'd been in the throes of suspicion and pain-induced insanity. But not at all as he'd expected. His father did know him far better than he knew himself. He knew Gabrielle as deeply. He'd known it would take Gabrielle to save him, bring back his humanity, that it would take *him* to heal, cherish and worship her. So his father had sent her to him.

And though it had started out as a mission for her, their magic had taken over from their first glance, fulfilling his father's prophecy.

But it had been the king's fault again that she'd kept secrets. He'd made her pledge secrecy, fearing the violence of his son's unreasonableness, the depth of his bitterness, things that would have made him blind himself to her true worth, costing him the one woman who shared his soul. Even when it had seemed that nothing could tear them apart, his father had still withheld the truth, fearing exactly what Durante had done upon finding it out.

Another verdict was as glaring. He might never know the true causes of his mother's decline and death, but whatever those diaries contained, something else must have caused her to write them. His father was no cold-blooded abuser. Thinking otherwise had poisoned him for five long years. But the heart that had led him to loving Gabrielle would never lie to him. His father, while guilty of many things, had never been guilty of hurting his mother.

He not only owed Gabrielle a lifetime of apologies, he owed his father, too.

"…but instead of exonerating your father," Gabrielle was going on, "I must have only added manipulating us to his offenses, in your opinion. Or rather, manipulating you, because I've been in on it, with the worst possible agenda, of course. So why not get on with your revenge? End your father's reign in humiliation, take the crown from him, take my company from me, throw me out on the street and leave me the hell alone."

"That was my rage talking," he insisted, urgency writhing in his chest. "I would never have carried out my threats."

"Really? So cancelling the wedding, telling the world why—"

"I told no one anything. And far from taking your company away, I'm here to give you these." He flicked open his briefcase, handed her a dossier. When she didn't take it, he explained. "These papers ensure that neither I nor anyone else can take your company away, that it will always be stable no matter what happens to any market in the world. And that's just the beginning. Make any demands. I'll do anything for you. *Anything*, Gabrielle. My father knew me, and you, too well— he knew we were made for each other. He did what he had to do, to bring us together, a debt I can never repay."

"So you won't dethrone him?"

"I was raving mad with shock when I said that. The moment I came to my senses, there was no question in my mind about your innocence."

"Sure. Until the next time something rouses your suspicions, and you turn on me and maul me to death."

"That is never going to happen again."

"I've heard that before, Durante. From Ed. Every time he abused me, he'd say it would never happen again."

"I'm *nothing* like him. Don't, *Dio,* please don't…don't put me in the same thought as him, *amore.*"

"You're worse than him." Her sob sliced into his brain, its agony, its import, insupportable. "I cared nothing for him. His abuse cut nowhere beyond the surface. Yours carved me to the marrow."

Her agony flooded his chest, became molten lead coursing through his left arm like the onset of a heart attack. He wished it would truly damage him. But self-abuse was self-indulgent. He needed to be at his fittest to undo what he'd done.

He wrestled with paralysis, surged forward to embrace her. She struggled like a cornered animal. He was distressing her more.

He staggered back, rasped, "I followed in my father's footsteps—this genetic compulsion we once spoke about—to the point that I suspected the worst of you, the keeper of my soul, and cast you away, as he'd done with your mother. But he let her stay away, compounded his mistake by marrying for the crown, and made a mess of so many lives. But I'm done being my father's son. I'm walking my own path from now on and I'm repeating no one's mistakes, starting with my own. Give me one last chance, Gabrielle. I'll never ask for anything more. I'll make amends, until the end of my days."

Tears no longer flowed from her eyes. She was no longer shaking as if she'd unravel, no longer breathing as if her throat were swelling closed.

Dared he hope…?

"Words are cheap, Durante." Her voice was steady, lifeless. "To you, everything is cheap. You can throw companies and fortunes at me, but the one thing I want is what you've failed twice to give me. The benefit of the doubt. Fair treatment. I once said, when you were as generous with superlatives, that 'never' has forever scope. I *should* have waited and seen.

"I thought at the beginning that I could handle it, if you were offering something simple and superficial, like no-strings sex. But you weren't, and even though I told you I wasn't in your league, I let you sweep me away, into all those powerful emotions and bottomless passions, let you seduce me into wanting—and expecting—too much, way too soon. I was right to be wary of your rash proposal, and again too weak to heed my wariness. I own my mistakes—whether it was falling into your arms then believing we could have forever, or abiding by a promise of secrecy, not only because I couldn't break my word, but because I feared for the fool's gold perfection of what I thought I had with you.

"Whatever you feel for me, it's not enough to overcome everything it has against it. You might think now that it's 'until the end of your days,' but give yourself, say, a month or two. *And* a woman or two. I bet you'll forget about me. Or maybe, when all the illusions have dissipated and nothing but desire remains, you'll walk back into my life like your father walked back into my mother's and be my part-time lover, too. If you're still single, that is. Whatever happens, the dream, the grand and unique and indestructible love, the guaranteed forever, is over. You ended it. And from where I'm standing, it's better this way."

He had no idea how he remained on his feet.

He'd thought he'd known how much he'd hurt her. Until she'd hurt him back. Caused him irreparable damage just by giving him a good look at her wound. He knew now. He also understood. Why his father had lost so much of himself when his lover had been suffering, why he'd almost died when she had.

He had broken her trust. Not just in his ability to always treat her with restraint and respect, but in the depth and constancy of not only his feelings but his character. More pledges now would mean nothing. Worse than nothing. His amends had to be undeniable, until she believed him and in him again.

And if she couldn't? If this was irreversible?

He laid the dossier on her desk, leaned burning palms and trained blind-with-tears eyes on it. He couldn't consider this. Not if he wanted to remain alive to see his plan through.

"Non rinuncerò mai ad amarti. Sono tuo per sempre."

I will never give up loving you. I'm yours forever.

His only indication that the words that had scraped their longing into his mind had actually left his lips was the lurch that shook her, the two wet trails that spilled down her haunted face. He filled his soul and senses with one last look at her, a sight that would fuel him during the desolation of being without her. Then he turned and walked away.

It felt as if he was walking away from life. As he was.

Sixteen

The door clicked closed. Durante. Gone.

She'd made him go.

Something skewered its way through her gut. An unvoiced scream. For him to come back. That she took back every word. About not trusting him. Not forgiving him. Not believing in his love. Not feeling as if she'd die if he forgot her, if he sought out others, if he sought her out again with nothing but lust in his heart and body. *She'd lied.*

But she'd had to.

She couldn't have let him prove to her how much he loved her. How much he regretted doubting and hurting her. For she would have believed again, surrendered all the way now that her last shackle—his father's secrets and her fear of their exposure—had been lifted.

But Durante's shackles would never be lifted. Not when they were created by her very identity. The daughter of the woman he believed had caused his mother's devastation and death. That knowledge would poison his love, would chip away at its foundations. Then his bitterness and paranoia would rise again and he'd decimate her, forever this time, under the brunt of his cruelty.

She crumpled to the ground.

She'd gotten home, somehow. She didn't remember how. She'd found herself there, weeping. She hadn't stopped since. It was morning now. She thought.

Her nerves flamed with impulses, her mind roiled with obsessions, her cells burned with longing.

She needed him back.

How could he not come back? Was that it? The extent of his all-powerful emotions? His unstoppable persistence? She'd slapped him with words, clearly trembling for a repudiation, and he'd taken them as cause to give up on her? He was really gone?

He *couldn't* be. He'd said he'd never give up. Why had he? Wasn't what they'd shared worth more than an hour's cajoling and a few pledges? Had all feeling been on her side, after all?

Which would make sense. More than a man like him feeling the same absolute emotions for her as she did for him.

But he'd said he *did*. And he never lied.

So had he faced himself with the truth, that in time he'd wonder how he'd disregarded who she was? Was he now wondering just how much of their rapport was real and how much had been his father's tutoring? Could suspicion be taking hold of his mind again?

If it was, then his mind was a time bomb and she shouldn't even think of coming within a mile of him again. She couldn't survive another blow up.

But…she could have carried on in her lifelessness if he hadn't shown up yesterday. How dared he jump-start her heart and hopes, then walk away again? This time she wasn't flatlining, as she had the first time. This time she was fibrillating, the spikes of chaos intensifying by the second, threatening to rupture her heart…

Stop. You're not doing this. You're not following in your father's footsteps. Or his mother's.

She had to behave as if she was alive, go through the motions. In time, it was bound to simulate life, maybe even re-spark it. She had to go through her morning routines, take them, and the rest of her life, one second at a time.

She dragged herself out of bed. One foot in front of the other. A shower, breakfast, morning show on TV, dress, work. Wait for him, pray for him to contact her again. She'd take him back if he did, grab at anything he offered, offer all of herself again come what may…

No, no, *no*. If she wasn't right for him, it would end far worse than any of their parents' stories had ended. For she was sure none had loved this intensely.

She walked back to the living room, taking a sip of her orange juice only to inhale one then spew it out in a fit of coughing.

His voice.

God, she was starting early, imagining hearing it.

Her eyes panned to where she thought she'd heard it issuing from, and she almost choked on her lungs in shock. He was… he was…

On TV. On the morning show she watched every day.

The gawking, swooning, hyper-excited female anchor was squeaking, "So why did you decide to break your silence with the press, Prince Durante? And in this spectacular way, too?"

Durante turned his brooding eyes from the woman's face to look directly at the camera. Gabrielle collapsed under the brunt of his stare. She knew every woman in the globe would be similarly affected, but she knew. He was looking at her.

Then he began to speak, dark, driven, unraveling her with each syllable and intonation. "I am here offering the love of my life a public apology, issuing a plea that she give me one last chance. I am announcing that Gabrielle Williamson's Le Roi Enterprises—besides publishing my biography, which will include the details of the situation that led to my…postponement of our wedding—will also have the exclusive on every public plea I'll continue to issue. Also, as a token of my total love and absolute trust, I have signed over all my holdings to her."

Among the bombs, she realized one more thing.

This was on air live. Right in front of her building.

She'd never thought anything solid could move so fast. She streaked out of her apartment, saw that the elevator was in use. She didn't even think of waiting, ran to the stairs and down the ten-floors, a missile set on Durante.

Once outside her building, she barreled her way through the barricade of human flesh he towered above. The crowd parted each time someone recognized her, and murmurs and exclamations spread like wildfire in dry tinder.

Her momentum slammed her into him. He barely moved under the impact. Hesitation, something she'd never felt from him, filled the arms that steadied her. His eyes devoured her as his face clenched with such longing, regret and entreaty that her chest heaved from their bombardment far more than with exertion.

His lips worked for a moment before they started to open. She just knew he was going to say more crazy, compromising things.

Her hand lurched up, clamped over his mouth. "This is all a publicity stunt, world," she panted. "A dare I didn't dream he'd take me up on. So…stockholders, don't panic. And tabloids, don't hold your breath. He will *not* be revealing anything, as there's nothing to reveal. And yes, the book is going to be great, and everyone should preorder their copy, but it will not contain any sensational confessions, just the secrets to this…this phenomenal powerhouse of a dreamboat's success, okay? What's more—"

"Non posso più vivere senza di te, Gabriella mia."

Her voice vanished, every electrical impulse powering her body shut down. She sagged in his arms. He was singing. Here.

I can't live without you, my Gabrielle.

The crowd gaped. All of New York City seemed to hold its breath. He continued the song he'd written for her, had proposed with, his voice setting the yearning lyrics on passionate fire, turning the evocative melody into all-encompassing enchantment.

A hush reigned after his last vibrato had died away.

Then a storm of applause and questions exploded.

"Did you write this song?"

"Will you be recording this song?"

"Will you release it as a single? Part of an album?"

He shrugged. "It's Gabrielle's song. She decides what I do with it." He turned his eyes down to her, his all-out surrender stoking the inferno raging inside her. "Just say the word and I'll turn it into a rock number and perform it in a jumpsuit—"

She surged up, sealed his lips with hers, shutting him up.

He sagged in her arms, groaned his relief long and shuddering into her mouth, shaking the foundations of her soul. Then he suddenly dropped down. She panicked. For a millisecond.

He wasn't fainting. He was bending for leverage. Then she was in his arms, feeling weightless, his gaze, the emanations of his whole being making her feel priceless.

The sea of bystanders parted, raged with hoots and applause. She vaguely thought New Yorkers must be reveling in the unfolding of yet another chapter in the fairy tale of their resident Castaldinian prince and his commoner American princess.

She missed the journey back up to her apartment. She only knew she was on her bed, her world once again anchored by Durante's beloved weight, the heat and hardness of his steel-fleshed body driving security and equilibrium back into hers.

A long time after the frenzy unleashed in the wake of the barely escaped catastrophe abated, she lay boneless and throbbing with satiation, cleaved into him, sighing her bliss. "That was quite a stunt you pulled down there."

FREE BOOKS OFFER

To get you started, we'll send you
2 FREE books and a FREE gift

There's no catch, everything is **FREE**

Accepting your 2 **FREE** books and **FREE** mystery gift
places you under no obligation to buy anything.

Be part of the Mills & Boon® Book Club™ and receive your favourite
Series books up to 2 months before they are in the shops and delivered
straight to your door. Plus, enjoy a wide range of **EXCLUSIVE** benefits!

- Best new women's fiction – delivered right to
  your door with FREE P&P

- Avoid disappointment – get your books up to
  2 months before they are in the shops

- No contract – no obligation to buy

We hope that after receiving your free books you'll
want to remain a member. But the choice is yours.
So why not give us a go? You'll be glad you did!

Visit **millsandboon.co.uk** to stay up to date
with offers and to sign-up for our newsletter

2 **FREE** books
and a
FREE gift

D0EIA

Mrs/Miss/Ms/Mr   Initials

BLOCK CAPITALS PLEASE

Surname

Address

Postcode

Email

NO STAMP NEEDED!

MILLS & BOON
Book Club

FREE BOOK OFFER
FREEPOST NAT 10298
RICHMOND
TW9 1BR

NO STAMP
NECESSARY
IF POSTED IN
THE U.K. OR N.I.

Durante pressed into her, almost entering her again "down there," purred, "Glad you approve."

She wanted nothing more than to have him inside her again. But this couldn't be put off. She dug her nails in his buttocks, stopping his movement.

He groaned in disappointment, rose over her, his eyes growing serious. "It wasn't a stunt. I was showing you everything I held dear, my privacy, my pride, my status, my achievements, are a negligible price for regaining your trust. None of them mean a thing without you."

Her heart swelled until it seemed to fill her down to her toes. Seemed it squeezed against her now ever-filled tear glands. "I won't let you do any of the things you said you'd do."

"I already did them.

"You're undoing them, right this second."

"I can't. It's all yours now."

"Okay, Durante, this long ceased to be thrilling and is getting pretty scary. Stop. Now! Before this crazy stunt backlashes, you crazy, insane man."

"I was insane to hurt you. I've never been saner or clearer about what matters. You, the restoration of your pride, your trust in me and my love. All I need is for you to let me be yours...yes, until the end of my days." His lips crooked. "I just hope you'll let me give you advice on what to do with your newly acquired wealth, so your stockholders don't suffer a cent's devaluation in the transfer. That's the only catch, really, that you can't give it all away to your favorite charities and causes."

"But I can give it to anyone I want, right? So I'm giving it to you. End of conversation." Something enormous mushroomed in his eyes, until she almost wailed. "What now?"

"I was just wondering. Who else would toss back something of that magnitude, without even pausing to make me sweat it first? Not that I am sweating it. I don't care about it at all. I made my billions, and I'll just make more. In fact, on the way here, I made a transaction that resulted in half a billion in my newly emptied account. I'm not destitute, if that what you're worried about."

"I'm not worried. I'm *disintegrating.*"

"While I'm rejoicing. If I managed to prove the extent of my trust. Even though you're making it so hard to prove anything by tossing everything back to me like that, I hope you know I wouldn't have risked anything with such catastrophic potential to so many if I didn't trust you more than I trust myself."

"Everything has to be larger-than-Jupiter with you, docsn't it? I toss around a few stupid words when I'm upset, and instead of giving me those couple of days—of hours you once suggested—to get my act together, you fling a whole financial empire at me."

"And my kingdom, for good measure." He sighed in contentment.

Suspicion sank its ice into her bones. She exploded out of his arms, sprung standing on the bed. "God, what did you *do?*"

He spread his magnificence like a replete lion, hooked his hands behind his head. "I told my father to go for his third candidate for the crown."

Her heart almost fired out of her ribs. "What do you think I am? An insane goddess appeased only with atrocious sacrifices?"

"You are my goddess, but you're regretfully too benevolent. You tried to stop my sacrifices, are trying to reverse them now."

He stirred, prowled on all fours to her, bent to kiss her feet. She cried out the surplus of emotion. He crooned worship, worked his way up her legs, her calves, the back of her knees, burning one fuse after another, congealing the valves of her heart. She collapsed at the first touch of his tongue inside the thighs that trembled again with the need to wrap around him.

He received her nerveless mass in his cherishing arms, cosseted all of her quivering flesh. "This has nothing to do with what happened between us. But it is the best course of action *for* us. We're both too much citizens of the world, too invested in our careers. As much as I love Castaldini and know you can come to love it, too, I don't see our life bound to it."

She squirmed. "God, no, don't even consider my career in this decision. I'll find a dozen ways to maintain it. I'm sure you can work out as many ways to run your empire by remote control. Take this back, *please*."

"I won't, because it's the right thing to do. If I'm crowned, it will pulverize the law that made Castaldini such a unique and prosperous kingdom until my father's personal life interfered with his being the formidable king he was. My reign would be the end of the crown for merit. And I truly think King Antonio had a great idea in making the king work for his crown, not be born to it."

"But the law is too absolute and unfair," she protested. "Many sons won't live up to their fathers' level, but you've surpassed yours. It would be glaringly obvious you were made king on total merit, that after you the law would be enforced again, until another king's son proves himself as worthy of the crown."

"Even if I'm worthy of it, I didn't grow up dreaming of it, wasn't fighting for it when I built my success and fortune."

"But that should only make you even more worthy of it!"

"It doesn't work that way in Castaldini. And then, I truly don't *want* the power and the responsibility, and that's a *huge* strike against me. All I want is to be yours."

There were no limits to the heights he'd make her scale.

She pitched herself from those heights into the depths of arms she knew would always be there to catch her. "It's too much!" He rumbled. She swallowed his protest, sobbed. "Don't contradict me. I'm stating facts here."

He chuckled. "Here's one more fact, *bellissima*. My father, too, believes the long-term repercussions of the precedent of my crowning would change the face of Castaldini, something we should all fight against. He was desperate for me to take the crown, not because I was Castaldini's last hope, but because he feared the Council's rigidity. They proved it by choosing me over the third candidate because he's an illegitimate D'Agostino, a factor that in this day and age shouldn't be a consideration. He still fears they'll let him, the one they know would probably make the best king go because of this stupid prejudice."

She raised an eyebrow, suspicion and hackles rising. "Going overboard alert. Losing all credibility here. Way to go to *de*-convince me. There can be no better king-material than you."

Delight crackled from his depths, rich and infectious and unbearably arousing. "Never stop saying things like that to me."

"No danger of that whatsoever. Just hope you can stomach all the nonstop adulation. So what's this exaggeration about this third candidate making the best king?"

"It's what I believe. We—my father's candidates—are on par as far as power and success go. But I believe Ferruccio is the one among us who has that most drive to lead. He's also the most… old-fashioned, if you will. And he might never admit it, but he craves setting down roots, which he's never had. That combination makes him the best choice for Castaldini's king. I pray they make him the offer and fast, and that he agrees to take up the mantle when they do. I'm not sure he will. If I were him, I'd probably courier the D'Agostino family and Castaldini to hell."

"What if he does refuse? Will you then take the crown?"

"I won't think of that unless I'm the last candidate left standing. But I agreed to be Leandro's co-regent. Once Ferruccio is crown prince, we'll be his main men on his new Council, continuing to do our utmost in Castaldini's service. That means many, many visits there. Would you like that?"

She plunged into his embrace, kissing him all over. "I would love that! And I love you, most of the time beyond endurance…"

She cursed herself for the tremor in her voice when he

heaved up, his eyes alert, alarmed. "What is it? Surrender all your worries, *anima mia,* let me erase them."

"I-I'm just so afraid…and that was the reason I…"

"The reason you said what you did yesterday."

"I always forget that you can read my mind."

"Just partially now. I can't tell what still pains you so."

"I-I…oh, hell…tell me the truth, okay? I'll know if you don't and it will prey on my mind. You *really* don't care who I am?"

"I couldn't care more." She jerked, and he gentled her, leaned her against his propped up thighs, stroked and kneaded her, at once mind-blowingly sexual and heart-meltingly emotional. "You are the one who has awakened my heart, reawakened my ability to care, to enjoy, introduced me to the full potential of life. You have nothing to do with our parents' choices. I was insane to suspect you of knowing of their affair, to doubt your motives toward me. But at the core of my madness was my fear that I didn't deserve you and all the happiness you bring me, that something would happen to prove it was all too incredible to be true."

"And even though you deserve to be punished, slowly, agonizingly…" She lunged at him, kissed her way down his body until he growled, thrust at her, drove convulsing fingers in her hair to stop her, to urge her on. "…you also deserve far more than I can possibly be or give…hush, don't contradict me again." She raised her eyes, found that his were rivaling Castaldini's shores in vividness and translucency, radiating pure azure adoration. "And that's the same fear that paralyzed me into keeping silent. I couldn't believe this could be happening to me. I was living in dread of ending the perfection."

His lips quirked. "So you don't think it was fool's gold?"

She fluttered her lashes. "So you don't think I seduced you?"

"You did seduce me. To the point that my mind unravels at the merest thought of losing you." Distress gurgled in her throat. A slash of bedeviling white lit up his dark gold face as he hauled her to him. "And *Grazie a Dio* that you did. You seduced me just by being yourself, with no motive other than being unable to have enough of me. But *ragazzaccia mia,* you stopped my amends too soon. Not that I'll stop. I'll just keep on making them, keep showing you, proving to you what you are to me, my everything."

"Them's fightin' words, Your Highness. Prepare to witness that you are this and more to me. For starters, I'll never withhold anything from you again, not facts, not the last shred of thought or emotion." She bit her tongue. "Uh…that sounded as if I'll be a blabbering, overemotional pain in the rear."

"This kind of pain?" He squeezed her buttocks, pressed her into his aroused flesh, groaned as if in suffering. Her insides clenched, needing, gnawing. She knew how he felt. "Or the other kind, where you agonize me by reassuring me I'm in your heart and thoughts, that I'm pleasing and pleasuring you? If that's the kind of torment you have in store for me, I beg you to never stop."

She opened herself to him, pledged with body and soul, to never, ever stop.

Much, much later, she was draped over her man, her lover, the most incredible gift in this plane of existence, feeling savagely pleasured and overcharged with satiation.

It was why the thought, when it came, ripped through her like a hot knife through butter.

He felt it at once, gathered her more securely. "Tell me."

She didn't hesitate this time. "You still don't know what really went on with your mother, what her diary meant."

"I know she was disturbed. From the thankfully little I saw of my grandfather, I can see why, now that I've opened my mind to other possibilities rather than the obvious ones pointing to my father."

"So you don't believe your father drove her to suicide?"

He shook his head. "Or your mother. It was a tragedy, but I believe my father now, that there was no villain."

"Do you *really* believe that, or are you just—"

"Manipulating history to get closure in a way that would exonerate both our parents for obvious self-serving purposes?"

"Will you quit finishing my thoughts and questions?" She scraped her teeth against the abrasion of his stubble.

He groaned his pleasure before he pulled back, his eyes solemn. "And no, I'm not deluding myself here. I punished myself and my father long enough for the failures I believed we were both guilty of. But finding you gave me the clarity to see that neither of us could have done anything to help her, just like neither you nor your mother could help your father. I also faced it that neither of us could have suspected Clarissa's ordeal, that we did intervene immediately when we found out. I was never able to forgive either of us for this. But loving you opened up my ability to forgive, to let only positive emotions thrive."

The serenity he exuded enveloped her, the freedom from darkness that blazed in his eyes lighting up the universe. Searing joy spilled from her eyes, as for the first time she knew the real meaning of security, of stability. This was unshakable.

He suddenly frowned. "*Dio mio,* what a fool I am!"

She jerked up. "What?"

"I dared presume you'll walk down the aisle on the strength of a proposal I effectively rescinded."

"It's okay. It's reusable. Like a 'get out of jail free' card."

He guffawed as he jumped up, scooped her up in his arms. "If you ran a jail, I'd never want to get out. Now, will you lend me your yacht? I want to reenact a certain proposal scene."

"Oh, God! You still haven't taken all your stuff back."

"You make it sound like some old clothes and a guitar."

"Just tell me how to get everything back in your name or I'll hold my breath until I pass out!"

He sighed, let her down on her feet. "I trust this won't be the way you operate with me from now on?"

She gulped a breath and he shook his head, grudgingly walked away, reached down to his strewn clothes for his cell phone.

He'd hit two numbers when she cried out. "Wait!" He cocked a daunting eyebrow at her. "You're penniless right now, right? Comparatively speaking?"

"Sì." His eyes flared and subsided like blue pulsars as he prowled back to her, running his hands suggestively down his chiseled body. "Why? Do you have a…position for me?"

She glowed up at him. "Many, permanent ones. In my bed. And everywhere else."

"Hmm. Do I get to be…on top sometimes still?"

"On top, under, behind, around. All positions are…wide open."

"I can say I'm interested." He licked his lips. "Rabidly so."

She hauled him to her in a ribs-cracking hug. "You just want me for my money." She giggled and sobbed and deluged him with kisses. "So, Your Scrumptiousness—now that I've proven, from my exalted upper-hand position, that I want you for you, will want only you, will love, cherish and defend you, be there for you with all that I am, for the rest of my days, *sposami,* Durante. Marry me, *amore mio.* Make me complete."

He hugged her off the ground, the elation and adoration radiating from him enough to power the whole city with years of love and wonder. "On one condition. If I say yes now, I still get to do my reenactment."

"Say yes now and you can do whatever you like, always. In fact, you'd better."

"You'll let me give you all that I am?"

"Oh, yes, please."

He let her down, kneeled, still hugging her, his eyes pledging more than his all. "Then, yes, *amore mio.* Love me and let me love you…forever."

She hugged him into her, body and being, bliss shaking her, gushing from her eyes. And she knew.

There'd never be doubt again.

This *was* unshakable. This was forever.

* * * * *

Another D'Agostino prince has found his soulmate,
but crown and kingdom are still at risk.
Don't miss the stunning conclusion to
THE CASTALDINI CROWN,
The Illegitimate King.
On sale June 2010 only from Olivia Gates
and Mills & Boon® Desire™.

THE HEIR'S SCANDALOUS AFFAIR

BY
JENNIFER LEWIS

Dear Reader,

Young, beautiful women who marry rich, older men are often treated cruelly in the press. These "trophy wives" seem to be objects of intense fascination and resentment, as evidenced by the ghoulish obsession with Anna Nicole Smith after the passing of her wealthy older husband.

The coverage of her life and tragic death made me wonder how it would feel to be subject to such envy and loathing. It sparked the idea for *The Heir's Scandalous Affair*, in which young widow Samantha Hardcastle has to find her way in the world after the death of her billionaire husband, Tarrant.

With the eyes and cameras of the world upon her, Sam finds herself falling in love with the one man she should stay far, far away from: her husband's illegitimate son. I hope you enjoy Sam and Louis's roller coaster romance.

Jen

Jennifer Lewis has been dreaming up stories for as long as she can remember and is thrilled to be able to share them with readers. She has lived on both sides of the Atlantic and worked in media and the arts before she grew bold enough to put pen to paper. Happily settled in New York with her family, she would love to hear from readers at jen@jen-lewis.com. Visit her website at www.jenlewis.com.

For my mother, who encouraged my love of books
from the beginning, and who was my on-the-spot
correspondent in New Orleans while I wrote this story.

Acknowledgement:
Thanks once again to the lovely people
who read my book while I was writing it,
including Amanda, Anne, Betty, Carol, Cynthia,
Leeanne and Marie, and my agent Andrea.

One

Samantha Hardcastle was wound tighter than her late husband's Cartier watch. The festive happy-hour crowd on Bourbon Street jostled and bumped her. Her new red Christian Louboutin sandals were supposed to lift her spirits. Instead they threatened to bring her down on her butt.

She pushed through the throng toward a less crowded side street, gasping for oxygen in the beer-scented darkness. Streetlights and neon bar signs blurred and jumped in her peripheral vision. Columns holding up the balconies above clustered around her like menacing trees in an enchanted forest.

She was dizzy and light-headed. Probably because she'd forgotten to eat since…had she even had breakfast before her flight?

Her ankle wobbled and she caught herself on a brick wall. She'd somehow lost her way between the shoe store and the hotel. The sun had set, transforming the unfamiliar city into a place of shadows, and now she couldn't find her way back.

Since her husband's death, she couldn't seem to do anything right anymore. Every day took just a little bit more energy than she had.

"Are you okay?" a deep voice asked in her ear.

"Yes, fine, thanks," she responded. She didn't take her hand off the wall. The dark street was spinning.

"No, you're not. Come inside."

"No, really, I…" Visions of being taken captive fired her imagination as a thick arm slid around her waist. She struggled against hard muscle.

"It's just a bar. You can sit down and rest a minute."

He guided her to a doorway. A light-filled archway in the hot darkness. A soothing string instrument filled the air, which—strangely enough—didn't smell of beer like the air outside.

"There's a comfortable chair over here." His tone was authoritative, yet soothing. The large room had the atmosphere of a turn-of-the-century saloon. Ornate gilding, polished plank floors and high tin ceilings. The colors were muted and mellow. Restful.

She let herself be helped to a leather armchair in a dark corner of the bar. "Thanks," she murmured, as he lowered her gently into the chair. "I don't know what came over me."

"Just rest. I'll bring you something to eat."

"But I don't—"

"Yes, you do."

She thought she detected a hint of humor in his firm rebuttal. Maybe she did need food. She kept forgetting to eat lately. She'd totally lost her appetite for—everything.

She glanced around. There were quite a few people sitting at tables and in booths along one wall. Unlike the jovial mob outside, they spoke in hushed tones, and their laughter tinkled in the air.

Two waiters set down a table in front of her armchair, crisp white cloth and gleaming flatware already on it. A strong hand brought a steaming white plate.

"Here, crawfish étouffée with dirty rice. Just what the doctor ordered."

"Thank you." She glanced up at the owner of the hand and the reassuring voice. "You're too kind."

"Oh, I'm not kind at all." Honey-brown eyes glittered with humor. "I don't like people passing out cold in front of my door. Bad for business."

"I guess dragging dizzy women in is one way to drum up customers." She risked a shy smile.

He smiled back with warmth that surprised her. He had chiseled features and tousled dark hair and was far too good-looking to be trustworthy.

Apprehension trickled up her spine. "Why are you staring at me like that?"

"I'm waiting for you to pick up your fork and eat."

"Oh." She grabbed the fork and scooped up a small mouthful of étouffée. Self-conscious under his penetrating gaze, she put it between her lips and attempted to chew. Flavor cascaded over her tongue as she bit into the tender crustacean, marinated in its spicy sauce.

"Oh, my. That's good."

A smile spread over his stern features. He gestured for her to continue. "Now, what can I get you to drink?"

He asked the question with a hint of seduction. Not like a waiter, more like…someone trying to pick her up in a bar.

A hackle slid up inside her. She'd dreaded being single again. Dreaded it with every cell in her body.

"Just a glass of water will be fine, thank you." She spoke in a clipped and officious manner. Like the wealthy Park Avenue matron she supposedly was.

He vanished out of her line of sight. With a sigh of relief, she fell on her crawfish étouffée, ravenous. She'd been walking around all day, trying to locate the man she hoped was her husband's estranged son.

She'd finally found Louis DuLac's house on Royal Street, with its tall windows and scrolled iron balconies. But he wasn't home. She'd tried twice.

The second time his housekeeper had shut the door rather firmly in her face.

Some festival was in full swing and the city was packed with tourists. She'd overlooked that when she arranged her trip. Her husband's private jet didn't require reservations, and the ten-thousand-dollar-a-night rooms were still available. It wasn't Mardi Gras, though. She knew that was in February or March, and right now it was October.

A loud pop made her look up. Champagne streamed over the side of a Krug bottle. Apparently Mr. Smooth had pegged her as the kind of person who could afford seven hundred dollars a bottle.

Probably her own fault. The red Louboutin shoes didn't help.

"Oh, I really don't—"

"On the house," he murmured, as he filled a tall, fluted glass.

She blinked. Even Tarrant's favorite sommeliers didn't hand over Krug champagne for free. "Why?"

"Because you're too pretty to look so sad."

"Does it occur to you I might have good reason to look sad?"

"It does." He handed her the glass and pulled up a chair. "Are you dying?"

There wasn't a hint of humor in his gaze.

"No," she blurted. "At least not that I know of."

Relief smoothed his brow. "Well, that's good news. Let's drink to it." He'd filled himself a glass and he raised it to hers.

She clinked it and took a sip. The expensive bubbles tickled her tongue. "What would you have said if I'd told you I was dying?"

"I'd have suggested you live each day as if it's your last." His eyes sparkled. They were an appealing caramel color, with flecks of gold, like polished tigereye. "Which I think is good advice in any event."

"You're so right." She sighed. Her husband, Tarrant, had such a lust for life that he'd far outlived his doctor's expectations. She'd vowed to follow his example, but wasn't doing very well so far.

Drinking champagne was a start. "Here's to the first day of the rest of our lives." She raised her glass with a smile.

"May each day be a celebration." His eyes rested on hers as he raised his glass. She felt a strange flicker of something inside her. A pleasurable feeling.

Must be the champagne.

"Do you see the guitarist?" He gestured to a corner of the room. "He's one-hundred-and-one years old."

Samantha's eyes widened. The musician's white hair contrasted starkly with his ebony skin. It was astonishing he even had hair at that age. And his spirit shone in his energetic finger movements that vibrated out into the air as music.

"He's lived through two world wars, the depression, the digitization of almost everything and Hurricane Katrina. Every day he plays the guitar. Says it reignites the fire in him every single time."

"I envy him his passion."

"You don't have one?" He cocked his head slightly. His gaze was warm, not accusatory.

"Not really." She certainly wasn't going to tell this stranger about her quest to find her husband's missing children. Even her closest friends thought she was nuts. "Shopping for shoes sometimes lifts my spirits." She flashed a smile and her new red Louboutins.

In a way, she hoped he'd sneer. That would squash the funny warm sensation in the pit of her belly.

Instead, he smiled. "Christian is an artist and art always lifts the spirits. He'd thoroughly approve."

"You know him?"

He nodded. "I lived in Paris for years. I still spend a lot of time there."

"I'm impressed that you could tell who designed a pair of shoes. Most men wouldn't have a clue."

"I've always had an appreciation for fine things." His gaze rested lightly on her face. Not sexual or suggestive, but she couldn't help but hear the words *like you* hover in the air.

Instead of feeling harassed she felt…desirable. Something she hadn't felt in a long time.

She brushed the feeling away. "Is New Orleans always this crazy?"

"Absolutely." He grinned. "Some people who come here have such a good time they even forget to eat." He glanced at her almost-empty plate of crawfish and rice.

She smiled. Let him think she was here for a fun vacation. In another life, maybe she would have been. Tarrant had loved jazz and they'd talked about coming for the spring Jazz Festival.

"Don't go looking sad again." He shot her an accusatory glance. "I think you need to dance."

She glanced over his shoulder where a cluster of elegant couples swayed on the dance floor. Adrenaline trickled through her.

"Oh, no. I couldn't." She took a quick sip of champagne. She was a widow. In mourning, though she'd promised Tarrant she wouldn't wear black even to the funeral. She flashed her shoes as an excuse.

He tilted his head and narrowed his eyes. "Christian would be horrified if he heard a woman had used his shoes as a reason not to dance."

"Then don't tell him."

"I most certainly shall tell him—unless you dance with me. I think it's the least you can do after I rescued you from the streets and fed you." A smile played around his mouth.

She chuckled. "You make me sound like a stray waif."

"A stray waif in Christian Louboutin shoes." He stood and extended his arm. Apparently he expected her to rise, too.

She took his hand and stood. She was nothing if not polite, the society-wife training ensured that. Besides, what was wrong with one little dance? Tarrant would rather see her moving than moping around.

He made a signal to the guitarist, who winked and struck up a new tune. Bluesy, but with a Latin flavor. Sam felt a shimmer of excitement as they stepped out onto the smooth wood floor. She hadn't danced in a long time.

The music hovered around them like smoke, filling the space between them. Through the sensual mist it created, she couldn't help but notice her partner was tall and broad shouldered. Her eyes were about level with his shirt collar, which had a fine pattern of irregular stripes. His jaw was solid, authoritative, like the rest of him.

He took her hand and clasped it softly, wrapping long,

strong fingers around hers. The warmth of his blood seemed to pulse through his skin and heat hers as the music beat around them.

"What kind of dance are we going to do?" She didn't dare look up at his face. Already she was too close to him. So near she could feel the heat of him through her clothes.

"Any kind you like. It sounds like a mambo to me."

Her feet slipped into the mambo rhythm, following the patterns she'd learned years ago at Ms. Valentine's dancing school. She tried to focus on the steps, on moving gracefully, and keeping enough distance between her and her partner. He smelled of spices, like the rich food she'd eaten, and of starched cotton.

"I like your shirt." She risked a glance at his face.

Those rich, honey-colored eyes gazed at her, twinkling with amusement. "You don't have to make polite conversation with me. I know you're nice."

"How on earth would you know that?"

"I can read people. It's a gift I got from my grandmother. She used to read tea leaves, but she told me her secret was always to read the people as they stared at the leaves."

"What do you look for?" She tried to ignore the steady warmth of his big hand on her back.

"Facial expression tells you what matters to someone, not just while you look at them, but every day. All the little dimples and wrinkles reveal something."

"Uh, oh. I'm getting self-conscious." Two plastic surgery consultations had reassured her that it wasn't yet time to get drastic, but at thirty-one, Samantha knew she was no longer at the peak of her once-prize-winning beauty.

"That dimple in your chin tells me you smile a lot. And the tilt of your eyes tells me that you like to make people happy."

"That's true." She let out a nervous laugh. "I've been told I try too hard to please. I'm a 'yes' woman."

"But you have strength of character. I can see that by the way you carry yourself. You care very much about everything you do."

She frowned, taking in his words. Was it true? Maybe she just had good posture from training for beauty pageants.

She'd tried hard to mature. To learn from her failed marriages and all the mistakes she'd made.

She'd given everything she had to make Tarrant's last years the best they could be.

"And you're very, very sad." His low voice tickled her ear. While they moved, he'd come closer.

"I'm okay," she stammered, trying to reassure herself as much as him.

"You are okay." His hand shifted on her back, stroking her. "You're more than okay. But my grandmother would tell you to breathe."

"I am breathing," she protested.

"Little shallow breaths." He leaned into her. She could feel his hot breath on her neck. "Just enough to keep you afloat, to get you through the day."

He squeezed her hand inside his. His penetrating gaze almost stole the last of her breath. "You need to inhale and draw oxygen way down deep into your body. To let it flow all the way through you, out to your fingers and toes."

Her toes tingled. "Right now?"

She swallowed. Glanced around his broad arm to where other couples danced, lost in their own world.

"No time like the present." He smiled.

He had a nice smile, warm and friendly. She might not be a tea-leaf expert, but she was no slouch at reading people, either. A survival mechanism she'd learned early on in her volatile household.

Of course, he was still far too good-looking. No man grew to adulthood with looks like that without an outsized and highly chiseled ego to match.

"Go on, breathe."

Their feet had been keeping time to the music, but suddenly he stopped. Holding her with one arm around her back, and one hand on hers, he waited for her to follow his command.

Aware that their nonmovement must be attracting attention, she sucked in a breath. Her breasts lifted several inches inside the thin, white dress before she blew it out, blushing.

"Nice try, but you need to draw it down into your chest." He tapped her back with his fingertips. "All the way down to my fingers."

She glanced over her shoulder.

"Breathing's not a crime in this state." He grinned. "Come on, let's do it together. One, two, three…" Eyes fixed on hers, he drew a breath deep into his chest, which swelled under his shirt.

Sam tried her best to match the length and duration of his breath. When she finally blew it out, she was gasping. "How embarrassing."

"Not at all. That was great. You'd be surprised how many people go through life every day holding their breath without realizing. You don't want to do that." He flashed a grin and swept her into the mambo rhythm again. Twirled her fast and tight until she had to suck in a breath just to keep her balance.

"You want to breathe it all in, everything, the good and the bad."

"The bad?"

"If you try too hard to avoid the bad stuff, you end up missing out on the good stuff, too." His narrowed eyes shone like a cat's in the dim interior. She tried to ignore a little tug in her belly.

Was it all the deep breathing? She couldn't tell, but something had changed.

Their dance became more intense as he pulled her closer, whipped her out and then drew her back in. A drummer had joined the guitarist on stage and the hypnotic, pounding rhythm of palms on bongos pulsed through her until her feet took on a life of their own.

She found herself moving faster, deeper, throwing herself into the dance. She drew air deep into her lungs as she whirled through the air, and came back to rest against his hard body. Somehow everything was effortless, flowing, and she found herself losing track of which part of the room they were in.

The drumming grew louder, then faded away, the clinking of glasses blended with the rhythmic strumming of the guitar, until the whole atmosphere seemed to throb, to breathe, in and out, round and round.

Sam laughed aloud with sheer delight. When the music stopped with a flourish, she fell into her partner's arms. "That was fantastic."

"You're an incredible dancer."

"I'm a very rusty dancer, but you're onto something with that breathing."

"In and out, that's all it takes."

"It's funny how we forget the little things that are most important."

He made another hand signal to the guitarist, who launched into a slow song with cascades of rippling notes. Sam let her body sway instinctively to the seductive sound.

The club's interior was warm and she could feel her skin—glowing, to put it delicately, but she wasn't embarrassed.

Her partner's reassuring gaze rested on her eyes, not probing or poking about the rest of her the way so many men did.

Without even thinking, she inhaled deeply and blew it out, and enjoyed the smile that stretched across his handsome face.

I don't know his name.

How odd. To be dancing with someone and have no idea who he was. She knew he owned the bar, so he had an identity, but without a name he wasn't quite…real.

Should she ask?

She blinked, strangely reluctant. A name seemed so formal, like a passport or driver's license that gave you official status. She didn't want to tell him that she was Samantha Hardcastle. Her name and picture might not ring any bells down here in New Orleans, but in New York they'd been plastered over the papers for months.

The Merry Widow, with her much older husband's billions now at her disposal. Like she'd *won* or something.

Bile rose in her gut. She didn't want this man to know anything about that. To form preconceptions about her as a gold-digging tramp who married a rich man for his money.

"Hey, you okay?" His hand slid around her back.

She realized her breathing had grown shallow again. She swallowed. "Sure, I'm fine. Sorry!" She drew in a deep and deliberate breath for his benefit, and they both chuckled as she blew it out.

The guitarist, joined by a saxophonist, as well as the drummer, launched into a swinging, bluesy number. His eyes were closed and his head bobbed in time with the music as if he were captivated by its spell.

Sam let that spell guide her feet as they danced without

touching, their bodies swaying to the rhythm. Sensual and muscular in his movements, her partner moved with effortless ease.

Maybe it was the sips of champagne, but Sam felt strangely weightless, like all her cares and worries had drifted up to the ornate tin ceiling and hovered there, leaving her free and light.

"Were you a professional dancer?" His breath warmed her neck as he leaned in.

She colored slightly. "I competed a few times. Does my dancing look too artificial?"

He shook his head, his smile reassuring. "Not artificial, just polished, like the rest of you."

She resisted the urge to glance down. She couldn't deny being polished. As Tarrant's wife, it had been her job. Her hours in between social lunches and dinners were filled with appointments to get her nails tipped or her hair trimmed.

She was so used to being buffed to a high shine that she had no idea what she'd look like without the carefully highlighted hair and couture dresses. If she stripped all the expensive enhancements away, would there be anyone there at all?

Right now it didn't matter. Her partner's expression shone with quiet appreciation. That honey-brown gaze didn't seem to accuse her or to find anything lacking.

She couldn't help but notice the way his hips moved. How they linked to strong thighs just visible beneath the smooth surface of his dark pants, to his flat belly.

A young, athletic body in the peak of health. A beautiful thing.

How old was he? Early thirties probably. Her age, though most of the time she felt about ninety.

He picked up her left hand and examined it. It felt very

naked without the big engagement and wedding ring Tarrant had given her with such fanfare only four years ago.

The engagement ring had a diamond too big to wear outside without an armed guard. The wedding ring had been buried with his coffin. Tarrant had wanted her to place it on his hand like Jackie Kennedy did when her famous husband died. He always enjoyed a dramatic flourish.

"You're smiling." His deep voice stirred something in her chest.

"Happy memories." How odd to have that as a happy memory. She was getting pretty strange in her old age.

"Now you're not smiling." He tugged her hand and pulled her closer. "I think you need to step outside your memories and into the present."

He slid his arm around her waist. Her breasts crushed gently against his chest and a warm surge of pleasure rippled through her.

"I love this song," he murmured. His low timbre vibrated in her ear, sending a shiver along her spine. "It makes me think of a lazy day out on the bayou. Sun shining on the water, cranes watching from the trees, the *putt-putt* of a shrimp boat in the distance."

The image formed in her mind, a peaceful scene, at odds with their rather urbane surroundings. "Do you go there much?"

"As often as I can."

She couldn't see his face because he'd pulled her too close. His arms wrapped around her waist and she found that hers had slipped around his neck. A quick glance confirmed that other couples danced the same way, wrapped up in each other, to the gentle strumming of the guitar and the low caress of the saxophone.

He lowered his cheek to hers and she felt the slight stubble on his chin. A delicious masculine sensation she'd almost forgotten.

Almost, but not quite. The familiar strains of desire echoed through her like the notes of the music. It stirred in the palms of her hands where they pressed against his broad shoulder blades, in her nipples as they bumped his hard chest, in her tongue, which wondered what his mouth would taste like.

The answer came as their lips touched, opened, and her tongue flicked over his. His sensual mouth was both soft and firm, his tongue at first tentative, then insistent, hungry.

Her fingers dug into the crisp cotton of his shirt. Her belly pressed against his firm hips, as she tilted into the powerful kiss.

Light and color crackled behind her eyelids, dazzling her, while their tongues danced together. Then, slowly, their tongues drew back, and his lips closed. She felt his warm skin part from hers, to be replaced by cool, air-conditioned air.

Still clutching his back, she opened her eyes and blinked in the dim light. Her breath came in unsteady gasps, her legs wobbled and her skin stung with arousal.

"Come with me." He didn't look at her and it wasn't a question. With one arm firmly about her waist, he led her off the floor and across the room. Faces and bodies blurred around her as she tried to get her bearings.

I only had two or three sips of champagne. The thought flickered through her mind then flew away on a low note from the saxophone. Under her flimsy dress, her body pulsed and throbbed, and if he wasn't holding her up, she wasn't sure she'd still be walking.

Maybe she'd be floating.

They left the crowded restaurant through a door behind the bar that led out into a dim hallway. Across the hall he opened a tall, polished wood door. "More private."

He ushered her into a beautiful room, decorated in the same prohibition-era style as the bar, as if Woodrow Wilson might wander in and start arguing with Franklin D. Roosevelt. Antiques gleamed in the soft light from a beautiful glass light fixture. The interlacing pattern of stained glass was so harmonious and unusual that she wondered aloud, "Is that a Tiffany lamp?"

"Yes, my mother collects them."

Her eyes widened. "Aren't they worth hundreds of thousands of dollars?"

He shrugged and opened a wood cabinet. "What use are beautiful things if you can't enjoy them?" He pulled out two crystal glasses and another bottle of Krug champagne.

"You do enjoy the good life, don't you?"

"I consider myself privileged to have the opportunity to enjoy the good life. I'd be a fool to squander it."

Sam smiled as he offered her the bubbling glass. "Do you live here?"

"No, this is more like…my office."

"It's lovely." She glanced around. Was there a bedroom?

And was it good or bad if there was?

"It's unchanged since 1933, when the original owner was shot dead by his lover."

Sam gasped. "Why'd she shoot him?"

"He slept with his wife."

She laughed. "I can see how a mistress would find that offensive."

Already they'd crossed the room and entered a large, high-ceilinged chamber with a grand, four-poster bed. Rich gold draperies glowed in the light from another jewel-toned Tiffany lamp.

He lifted the arm of an old Victrola phonograph and placed

it on the record. The mellow tones of a big band orchestra swelled from the brass horn.

His sensual gaze rested on her mouth. "I love your smile."

"Thanks, I love it, too. I haven't used it enough lately."

His eyes fixed on hers for a second, stalling her breath. Her lips buzzed with sensation. Had she really kissed him?

He stepped toward her and placed his glass on the polished sideboard.

Her insides trembled with long-forgotten desire. Anticipation mingled with fear as she watched his mouth, watched his eyes caress her body with their soft gaze.

Was he going to kiss her again?

Her answer came as his lips closed over hers in a swift motion that stole her breath.

Louis DuLac had kissed a lot of women.

He'd run his fingers over a lot of smooth skin and stared into a lot of desire-darkened eyes.

But this was a first.

He'd never met a woman whose every glance and movement resonated with passion and intensity that threatened to make sparks in the air.

She was blond and blue-eyed, his mystery woman, not so unusual.

She was slight, frail even, her limbs so thin his grandmother would have pinched them, clucked, and brought her some food.

Which, of course, is pretty much what he did.

"Why are you smiling?" Her mouth was pink from kissing, pursed with slight shyness.

"You'd be smiling, too, if you enjoyed this view."

She lay naked, half hidden under the crisp sheets, her body

softly illuminated in the ruby glow of a nearby lamp. Small, high breasts gave her a girlish aspect, but the far distance he glimpsed in her eyes spoke of a thousand lifetimes lived.

He almost regretted bringing her here.

Almost.

Her rosy nipple thickened between his thumb and finger. Her heart beat visibly just below her rib cage, and he saw its pace pick up as he trailed his fingers down toward the triangle of golden hair at the apex of her thighs, which writhed under their thin cover.

Her arousal was palpable, a primal hunger crouching below the surface. He could see it in the glitter of her dark pupils, in the silver sheen of her skin. He could taste it in the hunger of her kiss and feel it in the heat pulsing through her slender limbs.

The scent of her drove him half-crazy. Some expensive French concoction, no doubt, but mingled with the fresh, clean smell of her skin and hair, it was perfect.

Louis flicked his practiced tongue over her sensitive nerve endings and, through narrowed eyes, watched her hips buck slightly.

He deepened his exploration with fingers and tongue. Her fine gold hair splayed on the pillow and her eyes slid closed as she gave herself over to sensation. He was gratified to see her draw deep, unhurried breaths while he pleasured her.

Her fingertips roved into his hair and along his neck as he licked her until her hips shuddered. Then he stopped and pulled back.

Her eyes flicked open in—dismay? He smiled. "No hurry. We have all night."

Or did they? He had no idea if she had somewhere to be. Someone to meet.

No wedding band. He'd checked. That didn't mean much these days, but it reduced the chance of him ending up like the bar's original owner.

She raised herself up on her elbows, eyes shining. "I want to kiss you." Her voice was soft and sweet, her request so simple and innocent, it belied the fact that she'd removed her clothes with the candor of a practiced call girl.

She certainly wasn't that.

But she was a mystery.

One moment shy and awkward, the next polished and witty. Dressed in her fine clothes, she reeked of wealth and privilege. But the Louboutin shoes and John Galliano dress didn't hide the ragged emotional edge of a hungry waif. You didn't have to be psychic to see she was burdened with a sadness so huge that it threatened to suck oxygen from the air.

He shouldn't have brought her here.

She was too fragile, too slender and delicate, too dangerously close to some verge he knew nothing about.

He had a strange feeling that, in unlocking her mysteries, he'd open a Pandora's box that would unleash chaos on his world.

But he couldn't stop.

Two

Sam awoke with a start.

She blinked, searching for the familiar night-light in her room, but finding only blackness. A brush of warm skin against her elbow reassured her that she slept next to her husband…

Her husband was dead.

She sat up, heart pounding. Images plucked at her mind: flashing honey-gold eyes, strong and sensuous hands, a wickedly seductive smile.

The sound of breathing was just audible in the thick darkness. She heard a car drive by outside. Why was it so quiet?

She was in New Orleans. In a strange man's bed.

Her breath caught in her throat. Her thighs were sticky and her insides still pulsed with the stray echoes of arousal.

She'd *made love* with this man lying beside her.

She didn't even know his name, or anything about him, but she'd stripped naked and dived into his bed like a…like a…

Her eyes had adjusted to the point where she could make out the shapes of furniture in the thin moonlight sneaking through a crack in the heavy drapes. She eased herself to the edge of the bed, dipped her legs over the side and felt for the floor.

Cool wood on the soles of her feet shocked her more fully awake.

What was she thinking?

She wasn't thinking, that was the problem. At least he didn't know who she was. Or she hoped he didn't.

She could see the headlines already. *Gold-Digging Tramp Back on the Prowl.*

Of course they wouldn't be far wrong. Her husband was dead less than six months, and already she was naked in the arms of a handsome stranger.

Was she insane? Like, really, truly crazy?

She'd had her doubts lately, but this was different.

Fear propelled her into action. She glanced back at the bed and saw the shape of him outlined by white sheets, still apparently asleep. She needed to get out of here before he woke up.

Heart thundering and pain lancing her temples, she groped around for her clothes. Luckily, since she'd removed them herself, she knew they were on a chair near the bed. She struggled into her underwear, then slid the dress over her head.

Carrying her sandals in her hand, she crept toward the looming dark outline of the door.

She didn't feel crazy. She felt dangerously sane, as she turned the ornate brass knob with painstaking care not to make even a single click. She pulled back on the heavy wood door, praying that it wouldn't creak.

A glance over her shoulder reassured her that he was still asleep.

Her lover.

Her hand shook on the door when she remembered the feel of his hands on her skin. How gentle his touch was, how careful, and then how hungry and naked and…human she'd felt in his arms.

She hadn't felt like that in a long time.

Sam swallowed hard and stepped over the threshold. She closed the door behind her with the same agonizing slowness. She wasn't sure whether to be relieved or sad when it slid into place without even a click, and she left her handsome stranger behind, still deep in dreamland.

Was he dreaming about her?

She walked over an air-conditioning register, and the cool breeze shot up her dress. Her aroused flesh tingled and her nipples tightened. Shimmers of awareness still crept over her skin.

The sensation of intense arousal was raw and uncomfortable. Unfamiliar and unsettling. An unsteady ache settled in her chest.

She picked her way carefully across the floor, avoiding the fine old furniture and priceless lamps.

Almost there. But relief didn't come even as she released a heavy bolt and opened the door to the hallway. First, she'd be leaving this man's door unlocked, which, in a city with a high crime rate, might have any number of consequences.

But that wasn't it.

There was an uglier word for what she'd done.

Betrayal.

She'd betrayed her husband. Betrayed her vows to him and all the promises she'd made before and after. She'd betrayed her purpose here in New Orleans, which was to find his missing son and heir and bring him home to the family.

And she'd betrayed herself. She'd prided herself on her sto-
icism. On her steady attention to duty and the fact that she
wasn't a foolish girl anymore.

Only to find out tonight that in fact she was so "easy"—
or desperate—that she'd go home with the first man to gaze
into her eyes.

She snuck along the empty corridor, through a heavy,
bolted door, and into the silent bar. There must be another way
out, but she didn't want to take the time to find it.

She tiptoed through the cavernous space, so recently filled
with sensual music and laughter, now empty and silent.

Accusatory.

Long shadows chased her across the floor as a car drove
by outside. She found herself ducking like a criminal, and
crawling the rest of the way to the door.

Shame soaked through her. What had brought her to this?
She'd thought herself older and wiser and better able to avoid
the mistakes she'd made in the past.

The latch on the door was old and heavy, with an unfamiliar mechanism. She struggled with it for a full five minutes,
silent sobs rising in her throat, before finally the bolt slid free
and she was able to tug the door open.

She waited until the next block to put her shoes on. Even
then the pathetic clickety-click of the narrow heels made her
feel like a target.

No one around. If they were, she was easy prey in her
foolishly thin dress and high heels, clutching her expensive
purse with far too much cash in it.

Would she find her way back to the hotel and her normal
life? Or would she spend eternity wandering the dark, humid
streets of a strange city?

She probably deserved the latter.

* * *

Still too sleepy to open his eyes, Louis reached out his hand, anticipating contact with warm silky flesh. His fingers found nothing but cold sheets.

His eyes flicked open. Empty sheets.

Louis tried to shake off the sensual fog that had followed him from sleep. He'd dreamed about her. In his dream, she'd been laughing, throwing her head back with abandon, eyes sparkling in the sun.

He propped himself up on one elbow and scanned the room. Her clothes were gone.

He sank back into the sheets, disappointment blooming in his chest.

Not a surprise that she'd vanished, his woman of mystery. For a moment he even wondered if he'd simply imagined her.

She'd never told him her name, or where she was from. He hadn't asked, mostly because he didn't think she'd tell him, anyway.

They'd had a wonderful night—no expectations, no obligations, no tearful goodbyes, just a few hours of intense pleasure.

He'd probably never see her again. Which should be fine.

Except that, for reasons he couldn't put his finger on, it wasn't.

Sam patted her hair and inhaled deeply as she approached the gates of Louis DuLac's beautiful French Quarter house for the third time. She'd reached unconsciously for the big gold ring on her middle finger. Tarrant had given it to her for their first anniversary, and she never went anywhere without it. For some reason, she'd forgotten to wear it last night. She'd forgotten almost everything else, too—propriety, duty, common sense. Only a few brief hours ago she'd been in bed with a total stranger.

She inhaled deeply as she stepped under wrought-iron balconies and reached for the bell.

She was here in New Orleans to find her husband's unclaimed son and bring him into the family, and she couldn't let a personal mistake interfere with that goal. Besides, last night was a silly indiscretion born of painful loneliness, and she was going to forgive herself for it.

An old-fashioned chime sounded inside the house. Her heart thudded as she prayed he'd be home. She didn't want to be turned away yet again and no one ever returned her calls.

No sound reached her from the other side of the door. Apparently even the maid was out today. She rang again. This time she heard feet coming downstairs. A voice talking. "…the terms were good, but the property needs to be completely renovated and if we're going to open in time for the season, I just don't have the time to…hold on."

Something about the voice sounded vaguely familiar, even through the heavy, black-painted door. Her scalp prickled with awareness.

A very uncomfortable awareness.

The door flew open and shock snapped through her as she stood face-to-face with the man from last night.

Bright morning sunlight illuminated his unmistakable chiseled features and glittered in his golden-brown eyes. Recognition lit his features and a smile started across his mouth. "Hold on," he said again into the phone.

"I—I—I'm sorry, there's been a mistake," she stammered, stepping backward.

"Come in." He stood aside and gestured for her to enter. She peered past him into a dim, cool hallway with a large, ornate mirror on one wall.

"No, I—I can't. I didn't mean to—" Her mind froze, and

she found herself backing away, glancing over her shoulder so as not to fall down the steps.

"I'll call you back," he muttered into the phone. He lunged forward and grabbed her wrist. His strong fingers closed around her arm. Her muscles tightened as she instinctively resisted.

He held her firm. "Don't think you can ring my doorbell then run out on me *again.*"

Guilt seared her. She had sneaked out of his room without saying goodbye. He must be angry.

But humor glittered in his gaze. "How did you know where I live? We never even exchanged names. I think the least you could do is introduce yourself."

Sam's mind whirled. "I—I'm Samantha Hardcastle."

The smile faded from his eyes. "What?"

"Samantha Hardcastle, I came here to find my husband's son. His name is Louis DuLac and this must be the wrong address so I'm not sure what happened, but—"

"It's not the wrong address." His features grew hard and he gazed at her through narrowed eyes. "I'm Louis DuLac."

Sam's knees almost gave out. If he hadn't been holding her wrist she might have plunged backward down the stairs.

"But you can't be." The words fell from her lips, dazed and barely coherent. "It's impossible."

"Impossible or not, it's a fact. Come in."

This time his words were a command rather than an invitation. He still held a firm grip on her wrist.

"Oh, boy." Sam felt herself struggling for breath. He tugged her, gently, and she stepped toward him. "You're my husband's…oh, no." Her heart sank right down in her chest as her rib cage closed around it like a fist.

"I confess I don't know exactly what's going on here, but

this time I plan to get to the bottom of it." He studied her face with a slight frown. "You're not going anywhere until you come in and tell me what's going on."

Sam gulped. Her body was screaming at her to turn and run—to save herself—but her brain struggled to behave in a more civilized manner. She put one foot in front of the other and moved toward the doorway.

He didn't let go of her wrist until she'd stepped inside the threshold and he'd closed the door behind her.

"You're Louis DuLac?" The surprise in her voice seemed to amuse him.

"Have been since the day I was born."

"Maybe there's another Louis DuLac. It could be quite a common name."

He turned. Crossed his arms over his chest. He wore a pale blue shirt with crisp cuffs and collar. "I know who you are, Samantha Hardcastle. I've been ignoring your letters and phone calls for months."

Sam inhaled. "Why?"

"Why don't you come up to my office and we'll talk."

"I really don't think I should."

"Don't worry, I won't tear your clothes off." He gazed at her through narrowed eyes.

Was that mischief or malice that glittered in their depths?

Sam felt her face redden. She'd torn her own clothes off last night, if she remembered correctly. She deserved his scorn.

"It's up one floor." He led the way up a wide, polished staircase with an elaborate carved handrail.

The cool air-conditioned interior contrasted starkly with the already hot and humid morning air outside. Fine antiques decorated the large space in a minimalist and appealingly modern fashion. A pleasant smell of lavender enhanced the calm and ordered atmosphere.

"Do you live alone?" Her question popped out before she could consider its implications.

He turned, frowning. "Yes, in case you're worried that I was cheating on my wife last night, let me reassure you that I am single and unattached with no existing obligations."

"That's not what I meant." Or was it? Her pulse jackhammered under her skin. "I was just wondering."

"Wonder away. Curiosity's no crime." A mischievous half smile slid across his mouth for a split second, then vanished. "My study. Please come in."

Sam walked past him into a large, high-ceilinged room with a massive walnut desk at its center. The walls were painted sky-blue, topped by ornate white cornices that hung like clouds near the ceiling. "This is a spectacular house."

"Thanks. I inherited it from my grandparents. I've been fixing it up room by room." He glanced at the chiseled cornice with obvious pride.

Then his attention snapped back to her. "Please, take a seat." His accusatory gaze undermined the smooth politeness of his request.

"And why don't you tell me *exactly* what you're doing here?"

Louis leaned back in his armchair, wove his fingers together and rested them on the desk. The blonde had some explaining to do.

First, she'd driven him half-wild in bed, then snuck out in the middle of the night without a by-your-leave.

Second, she was apparently the crackpot sending him all these strange messages about a long-lost father wanting to welcome him back to his bosom.

She balanced precariously on the edge of her chair, pulse

visible at her slender throat, light wisps of hair fluttering in the breeze from the air-conditioning.

Nervous. As well she should be.

She twisted a big gold ring on one of her long, elegantly manicured fingers. "I came here to find you. To New Orleans, I mean. You haven't returned my calls or letters."

"And you thought it might be a good idea to sleep with me first?" He couldn't figure that part out.

"I had no idea who you were!" A flush of color spread from her sharp collarbone up her neck. "I didn't intend to sleep with anyone, least of all…" She swallowed hard.

Your stepson?

His mind boggled. "What makes you think I'm your husband's son?"

"*Late* husband. He died six months ago." Grief, still sharp, was evident in the suddenly taut lines of her face.

Pity surged through him. "I'm sorry."

"When he found out he was dying, we decided to try and find the children he'd fathered. We hired a researcher and gave her all the information he had. We then tracked down the individuals indicated in the research and administered DNA tests to see if they really were related. We found his sons Dominic and Amado this way."

"And how did your research lead to me?"

"Your mother is Bijou DuLac."

"I am aware of that, yes."

"She had an affair with Tarrant—my late husband—in the winter of 1977."

"In Paris?" His mother had lived in Paris since 1969.

"In New York. She was visiting the city for a series of concerts. They spent a month together, then she moved back to Paris. According to our researcher, she gave birth to a son exactly eight months later. We believe you're that son."

Something hot and uncomfortable slid down his spine.

"I am my mother's only child, so if she had a son, it's me." He couldn't keep the edge out of his voice.

Who were these people sitting in offices analyzing his existence?

He'd never known who his father was and he'd gotten along just fine without that knowledge. He certainly didn't need someone shoving a parent—a dead one, at that—down his throat now that he was long past needing one.

He cocked his head. "My mother told me I was born of the chance meeting between a double bass and a saxophone."

Samantha Hardcastle blinked. "Which one was she?"

He laughed. "I don't know. She didn't say."

Her expression softened and the sparkle in her eyes reminded him of how she'd looked last night. Beautiful. So feminine and alive.

Right now she wore a cool, mint-green dress with short sleeves and a scooped neck. Fresh and edible as a mint julep.

He leaned toward her. "I don't know if I'm the person you're looking for, but I'm glad that your search brought you back. It was rude of you to sneak out without a goodbye kiss."

Maybe he'd hoped to see a pretty flush of color light her cheeks, or a flutter of remorseful eyelashes. Instead, the shine left her eyes and her mouth tightened.

"I'm so sorry." She looked down, twisting her hands in her lap. "I don't know what to say. What a terrible thing. It should never have happened."

Her voice shook and he saw her hands tremble. He wanted to take her in his arms.

But she'd just told him that the night she'd spent in his bed was regrettable.

He wanted to be mad, but she looked like she was about to cry.

"You're lucky my feelings aren't easily hurt." He managed to keep his tone light. "Women don't usually look back on a night in my bed like they screwed up and spent a night in jail."

"I had no idea who you weren't." She stared at him, blue eyes wide and brimming with tears.

"You still have no idea who I am. We didn't do all that much talking. But I'll start. I was born in Paris and grew up both there and here in New Orleans. I own six five-star restaurants and when the mood is right I play a little guitar." He narrowed his eyes. "But maybe you did know all that?"

She gulped. "All except the guitar."

"Thing is, I don't know anything at all about you. Maybe we should correct that."

She drew in a shaky breath, which had the unfortunate effect of filling the bodice of her minty dress with her perky breasts. His pants grew tight.

"Have you heard of Tarrant Hardcastle?"

"Of course. I've eaten at The Moon in New York. It even inspired the name of my newest restaurant."

"La Ronde," she murmured.

"You have done your research."

"It's supposed to be the best new restaurant in New Orleans."

"In the world," he challenged.

Still no smile.

"I'm…I was his third wife. He has a daughter from a previous marriage, but after he was diagnosed with cancer, he told me about a woman who'd tried to sue him for paternity decades ago. He said he'd been wondering about the child—a boy—and what happened to him. Once he got a sense of his own mortality, I think he became obsessed with finding an heir."

"His daughter wasn't good enough?"

"She's young, and probably not cut out for running a

luxury retail empire. God knows I'm not cut out for it, either, so I encouraged him to begin the search. Then he recalled other incidents—such as his affair with your mother—and we began to suspect that he might have a whole network of heirs out there."

"How encouraging."

"Don't judge him too harshly."

"I can't judge him at all. Apparently I'm no better than he is, though at least we used a condom, so we didn't make any heirs."

She blinked rapidly and color flooded her cheeks. "I'm so ashamed. Honestly, I can't even wrap my mind about it. That I slept with my husband's son." Her throat dried on the last word and it came out as a strangled sob.

"Calm down. For all we know I'm the result of a different one of my mother's many lovers. Let's not kid ourselves that we live in a kind of world where people mate for life, like swans."

Sam hesitated, probably taken aback by his bluntness. "Did your mother ever marry?"

"No. She said slavery was over and she wasn't going to chain herself to a man for any reason, ever."

Her pretty blue eyes widened. "She sounds like a character."

"She was a very unconventional mother, let's put it that way. She showed me how to live my life without being cramped by other people's expectations."

She nodded, looking thoughtful.

"So, a little thing like accidentally sleeping with my step-mother doesn't put a hitch in my stride."

Her mouth flew open, then snapped shut.

"But as we've already established, we don't actually know if you're my stepmother or not, so why don't we just assume you're not." He wove his fingers together and mastered his features in a pleasant smile.

"Will you take a DNA test?" The words rushed out.

Louis hesitated, his flesh crawled at the thought of someone spreading his genes out on a laboratory table and delving into them in search of whatever mysterious information was hidden there.

His father. Sure, he'd wondered who he came from. Was someone out there, walking around, with the same unusual eye color or with his feeling for music or his passion for food?

As a kid, being hustled from one country to another and allowed to do things most parents would never permit, he'd dreamed of a traditional father who'd pat him on the head and be there for him no matter what.

Mercifully, he got over it.

"Why take a test now? What good would that do? If the man you think is my father is already dead, there's no point." He narrowed his eyes. "Unless you're planning to snap off a chunk of the Hardcastle empire and hand it to me on a gold platter."

Her face was strangely impassive. Was that part of the plan?

"And you can shelve that idea because I've already made all the money I'll ever need and I have my hands full with my six restaurants and coaching the Little League team."

"Will you take the test anyway?"

Her question, deadly serious, knocked him off-kilter.

"Why? What does it matter if I'm his son or not?"

"Maybe it doesn't matter, maybe it does." She shrugged her slim shoulders inside her mint-green dress. Her calm voice was thoroughly undermined by the intense look in her eyes. It mattered to *her*.

"Maybe it would make you feel better if I take the test and

we can determine that I'm not your stepson." He found the whole thing rather funny. Maybe the situation was just too ludicrous to take seriously. What in the world was his supposed father doing married to a woman young enough to be his daughter, anyway?

"There's a lab a few blocks away. We could walk over there right now. It's totally painless and only takes a minute. They swab a few cells from inside your mouth."

"Something tells me you're not going to quit until I agree."

A smile tugged at her pretty mouth. "Just say yes."

DNA. A father.

He sucked in a breath. The prospect of actually knowing who his father was sent prickles of energy dancing along his nerves.

Family came with obligations, expectations. People could disappoint or could let you down. "What if I prefer being rootless and freewheeling?"

"Taking a test won't change that." She'd already picked up her clutch purse off the floor. Apparently, she'd declared victory and was ready to head for the lab.

His pride and some other even more primal instinct fought back. "I'll think about it." He cocked his head. "Maybe we could discuss it some more over dinner tonight. Have you eaten at my restaurant, La Ronde?"

She swallowed. "I don't think that's a good idea."

"You think I might seduce you again?" He lifted a brow.

Her cheeks paled.

Ouch.

"Or maybe you're worried you might seduce me."

"I'm beginning to think I have no idea what I might do, so I'd better barricade myself in my hotel room and hope for the best." She managed a bright smile.

"It might be more fun if you barricade me in there with you."

She shot him a warning look. "Please take the test. You won't regret it."

The plea in her eyes won him over.

At that moment, he decided to take her damn test. For reasons he didn't care to examine, he wanted to make the lovely Samantha Hardcastle happy. Something about her snuck right under his skin and grabbed him where it hurt.

He'd take her test and if he did regret it, it wouldn't be the first or last regret of his life.

Still, he wasn't going to give up his DNA without the promise of a second date. "You join me for dinner, I'll take your test. Deal?"

She blinked. Her mouth moved, but no words came out. She looked panic-stricken.

Louis didn't like the nasty feeling in his gut that came from a woman apparently desperate enough to refuse a fine dinner with him at his own five-star restaurant. "The food's good."

"I'm sure it is."

"And the company's all right, too."

She swallowed. Twisted her big ring. Suddenly she stood. "I have to go. Do you have a number where I can reach you?"

He scribbled his cell number on a piece of monogrammed notepaper. A warm sense of satisfaction and anticipation crept through him. Her resistance had only inflamed his desire.

She'd call. And she'd eat dinner with him.

And as far as he was concerned, that was just the beginning.

Three

Samantha dived out Louis DuLac's front door into the street. Thank heaven she didn't have a car waiting, because she needed to walk. Tension strung her muscles tight and vibrated along her nerves.

So, she'd found Tarrant's missing son.

And slept with him.

Shame soaked through her like acid. Part of her wanted to fly back to New York and never see Louis DuLac again.

But then she'd have failed everyone. Dominic, Tarrant's first son, was thrilled that a world-class restaurateur might be his brother.

Dominic had owned his own chain of gourmet markets before joining Hardcastle Enterprises. His newfound half brother Amado owned a fine vineyard. Just by dint of his occupation, they were sure Louis would turn out to be one of Tarrant's sons.

Fiona, Tarrant's daughter, had exclaimed that she traveled to Milan at least once a year to shop and always ate at Louis DuLac's restaurant there.

They'd all been excited about her trip down here to find him. And she'd promised Tarrant.

She drew in a long breath of sticky, humid air. Why did Louis have to insist on dinner as a condition for taking the test?

Then again, why not? If he were her stepson, it would no doubt be the first of many family dinners she hoped to enjoy.

Unless she'd destroyed that possibility forever with her foolish behavior last night.

Maybe she could get him to promise that they'd never mention their indiscretion to anyone.

It would be their secret that he'd run his lips over her skin until it tingled with arousal. That he'd kissed her breathless and whispered erotic suggestions in her ear. That he'd licked and sucked her almost to the point of madness, then made love to her until she cried out with joy.

Her skin heated and her insides roiled with an agonizing jumble of passion and humiliation.

She marched along Royal Street, not sure where she was going. Adrenaline crackled through her, propelling her feet forward.

She turned a corner, then edged around a crowd gathered to listen to a sidewalk guitarist.

The bluesy music combined with the hot air, the sounds of laughter and a spicy food smell wafting from somewhere turned the whole city into an exotic cocktail of temptation.

What next?

As she stood waiting to cross the street, a sign in a window opposite her caught her eye.

Need advice? asked the scrolled letters, painted on a white board. *Madame Ayida ~ Palmistry and spiritual consultations.*

Yeah, that's just what I need, Sam muttered sarcastically under her breath. Yet the sign arrested her gaze. The simple black letters beckoned her to look closer.

She paused and frowned.

She did need advice. Should she take Louis up on his offer of dinner in exchange for the DNA test? Or should she run back to New York with her tail between her legs and forget she ever met him?

She stared at the sign from the opposite sidewalk.

Could it hurt to ask?

She checked for traffic and crossed the road, and her legs seemed to march to the door of their own accord. Next she was turning the brass handle.

If talking to yourself was the first sign of madness, surely asking someone called Madame Ayida for advice was the second.

Nevertheless, Sam stepped through the door into a small, curtained foyer. "Hello," she called. "Anyone here?"

"Madame Ayida is always ready to help you," came a voice from the far side of the curtain. Black velvet, as clichéd as the name. Probably Madame Ayida was taking a break from the rigors of touring with the circus.

The curtain lifted and Sam found herself staring into a pair of dark brown eyes. "Please, come in and sit down."

Sam obeyed. Instead of the mole-covered crone she'd anticipated, Madame Ayida was young, with milk-chocolate-colored skin and a wide smile. A yellow silk scarf covered her hair in a strangely reassuring fairground touch.

"I don't really know why I'm here." Sam followed the garbled words with a breathy laugh.

"That is not unusual," said Madame Ayida. She had a slight accent, but Sam couldn't put her finger on it. "Together we will discover the reason for your visit."

Sam lowered herself gingerly into the single gold-painted chair opposite Madame Ayida at a small, wood table with a scarred top and scuffed legs. "So, um, do you read my palm, or what?" She glanced around. There was no sign of a crystal ball or tarot cards.

"If you like." Madame Ayida smiled enigmatically.

Sam held out her hand, suddenly embarrassed by her shiny manicure and big gold ring.

Madame Ayida closed soft fingers around her hand and lifted it for examination. Sam's heart fluttered in the long silence.

"A long life, but not without heartache," murmured Madame Ayida at last, her gaze lowered.

"That's for sure." Sam tried to keep her tone light. "Twice divorced and once widowed. Please, tell me it gets better."

Madame Ayida looked up, compassion in her eyes. "You're at a crossroad." She lowered her lashes, studying Sam's palm. "There's a risk that you'll make a terrible mistake."

An image of Louis's naked body, glistening with a sheen of perspiration, flashed into her mind. "I think I might have already made it."

"No." Madame Ayida shook her head slowly. "You're facing a choice and you haven't made it yet."

Sam's throat tightened.

Madame Ayida looked down at her hand, her forehead puckered with worry. "A difficult decision. I see a familiar road and one that is strange."

Sam frowned. There wasn't any sign of familiar roads in her life right now. If there was, she'd put her foot on it right away.

"Neither will be easy." Madame Ayida smoothed a forefinger over Sam's lifeline.

"Oh, great. Story of my life." Sam forced a laugh. "Then I guess it doesn't matter much which way I go."

"Oh, it does." Madame Ayida's eyes fixed on hers, dark pupils wide in the dim light. She seemed to look right through Sam and into some other realm beyond. "This choice will determine the course of the rest of your life."

"No pressure, then." Sam stared at her palm. It was hard to even make out the lines in the gloomy storefront. Probably Madame Ayida was making this up off the top of her head.

Those wide, intense eyes refocused and stared directly at Sam, making her breath catch at the bottom of her lungs.

"You *must* follow your heart."

Sam shivered, which was strange since the room must be at least eighty-five degrees.

Something in Madame Ayida's voice reached right into her mind and echoed there.

But how could she follow her heart when she wasn't even sure she could find all the broken pieces?

Tarrant's death had left her feeling so empty and cold. Sometimes she felt like her future had shriveled up and died with him.

"You belong with the living, not with the dead." Madame Ayida's soft voice penetrated her consciousness.

Sam blinked, startled. Had this strange young woman read her thoughts? "This terrible mistake you spoke of, how can I avoid it?"

"Listen to your heart." Madame Ayida's soft fingers palpated her palm for a second, as if Sam's heart might be found there and resuscitated.

Her blood pumped so hard she could almost hear it.

She had the chance to bring another member of Tarrant's family home to meet his siblings. Would her terrible mistake be squandering that opportunity just to salvage her own pride?

What was left of her heart pounded in her chest. It seemed to beg her not to blow the chance to bring Louis into the family.

At that moment, she decided to accept his invitation to dinner.

She'd find out if he really was Tarrant's son, and if he was, she'd start over and form a new relationship with him.

One with absolutely no hot, steamy, sweaty sex involved.

She realized she was staring into space. "Thank you. You've helped me a lot."

Madame Ayida smiled enigmatically. "Twenty dollars."

Sam fumbled in her purse. She was a grown-up. She could handle this. She could put that one accidental night behind her and start over, just as she'd started her life over after each of her failed marriages.

She certainly wasn't going to make the mistake of falling into bed again with a man who might be her stepson. She didn't have to worry about that.

Did she?

She pushed out into the blinding sunlight with a fresh sense of resolve. Madame Ayida might or might not be a rip-off artist, but she'd helped Sam organize her own thoughts, which was probably all these fortune-tellers ever did anyway.

She snapped open her phone, fumbled in her purse for the paper with Louis DuLac's number on it and dialed with shaking fingers.

His deep greeting made her throat dry, but she managed to blurt out, "I'll go to dinner with you."

She could hear his smile widen in the silence.

"Great. I'll pick you up at six."

"I'm at the Delacorte."

"I know."

"Oh." Sam frowned, then decided she really didn't want to know how he knew. She could wear the black Chanel dress with the white trim. That was probably the closest her wardrobe came to resembling a nun's habit. "Just so you know, we're not going to…uh…do anything, okay?"

It didn't make sense, but she could swear she heard silent laughter. "I promise we won't do anything you don't want to. I can be a perfect gentleman, when I try."

Sam heaved a shaky sigh. "Good." Still, fears nagged at her. "No touching. Like, not even to shake hands."

"Don't trust yourself, huh?"

"Not really." She swallowed and tried not to picture the light shining in those honey-gold eyes.

Better not to touch at all. You never knew what could happen.

Or rather she had some pretty vivid memories of exactly what could happen.

"Well, you can relax. I'll take good care of you. Be sure to wear something you don't mind getting dirty."

"What?" Her question was greeted by the steady sound of a dial tone. Dirty? Weren't they going to La Ronde? Unless it was under construction, she couldn't imagine how you could get dirty there. Unless maybe lobster was involved. With a lot of butter.

She closed her phone and put it back into her purse. Maybe not the Chanel, then.

Sam was already in the dim, quiet lobby of the hotel, seated in a leather chair with her eyes on the door, when Louis arrived. Her skin pricked with a mixture of fear and anticipation. Part of her was terrified to even be in the same room with him.

Another part of her was gloriously relieved to see him again.

She hadn't blown it. Yet.

There was still a chance to welcome him into the Hardcastle family. As her son. And she was just fine with that.

Or at least she would be if that's how things worked out.

She rose from the chair, smoothing wrinkles from her hastily purchased Calvin Klein pantsuit. She'd tried for casual elegance, so she'd look okay if they went to a restaurant or if they…

"Hi, Sam." A wide, warm smile lit up his face. His caramel-colored eyes shone with good humor.

He approached with long, easy strides, as if he intended to put his arm around her and kiss her on the cheek. The way one normally would.

But he slammed to a halt about a foot from her like he'd hit an invisible wall. His smile morphed into a wicked, challenging grin. "See?"

His hands hung by his sides. For a split second, her body ached at the lack of touch.

She bit her lip. "Hi, Louis."

"You decided to take a chance on dinner."

Sam glanced around, to make sure no one was in earshot. "I came here with a purpose, and I'm trying to get back on track."

He studied her for a moment. "Sometimes it's a good idea to get off the track and reassess."

Sam shook her head. "Some days it's all I can do to put one foot in front of the other. A track is reassuring for me right now."

He nodded slightly. "I won't derail you."

The golden glitter in his eyes contradicted his reassuring message. But that was probably just her overactive imagination.

"So, where are we going?" She glanced at his clothes. Khakis and a button-down shirt. Neutral, conservative attire. Yet somehow on him the generic outfit looked strangely hip and…

No. Not sexy. She was not at all aware of this man's sex appeal. Besides, the loose-cut cotton totally concealed the thick, strong muscles of his arms and chest. And his powerful thighs. She could see a hint of his slim waist and flat belly, but really, she wasn't at all interested.

She sucked in a breath. "Shall we get going?"

Louis held out his arm to take hers, then whipped it back as if stung. "Follow me," he murmured.

He was taking this no-touching thing seriously. Good.

Sam nursed her untouched arm. She'd instinctively lifted it an inch or two and it hung there in midair for a moment before she plastered it back to her side.

Excellent. Much better this way. She held her chin high as she marched out of the hotel lobby two steps behind him.

He pulled open the passenger door of a sleek, pale-yellow, open-topped sports car parked next to the sidewalk outside. He stood aside, so as to avoid any accidental brushing of skin, while she climbed in and sat on the tan glove-leather seat.

"What a beautiful Jaguar. How old is it?" Sam stroked the polished dashboard. Maybe she just needed to touch *something*.

"It's a 1967 XKE. It belonged to my grandfather."

"And it still runs?"

"It was his baby. He saved her for special occasions, and I do the same." He flashed her a golden glance before walking around to the driver's side.

A special occasion. "Where are we going?"

He settled behind the sporty wheel. "You'll see. Just sit back and enjoy the ride."

Sam fumbled with her seat belt, and tried not to notice that her nipples were almost painfully sensitive as she brought the strap over them.

Deep breath. Remain calm. Keep focused on your goal.

She snuck a glance sideways to see if he looked like Tarrant. Maybe he wasn't Tarrant's son at all?

But on close inspection, she could see Tarrant's determined jaw. His high cheekbones. The lofty carriage of a man with limitless confidence.

She sank into her seat, her breath shallow. How had she not noticed last night?

Louis's features were more generous, his mouth wider and quicker to smile than Tarrant's. His eyes were a totally different color with a more catlike shape. And his smooth olive skin made a mockery of the freckly tan that Tarrant so painstakingly cultivated to hide his natural pallor.

There was no avoiding the fact that Louis DuLac was a breathtakingly handsome man.

What a terrible shame Tarrant would never meet him.

A rush of emotion threatened to get the better of her and she reached into her pocket for a tissue.

"You okay?"

"I was just thinking how it's awful that you'll never meet your father."

"I don't know who my father is."

The admission didn't seem to faze him at all. Louis DuLac was obviously comfortable with himself, and didn't need to cling to anyone else for support.

She wished she had that kind of strength.

"And you don't know who my father is, either," he continued. He shot her a bright smile. "Does it matter? I'm the same person either way."

"You don't want to know, do you?"

"Not really."

"What are you afraid of?" She stared at him, trying not to admire the sculpted perfection of his cheekbone.

"Afraid?" He flashed an aggressive glance at her and laughed. "I'm not afraid of anything."

"I don't believe you. You must be afraid of something. Snakes? Spiders? The dark?"

"Three of my favorite things." A smile settled over his mouth as he watched the road. The city streets had leafed out into a lush suburb.

"Then you have nothing to lose by learning who your father is." She smiled and tossed her hair.

He'd backed himself into a corner.

"You're tricky." He shot a glance at her.

"I'm smarter than I look."

"You certainly always look very smart. Didn't I tell you to dress casual?"

"This is casual. It's Calvin Klein." She raised an eyebrow.

"Did you buy it today?"

"I might have. Or I might have had it for years." She crossed her arms over her chest. "Don't flatter yourself that I bought it to impress you."

"That wouldn't flatter me at all. I don't want to be impressed." He kept his gaze on the road.

"What do you want?" Nothing like getting to the bottom of things. Especially since there was no touching involved.

Though, maybe she was flattering herself by thinking he wanted to touch her again.

"I want you to be yourself. Take it easy. Feel the wind in your hair."

Be yourself? If only she knew who that was. She'd grown so used to trying to please everyone else she wasn't sure who was in there under all the smiles and smart outfits.

Time for a diversionary tactic. "Where are we going?"

"My very favorite place."

Louis decided not to tell her that his favorite place was well-stocked with snakes and spiders, and that it was most magical after dark.

He glanced sideways at Sam. Fresh and pretty, her pale gold hair tossed in the breeze. She didn't fuss over it and try to fix it like some women. He liked that.

"You're looking more relaxed already."

"It's beautiful here."

They'd left the city limits and headed out into the bayou on Belle Chasse. The air was warm and Sam had taken off her jacket. The wind pressed her textured cotton top to her skin, tracing her girlish curves.

It was okay to look, as long as he didn't touch.

Louis felt a bit like a kid in a toy store who'd already spent his whole allowance. He could look at all the pretty, shiny things, but he couldn't take them home.

At least not yet.

"Just last night, you were naked in my arms."

She swung her head around to look at him. Panic shone in her eyes. "I've never done that before."

"Had sex?" He raised an eyebrow. Couldn't resist teasing.

She shot him a scolding look. "Had sex with a man I just met."

"I hope it was a memorable first." He glanced at the road,

reluctant to take his eyes off her face. "I'll certainly never forget it."

Her neck turned pink. A very pretty pink that made him want to layer kisses over it.

She didn't say anything.

"A guy could feel quite rejected by your silence."

She flicked her hair back. "I did say we weren't going to do anything tonight."

"And we're not. No touching at all." He slid his fingers over the wheel, as if taking out his desire to fondle on the punched chestnut leather. "But no one said anything about no reminiscing. That was a beautiful night."

"I don't know what came over me last night," she said, her words slow and careful. "But I do know that it won't happen again."

As they drew close to the shed where he kept his boat, Louis wondered what on earth he was thinking when he came up with the crazy idea of bringing her here.

This was his special place. His sanctuary away from all the drama and intrigue of his everyday world.

The mysterious Samantha had closed up like a snail pulling into its shell. She wasn't rude, exactly, but his questions about her life were met with brief, colorless answers that told him nothing about her.

She was going to hate it here. There weren't any boutiques or musicians or celebrities and her high heels would sink into the wet ground. He should have taken her to La Ronde, as she'd expected.

Or not taken her anywhere at all, as she'd have clearly preferred.

"Where are we?" She peered around when they pulled up in front of the boathouse.

"The middle of nowhere." He jumped out of the car. The air was clear and cooler already, the sun sinking below the shiny, wet horizon. "Are you nervous?"

"It does occur to me that I know very little about you." She glanced around. He saw her notice that the road ended only a hundred yards or so away.

The boat shed was the only structure visible among the messy web of canals and grassy land that stretched out as far as the eye could see.

She opened her car door. "But you've got an honest face."

He laughed. "That's a first."

She stepped out onto the road. "Is this where we're having dinner?" Doubt hovered around the edges of her question.

"We've got a little farther to go, but we're bringing dinner with us." He unlatched the XKE's tiny trunk and pulled out the wicker picnic basket. His friends teased him for not using a plastic Igloo ice chest that would actually keep the champagne cold, but both his lovely old car and this beautiful woman deserved a bit more style than that.

She smiled. "A picnic."

"Is that okay?"

"I haven't had a picnic in…I don't know when I last had a picnic."

Maybe almost as long ago as you last had sex.

He didn't say it. But she had bottled-up fire and hunger inside her that must have taken years to accumulate. Maybe she'd never even had sex with her late husband.

The man she believed to be his father.

"We're going out on my boat." He ushered her into the dim, cool boat shed, restored and painted to look just as it had when his great-grandfather first erected it to house his beloved shrimp boat.

Louis's handmade reproduction of the old Lafitte skiff rested lightly on its rails, polished wood shining in the sunset glow that snuck in through the open doors out to the water.

Samantha's silence made him glance sideways. She stood, frowning at the boat. "I can't swim."

"You won't have to. This boat is the smoothest ride ever made and there's not a wave to be found on these waters."

Fear glimmered in her eyes. He wanted to put his arm around her and reassure her. To whisper that he'd take great care of her and he wouldn't let anything hurt or even scare her.

But he'd promised no touching.

"If you're not comfortable on the boat, we'll come right back. We can always eat in here."

Samantha bit her lip, a girlish gesture. "No." She sucked in a breath. "I'd like to go on the boat. I'm trying to step outside my comfort zone more often."

"An admirable thing to do." He held out his hand to take hers. She looked at it, then up at him.

He dropped his hand to his side. It prickled with the frustrated desire to touch her. "Old habits die hard."

He managed to resist offering to help her into the boat. She climbed on while it was mounted on the rails, then he removed his shoes, lowered the boat and its precious cargo gently into the water and climbed in himself.

Sam laughed at his soaked pants. "You're all wet."

"I'll dry. It's refreshing. You can go for a dip if you like."

She glanced over the rim of the boat into the dark, glittering water. "No, thanks. I don't want to go that far outside my comfort zone. Is it deep?"

"Not very. A lot of this was solid ground a few years ago. The water levels keep rising. Every year I'm closer to owning oceanfront property."

"This is nicer than the ocean. It's so quiet. And I love the sound the grasses make, like they're whispering secrets to each other." Her blue eyes shone with pleasure.

Louis felt a knot form in his gut. This was *exactly* why he'd brought her here.

Already he could see the tension slipping out of her shoulders and her hands spreading out over the wood gunwale as she relaxed into the boat.

The late afternoon sun shone on her skin and picked out flecks of sparkling gold in her hair.

Momentarily sorry that it would drown out the gossip of the grasses, he started the engine and guided the boat into a wide canal, where water shimmered among the grasses on either side. "You could open the basket for us."

She unlatched the leather buckle and reached in. "Goodness, what beautiful dishes. Are they silver?"

"My great-great-grandfather was a silversmith. I like them for picnics because they don't break."

She nodded, a smile flicking across her lips. "Tarrant would approve."

Louis's shoulders tightened at the mention of the strange man's name. "He liked nice things?"

"Only the best." She picked up a plate and he felt a familiar flash of pride as she traced the intricately carved pattern with her fingertip.

"I guess that's why he chose you." The words slipped out. He wasn't looking to flatter her.

She blushed. "I don't know why he chose me at all. We met at a party I was catering. It was my first night on the job and I spilled white wine all over his pant leg. The other caterers were sure the firm would never be hired again. They got me in such a panic that, when he asked me out while I was mopping him up, I didn't dare say no."

"A Cinderella story."

She laughed. "Yeah. I guess it was. I didn't have a penny to my name at the time because my second husband wouldn't let me take anything with me when I walked out."

"That's not too nice."

"He wasn't. That's why I left." She shrugged. "Best thing I ever did. Well, after leaving my first husband."

"He was a rat, too?"

"Most definitely. Ooh, is this potato salad?" She'd pulled the lid off a crock and dipped her nose down to inhale.

He watched her one tiny dimple deepen at the whiff of Creole mustard. "Great Aunt Emmeline's recipe."

"You have a lot of relatives."

"Maybe that's why I'm not looking to find any more."

She gave a little pout. She knew he wasn't serious.

"There's a spoon in the bottom, help yourself. And there's some andouille sausage in the warmer, and fresh rolls. And champagne, of course, in case we get thirsty."

Samantha eyed the champagne and flashed him a nervous glance. "I think I'd better stay away from that."

"You're afraid you might decide it's okay to touch me after all?" He leaned in, so close he could smell her lovely smooth skin and the natural feminine scent hiding under her elegant perfume.

"No." She spoke too quickly and he heard a ripple of hesitation in her voice.

The uncertainty hung in the air like smoke.

He felt it creep into his lungs and spread throughout his body as the image of her naked in his bed—just last night— flashed across his mind.

He wanted Sam back in his bed, preferably tonight.

But he was a patient man. Some things were worth waiting for.

She handed him a plate with a knife and fork. He reached into the basket and unwrapped the fresh smoked sausage and the crusty bread.

Their arms moved within inches of each other. Louis teased her by reaching so close that she drew back a little to avoid contact. The hairs on their arms almost brushed.

But not quite.

The warm air between them crackled with volatile energy created by the absence of contact. He couldn't remember ever hurting so badly for a woman's touch.

A woman who might be his stepmother.

Four

Sam took a bite of the spicy sausage. The boat engine throbbed in a steady pulse, and water slapped against the sides.

She could feel Louis's eyes on her as she licked her lips. His gaze oozed over her like fresh honey. She should be offended that a man she barely knew felt free to stare at her like that.

Except that she'd already slept with him.

"Were all your husbands older than you?"

Louis's strange question jerked her out of a sensual fog. "*All* my husbands." She grimaced. "You make me sound like Zsa Zsa Gabor."

"I think she made them wait until they put a ring on her finger before she slept with them." He winked and bit off a chunk of bread.

Sam's mouth fell open. Then she drew in a breath and reached for her sense of humor. "You're right. Why buy the cow when you can get the milk for free?"

Her mother had repeated that phrase many times during her teen years, when Sam was competing to be Miss Corn Dog or whatever title came with the pageant of that week.

She frowned. "In fact, I was a virgin when I married my first husband." She looked right at Louis. "And yes, he was older."

Louis's expression didn't reveal any opinion, negative or otherwise. "What went wrong?"

"Who knows?" She shrugged and looked out at the waving grasses. The sun hung low on the horizon, bathing land and water in a thick golden soup of light.

"*You* probably do."

She glanced up. People didn't usually talk to her like this.

Like what?

Rude.

But Louis just watched her, eyes twinkling with mischief as he ate.

"Okay. Let's see. I married him so I could get away from home because my mother ran me on the pageant circles like I was a prize bull and I knew I'd never get to go to college as long as there was a penny to be earned from parading me in front of an audience. To be brutally frank, I'd probably have married anyone."

"I doubt it. Who was he?"

She rankled at his dismissive comment. "He owned a car dealership in our town. He was safe and solid, and he treated me nicely."

"Did you get to go to college?"

Sam's gut tightened. *He's already figured out the answer.* She studied his face for mockery, prepared to defend herself, but all she saw in his eyes was warm interest.

"He didn't want his wife working or going to school."

"Jealous."

"Exactly. And after two years of trying to be the perfect little wife, I'd had enough."

"See? You know exactly why you divorced him." Louis shifted his legs as he cut the engine. The wet cotton of his pants clung to his muscled calves. A reminder of the strength and power of his body. How he'd held her close and...

She averted her gaze. She'd certainly never had feelings like that for her first husband.

Or even her third.

Guilt snaked through her. How could she have fallen so quickly into another man's arms? She'd promised Tarrant that she didn't miss sex. That she didn't need crude lust or grace-less fumbling to be happy.

So why did her skin tingle at the simple nearness of this man?

Sam inhaled deeply and tried to drag her mind back to the conversation. "You're right. I do know why I divorced him. It's amazing I lasted two full years. He barely let me leave the house. I'd been so looking forward to figuring out who I was, without my mother telling me what to wear and say and do, but he was even worse. My every move reflected positively or negatively on the Bob MacClackery Automotive empire. If he could have bought a Barbie doll and dressed it himself and called it Mrs. MacClackery, that would have been heaven for him. Lord knows I tried to please him, but it just wasn't possible. Finally I gave up."

Funny how she could look back with detachment now. Things that had been so painful and hard to cope with at the time now seemed funny. Her desperate attempt to be little Mrs. Perfect, polishing linoleum and hovering over racks of lamb.

And answering to the name of Samantha MacClackery.

"I'm glad your smile is back, but don't forget to eat." Louis spooned more potato salad on her plate.

"How can I eat when you're distracting me with all these bad memories?"

"My humble apologies. Champagne to celebrate your freedom?"

She started to raise her glass, then her hand froze in midair. Samantha's gut clenched as another drop of pure guilt splashed inside her. "I didn't want to be free. I didn't want Tarrant to die."

The smile faded from Louis's eyes. "I'm sorry, that was insensitive. You loved him a lot."

Chest tight, Sam reached into her pocket for a familiar hankie and dabbed at her eyes. "More than I'd ever imagined. And I'd had a lot of practice by then."

He didn't smile at her attempted levity. "It's great that you finally found someone who made you happy. I guess the third time was the charm, or however that cliché goes."

His words sounded insincere, like he was just being polite. Suddenly she needed him to know that her late husband was not just some old man with a yen for young women.

"Tarrant Hardcastle was the kind of man who adds color and style to the history books. He was brimming with ideas and dreams and schemes and glorious visions, right up until the day he died. It was an honor to be in his presence. I still don't know what he saw in me." She fixed him with a steady gaze, defying him to disagree.

Louis met her gaze, his expression serious. "Maybe he saw someone who could love him for himself, not for his money."

She raised an eyebrow. "How would he know?"

"As a man of vision, I bet he could just tell." A dimple appeared as he smiled. "And you are pretty."

Sam felt herself blushing. What for? It's not like she didn't know she was pretty.

That's what got her roped into all those stinking beauty pageants that had her strutting about like a champion heifer when she should have been taking courses at the community college so she could get a real job.

And she knew she was still pretty now, at thirty-one. She should be, what with all the money and effort that went into it. She supported a whole army of personal trainers and massage therapists and colorists and manicurists.

And Tarrant had insisted she only wear couture originals. He called it a quirk of his.

She'd readily humored him. At the time, she'd explained it to herself and others as another example of his visionary approach to life.

Suddenly her perspective was different.

"Maybe he married me because he wanted to dress me up like a Barbie doll, too?"

"I think you enjoy the Barbie thing yourself. I asked you to dress casual and you look like you're ready to hit a runway somewhere."

Sam glanced down at the rather chic linen outfit she'd chosen. "I guess I can't help it. It's an ingrained habit. I'd probably need a twelve-step program to get me into a pair of Levi's at this point."

Louis grinned. "I bet you'd look cute in a pair of Levi's. But if dressing up makes you happy, what's wrong with that? You can't live your life to meet other people's expectations. You have to do what's right for you."

"Sometimes that's hard to figure out. I guess I'm so used to trying to meet other people's expectations that it's natural to me now."

Louis put his plate down on the floor of the boat. He crossed his arms on his knees and leaned forward. She shrank from the intensity in his gaze, from the focused attention of his sharp mind.

"Sounds like you've spent your life looking for a father figure who'd tell you what to do." Again, his gaze wasn't accusatory. If anything, it was compassionate.

She lifted her chin. She didn't want his pity or anyone else's. "As it happens, my father didn't tell me what to do. He mostly ignored me."

Louis scraped his plate into the water. Sam watched in awe as several fish spooked to the surface and snatched at morsels of potato and sausage.

She clung more tightly to her own plate.

Why was she here? She didn't need to be psychoanalyzed by some guy who thought he was God's gift to women. She was just trying to make it through the day in one piece.

Louis cocked his head. "Maybe you were subconsciously trying to get your father's attention by reenacting the scenario."

Sam narrowed her eyes. "I got his attention all right. He hasn't spoken to me since my first divorce. He said I was a sinner for leaving my marriage and doomed to hell." Sam's heart still clenched at the memory. Her plate shook in her hand and she clutched it tighter.

Louis winced. "Some people shouldn't be parents."

He took her plate from her and cleaned it with the same deft move. She watched the fish dart to the surface and inhale her uneaten morsels.

"Recycling in action," he murmured, as he wrapped the plates in a pretty dishcloth and returned them to the basket. "Don't let your dad get you down. I survived just fine without one."

His level gaze challenged her to alter that bare and apparently comfortable fact of his life.

For a second, she felt a twinge of remorse that she'd invaded his comfortable existence and inserted a new possibility into it. "Family can be a wonderful thing."

"In moderation." Louis winked.

Sam smiled. His warm expression disarmed her. The rich copper rays of slow sunset shone on his too-handsome face and glittered in the droplets of water that splattered his powerful forearms.

She tried not to notice the funny ticklish sensation in her belly.

"At least I don't have to worry about making a child miserable by inflicting my own traumas on them."

"Why not?" he asked. "Isn't that part of the fun of parenting?"

Sam felt her smile fade. "I don't have any children." She could say it calmly, all emotion buried beneath a composed exterior. She'd officially given up all hope and she was fine with that. She'd known when she married Tarrant that he was not capable of giving her a child, and she accepted it as her fate.

She'd actually felt calmer since then.

"Me, neither." Louis sipped his wine.

"Do you want children?" It didn't feel forward to ask. They weren't dating. She was just curious.

"Nope."

"Why not?"

"I already told you I'm the product of a chance meeting between a double bass and a saxophone. I grew up like a stream of notes in the air. I don't think I finished an entire year of school in the same place. I certainly never did homework or ate square meals or tried out for a team. I wouldn't have the first clue about raising a child." His eyes sparkled, still squinting slightly against the low rays of sunlight. "So, it's lucky I've never wanted to try."

"You are lucky. It's kind of pathetic how badly I used to want one. And when I married my second husband, who was also keen to have a child, we couldn't get pregnant. We tried day in and day out for months on end."

She reached for her glass and swiped a sip. Ugly memories rolled over her. "He blamed me. We had me tested and everything looked fine, but he wouldn't get tested himself. One day we just stopped having sex. He said he didn't want children anymore."

Louis listened with compassion in his eyes.

"After that, he started staying out a lot. I dressed up in all the lacy lingerie I could find, but he just wasn't interested. 'Working late,' he said, but I soon found out different. And that's when I left him."

Louis whistled. "What a jerk. He didn't know how lucky he was just to have you."

Sam shrugged. "Or not. Apparently I couldn't give him what he wanted." Goose bumps sprang up on her arms and she raised her hands to rub them. "Tarrant appreciated me just for being me. And, oh, boy, was I grateful for that after my first two husbands."

"Finally, you found the father who gave you the love and approval you wanted." Louis looked steadily at her.

Sam recoiled from his suggestion. "No! It wasn't like that at all."

"Did you have sex?"

"Well, no, but… He was ill."

Louis made a small movement with his mouth. Like he

couldn't quite find the right words. Or maybe he could, but he didn't like to say them.

"He was my *husband,* not my father." Her voice rose high as emotion snapped through her.

Louis simply nodded. "And you were a good wife to him. Every man should be so lucky."

Samantha didn't offer any sign of acknowledgment. She didn't need his condescension. She *had* been a good wife.

"I'm not mocking you." Louis frowned. He scratched at something on his arm, pulling his shirt cuff up to reveal a stretch of tanned forearm.

Not that she cared.

He looked up at her. "You're a very giving person. That's a rare and beautiful thing. It's something not everyone appreciates."

Sam found herself wanting to take the compliment and bask in its unfamiliar light. But she managed to resist. "Well, it's been fun analyzing my personal failures and foibles, but let's shine a spotlight on yours for a moment, shall we?"

A wicked grin crept slowly across his mouth. "You're assuming I have any."

He leaned away and started the engine. The movement gave her an extravagant view of the thick muscles of his back under the strained cotton of his shirt.

He wasn't perfect. He probably had all kinds of things wrong with him.

On the other hand, she certainly couldn't find fault with his performance in bed. Of course, her experience in that realm hadn't been of the highest quality.

Until last night.

Okay, so maybe he had the right to be a little cocky.

His honey-toned eyes gazed at her from under thick black lashes that were wasted on a man.

The nerve! He was flirting with her.

She flicked an imaginary crumb off her lap. "I'm sure you're not quite as perfect as you'd like to think you are."

"Probably not, but you'd have to get to know me better to find out." He raised a brow.

"If it turns out that you're my husband's son, then I hope we'll become very close."

"And if it turns out I'm not, you'll cast me aside like a used Ziploc bag?"

A smile tugged at his sensual mouth. Sam blinked.

What if he wasn't Tarrant's son?

Then it was okay to have slept with him. She could even sleep with him again.

A thick sensation swelled inside her and her nipples tingled. She'd never felt *anything* like last night. Every millimeter of her body had come alive with pleasure. A stray throb of memory stirred inside her.

Sam dragged herself back to the present. "I guess we'll cross that bridge when we come to it."

Louis made a show of looking around. The sunset shone like spilled champagne over the wide, shimmering swamp.

"I don't see any bridge. Just a boat, with a man and a woman in it."

Sam glanced around. There really was nothing out there. They'd motored far away from the boathouse and there wasn't a visible structure anywhere. Just sky and bayou, with the sun hovering at the horizon like a cherry floating in a cocktail.

"It's going to get dark any minute."

"Yes."

"Won't we get lost? Or eaten alive by bugs?"

"You're not worried about alligators?" He cocked his head.

Sam shivered. "Thanks for reminding me. Shouldn't we be getting back?"

"We could. Or we could spend the night here." He inclined his head. A wooden structure appeared among the grasses like a mushroom sprouting. A tiny cottage of some sort, on stilts that raised it over the swamp.

"What is it?"

"My granddad's fishing retreat. I renovated it a couple of years ago. It's a lot more high-tech than it looks. I'm embarrassed to say that there's even solar-powered air-conditioning." He shot her a wry smile.

She stiffened. "I'm not sleeping here. You need to take me back to the city."

"Why? It's a beautiful night. You already agreed to spend the evening with me, so I know you don't have anywhere to go. I've proved to you that I can keep my hands off you, and I promise to keep them to myself all night long."

He held up his hands and examined them, as if making sure they were going to behave. "Don't you trust me?"

"I don't have any…stuff with me. Makeup remover. That kind of thing."

"What happens if you don't take your makeup off?" He looked genuinely interested.

Sam hesitated. "I have no idea. I've never tried."

"Then maybe it's time you did. You said you wanted to step outside your comfort zone, didn't you? And really, you can trust me."

Sam rubbed her arm. She felt chilly, though the air was still warm.

"Or maybe it's yourself you don't trust." He squinted

against the sun's rays, looking unbearably handsome. Somehow the fact that he knew it didn't diminish his appeal at all.

"It's peaceful here. No TV, no radio, no Internet. No outside world." The boat had somehow sidled up alongside the building, and he cut the engine.

Water lapped against the wooden stilts holding the structure above the shimmering water. The pinkish cedar looked fresh and new, and she could smell its pungent scent, crisp and inviting amid the fecund funk of the bayou.

The boat rocked in the water. Could it hurt to go inside for just a minute?

"Take a look. See what you think. If you don't like it, we'll head back."

"Okay." She could hardly believe she'd agreed, but suddenly she had to see what Louis DuLac's special place looked like inside.

She could tell it was special. Even from the boat, she could make out images of cranes carved right into the wood of the corner boards and the door, which gave the building a Japanese feel. Steps came down right to the water, each riser carved in a distinct shape, almost like stepping stones.

She hesitated, wondering how to get from the yawing boat onto the solid wood of the steps.

"Since you don't want me to give you a hand up, I'll pull the boat up close to the steps, and you can grab on to the railing."

Louis leaned forward and grabbed the railing himself, then tugged the boat alongside it with the sheer strength of his body. Sam tried not to notice the way his muscles rippled under his shirt and how his powerful thighs braced to hold the boat steady. "Go ahead."

Sam climbed shakily to her feet. She leaned out of the boat

to grab the railing. True to his promise, Louis held the boat steady against the steps while she pulled herself up onto them.

Apprehension prickled along her spine as she stood there on the steps of the only structure visible for miles around. If he turned the boat around and left, she'd be stranded.

But he lashed the boat to a stilt with expert ease. "Go on in, it's unlocked."

"You just leave it open?"

He shrugged. "If someone's determined enough, they'll get in anyway."

Sam pushed open the smooth door, with its lovely square carving of two cranes amid tall grasses.

"Oh, goodness." It was beautiful. Dark golden light filled the space, streaming through a wide window on the opposite side that framed the sunset. Considering the warmth of the afternoon, the interior was wonderfully cool and comfortable.

The plank floor invited her feet to step inside. The single room smelled of fresh, new wood. The scent of new beginnings.

Louis came in behind her and hesitated. She shifted aside, giving him room to pass without touching her. Her skin tingled as he eased into the space, sliding by her *almost* close enough to touch, but not quite. His male scent mingled with the fresh aroma of cedar to push her senses into overdrive.

She watched as he flipped a latch on the paneled wall and pulled down something like a Murphy bed. It opened to a low sofa, Japanese style, with a patterned covering of dark purple and gray. He pulled a couple of cushions out of the cavity in the wall where the sofa had been. "Take a load off."

Sam eased herself down onto the sofa. Its cushiony soft surface felt blissful after the hard bench of the boat. Louis moved across the room and pulled down an identical sofa on the other side. "See? No touching required. His and hers."

"This place is amazing. What else is hidden in these walls?"

Louis beamed with what looked like pride as he pulled open another paneled cabinet to reveal the interior of a fridge, stocked with drinks. "What can I get you?"

"Oh, my." Sam stretched out on the cushioned surface. Her muscles crackled as tension slipped from them. "This does feel good. Maybe a soda water."

The delicious whoosh of the soda bottle cap popping off made her mouth water. She took the bottle and again their fingers almost touched, but not quite. She could swear she'd felt a snap of electrical current right at the tip of her fingers.

She smiled. He smiled back. A warm sensation stirred in her belly.

Uh-oh.

Get a grip, Sam. You're probably the fourth woman he's brought here this week. "This is quite the romantic hideaway. I'm guessing it gets a lot of use," she said drily. She took a sip of her soda water. The bubbles crackled over her tongue.

"I come here a lot." He looked steadily at her. "More all the time."

A prick of jealousy stuck her somewhere uncomfortable.

"But you're the first woman I've ever brought here."

"What?" A weird shiver sprang across her skin.

"This is where I come to be alone. Don't get me wrong, I like people. I love the hustle and bustle of my restaurants and organizing events and bringing people together. That's been my whole life."

He pushed a hand through his hair and turned to look out the window. The sun was now a slim chip of glowing amber, resting delicately above the dark purple horizon. "Maybe I'm getting older or something." He looked at her, humor shining in his eyes. "Who am I kidding? Of course I'm getting older.

But lately, I find I need to step off the carousel and reconnect with nature. With myself."

He frowned, as if embarrassed by his confession. "And I thought you might like to do that, too."

A very strange sensation rose inside Sam. She absolutely believed him. He'd chosen her, out of all the women in the world—a good percentage of whom would no doubt be willingly at his disposal—to share his special place with.

Without the promise of even a touch, let alone a kiss.

That touched her somewhere far more powerful and vulnerable than her skin.

She covered her confusion with a sip of her drink. She wondered if she should say something, but Louis didn't seem to expect her to. He'd brought in the picnic basket and he opened it and unloaded some supplies into the small fridge. "We have fruit and cheese if you're hungry, and there's plenty of bread left. If you like, we could catch some shrimp. There's a grill out on the deck."

Sam laughed. "That's self-sufficient! Let's leave the shrimp alone, though. They deserve some peace and quiet, too. How did you come to build way out here?"

"My granddad owned the land." Louis popped the cap off a second bottle of soda water. She watched his powerful neck swell as he took a swig. "Or at least it used to be land." He smiled ruefully. "It's been underwater for as long as I can remember, but he said it used to be dry and that you could walk out here from the road."

"That's hard to imagine."

"I like it better like this. Somehow a destination seems more worthwhile if there's a bit of a journey to get there."

"I guess you'd have to have that perspective if you have restaurants all over the world and travel a lot."

"I grew up traveling. My mom's a singer, so I went with her on tour every summer."

"That must have been fun."

"Fun, exhausting, confusing, exciting. A little bit of every-thing. Made me who I am, though. I make friends easily and I can settle in pretty much anywhere at a moment's notice. One of my friends teases me that the whole reason I opened my restaurants is so I can have a roomful of friends to drop in on in any city I visit."

"That's a nice idea."

Louis chuckled. "I think she might just be right."

Sam's smile faltered at the mention of a "she." Which was ridiculous. How on earth could she be jealous of some woman she'd never even heard of who probably really was only a friend?

Especially when she had no real personal relationship with him *at all*.

Other than being the first woman invited to his special place.

And having spent one night in his bed.

The memory of his strong arms around her assaulted her like an anxiety attack. He'd rolled up his sleeves and she could see his powerful forearms clearly, even in the dusky gloom. The exertion of their journey had rendered him rather rumpled. His hair curled untidily over his forehead and his pants had dried into wrinkles. He looked more boyish and innocent than he had yesterday, as the elegant and worldly host of his own smart restaurant.

She probably looked pretty rumpled, too, though she man-aged to resist peeking down at her clothes to check. Lord knew what this humidity was doing to her hair.

Then again, maybe she also looked cute and girlish.

She tried not to giggle. Suddenly she felt like a teenager.

For the first time in her life, she was alone, in a sexually charged situation—let's face it, the sexual tension was so thick in the air she could smell it even over all the cedar—with a man her own age.

"I bet you're a painter." Louis's low voice jarred her out of her contemplation.

"You mean, painting pictures?"

He nodded. "When you look at things you seem to linger and take in all the elements of the image in front of your eyes."

Sam blinked. Her heart started pounding. "I, uh, used to paint…a little."

"What did you paint?"

"Landscapes, flowers, that kind of thing. Nothing at all serious or important."

"In whose opinion? One of your not-so-nice ex-husbands?"

She swallowed. "Well, yes. Tarrant always said I should paint, though. He offered to set up a studio for me in our house."

"But?" He cocked his head.

"I was too busy." She shrugged. "Being his wife was a full-time job."

"All the ladies' lunches, the pedicure appointments, the charity fund-raising meetings, the gala evenings." His voice trailed off.

Sam flushed. He'd reduced her whole busy life to a dismissive sentence. She lifted her chin. "Exactly."

"Now that you're alone, you could make the time."

"Maybe I don't want to." She fiddled with her ring.

"Afraid to see what might pop out of your imagination with no one to tell you what to do?"

"I'm not sure I even have an imagination anymore."

"Of course you do." Louis narrowed his eyes. "It's just

been lying dormant, letting ideas and fantasies and dreams stockpile in there, waiting for the moment you choose to set them free."

Sam frowned. Her mind felt as blank and lusterless as an unprimed canvas. Something she never could have imagined when she was a teenager with a million dreams. "I don't think so."

Undeterred, Louis leaned forward, a gleam in his eyes. "If you could paint something right now, anything, what would it be?"

The warm glow of the last rays of sunset picked out the smooth, strong planes of his face, molding them like a fine statue. How magnificent he'd look standing there, nude, with those coppery rays chiseling the sturdy musculature of his body.

Uh-oh. Her imagination appeared to be working after all.

"Come on. Anything."

"The sunset, maybe," she said, hesitant, afraid to meet the pull of his gaze.

"Then let's go look at it." He rose to his feet and stepped toward her, then stopped, as if he'd just remembered that invisible glass wall between them. Sam's skin tingled once again at the absence of natural contact.

He pushed open a door in the wall, and the room flooded with light like thick golden honey. "There's a deck out here. Come on."

Squinting against the sudden brightness, Sam followed him outside. The entire bayou was aflame with gold and copper. Rich dark reds and purples hung in the trees, the water shimmered and glimmered as its black depths reflected the last rays of sun with diamond brightness.

"I challenge you to find anything more beautiful than that

in the whole world." Louis gazed out at the jeweled world before them.

"It's magical."

He turned to her, and a laugh escaped. "It is magic, and it's going to work its magic on you. The old voodoo everyone talks about. It's going to flood your imagination with beauty until it overflows and you just can't keep it locked up anymore."

Sam tried to suppress a giggle, but it came out anyway. She imagined attacking her dull life with a brush loaded with bright golden-yellow paint.

Not that she'd know where to begin.

"I couldn't paint this. I don't have the skills. I always wanted to take a class, but somehow it just never happened."

"So start tomorrow."

"I can't."

"Why not?"

"For one thing, I'm too old."

Louis snorted. "Unless you've had some really fine plastic surgery, I wouldn't put you a day over thirty."

A flash of vain pride swelled inside her, and she cursed herself for it. "I'm thirty-one."

"See? You're practically a kid."

"I'm not. I'm a widow with a large charitable trust to manage. It's an important responsibility."

"And I admire you for taking it on, but trust me, there is absolutely enough time, both in your day and in the rest of your life, for you to become the painter you always wanted to be."

"What if I stink at it?"

"That kind of thinking keeps people glued to their TVs watching other people live while they wonder what real living would be like. You're not going to do that. You've got a decade or two of living to catch up on, from the sound of things."

Sam looked out at the bright palette of colors shimmering around her. Suddenly the world felt rich and heavy with possibilities.

Louis leaned over the railing. "I've got a friend in New York, Margo, who teaches at Pratt Institute. I'll give her a call and she'll help you get started."

Excitement crackled through Sam. Could it really be that easy? To just pick up a brush and get started? "I might need a good supply of nude male models."

Louis grinned. "I can see your imagination's up and running."

"Once again, I can see you have an unsettling amount of insight into me."

He shrugged. "Someone's got to set you free."

"I am free. I make my own decisions."

"Do you? Or are you going to unwittingly start looking for another father figure to tell you what to do?"

Irritation prickled over her. "Seriously, Tarrant was not a father figure."

"I'm just calling it the way I see it." He opened the door to the cabin. "We'd better go back in before the bugs start biting."

Sam followed him into the dimly lit space.

Although she hated to admit it, her previous partners had all been at least ten years older.

She'd always felt older than her peers. With her strict and easily angered parents, she hadn't had the opportunity to be a moody teenager. One time, she'd broken a vase while dancing around the room to the radio, and she'd eaten only cold cereal with water for a week as a punishment.

Her mother had pointed out that in addition to making her more careful in the future, it would slim her down for the upcoming teen pageant she was entered in.

She'd learned to toe every line like an infantry recruit out of sheer self-preservation. She'd never even attempted to do anything wild and irresponsible.

Like sleeping with a man she'd just met.

Sam knew Tarrant had wed her because she'd refused to sleep with him until they were married.

He'd said that was so audacious that he fell instantly in love with her. They were married a week later.

Louis was the only man she'd ever slept with that she wasn't married to.

The final fiery rays of the setting sun licked around him, setting her imagination aflame with how sensational he'd look and feel if he were naked in her arms. Right now.

God help her, she wanted to sleep with him again.

"I need to go back. *Now*."

Five

"No problem." Louis moved back inside and closed up his sofa.

Sam stared at him. He was just going to agree and take her back without a fight? Her heart sank a little.

She followed him in. It was almost dark and she felt disoriented. Louis closed her bed and ushered her to the door.

Didn't he want her to stay?

Goose bumps rose on her skin at the thought of leaving the comfortable cedar-scented haven for the dark and murky swamp.

He held the door open. Their arms almost brushed as she passed him and the tiny hairs on her skin stood up as if trying to reach out and touch him.

He latched the door, eased by her on the steps—so close she could feel the heat from his skin—and jumped lightly down into the boat moored off to one side. "Stay there, I'll bring it right under the steps for you."

Sam hesitated. Surely if she stepped down, the boat could rock and she'd lose her footing? Night creatures chattered and chirped in the bayou all around. Louis crouched in the boat, looking at her, his expression unreadable in the deep dusk.

It would all be so easy if she could just take his hand to steady herself while she stepped down.

But she'd made the rules so she had to stick to them. She sucked in a shaky breath. One, two, three, she launched herself forward and managed to land one foot on the wooden floor of the skiff. The other foot, however, caught on the rim of the boat and she lost her balance and stumbled forward.

"Whoa!" Louis caught her in his arms before she could plummet to the hard wood.

Her body collided with his in what felt like slow motion. First, her hands crashed into his chest, then somehow slid under his armpits to grab around his waist.

Louis almost lost his balance, too, as she fell into him on the uneven surface.

Her breasts crushed against hard muscle before she finally came to rest, sprawled over him like a car wrapped around a lamppost.

"Whoops," she murmured. A hot shiver of desire flashed through her at the feel of his hard muscle under her.

Her pelvis rested awkwardly on his. A sudden thickening beneath his zipper aroused feverish memories that made her insides start to throb.

Sam sprang back, her face heating. "I'm so sorry."

"I'm not," he croaked. "I'm just sorry you're on this no-touching kick. Unless this is your way of telling me you didn't really mean it?"

Even in the semi-darkness, she saw a wicked gleam in his eye.

Heat crept through her like fire along a fuse. Her breasts felt heavy, and her skin stung with awareness.

She scrambled backward, her hands pressed to his hard chest and belly as she peeled herself off his strong body with painful regret.

"I meant it."

I wish I didn't, but I did.

"Just think, I might take this DNA test and you'll find out I'm not related to your husband."

Sam blinked. "It's a possibility."

A very attractive one.

He cocked his head. "Then things would be different." His smooth voice caressed her in the near darkness.

"Very different. But for now, let's just get back, okay?"

"Okay."

In less than five minutes, she was clambering out of the boat onto dry land and back into his vintage car. Her legs felt hollow and her chest strangely empty.

Even if he wasn't Tarrant's son, she'd still only been widowed six months. It was far too soon for any kind of…affair.

And hadn't she promised herself she was done with all that stuff? Three husbands were enough for one lifetime. She planned to devote herself to managing Tarrant's charities.

And get a nice cat.

"Buckle in." He slid in beside her. Painful awareness of his body only inches from hers made her fight not to squirm in her seat. He was so healthy and strong and young and…sexy.

Different from Tarrant.

Guilt tightened her gut again. Her love for Tarrant had been based on so much more than mere physical attraction. He was a handsome man, of course, but older and unwell. The appeal was more cerebral. Spiritual, even. She'd wanted to help him.

To save him.

And in a small way she had, at least for a time.

Finding his two long-lost sons had awakened something in him that made him better able to handle his own mortality. He had a sense of the future, a conviction that he'd left behind a legacy more powerful than bricks and mortar and money in the bank.

And Louis could well be a part of that legacy.

"You will take the DNA test, won't you?"

"Of course. I promised I'd take it if you had dinner with me. You held up your part of the bargain, so I wouldn't be a gentleman if I didn't hold up mine." He turned to her and she could see his appealing grin in the light reflected from the headlights.

The sun had disappeared, leaving them shrouded in darkness. A cool breeze whipped her hair as they drove along the winding, lonely road through the bayou country.

"Thank you. I appreciate it." Although it was obvious he wasn't a man used to taking orders, he'd literally obeyed every single one of her stipulations.

An odd feeling snuck through her. She wasn't used to that kind of respect from a man. Much as she'd cared for Tarrant, he made all the rules and everyone else fell into line. A pattern she was familiar—even somewhat comfortable with—from her first two marriages.

But Louis let her call the shots. He didn't feel the need to bully her or exert his manly dominance. Yet he exuded natural self-possession. Effortless confidence.

Which of course was how he had managed to get her out in a boat on a swamp in the dark.

"Why are you laughing?" His rich voice trickled into her ear.

"I'm just trying to figure out how you talked me into this."

"I didn't talk you into anything. You wanted to come. You just weren't aware of it at the time."

"Oh. Is that it?" She chuckled. "I guess you can tell all this because you inherited your grandmother's psychic abilities. What do I want to do next?"

"Well, you want to come back to my home and spend the night in bed, then wake up early and eat beignets and milky coffee on the riverbank with me, but you're not going to."

"I don't even know what a *beignet* is."

"And you're not going to find out, either, since you have no intention of staying over at my house. Which is a shame, because we'll both miss out on another wonderful night together."

The way he said it, soft and wistful, tugged at something deep inside her. "It was a nice night. And so was this. But you do understand, don't you?"

"I respect your wishes." He flashed a glance at her. "And I have a feeling you're not used to that, so I'm hoping it helps my case." A wicked smile flashed across his mouth.

"Your insight into me is a little frightening, truth be told."

He looked out into the distance. "Don't let it worry you. I can see into everyone." He turned to look at her again, and even in the dark she could see the honeyed shimmer of his eyes. "And in you, I like what I see."

Sam rubbed her arms as a strange hot-cold feeling cascaded over her.

Why did it feel so good that this almost-stranger liked her? That he cared enough to chase her, and then to respect her wishes?

Maybe she was just relieved that someone could spend the night with her and still want more.

She fiddled with her ring, not sure how he'd react to her next request. "I'd like to come with you to the lab. Then we can arrange to have the results sent to both of us, if you agree."

"Don't trust me to tell you my secrets?" He smiled, looking out the windshield. "And there I flattered myself thinking you might be starting to trust me."

"I am."

And that's why I need to know the truth.

Shivers of excitement rippled through her at the possibility that he could be no relation at all. That maybe they could…

She fanned her face, suddenly hot. She was getting way ahead of herself.

What if he was Tarrant's son?

How on earth would she explain to Tarrant's daughter, Fiona, that she'd slept with her half brother?

Her insides clenched into a knot at the thought.

Fiona had hated Sam for marrying Tarrant despite being young enough to be his daughter herself. They'd eventually formed an uneasy truce, which had lately warmed into a careful friendship as a result of Sam's persistent efforts.

A revelation like this could be catastrophic.

She wouldn't tell her. She couldn't. Keeping Tarrant's family together was the *most* important thing in her life.

Without them she had no one.

"You can come with me. I won't even put any conditions on it." He glanced at her, and she tried to ignore the heat that flared inside her, despite her fears. "And you can have them send you the results directly. I don't have any secrets."

Sam's stomach tightened. "Will you keep our…encounter a secret? Just for now, until we know?"

Louis frowned at her. "I don't go around bragging about

my personal business. But it doesn't sit right with me to be secretive. We don't have anything to be ashamed of."

The "we" gave her a strange thrill, followed by a rush of shame. Was she so lonely and desperate that she craved even such an unsuitable encounter?

"It's just that…Tarrant's daughter. She wouldn't understand."

"She wouldn't understand that two consenting adults can enjoy each other's company?"

"Not if we're related."

Louis laughed. "It's not like you're my first cousin, sweetheart. I know you New Yorkers hear all kind of stories about us down here in the deep South, but you and I aren't related by blood."

"You know what I mean. It's taken me a long time to get close to her. Please." She hated the pleading tone in her voice.

Louis stared out over the wheel. The headlights created twin yellow flares on the road surface. The hum and flutter of nature was almost deafening in the darkness around them. "I won't say anything."

His gruff tone underlined his reluctance. Sam felt a momentary stab of guilt at making him undermine his principles, but really, who would he tell anyway?

They passed the rest of the drive chatting about music and movies. Careful conversation. Witty, but guarded, like two acquaintances at a party.

Which was what they were. She didn't know him, and he didn't know her. Not after one night. Or even two.

He parked near her hotel. Nervous energy fluttered through her. He opened her door and stood aside with mock deference to her insistence on no touching.

Her body ached at the lack of even conventional contact.

"Good night," she said, her voice shaking. She glanced at the brightly lit entrance of the hotel. They stood in the muted glow of a vintage streetlamp.

"It was a good night. And I think a good-night peck on the cheek would only be polite."

Sam hesitated. Swallowed. Her rules were a bit silly, rude even. And he'd been so understanding and wonderful about it. Surely just a little, tiny, goodbye type of kiss wouldn't be so bad?

Anxiety and excitement snaked through her. He stepped toward her and she instinctively tilted her chin.

An electric sensation zapped through her as her cheek brushed his. *Uh-oh.* Before she could stop, her lips found his.

Hot relief rushed through her when their mouths met and mingled. Her arms found their way around his waist and her fingers buried themselves in his cotton shirt, gripping the sturdy muscle underneath.

Louis's arms closed around her back, soft and reassuring. He kissed her tenderly, with restraint, even as passion snapped and sizzled in the air around them.

Oh, dear.

When they finally parted, disentangling their limbs with agonizing reluctance, her whole body throbbed and tingled with painful arousal.

"I'm not sure that was such a great idea," she rasped.

Louis didn't say anything. He just looked at her, his expression…pained. His arousal was visible even in the dim glow from the streetlight.

She could tell he was thinking, *If it wasn't for your neurotic reluctance, we'd spend the night in each other's arms the way you know we both want to.*

But she couldn't.

"Um. The test. What time is good tomorrow?"

Louis raised an eyebrow, then blew out a hard breath. "Let's get it over with. The earlier the better."

"The lab opens at nine."

"I'll pick you up here."

"Great." She managed a fake smile and practically ran for the bright sanctuary of the hotel lobby. She didn't dare look back. She knew he was standing there, looking after her.

Waiting for her to weaken and run back into his arms.

Her hands trembled as she pulled her key card from her pocket. She stepped into the glittering, polished interior of the elevator and the doors closed, leaving her alone.

Phew. She'd done it. He'd agreed to take the test and she'd managed the entire evening without any inappropriate contact.

Except that kiss.

But really, it was just a kiss. Practically a peck on the cheek.

A sound escaped her mouth. A snort of disbelief. Her whole body still stung with stray energy that snuck over her skin and along her nerves, from her lips to her fingers and toes and everywhere in between.

She stepped out into the silent, carpeted hallway and shivered in the air-conditioning. She fumbled with the key in the lock, but managed to open the door and step into her luxurious suite with its magnificent scrolled bed and five-hundred-count sheets.

Alone.

Oh, Tarrant. Why did you have to die and leave me?

The familiar lament rang through her mind. It hurt so much to go to bed by herself every night, the cold sheets a reminder that she had no one to comfort her. No one to hold her. No one to mutter and sigh over the day's mundane events or admire the silly new lingerie she'd bought just to make him smile.

Louis might do all those things, if she'd let him.

But for how long? A week? A month?

Then he'd be off to Paris or Milan and the busy whirl of his life. Back to all the other women he no doubt charmed and delighted just like her.

She and Louis were the same age and while she'd been married three times, he'd never taken the plunge once. *That should tell you something.*

Even if he wasn't potentially her stepson, there was no possibility of a lasting relationship.

He was exactly what she didn't need. Another opportunity for the papers to fill their pages with humiliating gossip and innuendo.

He was *all wrong*.

But that didn't stop her from clutching the sheets around her and wishing with every ounce of hope she had left that he wasn't Tarrant's son after all.

Morning sunlight sparkled off the sidewalks and windows as Sam and Louis walked the few blocks from the hotel to the lab. She was glad of the excuse to wear large, dark glasses that hid her emotions.

She noticed with a start that they paused to wait for a car to pass at exactly the same spot where she'd seen the sign for *Madame Ayida ~ Palmistry and spiritual consultations.*

The black letters danced in front of her eyes.

"I went to that fortune-teller yesterday." She pointed to the sign. "Madame Ayida. What she told me made me decide to have dinner with you so you'd agree to the test."

"I owe Madame Ayida a debt of gratitude."

"She told me to follow my heart." Sam frowned as she remembered the gravity in the young woman's voice.

"That's good advice. Did your heart tell you to keep your hands off me, or did it tell you to kiss me?"

Both.

Sam brushed away his question with a laugh. "She also said I had to choose between two roads, one familiar and one strange, and that the choice would determine the rest of my life."

Louis looked at her. Sunlight glittered in his honey-gold eyes and the force of his gaze made her belly quiver.

She bit her lip. "Do you think fate is determined in advance by forces we can't control or do you think we create our own destiny?"

"Definitely the latter. Every decision you make shapes your life."

"Sometimes I feel like I'm on a roller coaster and the best I can do is hang on. Every plan I make gets derailed." She sighed. "I used to think I just made the wrong choices in the first place, but since Tarrant died, I don't feel in control at all. I feel I could have saved him, somehow. That I should have."

He frowned. "I guess you're right that we have no control over some things. I don't have any control over who my father is."

"Or isn't."

Louis had a strange expression in his eyes. "I have a funny feeling the tests are going to tell you what you want to hear."

Sam froze. He assumed that she wanted to find out he was the missing heir she sought.

But he was wrong.

"You never know. You don't look all that much like him."

"I take after my mother."

"You do. I've seen her album covers. She's very beautiful." The dark, exotic beauty fit the mold of so many of Tarrant's former lovers. Sam felt a bit pale and colorless by comparison.

Or maybe just jealous.

Tarrant had played Bijou DuLac's albums quite often, and they'd even gone to see her in concert at Carnegie Hall once—before Sam knew she was likely the mother of one of his children.

A joy Sam would never personally experience.

The familiar hollow emptiness inside her opened up like a sudden chasm. Sam kept her eyes dead ahead, hoping Louis wouldn't look at her until she got her emotions under control.

"My mom would throw an opera-diva-style tantrum if she knew I was about to take this test."

"She wouldn't want you to know who your father is?"

"She'd see it as irrelevant. She can't stand looking at the past, or even toward the future. She's big on living in the present. Enjoy each day as you meet it head-on, all the ones behind you are irrelevant, and the ones ahead are an adventure you'll greet when you come to it."

"I get the sense you share her philosophy."

"I do. And I've had a pretty damn good life so far, so it's working for me."

Sam's skin prickled as they walked past Madame Ayida's storefront. "How do you feel about finding out who your father is?"

"I guess it's an adventure I'll greet when I come to it." He flashed her a mischievous grin.

They both grew quiet when they reached the door of the lab. A smiling redheaded nurse bustled out to the reception desk to greet them. Sam explained that they needed to collect Louis's DNA and have the results sent to both of them. She didn't bother to explain they'd then be compared to Tarrant's data at the company labs in New York.

She nodded sympathetically. "Of course." She looked at

Louis. "And if the results prove you're the father, you be sure to make your payments on time, unlike my louse of an ex-husband." She turned to wink at Sam.

Sam cringed. "Oh, it's not like that at all."

The redhead shuffled through some papers. "You think he's the father of your child, right? That's why you need the results, too."

"No. We think he's my husband's son."

The nurse glanced up, and squinted at Louis. Then back at Sam, who felt heat rising to her face.

Louis looked totally unruffled. If anything, she saw a gleam of humor in his eye.

Why did she feel the need to explain? "It's complicated."

"I'll bet."

Sam waited in the lobby while Louis went into the back to have his cheek swabbed for cells. The nurse's unprofessional behavior left her rattled. Why did people have to butt into someone else's personal business?

She could just imagine the newspaper headlines if this little story got out.

Louis emerged with a guarded expression on his face, and they didn't talk at all until they were back out on the street.

"I have to go catch a plane," she said quietly to forestall any suggestions he might tempt her with.

Or maybe she was flattering herself that he'd try.

"I'm flying to Paris myself. Big party at my restaurant there tonight. A lot of my oldest friends will be there."

Sam tried to ignore a twinge of jealousy. "Sounds like fun. I hope you have a wonderful time."

He looked at her, golden eyes shining with wary appreciation. "Thank you. I'll call you and we can talk when the results come in."

"Sounds good."

There was no suggestion of even the faintest peck on the cheek. No doubt Louis was also aware that any contact between them might explode into a conflagration neither of them could handle right now.

Sam managed a cheery wave that later seemed forced and phony, but it was the best she could do. Then she hurried away down the sidewalk, heart pounding, wondering if she'd ever see Louis again.

Six

Sam knew the results were due today, so she deliberately lingered in bed, away from the prying eyes of the household. Still, she gulped when her phone rang. Her hand shook as she reached for it and flipped it open.

"Sam, guess what?" Bella's cheery voice sent her pulse into overdrive. Bella ran the Hardcastle lab and was personally overseeing the DNA-test analysis.

"What?" she croaked.

"It's a match! Isn't that great? You found another of Tarrant's sons."

"Oh, fantastic." Her voice seemed to echo in a hollow cavern. "Are you sure?"

She'd almost convinced herself Louis wasn't related. That he was just another one of the billions of people walking the face of the earth who had no relationship with Tarrant Hardcastle.

That he could be simply…hers.

"The results are incontrovertible. Nearly a hundred percent. Which is hardly surprising considering that Louis DuLac is a successful restaurant entrepreneur. Isn't it funny that all three of Tarrant's sons are movers and shakers in the same field? Dominic in food retail, Amado in the wine business and now Louis with an international chain of restaurants. I guess it proves the apple doesn't fall far from the tree, even if the tree wasn't actively involved in its development."

"Yeah. Strange." Sam swallowed. Her heart bumped painfully against her ribs. "Well, that is great news." She tried to inject enthusiasm into her voice, which only made it waver.

It was over. All over.

Well, the self-indulgent stage of their relationship was. No more flirtatious glances or kisses or passionate embraces. The next stage, where she was his cheerful but sexless stepmother—that was just beginning.

She slid a little deeper under the covers. "I'll call and tell him myself."

"May I speak to Louis DuLac, please?"

Pleasure flooded Louis's body at the sound of Sam's voice. Her formal tones brought a smile to his lips.

"Speaking." He sat in his restaurant, going over some orders before the early-lunchtime crowd started to arrive. The ceiling fan wafted air over his skin, which heated at the memory of Sam's sparkling blue eyes and lithe body.

"Great. It's Samantha." Again the clipped voice. As if they were business acquaintances. Like he'd never held her in his arms and made love to her all night long.

"I know. Hi, Sam." He let a hint of flirtation slide into his voice.

"You're Tarrant's son. I just heard the results of the analysis. There's no doubt at all, you're definitely his." The barrage of words ended abruptly.

No words came to his tongue. *Tarrant's son.*

He had a father.

He blew out a snort. Of course he had a father; everyone did. Hard to be born without one. Still. A real person, who probably shared traits with him that he'd never even noticed in himself.

"Are you there?" Sam's voice jerked him out of the strange rush of thoughts.

"Sure, I'm here. It's taking a while to sink in."

"Isn't it wonderful?" Her voice rang with false cheer.

"Yeah, I guess so." She'd wanted so badly for him to be the son she sought. Or did she? Now that they'd been intimate, everything was complicated.

"I'm thrilled." Her voice reached such a high note that it actually cracked. "It's just what I was hoping for. You must come to New York as soon as possible. Your brother Dominic is anxious to meet you, and so is your sister, Fiona. Amado told me he can fly up from Argentina anytime."

"I have two brothers and a sister?" He couldn't keep the excitement out of his voice. She'd mentioned Tarrant's other children before, but they hadn't seemed real until now. A thick rush of emotion flooded his body and made his skin prickle.

Since the loss of his grandparents, he's felt painfully alone sometimes. His mom was…well, she was a law unto herself, and woe betide anyone who tried to count on her for anything other than a spectacular stage performance. His grandma and granddad had been the people he'd turned to for love and support, until suddenly they were gone—dead within weeks of each other.

Adrenaline and excitement pulsed inside him at the prospect of meeting the siblings he never knew he had. "I can't wait to meet them. Truly. Where do I show up? Just tell me when. I'm coming."

"Oh, Louis. I'm so happy. Really, I am." He heard tears in her voice. "Tarrant would be so pleased. It's such a shame you'll never meet him."

"I have a feeling I'll get to know him anyway."

I've already slept with his wife. Regret, mingled with stray longing, stuck in his craw.

There was a pause. "Um, I hate to ask this, but, ah…"

"Will I keep my hands off you?"

"Exactly." The relief in her voice pricked his balloon of enthusiasm a little.

Gain two brothers and a sister…lose a lover.

Not that Samantha had ever been his to lose in any real sense. *His stepmother.* "I'll be the very soul of discretion."

"Sam relax. Why are you so jumpy?" Dominic looked up from the large desk where he was signing some kind of contract. "It's fantastic that you found another one of our brothers."

Sam gulped and glanced around Dominic's spacious office at Hardcastle Enterprises. What on earth would she say if he knew she'd also *slept* with Louis? Tarrant's first son was highly principled, to the point where he'd at first rejected his father out of hand, disgusted by the man who'd abandoned his mother and neglected his responsibilities.

"What time's he coming?" Amado had flown up from Argentina to meet his new brother, and was clearly excited.

"He'll be here any minute," she said, trying to keep the tremor out of her voice.

Dominic surprised her by crossing the room to take her in his arms for a hug. Though standoffish and reluctant to join either the family or the corporation at first, to her great pride and happiness, he'd become their enthusiastic leader. "Sam, you do realize that none of us would be here without you. You're a miracle."

She laughed off his compliment. "Don't be silly. It was all Tarrant's idea."

"You can say that all you like. We know better."

"You're the mother of all of us, Sam," said Amado, while crunching a crudité. "Whether you like it or not." His mischievous grin revealed how happy he was to be here, though at first, he'd refused to even meet his famous father.

Sam blanched. Of course he had no idea how deep his well-meant comment cut her. "Oh, don't be silly." She waved her hand in the air. "I'm more like your sister."

Not that being Louis's sister even by marriage made sleeping with him any more excusable.

"In age, yes, but in wisdom and caring? No. You're our mom." Amado wrapped his arm affectionately around her shoulders and squeezed.

Warmth flooded Sam and made tears well in her eyes. Honestly, she did feel maternal affection for these strong and capable young men.

So how had things gone so horribly wrong with Louis?

Her feelings for him were anything but maternal.

Sam almost jumped out of her skin as the door to Dominic's office opened. Fiona, Tarrant's daughter from his second marriage, marched in. "Louis DuLac has arrived in reception. He's on his way up."

"Oh, goodness." Sam's hand flew to her chest. "That's great. Wonderful." She smiled at Fiona, but the pretty redhead was fiddling with the buttons on her new lavender iPod device. Probably pretending she didn't care one way or another that yet another sibling had shown up to displace her from her former position as Tarrant's only child.

Sam felt for her. She'd managed to become close to the prickly young woman, and didn't want anything to damage their delicate relationship. Yet another reason her accidental liaison with Louis had to remain secret.

She glanced around the bright, comfortable office. Dominic and Amado stood, expectant grins on their faces.

Their wives, Bella and Susannah, were at this very moment helping Fiona hastily arrange the details for a celebration party tonight.

How would Sam react when she saw Louis? His face had haunted her in dreams. Worse yet, so had the touch of his hands and the press of his hard body against hers.

Would she be able to keep her emotions and physical reactions under control when he arrived, or would the bright flush of her face or a sudden tightening of her nipples give her away?

She checked the buttons of her thick Chanel suit. At least no one would see the nipples.

The door flung open again and Sam tried not to topple off her heels. Melissa, Dominic's admin, peered around it. "He's here!" Her smile radiated the joy everyone in the company seemed to feel about the exciting news that Sam had found a new family member.

She should be happiest of all, since it was her avowed mission in life to gather Tarrant's scattered children.

So why did she feel dread trickling through her veins?

Louis appeared in the doorway and his eyes locked instantly onto hers.

"Welcome!" she stammered. "Louis, this is your brother Dominic."

Dominic strode forward and shook his hand, then broke the

tension by pulling Louis into a hug. "We're so glad Sam found you."

"Yeah, me, too." Louis glanced up at Sam with those familiar honey-gold eyes.

Anxiety pooled in her belly, along with the unwelcome thickening of arousal. "And this is your brother Amado. He flew overnight from Argentina to be here when you arrived."

Amado clasped Louis's hand in both of his and shook it forcefully. "I know you probably feel strange right now meeting a crowd of relatives you didn't know you had." His English was accented, but flawless. "Trust me, you get used to it."

"To be honest, it doesn't feel strange at all." Louis looked from Amado to Dominic. "Sam was so convinced I'd be Tarrant's son, that when the DNA test results came back, I wasn't the least bit surprised."

Sam swallowed hard. "Goodness, look at the three of you together." Tarrant's three sons were all so tall and handsome. With their dark hair and olive complexions, they actually looked more like each other than any of them resembled Tarrant. But there was no denying they all had the air of commanding authority that had struck her so strongly when she first met her husband.

Emotion swelled in her chest. "What a wonderful sight. If only Tarrant was here to enjoy it."

Dominic stepped toward her and wrapped his big arm around her shoulders. Probably because he knew too well that memories of Tarrant easily reduced her to a blubbering wreck.

She grabbed his strong hand, sucked in a breath and tried to pull herself together.

I can do this. Her role here was to honor Tarrant's memory as she gathered his family together. She could forget about Louis as a man, and think of him purely as her...son.

Couldn't she?

She sought his face, hoping to reassure herself. But when his eyes locked onto hers, energy flashed between them with defibrillator intensity.

Uh-oh.

"This is the lab." Bella, the head of technical research at Hardcastle Enterprises, beckoned Louis and the others into the bright space, with its gleaming instruments and rows of computers. He'd been in the building for less than an hour, but already Louis thought it was the most outrageous place he'd ever seen.

"When I first showed up, Bella called Security to get me thrown out," Dominic said with a grin.

"And now you guys are married?" Louis was still trying to wrap his mind around the relationships between the dynamic and intriguing people who were now his family.

"It's a long story," said Bella with a wink. "But the path of true love never did run smooth, isn't that what they say?"

"That's what they say." Louis glanced behind him, hoping to see Sam.

Amado and his wife, Susannah, were there, arms looped around each other's waists, but there was no sign of Sam. She'd slipped away as they'd left Dominic's office, murmuring something about caterers for the party that night.

Since the moment he'd shown up, he'd wanted to take her in his arms. But every time he looked at her, something in her gaze warned him to keep his distance.

"How did you react when Sam first found you?" Fiona picked a clear glass container off one of the polished counters and swirled an imaginary liquid. "Was it a big shock?"

In more ways than you know.

"She'd sent me letters telling me about Tarrant, but I'd ignored them. I guess I wasn't ready. But you can't ignore Sam in person." A grin spread across his mouth.

"Dad sure couldn't." Fiona winked at him. "But I can't complain. As wicked stepmothers go, she's a pretty nice one. How does it feel to have a new, instant stepmom?"

Something in Louis's chest tightened. "I can't think of her that way. She's too young."

Fiona laughed. "That's what they said when she married Dad." She set the glass container down on the counter with a thunk. "But everything's a little different around the Hardcastles, in case you hadn't figured that out already."

Louis could see that Fiona didn't set out to make life easy for Sam. It touched him that Sam was so concerned about building a relationship with the outspoken redhead. *His sister.* Fiona had been Tarrant's only child until recently, and the adjustment must be hard for her. Louis fought the urge to take her in his arms and give her a hug. "Hey, Fiona, how do you feel about suddenly having all these big brothers?"

A wry smile slid across her face. "I always heard that big brothers are great for hooking you up with hot guys. I'm still waiting."

They all laughed. Louis glanced at his brothers, Dominic and Amado. The resemblance between them was striking, unmistakable. There was no doubt they were flesh of the same flesh. Something hot and hard welled up inside him, and emotion threatened to get the better of him.

Brothers.

As a kid he'd sometimes longed for siblings. Someone to share life's dramas and joys with. Suddenly they'd appeared in his life overnight.

"Come on, guys, we've got a lot more to see." Dominic

clapped a hand on Louis's back. "I'm sure Susannah wants to show you the wine cellars she's so painstakingly stocked with the best wine in the world, including her husband's."

"Is that how you two met?" Louis knew that Amado and Susannah were recently married. Romance was apparently thick in the air at Hardcastle Enterprises.

"Susannah came to my estancia in Argentina bearing the news that I might be Tarrant Hardcastle's son."

"Which came as a big shock to him." Susannah shot him a mischievous glance. "Since Amado had been raised to believe his grandparents were his parents. He had no idea his long-dead sister was actually his mother."

"I wasn't all that happy about it, either." Amado gave Louis a wry look. "But Susannah showed me that sometimes having your life turned upside down can be a good thing."

"I agree." Louis looked around at his new family, affection—love—swelling in his heart. "I'm still feeling a little upside down right now. But it's a real good feeling."

Music throbbed over the high-tech sound system and bodies gyrated on the round dance floor cleared in the center of the circular space.

"Fiona," Louis grabbed Fiona as she whirled past him. "Have you seen Sam?"

The pretty redhead glanced around the crowded restaurant.

The party at The Moon, on the top floor of Hardcastle Enterprises' Fifth Avenue headquarters, was supposed to be an intimate gathering of family and close friends. Somehow it had turned into the event of the year, with people jetting in from all over to join the festivities.

Louis wasn't complaining. He loved a good party. Didn't mind being the guest of honor and center of attention, either.

But he was beginning to worry Sam had snuck off to avoid him.

No kiss hello. Not even a polite handshake. Now, wasn't that downright rude?

"I saw her about half an hour ago, fussing over some crusty old friend of Tarrant's who showed up. She's here somewhere, though. She'd never leave a family party."

True. Sam was not the kind of hostess who'd abandon her guests.

Even if she was trying very hard to avoid one of them.

A flash of fine blond hair caught his eye on the far side of the room. Louis excused himself and dived through the elegant crowd. She was chatting with an older woman, and he kept his eyes locked onto her slender back, zipped into a fitted black dress, until he was so close he could smell her expensive scent.

"Sam." He laid his hand on her arm.

She spun around. "Hi, Louis." Her cheery tone was undermined by the panic in her eyes. "Are you enjoying the party?"

"I'm having a wonderful time. There's just one thing missing."

She licked her lips, nervous. "What?"

He leaned in and whispered in her ear. "You."

"I'm sorry, I've been very busy with all the guests." She excused herself from her conversation and the older woman smiled and disappeared into the crowd.

Louis cocked his head. "I'm a guest."

"I asked Dom and Amado to take care of you."

"They did, but now they're both dancing with their wives." He indicated the dance floor with a nod of his head. Dominic swayed to the music, his hands resting on Bella's shapely hips, and Susannah and Amado were locked in a romantic embrace.

"I see what you mean."

"And I don't have a dance partner."

Sam's eyes widened. "I can't… Many of these people are Tarrant's personal friends."

"I'm not asking you to strip naked with me here. Just a friendly dance, that's all."

She stared at him, frozen. Her eyes fell to where his hand still held her slender arm in its firm but gentle grip. "I guess one dance wouldn't hurt."

"You won't even feel a pinch."

A smile crept across his mouth. Without asking, he slid his arm through hers and guided her onto the dance floor.

An inventive DJ was mixing old-school house beats and North African folk music into a pulsing and sultry brew. Dancers swayed and writhed in a fog of sensual heat.

When they reached the center of the crowd, Louis leaned in until his lips almost brushed Sam's ear. "Can you blame me for being hurt that you tracked me down, roped me into a new family, then abandoned me?"

"I'm sure you understand." She started to sway stiffly to the music, standing a good foot away from him.

She looked so nervous and tight. Breathing in shallow gulps and barely able to look at him.

His muscles ached with the desire to take her in his arms. That's what she needed. What they both needed.

But he could see her point. "I do understand. The family you've created here is beautiful. It's powerful, and I can see how you'd do anything to protect it."

She bit her lip again and her eyes welled with tears. "Thank you. It does mean so much to me that you're part of it."

"Me, too." He was surprised by how much emotion he felt meeting his half brothers and half sister. He'd spent the day with them and already felt closer to them than some people he'd known for years. "I feel blessed to have met all of you, no matter how it happened."

Sam's lovely face brightened with a smile that lit the room like rays of sun. Or maybe like the rays of moonlight pouring through the circular skylight open to the stars above.

Then her smile wobbled. "I just wish things had started out differently."

"Maybe you should take the fatalistic approach—that things happen the way they do for a reason."

She frowned, thoughtful. Her body moved more naturally to the music as she got lost in her thoughts, and he tried to keep his eyes from wandering to her breasts or her hips.

"Do you really believe that?"

He sucked in a breath. She deserved his honesty. "Nope. To tell you the truth I think things just happen and you have to deal with them the best you can. I can't think of one single good reason for the city I love to be ravaged by a hurricane." He shrugged. "On the other hand, if it hadn't happened, I'd still be living in Paris."

"You moved back after Katrina?"

"Yes. At first I came to help my grandparents. They were elderly, and the disaster took a big toll on both their health and spirits. Their house had pretty minimal damage since the Quarter stayed dry, so they invited friends to come live with them. I helped sort out meals and beds and all that stuff, and then I got sucked into the magic of the place and its people."

Her blue gaze fixed on his, inviting and encouraging.

"I bought some beautiful old buildings and fixed them up to create new homes for people who'd lost theirs. When things settled down, I helped my granddad rebuild his old boathouse and fishing cabin. By then I knew New Orleans was my home now, not Paris."

Sam had edged closer, probably to hear him over the steady throb of the music. "We read that you've done a lot to help the rebuilding effort."

He frowned. "It feels strange that you guys were researching me when I didn't even know you existed."

She leaned in and he could sense the heat of her skin. "We read about the houses you renovated and the restaurants and bars you opened to create jobs. All that only made us more anxious to meet you. It hurt when you didn't respond to our calls or letters."

A prick of guilt stuck him. He'd dismissed the letters as time-wasting foolishness.

Or had he?

Maybe he'd been afraid of what they might mean.

"I was busy, but perhaps the real reason I didn't respond is that I lost my grandparents last year. They died within a month of each other, and I guess I didn't want to hear or think about any other family right then."

"I'm sorry."

The compassion in her eyes made emotion gather in his chest. "I'm glad I got the opportunity to spend time with them before they passed. That's another blessing that came out of a nightmare."

Dancing had warmed Sam's skin, releasing her scent into the air around them. Her closeness was a delicious torment. All this talk about what he'd lost only made him want to cleave closer to what he'd found.

"You know how it feels to lose someone close."

She looked up. "Like you've lost a part of your own body. It hurts."

"And from what I can see, we both have the same strategy for dealing with the pain. Keep busy."

Sam laughed. A sound that made his heart beat faster. "You're right. I've been like a windup toy since Tarrant died. I try to keep moving every minute of the day."

"You're afraid that if you stop you might fall apart."

Her eyes widened. "Exactly." Then she frowned. "And I don't want to fall apart. I've had enough drama and crisis in my life over the last decade. I'd rather lift my chin up and keep dancing. Does that sound crazy?"

Sympathy swelled in his heart. "Not at all. It sounds brave."

Her strength of spirit moved him, and the desire to take her in his arms became a steady ache, throbbing in time to the lilting and sensual music that filled the air around them.

"We're a lot alike, you and I, Sam," he whispered into her ear, leaning close. "I think we're both most comfortable in a crowd, surrounded by laughter and chatter and people having a good time. Or even people pretending to have a good time."

She looked up at him, blue eyes sparkling. "We're people people."

He chuckled. "Yes. And sometimes it's easier for us to spend our time greasing the social wheels so we don't have to think about what we truly want."

Emotion flickered in the depths of her eyes. She bit her lip.

He inched toward her, enjoying the heat of her skin through her stiff black dress. "Or about what we *need*."

He'd had enough of her no-touching routine. Right now he needed to hold her more than he'd ever needed anything. "Come with me."

He grasped her hand and she didn't fight him. Slowly, without betraying the urgency he felt, he led her through the crowd of gyrating bodies and toward the exit.

She didn't protest as he led her past the uniformed waiters

handing parting gifts to the guests. Or even when he ushered her into a waiting elevator.

The doors closed leaving them alone for the first time since his arrival in New York. His lips and hands fought the urge to take hold of her and kiss some sense into her.

A glance up at the ubiquitous security camera restrained him.

Sam looked at him, nervous and expectant, as they stepped out into the silent lobby. She muttered a nervous goodbye to the security guard at the desk.

Outside the elegant Hardcastle building that took up most of a Fifth Avenue block, lamplight created pools of golden light in the darkness. "We'll go to my hotel," he murmured, shielding his voice from the scattered passersby. "It's only two blocks away."

Sam didn't protest. She kept stride with him in the warm fall air. "I wonder what they'll say when they realize I've gone."

"I hate to say it, but they're probably all having too much fun to notice."

Her pained expression made him regret his words.

She looked away. "You're right, of course. I sometimes get an exaggerated sense of my own importance. I forget everyone else has a full life of their own to occupy their time." Her voice shook and he felt her hand cool in his.

Louis stopped walking, spun in front of her and took both her hands. "You are important. You're the reason we're all here tonight. Your energy and vision and heart made it happen. And you're important to me." He said the words with force. He felt so much more than he could put into mere words.

As her delicate pink mouth quivered, no doubt preparing a rebuttal, he leaned in and kissed her.

Her lips parted and welcomed his mouth to hers. His arms instinctively slid around her waist and he held her against him, kissing her with all the painful longing he'd stored up over the past days and nights.

A shudder rippled through her, the force of her relief so strong he could feel it like an electric jolt. She was every bit as hungry and desperate for this kiss as he was.

Finally the synapses of his brain started firing again and he managed to pull back. Sam blinked like an animal startled out of its burrow. Her mouth opened to speak, but no words came out.

"We'd better keep walking." He slid his arm through hers. "We're nearly there."

Sam put on dark glasses when they approached the entrance to the elegant hotel.

"Shades at night?" Louis couldn't resist teasing. "Worried the lobby lights will be too bright?"

"I could run into someone I know."

"So? We're not doing anything criminal."

She glanced at him. The wide, black lenses hid her eyes, but the muscles in her jaw were rigid. "Maybe not criminal, but…*scandalous*." The final word came out as a whisper.

Truth be told, it shot a bolt of lust right through him. Apparently the scandal thing just didn't get under his skin the way it did with Sam.

But he respected her wish for privacy.

He guided her across the shimmering marble floor of the hotel lobby, enjoying the elegant sashay of her tight behind as she walked in front of him. The prospect of seeing her naked in his bed again made his skin hum with excitement.

She stood in the back of the elevator, dark glasses still covering her beautiful eyes, while the doors closed.

"I think the sunglasses make you look like you have something to hide."

"I do."

"At least you can't hide it from me." Again, only the security camera made him keep his hands off her luscious body, pressed so enticingly against the marble wall of the elevator.

His fingers stung with anticipation as he unlocked the door and ushered her in. He'd ordered champagne and caviar at the front desk and it was already being delivered when he and Sam arrived at the room. He tipped the waiter and ushered Sam inside.

Heat flared through him as the door closed behind him with a click.

"I do hate eating caviar off dry saltines. A beautiful woman's naked body is so much more *sympathique.*"

"You're wicked." She lowered the glasses to reveal a mischievous gleam in her own eyes.

"With my wild upbringing, how could I not be? Take pity on me anyway." He cocked his head and allowed a grin to slip across his mouth.

"Apparently I can't help myself."

Somehow they'd already drifted together and his hands found their way to her hips. Her dress was black and structured, and hid the soft curves of her body under taut seams and crisp peaks of fabric. "We need to get this off."

His voice came out a little huskier than he intended, but his request had the desired effect. Sam nodded and started to struggle with a zipper buried in a side seam.

Louis's arousal thickened as he tugged the zipper pull along the hourglass curve of her waist and snuck a fingerful of silky skin on his way down.

Sam wriggled under his touch and a soft moan escaped her

mouth. Together they struggled with the stiff silk, tugging it down over her pert breasts, past her slim hips and over her sweet, tight ass.

"Much better," he breathed, when she stepped out of it. Now she wore nothing but a skimpy black lace bra and panties.

She blushed. "I hate panty hose in summer."

"Me, too. All that nylon makes my legs itch."

Sam giggled. Her eyes zeroed in on his crotch, which hardened when she reached for the button on his pants and boldly unfastened it.

With careful concentration, she unzipped and pushed the fabric down over his thighs and calves. "I'm going to have to take my shoes off," he said, as the touch of her soft fingers on his skin almost deprived him of rational thought.

"Oh, yeah. Let me unlace them."

The view from above, as she crouched to unlace his shoes, was magnificent. Her delicate panties only had a slim string in the back, revealing her well-exercised backside in all its taut perfection.

Sam turned her attention to the buttons of his shirt, pressing her thighs to his as she unbuttoned them. Louis grew as hard as the bedrock under Manhattan.

He couldn't keep his hands off her. Her slender body was an enticing combination of soft curves and strong muscle. His fingers roamed over her smooth, warm skin, reveling in all the sensations he'd missed during their agonizing evening of no touching.

Sam's fingers shook as she struggled with the buttons. Her breath came in unsteady gasps. Her urgency was palpable.

Which gave him a wicked idea.

"You know, Sam," he murmured, watching her fingers undo the last button and push the shirt back over his shoulders.

"What?" She didn't look up from her task. Apparently she was too engrossed in pushing the rumpled broadcloth down over his arms.

"I think maybe you were right."

"Right about what?" She fumbled with one of the cuffs, which was buttoned.

"Maybe we shouldn't touch each other."

Now she looked up. Her blue eyes narrowed. "You're kidding."

The shirt, hung up on that last button, came free and fell to the floor, leaving him dressed only in a pair of boxers that did absolutely nothing to hide his intense arousal.

The look of sudden desperation on her face almost made him reconsider.

But not quite.

She'd put him through the hell of keeping his hands off her, when he wanted nothing more than to take her in his arms and hold her.

Let's see how she liked it when the tables were turned.

"I obeyed your rules when you decided we shouldn't touch." He cocked his head. "Now I think it's only fair that you obey mine. Don't you agree?"

She licked her lips. Her nipples had tightened to rosy peaks beneath her transparent bra and her belly trembled visibly with arousal.

"Why?" she rasped.

"For fun." He let a naughty grin slide across his mouth. "Go lie on the bed."

It was a command, not a question.

She peered at him for a second, then crossed the room with elegant strides. He couldn't peel his eyes off the delicious view of her backside in its provocative underwear.

Mrs. Hardcastle clearly had a wild streak that she kept very firmly under designer wraps.

He was going to make it growl.

She eased onto the bed on her stomach, all lithe tan curves and thinly veiled enthusiasm.

"I don't know if I can trust you," he said, standing over her so that the light cast his shadow on her skin.

He wasn't sure he could trust himself, either. But it would be fun trying.

"I'll be good." She blinked innocently.

"If you're not, then do I have the right to take appropriate corrective measures?"

She peered at him, mischief sparkling in her eyes. "Of course."

"Excellent. I can see we understand each other." He walked to the table where the champagne sat cooling in a silver ice bucket. He poured a single flute.

He walked back to the bed, carrying it between his thumb and forefinger. "Since we're avoiding touch, we'll explore the other senses. First, taste."

He held out the glass. "I want you to take a sip." She reached for it. "Don't swallow any of it. Just take the champagne into your mouth and enjoy the taste of it. Then, you'll pass it to me."

"Without touching?" She looked doubtful.

"Not even a tiny brush of skin."

Wary blue eyes on him, she rose onto her knees and took the glass—avoiding his fingers with care—and took a sip. He watched her face as the bubbles tickled over her tongue.

Louis climbed on the bed, careful to keep a few inches between them, which was a challenge given the movement of the mattress.

He lay on his back and maneuvered his head between her parted legs. The scent of her silky skin wrapped around him.

Just who was he trying to torment, here?

Sam leaned forward, a cautious smile on her face, her cheeks slightly swollen with champagne. She poised her mouth about an inch over his—which nearly killed him—and he opened his mouth so that she could drip the champagne into it.

Warm and sweet from her mouth, the sparkling liquid felt like a taste of heaven on Louis's parched tongue. Only one drop spilled and rolled over his chin.

He swallowed and licked his lips. "Thanks."

Sam grinned. He saw her glance down at his shorts, where his intense arousal must be very evident.

"Name another sense."

"Um," she bit her luscious pink lip. "How about hearing?" She narrowed her eyes, apparently doubtful that he could manage it.

"Excellent choice. You're going to listen to my heart rate while I tell you some of the things I could be doing to you right now."

Her eyes widened.

"Lie on your side." He waited for her to shift to one side of the bed, then he positioned himself alongside her, so his chest was level with her head. "Come close," he whispered. "But remember, touching has its consequences, so be careful."

She edged toward him, bracing herself on the soft mattress with manicured fingertips, wary as a hunter. She paused an inch or two from his chest, tucking her silky hair behind her ear. A diamond glittered in her soft, pink lobe and he fought a sudden urge to forget this stupid game and just kiss her.

"Oh, my gosh," she exclaimed. "I can hear your heartbeat and it just sped up!"

Louis grunted. This whole stunt might reveal too much about him to a woman who obviously had way too much power over him. He was pretty on edge after all the emotion of the day and the excitement of meeting his new siblings.

"Go on, do tell. I want to know what revs your engine." Sam grinned, clearly relishing his disadvantage.

"You do," he growled.

"So I see. And I want to hear exactly what you'd like to do to me." Her blue gaze challenged him to lie to her.

Louis stretched a little, causing her to pull back a bit or risk touching him with her cheek. "First, I'd like to trace my tongue all the way from your glittering earlobe, down your sensitive neck, to your nipples."

"Oh, yeah, faster still."

Her grin irked him. "I'd like to undo your bra with my teeth." She raised a brow. "This one has a tricky hook."

"I have talented teeth."

"Ooh." Her dimple grew deeper. "Then what?"

"I'd like to lick your nipples until they grow hard."

"Won't take long."

"Then trail my tongue over your belly and down past your waist, until I reach the top of your thighs…"

"Your pulse is thumping."

"I'll bet." Louis could barely think. His blood had departed his brain for lower regions, which throbbed painfully. "And then…all right, enough of this one." He rolled off the bed, away from her.

Whose dumb idea was this?

Sam's eyes shone. "Which sense is next?"

She was enjoying this far too much. She was supposed to be the one suffering.

"How about smell?" she continued. She'd flipped onto her back and lay supine, arms behind her head, giving him a dangerously enticing view of her gorgeous body. "I'd like to smell you. All over."

Louis gave her a funny look. "I don't know if that's a good idea. It's been a long day."

"All the better. Come on. It's not fair for you to have all the fun."

"All right, knock yourself out." Louis eased himself back onto the soft covers. At the very least, this should diminish his agonizing arousal.

At least that's what he thought until Sam climbed over him.

"Hey, wait, your hair's touching me." The fine strands brushed his chest like butterfly wings, making his skin twitch.

"Doesn't count." Sam leaned closer. Her hair brushed higher as her nose sought out his neck, then his cheek.

Worse than the silky fall on his chest was the fact that he could smell *her*. The familiar French scent blended exquisitely with her own delicately erotic, feminine fragrance. The result was magic, like a thousand-dollar bottle of wine, the perfect freshly dug truffle or the finest handmade Swiss chocolate.

Did her husband choose that scent for her?

His *father?*

His muscles knotted and he jerked up. Their cheeks clashed and his chest collided with hers.

"What?" She sprang back.

"Enough," he growled. "This is killing me."

"It was your idea."

"I'm an idiot."

She shot him a sympathetic look, but excitement danced

in her eyes. "But you still have to pay the consequences, so it's only fair if you tell me what you were going to do to me if I touched you."

Oh, yes. He'd been right about that wild streak. Desire flashed through him. He'd unleashed the real Sam, the energetic and creative person who'd kept quiet and played nice all those years.

She excited him more than any woman he'd ever met, and his desire for her stung his veins and drove him half mad.

To complicate matters, they were already "family"—in the most unconventional way—so there was no disappearing over the horizon when the party ended.

But he didn't care. They were on this adventure together and he intended to strap in and enjoy the ride, wherever it took them.

Even if it meant letting her tie him up.

Seven

Sam laughed at the look on his face. Cocky and apprehensive. She wouldn't have thought those two could go together.

But she'd never met a man like Louis before.

"Go on, spill." She leaned in, giving him a view of her cleavage that attracted his eyes like a hypnotist's pendulum. "What should I do with you?"

She probably should be surprised by the flirty tone in her voice, or by the way she kept edging closer just to torment him, but for reasons she couldn't explain she felt totally... *comfortable.*

"Well." He licked his lip, which caused a pleasurable throb between her legs. "I had intended to tie you—very gently—to the bedpost so I could have my wicked way with you."

A rakish smile crossed his mouth.

"Ooh. Sounds like fun. I'm sorry I'll miss out." She pressed a finger thoughtfully to her lip. "Now, what shall I tie you with?"

"Your bra." He seemed to be struggling to tug his eyes away from it. In fact, his obvious appreciation for her entire body was more arousing than she could have imagined.

Under his gaze she felt powerfully female and desirable, maybe for the first time in her whole life. "What was that you said about your talented teeth?"

He raised a dark brow. "Is this some kind of dare?"

"Absolutely." She thrust her breasts under his chin. His obvious pleasure in her action only encouraged her to wriggle a little under his gaze. "I'm waiting."

"I don't think I can do it without touching," he rasped, eyes still riveted on her breasts.

"Touching is okay, just no hands."

Her skin craved his touch with an intensity that made her body sparkle with anticipation.

Louis eyed the clasp in front of her bra like a jewel thief studying a challenging safe combination.

Sam managed not to squirm as his face lowered between her breasts and he closed his mouth over the clasp of her bra. His lips brushed her skin and sheer pleasure shivered through her. Her nipples hummed at his nearness, and in anticipation of being freed from their lacy cage.

In about three seconds, Louis had the clasp undone. He looked up, triumph gleaming in his eyes.

"That's some talent." She slid the bra down her arms and dangled it from her fingertips. "Now come on over to the bedpost."

Louis eased his muscled body across the bed, and she bound one hand to the polished mahogany by winding her bra around it a few times and fastening the clasp. He would have no problem wiggling free if he wasn't man enough to stand up to his own challenge.

But she had a feeling Louis didn't back down on a promise.

She began by layering floaty kisses over his stomach, then his thighs. Just as it looked as if his shorts might burst at the seams, she pulled them down and let him spring free.

Her own excitement made her giggle more than once. It was torture to be so close to making love with this man, yet to keep delaying it.

But it was so much fun.

Sam wasn't sure she'd ever actually had *fun* in bed with a man before.

Tarrant hadn't been able to…well, get it up, for want of a less blunt description.

And she hadn't minded. Really, she hadn't. Her first two marriages had left her with the impression that sex was a tiresome marital obligation in the same category as starching and ironing shirts, and it was a relief not to have to do either for Tarrant.

Last time with Louis had been intense and explosive, but too edged with her own desperation to be described as "fun."

This was totally different.

Louis knew all about her. About her past relationships and the experiences that had made her who she was. There was nothing to hide from him. She could think about her former husbands right now, as she hovered over his dangerously aroused body, and not feel guilty or ashamed about anything. She didn't have to fake innocence or experience she didn't have in order to be "perfect."

He'd invited her to be herself, and told her that was all he wanted.

Now here she was. All her usual doubts and fears and

worries were still there, but they didn't seem that big and important anymore.

Which made licking his skin and enjoying his warm, male scent all the more enjoyable.

"You know you're killing me." Louis's pained expression was undermined by the glitter of pleasure in his eyes.

"I never knew I had such a taste for murder." She looked up from kissing his belly. His arousal was so raw and visible, it made her heart jump in her chest.

He was this excited about being here with *her.*

His strong, young, muscled body was having a pretty dramatic effect on her libido, too. She'd never seen a more beautiful physique.

Athletic, but not in the heavy, gym-pumped manner of a bodybuilder. More natural and sexy. His tan skin was smooth, which made it glow in the warm light from the bedside lamp.

As she tormented him with her lips and tongue, she enjoyed watching his muscles tense and tighten as he tried to keep control.

"Sam." His guttural voice betrayed his urgency. His free hand fisted into the sheets and the bound one strained against her flimsy bra.

The bra snapped.

Louis flinched when the elastic smacked his wrist. He rubbed it, then looked up at her with a predatory grin.

Sam's whole body convulsed in an involuntary shiver. The next thing she knew she was climbing over him, clawing at his skin and pressing herself against him.

Louis's arms circled her waist and she let out a shuddering sigh as he gathered her into his hot and hungry embrace.

"You don't know how much I've craved this," she murmured.

"Yes," he replied, breath warm on her ear. "I do."

In less than a second he was inside her, filling her with all the desire and longing and hope she knew she'd created in him. It was blissful agony to finally give into the yearnings she'd tried so hard—and failed—to master.

They rolled on the sheets, switching roles, enjoying each other's bodies with abandon. The pleasurable sensations grew so intense and overwhelming that Sam heard herself laugh out loud.

Louis's obvious delight in her pleasure only heightened it. He kissed and caressed her, touched her with tenderness that made her heart flutter, then groped her in rough excitement that made her pulse throb faster and her breath come in unsteady gasps.

Her orgasm blew out of nowhere like a tornado on a clear day. It whirled her around—twisting and turning and picking up cows and houses and the roofs of strip malls—then flung her down on the rumpled sheets in a heap, unable to move or even speak, her limbs weighted with blissful relief.

She opened her eyes to see Louis next to her, chest heaving with exertion. His closed-eyed expression had a strange intensity to it, like someone deep in meditation.

"You okay?" she rasped.

"Very much so." The smile appeared around the edges of his sensual mouth, then his eyes slit open, sparkling gold. "Aren't you glad you finally got some sense and came to my bed?"

"Yes," she admitted. "I'm honestly not sure how I'll feel in the morning, but right now I'm very glad to be here."

He slid his palm over her belly and let it lie there, warm and reassuring. "Just take it one minute at a time."

She drew in a deep breath and let it out. "I'll try."

Louis nuzzled close, resting his nose and mouth in the

crook of her neck, where they fit perfectly, his breath soft on her skin.

What a relief not to have to fill the air with false promises and phony reassurances. Around Louis it was okay to be confused and uncertain. To be truthful. Maybe if she spent enough time with him, she really would be able to figure out who she was and actually have a shot at "being herself."

With that rather exciting thought floating around her brain, Sam drifted off to a peaceful sleep.

"Room service" were the first words Sam heard on waking the next morning. They were coming from the other side of the door and they barely penetrated her consciousness, but she still gathered enough sense to pull the sheets over most of her head and freeze in a panic.

Did Louis not care if people saw them together? It was one thing for them to enjoy intimacy in private, but quite another for the rest of New York to find out about it.

She heard Louis exchange pleasantries with the waiter, and when the door clicked, she emerged. "You could have warned me," she murmured, pushing hair out of her eyes.

"You looked so peaceful, I couldn't bear to wake you. And I'm starving." His mischievous grin melted her pique.

"I can believe it. You were pretty athletic last night." She blew out a breath, remembering some of the Kama-Sutra-style moves he'd introduced her to. Her insides shimmered at the memory.

"So I need some ham and eggs."

"I'm surprised. That seems very traditional for you."

"Every now and then I even surprise myself. I ordered plenty for you, too, and a basket of breads and pastries. We can call down for anything else you want."

The smell of freshly baked brioche tickled Sam's nostrils. "I'm sure I can manage with what you ordered." Suddenly she was starving, too. She glanced around for something to wear, then remembered she had nothing but her rather uncomfortable little black dress from last night.

"Here," Louis winked and threw her a robe with the hotel logo emblazoned on the pocket.

"Thanks," she rasped, and pulled it on. She scanned the room for mirrors. "I'm sure I look pretty scary."

"You look devastating, as usual." Louis helped himself to a heaping plate of ham and eggs. He wore only a pair of cream-colored cotton pajama pants, and his bare, muscled chest made an attractive backdrop for the feast now spread on the table.

Sam's stomach grumbled and she climbed over the bed. Louis abandoned his plate long enough to kiss her good morning. Her insides buckled at the soft touch of his lips on hers.

"Oh, goodness. What a night." She smiled shyly at him.

"What a night." He smiled back. "Now help yourself to some food and rebuild your strength."

Sam chose a croissant and spread it with butter. Her personal trainer would have a heart attack at the sight of so much cholesterol, but if you were going wild, then why not go all the way?

Louis poured her a cup of coffee and she took an invigorating sip. A stack of newspapers rested on the far side of the table, and she wandered over to glance at the headlines. *The New York Times* newspaper was on top with an article about a corporate bigwig she knew slightly who'd apparently been nailed for tax evasion.

She shook her head. How could smart people be so stupid? She lifted the *Times* to see what was underneath.

Merry Widow Makes Out.

Her heart froze at the sight of the tabloid's familiar moniker—for her. She grabbed the paper and managed to focus her eyes on the grainy black-and-white image underneath the headline.

"Oh, no." She could make out a blurry outline of herself and Louis, locked in an embrace. The one clear and unmistakable thing in the photo was her face, lit up against the darkness, eyes closed in an expression of rapture.

Her legs grew shaky and she reached for a chair.

"What's going on?" Louis looked up from a sip of coffee. At the sight of her face, he rose from his chair and moved around the table.

He took the paper from her hand and muttered a curse when he saw the headline and picture. "That's not right."

Sam's temples started to throb. "I should be used to it by now." She shook her head. "But at least in the past, it was all lies and innuendo. Now they actually have a story."

"Do they know who I am?" Louis scanned the paper. "Damn."

"They do?"

"Yeah. I'm your 'handsome stepson.'"

Sam pushed her face into her hands. She didn't want to see anything. She could feel the walls closing in on her as her delicately ordered world began to crumble.

She was dimly aware of Louis crouching down next to her chair. "Sam, I'm sorry this happened."

"Me, too," she breathed, her words barely audible.

"I mean, I'm not sorry I kissed you. I'm sorry those idiots made a story out of it." She felt his hand on her spine, rubbing gently.

Her back stiffened. "I'm sorry about both."

She turned to face him, angry at herself and angry at him, too, for letting her do something so stupid.

She reached for the paper and Louis pulled it back. "Why read it?"

"Because I need to know what's being said." She heard the same clipped tones she used when her assistant, Kelly, tried to keep the morning papers away from her on one pretext or other.

Louis handed her the paper and she scanned the lines.

Speculation has it that the widow isn't content with the mere millions she inherited from late retail tycoon Tarrant Hardcastle, and that she wants to get her manicured fingers on the rumored billions stashed away for his heirs. If this kiss is any indication, she's struck the jackpot.

Sam let out a fierce growl. "Ugh! How do they come up with this stuff? It was my idea to have Tarrant set aside money for his heirs."

Louis took the paper and read it, then shook his head. "They're mad at you because you're young, beautiful and rich. Simple jealousy. You can't let it get to you."

"Trust me, I try not to, but this time it's my fault."

"Because you kissed me?"

"Because I kissed anyone out on a public street in New York. I must be losing my mind. Right on Fifth Avenue." She shook her head in disbelief at her own stupidity.

He was a grown-up, too, and old enough to know better, even if he was her *handsome stepson.*

She cringed and hurried around the bed, looking for her dress. She shook it out and stepped into it, then crammed her bare feet into her high black stilettos.

"I guess everyone out there will know I unexpectedly stayed the night somewhere anyway, so no big deal trying to look decent."

She didn't like the bitterness in her voice, but she couldn't help the way she felt. How could she have been so stupid as to hand her head on a stake to the tabloid press?

Fiona would see it.

And Dominic and Amado.

All the staff at Hardcastle Enterprises.

Not to mention her personal staff at home.

Her face burned with shame and tears pricked her eyes.

"I wish I could do something to make it all go away," said Louis softly.

"You can't." The angry shrew voice sprang from her mouth again. "Gee, I thought New Orleans had all that old black magic and voodoo stuff. I'd think a carefully laid curse here and there—maybe a couple of stringer reporters turning into toads—wouldn't be too much to ask."

Louis shot her a pained smile.

"I guess that would be bad for my karma or something. Not that it could make much difference, really. How much worse can it get?"

"Sam, calm down. Nothing has actually happened. No one's hurt, no one's died. Put it in perspective." Louis stood in front of her, sculpted arms hanging by his sides, his handsome face set in an expression of easy confidence.

She hated the fact that heat flashed over her—even now, when arousal should be the very last thing on her mind.

The unwelcome desire morphed into a kind of crazed fury. "Nothing has happened?" she spat the question at him. "I'm hurt. You're hurt."

She paused, gasping for breath. "And Tarrant has died. If

he hadn't died, none of this would have happened. Why did he have to die?"

The last part emerged on a wail. She grabbed her dark glasses off the table and tears blinded her as she rushed for the door.

"Sam, wait." She heard Louis's voice behind her while she struggled with the knob and crashed out into the hall. "Sam."

She cringed at the sound of his voice calling down the hall as she stood waiting for the elevator, then the doors opened and she stepped in.

In the elevator she tried her best to fix her hair in the reflection on the mirrored walls. She adjusted her big sunglasses over her tear-filled eyes. Then she breathed in as deeply as she could and prepared to face the worst humiliation of her life.

Eight

Sam could hear her cell vibrating in her clutch purse on the side table.

Or maybe it was just the whole mansion vibrating with distress.

The staff slunk along the walls, trying to be invisible. No one would look her in the eye. Except Fiona.

"How could you do this?" Her stepdaughter's face was blotchy and pale. "I mean, he's my brother! That's just sick." Her pretty features contorted with disgust.

Sam's gut twisted. "It was an accident."

Fiona blew out a snort. "Good one. Try again."

Sam shoved a hand through her tangled hair. "I had no idea who he was when I met him. I didn't even know his name."

"And you thought it would be a good idea to sleep with him?" Fiona scowled. "Jeez, and don't I remember you giving me a maternal lecture about choosing my partners carefully just a few months ago? I guess it's *Do as I say, not as I do.*"

Sam felt tears prick her throat. She'd tried so hard to be a good role model for Fiona, whose own mother was a preoccupied socialite with little time for her "plain" daughter.

It had taken her three full years to gain Fiona's trust, and they'd bonded even more closely since Tarrant's death. She'd cried on Fiona's shoulder more than once in the emotional aftermath, and she'd come to think of her as a younger sister.

Now their hard-won relationship lay in ruins.

Fiona glanced over her shoulder at Sam's bag. "I think your phone is ringing."

"I'm so, so sorry."

"Don't apologize to me. It's not even my business." Fiona crossed her arms over her green T-shirt. "But that buzzing is driving me nuts. Are you afraid to answer it in case it's the press? There must be twenty of them gathered on the front steps."

Sam froze. "You're kidding."

"Didn't Beatrice tell you?"

"No." The housekeeper had been avoiding her glance as if she couldn't even stand to look at her. "Is it just newspapers or are there TV cameras, too?"

Fiona cocked her head. "Why? Want to know what kind of direction to give your makeup artist?"

Irritation flared in Sam's chest. "Fiona, did you leak this to the press?"

Fiona cocked her head. "Do you really think I would do that?"

"You're the one that leaked the story about Dominic and Bella, aren't you? No one else could have known the details."

The younger woman froze.

Anger and hurt rose in Sam's chest. "I've tried so hard to be a friend to you, Fiona. I do think you've had a raw deal around here and I can see why you feel sidelined by all these new siblings you never asked for. But it's not fair to try and destroy other people's lives as revenge."

Red blotches stood out on Fiona's pale face. "I admit, I did leak the story about Dominic and Bella. I was so mad! Dominic came out of nowhere and suddenly Dad's all dewy-eyed and can't wait to hand over the whole empire to him. I felt invisible. But I swear I didn't say anything about you and Louis. How could I? I had no idea." Her voice cracked with desperation—and what sounded like honesty.

"Really?"

"Really. Who on earth would imagine you, little Mrs. Goody Two-shoes, would be shacking up with her own stepson?"

Sam gulped. "You have a point."

"And Sam—" Fiona swallowed "—I really do like you. You've been so kind to me, even though I've tried my best to make you hate me. Sad as it is, you're probably the best friend I have." Fiona's lip quivered.

Sam's heart squeezed. "I like you, too, Fiona. I really do. Oh, dear. What are we going to do now? Is it just local press?"

"It's national. You'd better pull yourself together. You're not looking your best. Breath mint?" Fiona pulled a tube of mints from her pocket and held it up.

Sam shook her head, but the strange humor of the gesture gave her a slim ray of hope that all was not lost. "I don't think a breath mint could do much for me now. I'm just going to barricade myself in the way I usually do." She paused and rubbed her eyes. "And believe me when I say that if I could undo what I did…"

"Well, you can't. But that's life, isn't it?" Fiona winked. "Honestly, it's a bit of a relief that you're not such a freaking saint after all. You're always so loving and giving and generous, with time for everyone, and never a hair out of place." She cast a glance at Sam's hair and chuckled. "Guess you're human after all."

The phone started to buzz again.

"If you don't get that, I will." Fiona started across the room.

Adrenaline flashed through Sam and she rushed after her. "I'll get it!"

"Afraid it's lover boy?"

Yes.

"It could be Dominic or Amado calling to find out what the fuss is about." She hadn't faced them yet, since they didn't live with her in the Park Avenue mansion like Fiona.

She shoved a hand into her purse and pulled out the vibrating instrument. "Hello."

"Hey, Sam." The soft, deep voice seemed to reach right out of the dark metal and caress her ear.

She recoiled from the sensation and her finger hovered over the disconnect button.

"It's him, isn't it?" Fiona stared at her, emerald eyes narrowed.

Sam nodded. "Hello," she croaked.

Part of her wished he'd just disappear to Europe, or even New Orleans, at least until this whole thing blew over. And part of her wished he was right here, holding her in his strong arms.

"How're you holding up?"

"I'm okay," she said, trying to convince herself. "I'm with Fiona. I think she's beginning to see the humor in the situation." She risked a cautious glance at Fiona.

Fiona shot her a little smirk.

"Not that it's actually funny, of course," she backtracked. "It's horribly embarrassing. The staff is avoiding me like I have bird flu. Tarrant's housekeeper has been with him for twenty years and I think she'd be glad to throw me out to the reporters."

"I'm watching TV," Louis interrupted. "They're broadcasting from the steps of your mansion."

Fear shot through Sam. "Right now?"

"Yes, there's a woman with apricot helmet-hair telling the story of your life."

"Oh, no." Heat flooded her face. She glanced at the windows, suddenly afraid helicopters might be hovering outside, looking to snap her picture.

They'd love that. She'd probably never looked worse. It would be a great "where are they now" shot in contrast with her old beauty queen pictures.

Sam cursed herself for the vain thought. "I'm just going to sit tight. They swarmed around right after Tarrant's death, when the news came out that he'd left me so much money, but eventually they got bored and went away."

"How long did that take?"

She rubbed her temples. "A couple of weeks."

"You're going to stay locked up in that house for two whole weeks? Besides, it could be longer this time. It's a juicier story." A hint of innuendo colored his voice.

Oh, boy, is it ever.

"Staying inside for a few days is no big deal."

She heard a snort of disbelief. "Sam, you can't let them keep you prisoner."

"Really, I have everything I need. There's a staff of fifteen."

"I'm coming over."

The conviction in his voice warmed her heart for a split second, then adrenaline rocketed through her veins. "Please, don't! You'll only make it worse. They'll be all over you. You have no idea of the kinds of things they'll say to make a story."

"I can handle myself."

"Louis, please." She sucked in a deep breath. "I hate to say it, since I brought you here to meet the family, but I think you should leave town. At least for a while."

"Sweetheart, I'm not going to let anyone run me out of town, least of all you." Humor deepened his voice.

Sam found herself wanting to smile. But it wasn't a laughing matter. "It might hurt your business. Restaurants are all about image and perception."

"And food. Are you eating? I bet you're not."

Sam glanced down at her stomach. She'd run from the hotel room before her first bite of croissant and since she'd been back at the mansion she hadn't even taken off the awful black dress from last night.

"Give me Fiona."

"What?"

"You heard me." Louis's tone brooked no contradiction.

Sam stared at the phone for a moment, frowning, then held it out to Fiona.

Fiona looked alarmed, but extended a pale, rather shaky hand and took it. "Hello?" she said slowly.

Sam rubbed her hands over her face. She felt quite light-headed. She really should eat. What on earth was he saying to Fiona? She could hear the low murmur of his voice on the other end of the phone.

Fiona listened with total concentration, nodding silently. She chewed her lip. "Are you sure that's a good idea?" she asked at last.

Sam's stomach knotted. "Sure what's a good idea?"

She could hear Louis's murmur again.

After a few seconds, she handed the phone back to Sam, who rushed it to her ear only to hear the grim drone of the dial tone. "He doesn't say goodbye politely on the phone," she muttered, remembering the time he'd hung up after issuing orders on what she should wear for dinner.

"No." Fiona grinned.

"What are you smiling at?"

"Nothing."

"Then stop it." She couldn't help smiling, mostly because she was immensely relieved to see Fiona smiling, too.

"Can't. You know, you really look *awful*." Fiona tilted her head as if to get a better angle on Sam's shocking awfulness. "I wouldn't have believed it possible. You're not even all that pretty without your makeup on. You have these funny little dark splotches under your eyes. Your hair looks like straw, and your nose is bright red, like a circus clown." She let out a laugh.

Sam's hand flew self-consciously to the straw. "So glad I can provide some comic relief at this moment of high drama."

"Yeah." Fiona chuckled. "I love it. Usually I feel like such a dumpy klutz around you. Little did I know the whole effect was painted on."

Sam put her hands on her hips. "I should be offended."

"Yeah." Fiona pressed a thoughtful finger to her lips. "You know, you really should let the press get a look at you right now. I bet they'd stop being so mean."

"Maybe I'll go to the door right now and weep all over them."

"Nah. Don't give 'em the satisfaction." Fiona slid her arm around Sam's shoulders. "We'd better get you fixed up before Louis gets here."

"He's truly coming?" Panic rippled over her.

"Of course he is. Did you have any doubt?"

"We've got to stop him."

Fiona laughed, as if Sam had suggested trying to turn back the tide. "Let's go get you something to eat."

Louis marched along Park Avenue with determination surging through him like liquor. Sam *needed* him. And not as a stepson, either.

Thick clusters of pink coneflowers and yellow black-eyed Susans bloomed their hearts out in steel planters along the facade of a tall office block. Their honeyed smell rose into the hot air, propelling him faster toward Sam.

Every moment they spent together, he could see her opening up like a flower, shedding the molds she'd crammed herself into in the past and finally transforming into the glorious, powerful woman who'd been crouching inside all along.

Even here in the concrete-covered heart of one of the largest cities on earth, bees buzzed around the plump centers of the flowers, gathering pollen to make the delicious honey that sustained them.

Louis felt like a bee around Sam, drinking in all her powerful energy and refreshing his own life force by helping her rediscover hers.

He laughed aloud. He could intellectualize it all he wanted; the truth was they'd had *great* sex together.

He pulled open his cell and punched in a number. A female voice answered.

"Margo, it's Louis."

"Hi, baby," her rich voice greeted him. "Are you coming up to New York for my opening next week?"

"I wouldn't miss it for anything, and I've found you a new student."

"Hmm, let me guess, she's brilliant and beautiful and you're on a mission to help her find herself."

He frowned. "Am I that predictable?"

"Yes," she chuckled. "But you're lovable, too."

Louis shoved a hand through his hair. Okay, so he'd dated a few wealthy and beautiful women who needed help finding themselves. But somehow the idea that Sam was another in his long string of lovely ex-girlfriends scratched at someplace uncomfortable inside him.

He marched faster along the street. "Sam's different. She's been through a lot. She's going to need all your encouragement just to overcome her self-doubt."

"Ah, a project. And who'll be mopping up her tears when you run off to Paris or Milan and don't call when you said you would? What was it you said last time? 'Every relationship has its season'?"

"That sounds like something my mother would say."

"You're more like her than you'll admit."

Louis dodged to avoid a cab speeding through a red light. "I am not."

"Oh, yes, you are, sweetie. Sipping the nectar from each pretty flower, then moving on."

Louis froze at her use of the metaphor he'd just been contemplating himself. He hated when the universe locked onto him like that. "The bee plays a valuable role in pollination. Bringing each flower to life." He shoved a hand through his hair as he resumed his marching.

He didn't say that since he'd met Sam, he found himself contemplating the deeper and more fulfilling pleasures of sticking around to make honey.

"My new student, is she madly in love with you?"

Louis stopped dead in the middle of the Park Avenue sidewalk. A rushing man in a suit slammed into him from behind and they muttered apologies.

"No, she's not."

"Or at least that's what you're telling yourself so you don't feel so bad when you leave her for the next pretty project."

Her comment cut to his heart. Sam was so different from anyone he'd ever met. "Margo, I'm going to stop inviting you to my restaurants."

"No, you won't. You love my refreshing honesty."

Louis laughed. Then he caught sight of a crowd of reporters gathered outside the beautiful stone mansion in the middle of the next block.

Sam's house.

"Yeah, Margo, I rely on you to prevent my ego from getting out of control. I'll call you."

"I'll clear my schedule any day for you, sugar. And if you ever decide you want a woman who already knows how to paint…" She hung up, leaving him with a smile on his face.

The smile faded as he wondered how to run this gauntlet of reporters and get to the door, let alone get someone to let him in.

Did he really want to stir up and inflame the reporters like that? Sam would hate it.

A familiar bar-restaurant on the side street between Park and Madison caught his eye, and he turned up the street.

He eased under the yellow awning and greeted the statuesque maître d' with a hug. "Hey, Venetia, the boss here today?"

"He's out on his boat, but I know he'd want me to take care of you. The filet mignon is shockingly good today."

"I've got something a little different in mind. Is there an alley behind this place?"

"Kind of an air shaft." She raised an elegant brow. "Why?"

"Do you have any experience with breaking and entering?"

Sam flashed the mascara wand over her lashes one more time for luck. Sitting at her dressing table, back in her familiar element, she'd managed to calm down considerably.

And embarrassing as it was to admit, she did feel better with her familiar "face" on.

"Ugh. You look disgustingly gorgeous again." Fiona lounged on a chaise in the corner. "I hate you."

A tapping sound on the window made them both turn.

Another familiar face appeared behind the casement. "Louis," they gasped in unison.

Sam darted from her chair. "This is the fourth floor. What the heck?" She yanked open the casement and gripped his arm. "Are you insane?"

"Obviously. If you'll excuse me." With a polite smile, he pulled himself through the opening and climbed down onto the carpet. Followed by a shower of black dirt.

"You need to clean up that wall back there. It's covered with soot from my friend Vincent's kitchen exhaust." Louis's white shirt was filthy, and black smudges disfigured his annoyingly handsome face.

Sam cocked her head and tried to prevent a smile sneaking across her lips. "Then don't you think Vincent should clean it up?"

"I'll leave it to you guys to duke it out." He winked. "So, how's everyone doing?"

"Surprisingly well, under the circumstances." Sam crossed her arms over her chest. Mostly to hide the thickening of her nipples inside her blouse. "But I have no intention of letting the press see you here. How did you know which room it was?"

"I didn't. I've been crawling about on your fire escapes for fifteen minutes."

"And no one saw you?"

"You need better security."

"I guess the staff are all hunkered around the front windows, staring out at the reporters." She squeezed her arms to stop the tingling in her breasts. How could she still be attracted to him even now?

Chemistry, perhaps. Or some other destructive force leading her down the road to ruin.

"You're getting soot on the carpet."

"What kind of nut chooses a white carpet?"

"It's very popular these days. All the chichi designers are installing them." She couldn't fight the smile that snuck over her mouth. "I guess you'd better strip off so we can scrub you clean."

"What a pleasant idea."

Louis reached for the button below his collar.

"I'm out of here." Fiona leaped from the couch with her iPod, and strode for the door.

No one tried to stop her.

Sam narrowed her eyes as the next button revealed an enticing strip of well-toned chest. "That wall has got to be twenty feet high."

"I'd put it closer to thirty." Louis mouth tilted up at one corner. "But it's got quite a few bricks missing."

"Good footholds, huh?"

"Almost like the climbing wall at the gym. You should put some barbed wire on top or something."

He tugged his shirt off and heat flashed through Sam. "I guess I should turn the shower on," she rasped. It was only a few hours since she'd been held by those sturdy arms.

So much had changed since then. Panic flickered through her. "Did any of the reporters see you?"

"I don't think so, but it'll make a good story if they did." He grinned and unbuttoned the fly of his dark pants.

Sam swallowed. "There are helicopters, you know." She could hear vibrating rotors right now.

A knock on the door made them both swing to face it. Louis hesitated, his pants already halfway down his powerful thighs.

Sam dashed forward. "Hold on! Who is it?"

"Mrs. Hardcastle, the security has been breached!" She recognized the high pitched voice of Beatrice, the house-keeper who'd been avoiding her all morning. "The alarms have gone off. There might be an intruder on the premises."

Sam put her hand on the handle to prevent Beatrice from opening it. "I don't hear any alarms." She glanced back at Louis.

Who had the nerve to wink at her as he slid his pants all the way off.

"They're silent."

Sam frowned. "What's the point of that?"

"To alert the staff, of course," said Beatrice, as if talking to an imbecile. "We've summoned the police and they'll be here any moment."

Sam's hand tightened on the handle. "I don't think that's necessary."

For a few, silent seconds, disapproval radiated through the closed oak door. "They're bringing sniffer dogs. They'll search the perimeter and ensure that no one's gained entry. There could be a reporter on the loose inside the house."

Sam could quite picture Beatrice, lips pinched together in disgust at her mistress's blatant disregard for basic safety. Tarrant had thought Beatrice "charmingly old-fashioned." Sam found her to be downright hostile.

She bit her lip. "I suppose it does make sense to check, but please make sure I'm not disturbed." She shot a wide-eyed glance at Louis. "I'm going to…er, take a shower."

"Let me bring some fresh towels. Those ones are from yesterday."

"They're fine, really. It's better for the environment if we use them a few days."

Louis chuckled audibly and Sam shot him a furious glance.

"If you say so, *madam*." The emphasis on the last word was anything but obsequious. "I'll make sure you're not disturbed unless it's absolutely necessary."

"Thank you, Beatrice, I appreciate that." She sank against the door as orthopedic shoes stamped back down the hallway.

She looked up to see Louis, stark naked and breathtakingly gorgeous. "I should throw you to the sniffer dogs."

"I do like dogs." He smiled. "I've never lived in one place long enough to keep one, but I've always wanted to."

"Maybe you should stop traveling so much."

He nodded slowly. "That's what I'm thinking."

She tried to process his words, but her brain didn't seem to be firing on all cylinders.

Hardly surprising with a naked man only feet from her and the house surrounded by reporters and police.

She noticed that he'd rolled up his dirty clothes and placed them carefully on an opened newspaper.

Thoughtful.

Desire unfurled in her belly. "The shower." She walked into

the large bathroom that adjoined her dressing room and turned the giant gold-plated faucets. A reassuring roar of warm water drowned out sound.

Louis followed her into the bathroom. Before she knew what was happening, his lips were over hers and his arms around her back.

She shuddered with a powerful mixture of relief and longing. Nothing felt more natural than being held tight in Louis's arms.

How could that be?

"What are we doing?" she asked, when they finally pulled apart.

"I think they call that kissing."

She blinked. "Your face is still dirty. You'll mess up my makeup."

"Too late." His eyes glittered. "But it's okay because you're coming in the shower with me."

"I just had a shower," she stammered.

"You can't be too clean."

His fingers were already unbuttoning the crisp, striped blouse she'd donned in her attempts to look and feel "respectable."

Why did she care so much about the respect of people who didn't even know her?

Her skin sizzled with awareness as his fingertips brushed her bra. His breath was warm on her neck, quickening along with his obvious arousal.

"What if we're interrupted?" she whispered.

"They won't interrupt you in the shower." He tugged her shirt from her fitted, A-line skirt.

Heat flickered deep inside her. "I suppose you're right."

The room was filling with steam, only some of it generated by the hot water pouring from the six ergonomically designed, gold showerheads.

She heard the *zwick* of her zipper, as Louis's hands moved lower. Her hands wandered of their own accord over his smooth, tanned skin.

A series of loud bangs made Louis freeze. "What was that?"

"It's the water pipes. They're from the 1890s. They get air in them or something. Tarrant always meant to get the house replumbed, but it would mean tearing out the old plaster walls and…hold on, let me stop it before the noise brings Beatrice back."

She leaned into the shower, which splashed her shirt as she turned the faucets off for a second.

In the momentary silence, she heard the wail of a police siren. Fear crowded her brain. "We can't do this."

"What, take a shower?" Louis's voice was muffled by her breasts. He'd crouched to lower her skirt and had somehow gotten distracted.

"No, *this*, anything! Are we insane? The house is surrounded by armed police and aggressive reporters who'll do anything for a story."

"You shouldn't let yourself get distracted by things you can't control." His lips brushed her belly button, making her insides flutter.

Desperation welled inside her. "I don't feel like I can control anything. Even my own body. Although my brain is screaming at me to take cover, all I want to do is get in that shower and…and…"

Make love with you.

Even in her feverish state, she didn't say the words. There had been no talk of *love* between them.

Louis rose and placed his hands on her waist. "Didn't you receive some advice to follow your heart?"

Sam frowned. "Madame Ayida? Oh, please, I'm sure she just makes that stuff up to entertain the tourists. What kind of a cliché is 'follow your heart,' anyway?"

"A powerful one." He buried his face in her neck and pressed his lips softly to her skin. "I followed mine here."

His deep voice penetrated her fog of anxiety. "Your heart?"

He looked up, and met her gaze with those haunting eyes. "I do have one, you know, despite what they say."

"And what is it telling you?" She spoke slowly, her voice shaking. Maybe he'd say something that would let them both off the hook.

That would be fine. Good even.

Her heart hammered behind her ribs.

"It's telling me I've met a very special woman. A woman so generous and caring that people assume she must have an ulterior motive."

Frowning, he looked into her eyes. "A woman who has so much love to give that the world can't seem to absorb it all and keeps throwing it back in her face."

He brushed her cheek with his thumb. "And I'm not fool enough to let you throw away what we've found together."

Sam's heart squeezed. She managed to keep her breathing under control. "What have we found?"

She cursed herself instantly after asking the stupid question. What did she want to hear? That he loved her?

How lame could she get? She didn't even want him to love her. They couldn't have any kind of relationship given the weird family situation, so the whole thing was just pointless and stupid and painful and...

A whimper escaped her mouth as Louis took her into his

embrace and held her so tight she couldn't possibly escape even if she wanted to.

Which she didn't.

In a swift motion he lifted her into the shower and kissed her hard as warm water cascaded over them.

"I'm still wearing my underwear," she protested, when he let her up for air.

"Not for long," he growled. He unfastened her bra with a deft movement of his fingers, and tugged her soaked panties down over her legs.

He rose, dripping. "Much better." His voice was hoarse with the longing that echoed between them. Louis's hands roamed over her body, smearing the water over her skin until she moaned and writhed under his touch.

His arousal had gathered into a hard arrow of need, pointing right at her. She took him in her hand, and he released a low groan.

"I want you inside me," she murmured, hardly able to believe she was saying it aloud. "Now."

Louis replied with his body, entering her with swift passion that made her gasp with pleasure.

He hadn't answered her question about what they'd found. He didn't need to. They'd found…this. Physical closeness, of a raw, intense and human kind that she'd never experienced before. It added a dimension to their emotional connection that made her feel…whole.

They writhed and twisted under the steady flow of water. She let her hands wander over the masculine curves of his body, into his damp hair.

Louis kissed her face and neck and held her steady in his arms as she let wave after wave of vicious pleasure wash over her.

It took her a moment to realize Louis was saying something. His voice blended with the roar of the water and the roar of sensation and emotion inside her, but his words snuck through the curtain of bliss and she realized he was trying to answer her question.

"We've found…" His words were guttural, filled with emotion. "We've found…" he repeated and then he hesitated, still moving inside her, talking to her with his body.

Then he stopped.

The interruption was jarring, and she opened her eyes. Louis stared at her, water cascading over his striking face.

"Sam, will you marry me?"

Nine

Sam disentangled herself from Louis and flew out of the shower, half skidded on the marble floor and grabbed a towel before fleeing into the bedroom.

Had he really asked what she thought he had asked?

No. It wasn't possible. Her mind was playing tricks on her. Her heart thundered and her brain raced like a roller coaster.

"Sam." Louis appeared in the steamy doorway, a towel wrapped around his middle. "That wasn't quite the response I was hoping for."

"I'm sorry. I had to get out. I thought I… I thought you…" She didn't know what she thought. Mostly she just wanted to get away from Louis and the alarming pull he seemed to have on her.

Louis moved up behind her, still dripping. She held herself steady and tried not to shiver as he buried his face in her wet hair. "Will you?"

Sam gulped. "Will I what?"

"Marry me."

He said it simply, with no roguish charm or humor.

Like he really and truly meant it.

Sam wheeled to face him. "You can't be serious."

"I've never been more serious in my life."

Sam's chest tightened. She stepped away from him. "There's a lot more to a marriage than great sex. Trust me, I've been married three times and there wasn't great sex in any of them."

"Maybe that's part of the problem." She could hear humor in his husky voice.

She recoiled from him. "It doesn't matter anyway, because I'm done being married." Her voice rose, trembling with emotion. "Three times is enough for one lifetime. I'll always cherish the memories of my time with Tarrant, but I'm not going to ever marry again."

"You don't mean that."

Sam wheeled around, heart pounding. "Don't tell me what I mean! I don't need a father and I don't need a big brother, either. I've lived and learned a lot of things the hard way and I can make up my own mind, whether you like it or not."

She stormed out of the room and slammed the door behind her. Too late she realized she'd just slammed herself into her walk-in closet.

Hopefully Louis would have the decency to *go away*. Preferably the way he came, so no one would see him.

Her breath came in ragged gasps. Marry him? Was this some kind of cruel joke at her expense?

All she wanted was to be left alone.

"Sam." His low voice filtered through the wooden slats. "You're in a closet."

"I know," she half shouted, so angry at him she wanted to scream. Who was he to play with her emotions? She was fragile before she met him and now—

A half sob caught in her throat.

"Let me in."

"No!"

"Then I'll huff, and I'll puff and I'll—"

"Louis, it's not funny," she panted. "Please, just leave me in peace. I need to be alone."

"No, you don't. You've spent way too much time alone and you need to be with me."

"Ha," was all she could manage to say, as his words rattled around in her poor overtaxed brain.

Then a welcome retort found its way to her lips. "You're crazy. You read that article. I'm *The Merry Widow*, remember? The *gold-digging tramp* who married Tarrant for his money."

She fisted her hands into a red crushed-velvet dress. "Everywhere I go, there's some maniac with a camera hoping to capture a picture of me in a compromising position so they can make money from my miserable existence." She tugged at the dress so hard that it popped off the hanger. "No one wants to be a part of that. No one should be a part of that." Her voice ended in a whimper.

She saw the knob turn and couldn't summon the strength to stop it. Louis eased into the dim space of the closet and closed the door behind him.

It was pretty big, as closets go, but there was still less than two feet of space between them. His freshly clean, male scent tickled her nostrils. Drops of water glistened on his skin and hung from his damp hair.

"You came after me, remember? I was just going about my own business."

Sam bit her lip. "Maybe it was a mistake."

"You opened Pandora's box." His eyes glittered in the half-light sneaking in through a crack in the door.

"The Greek myth where a woman gets curious and unleashes evils on the world?" She clutched her towel closer.

He did blame her.

"Yes, slander, greed, vanity, envy, falsehood, scandal..." He cocked his head. "Those things do seem to be loose in our world right now."

She avoided his glance. "I should have left you alone."

"No." He seized her hand. Her fingers trembled inside his hot grasp. "There was one more thing in the box, the most important one, that didn't escape. She didn't let it." His eyes met hers. "Hope."

Something flashed between them as he held her gaze and mouthed the word, so soft she could barely hear it.

"Hope," she repeated, unable to stop herself.

"You awakened something in me, Sam, something that wasn't there before." A flicker of confusion crossed his brow. "I always thought I knew what I wanted in life, and that I had it, too. But since I met you, I know I want more." He squeezed her hand. "I *need* more."

Her heart constricted, as if he held it in his hand, too. "I'm sure you'll find it." Her voice sounded thin. "With some nice girl who doesn't have a cartload of baggage and a crowd of vultures circling around her head."

"I don't want a nice girl." He edged closer to her. The closet was getting hot, water drops on their skin almost evaporating into steam. "I want a woman. One who isn't afraid to make the life she wants. That's you, Sam. You've been brave enough to start over again and again, and you're not done yet."

She looked past him into the gloom, where her much photographed outfits, each one laced with memory, hung in regular rows. "I'm not done with life, but I'm all done with marriage. Three is enough."

"Says who? Zsa Zsa would disagree. And you two have a fair amount in common if this wardrobe is anything to go by." He fingered a bold-patterned Gautier gown.

Sam lifted her chin. "You're very argumentative."

"It's part of my charm."

His hands wandered through her clothes, plundering them, his fingers roaming through the luxurious fabrics just as they'd roved over her skin. Which tingled with…annoyance. "Why are you in my closet?"

He hesitated, his eyes wandering to her mouth, which twitched, and her throat, which gulped, before replying, "because you're here." Louis lifted his hand and cupped her cheek. "I love you, Sam."

The words closed around her heart like a fist, then swept away on a wave of panic. "You can't."

"I don't take orders well." His golden eyes glinted a challenge.

"Everything's too complicated."

"Nothing complicated about love." He brushed a drop of water from her lip with his thumb. "Do you love me, Sam?"

She froze. *Yes* screamed across her brain. "No."

He cocked his head. "I don't believe you."

"You're shockingly arrogant, you know that?" Her voice rose.

"Yes." A smile flickered across his lips. "I know what I want and I'm not afraid to go after it."

"Maybe you should think about someone else for a change." Her hands shook. "I have responsibilities to this family and to the whole Hardcastle corporation."

His eyes narrowed. "And to yourself."

"Exactly." Sam shoved a hand through her tangled hair. "I'm thirty-one and I've been through three husbands. There's something wrong with that picture, don't you think?"

"I don't think there's anything wrong with it at all." He held her gaze. "It's unique. It's your journey and you're a beautiful person."

Beautiful?

Sam cringed at the thought of what she must look like right now. Lucky she couldn't see herself. Louis of course looked breathtaking. The shaft of light through the closet door sculpted his torso in gold, while water dripped erotically from his shiny, dark curls.

"What is going through that intriguing mind of yours?"

She tilted her head. "Just mulling some artistic options."

A smile slid across his lips. "As you should be. You've a lot to accomplish, Sam, and some lost time to make up for."

"As it happens, I agree with you there. I've decided that I will take up painting. And I won't even be mad at myself if I stink at it."

"That's the attitude. I knew you'd see it my way eventually. Now, back to my other question."

Sam shrank into her towel. "I can't marry you. It's preposterous that you even thought of it. Even if you weren't my *stepson*." She shuddered involuntarily. "We barely know each other."

"We have a deeper connection than most people."

She narrowed her eyes. "Is this some New Orleans voodoo psychic angle you're working here? I'm not as gullible as I look."

"Remember what Madame Ayida said?"

"Follow my heart. Yeah, sure. I'm not even sure there's one

in there after all this time." She glanced mockingly down to where her hands crossed over her towel. "Don't forget she also mentioned the two roads, neither of which seemed to lead anywhere I'd want to go."

Louis looked at her for a second, then laughed. "How do you know if you haven't walked on one yet? Didn't she say one is familiar and one is strange?"

Sam crossed her arms over her chest, which left her fumbling for her towel. "If you look at it that way, then it's getting married that's familiar, and not getting married that would be strange. I'll go with strange."

"Fine. We can live in sin."

She couldn't help laughing at his deadpan comeback.

Then her smile faded. "I'm sure the tabloid press would enjoy that."

"Absolutely. We'll really help 'em sell some copies. Just think, if we have a bunch of kids, they could accuse you of being mother to your own grandchildren." His eyes shone with humor.

Sam froze. *Children.* She'd told him how much she wanted a child, so his comment was a low blow.

"Tarrant's children are my children," she said stiffly.

"Including me, I guess."

"Yes." She gave him the hardest stare she could muster. "That's my preference."

"You can't have kids your own age."

"Sure you can."

They stared at each other.

He blinked first.

"You think *I'm* stubborn," he said, eyes glinting. "You're downright delusional."

"Then leave me alone with my delusions. We're happy together."

Louis stared at her for a moment, then laughed, slowly. "You've certainly got the wardrobe to be a delusional billionaire widow." Then his eyes narrowed. "But I won't let you throw your life away."

He leaned in until his words vibrated off her skin. "You're meant to be a mother, and not some kind of fake, fairy-godmother type of mother, but a real mother who has to get up in the night because her baby is crying, and has to miss an important meeting because her toddler has a fever and has to relearn long division to help her nine-year-old with his homework."

A flash of pain almost blinded her. How would he know that she craved the challenges of parenthood as much as the photo-album moments people raved about?

She tried to keep her breathing steady. "I thought you didn't want kids."

"I didn't know what the heck I wanted until I met you, Sam." Emotion darkened in his voice and shone in his eyes.

Her insides churned and she felt her grip on reality growing more fragile.

"This is insanity. Why are we standing here with no clothes on?"

"I don't have any clean clothes." He looked at her, eyes glinting. "And I don't think yours would suit me."

Sam blinked. Swallowed. "Some of Tarrant's are still in the other closet." She pointed to the door. The air was so thick she could barely breathe. "Help yourself."

She collapsed against the rack of clothes as he opened the door and slipped out.

Her heart rattled like a runaway train.

Why did the craziest things seem possible with him around?

Get dressed. She didn't want to be standing around in a

towel when the police came to the door with their sniffer dogs searching for an intruder.

Especially since she was harboring one.

The racks of couture originals usually comforted her, the rich colors and fabrics a balm to her spirit. Today they seemed to hang around her like carcasses.

I bet you'd look cute in a pair of Levi's.

Louis crept into her consciousness. Of course there weren't any Levi's to be found. There was one pair of Circle of Seven jeans folded up on the top shelf. A gift from Fiona that she'd never found occasion to wear.

Sam pulled them down and climbed into them. She tugged on a fitted black shirt and buttoned it, fingers shaking. Maybe she could just stay in the closet all day and not go out to face the mess that she'd made of her life.

Or Louis.

"Are you still in there, or is there a secret tunnel to Barneys?" His voice resounded through the wood door.

Sam smiled. "I wish there was a secret tunnel."

She braced herself as the door opened. He stood there in a pair of pale linen pants and a loose shirt. She couldn't recall ever having seen Tarrant in that outfit, which was no surprise since he'd had almost as many clothes as she did. "You look nice," she stammered, to cover the awkwardness she felt.

"I am nice."

"I'm not so sure about that."

"I want to spend the rest of my life proving it to you."

He reached for her hand, but Sam shrank back. "Be sensible. They're looking for an intruder, remember?" Suddenly her mind was clear and clicking. In crisis mode. "We've got to get you out of here somehow. Now, how can we do it without the staff seeing you?" She pressed a hand to her temple. "Maybe we can get you down to the underground garage and into the car with the tinted—"

A high-pitched noise made her jump. "My phone."

She ran forward and snatched it off the dressing table.

"Where the hell have you been?" cried Fiona, the moment she pressed it to her ear. "I was pounding on the door. I figured maybe you went out on the fire escape or something. What's going on?"

Sam gulped. "We… I…" She didn't dare look up at Louis.

"On second thought, I don't want to know. I've been trying to find you because Dominic and Amado are here."

Sam's heart stopped.

"They're out in the street arguing with the reporters. Turn on your TV to Channel Five. Or heck, just open a window."

Sam ran past Louis, grabbed the remote from her dressing table and flicked on the TV above Tarrant's dressing table on the opposite wall. It reflected into her mirror right next to her own startled expression.

In a surreal montage, her own front door floated above her cosmetics bottles, decorated with a familiar network logo. Dominic stood on the steps, his proud features rigid. "This rumor is ridiculous, and neither Hardcastle Enterprises nor the Hardcastle family will take it lying down."

His face loomed as he neared the camera lens. "If you don't retract this ludicrous story about my stepmother, Samantha, having an affair with my brother Louis, we'll sue you for libel." His lips settled into a hard line.

The reporters exploded into a blur of sound and motion. Sam staggered back, heart pounding. "Oh, no. We've got to stop them…" she murmured into the phone. "How can we get him inside?"

Just then an incensed Amado took a swing at a reporter who'd shoved a microphone in his face.

Worry propelled her out of the room, phone still pressed to her ear. "Beatrice, open the front door!" she shouted down the wide stairs as she shoved out into the hallway.

"We can't. The mob will break in."

"Dominic and Amado are out there. They could be hurt." She ran down the stairs, bare feet cool on the limestone.

If no one else around here was brave enough to open the door, she'd do it herself.

"Madame, don't go out there!" Beatrice and Sam's assistant Kelly mobbed her in the front hall.

She pushed past them, single-minded, tugged on the heavy brass locks and yanked the door open, then blinked as light flooded in from the street outside. "Dom, Amado!"

She couldn't even make them out in the throng of bodies. Microphones and cameras thrust toward her. Voices and clatter and commotion rose into a roar of sound that assaulted her ears. *Is it true? Are you having an affair? What about the photographic evidence?*

The clamor assaulted her ears and she shrank back. "Dominic, Amado, where are you?"

Dominic's dark head thrust through the crowd. "Sam, thank God you've come out to defend yourself. I won't let them treat you like this. Tell them it's a lie."

Sam's mouth opened, but no words came out.

To tell that it's a lie would be...a lie.

"Come here, Sam." Dominic stood right in front of her on the top step now, his face dark with anger. "Tell these vultures that you won't put up with their bull anymore."

"I...I...I..."

Amado pushed through the crowd, looking disheveled and

irate. "This is a crime. An assault on an innocent woman in her own home. These people should be behind bars."

Dom and Amado flanked her, and she felt their strong hands holding her up. "Go on, Sam, tell them."

Silence throbbed as the gathered throng waited for her reply. Even the birds seemed to stop singing, and the traffic on Park Avenue ground to a halt.

"Come on, Sam, defend yourself," murmured Dominic.

She hesitated, blood pounding in her brain. "I…I…I can't."

She turned and plunged back into the house. She heard Dominic and Amado, pressing the reporters back. They both managed to get through the door and closed it behind them.

All of them stood, panting, in the hallway for a split second.

Then Dominic moved forward and put his hands on her shoulders. "Sam, what do you mean?" She shivered under his forceful touch.

Her voice wouldn't come out. She dragged in a shaky breath. "I can't deny it."

"Why not?" His dark eyes peered into hers.

"Because it's true."

Shock washed over Dominic's face. "It can't be."

He pulled his hands from her shoulders, a move so sudden it made her flinch.

Confusion contorted Amado's handsome features. "What do you mean, Sam?"

The entire household staff gathered in the hallway; Beatrice and Kelly, the cook and her assistant, even Raul the ancient repairman who'd been with the house since its previous owner. Fiona stood behind him, her iPod unplugged from her ears and her face pale.

All hung on her reply.

"Louis and I have…have…" She cursed herself for being unable to form a whole sentence.

But what was a polite—or even halfway decent—way to tell them what had really happened?

"We're in love." A deep voice resonated along the marble hallway.

Sam looked up and saw Louis at the top of the stairs.

Something hot and unfamiliar swelled inside her.

She crushed it down, angry that he'd made a public declaration even though she'd made it clear she couldn't marry him. Some things weren't meant to be.

Dominic and Amado stared at each other, then back at Sam.

"I'm so sorry," she whispered to them. They were both so traditional, so worried about honor and the family reputation. They made her feel safe and protected.

And she'd betrayed them.

"Is it true?" Amado took her hand.

"I…" What exactly was he asking? Was it true that she was in love with Louis?

Panic surged through her. She was recently widowed and still grieving her dead husband, she had no idea what she felt about anything.

"It started by accident," she stammered. "When we first met I had no idea who he was, and I tried to stop, but—" The words jammed in her throat.

"But we couldn't." Louis materialized beside her, tall and self-assured.

He shrugged, maybe a hint of apology in his expression as he looked at Dominic and Amado. "We should have told you earlier, so you didn't waste your energy arguing with the rabble out there."

His casual "we" stirred a warmth, mingled with fury at the

way he spoke so easily for both of them. Couldn't she even express her own thoughts without someone jumping in to put words in her mouth?

She glanced at Dominic. His face would make quite a painting. A baroque mask of horror somewhere between Goya and El Greco.

Her stomach curled into a knot.

Then he started to laugh. The sound boomed through the wide marble entrance hall and up the stairs. Contagious, it rippled first to Amado, then Fiona, then to the junior staffers.

Louis joined in, then even Sam found herself unable to control the explosive release of tension.

"They are going to *love* this."

"It really isn't funny," gasped Sam. Horrible, breathy bursts of laughter exploded from her throat. Hysteria. Everything was moving too fast, going all wrong.

"It is, though," Dominic's often serious face bore a huge grin. "And it's wonderful. I thought you had a mysterious glow ever since you came back from New Orleans. I figured it was because you were so excited to find Louis, now I can see it was a little more than that."

Sam wrung her hands. "I didn't want anyone to find out."

"Why? You're not related," said Amado. "It's a family tradition to fall madly in love with the wrong person. Look at Dominic, getting involved with a corporate spy planning to sue his father, and me, crazy about the woman who showed up to destroy my family." He grinned. "Welcome to the club, Louis."

Louis, standing calm and unruffled, smiled and glanced at Sam. "You okay?"

"I have no idea," she said honestly. She suspected not. There was an unpleasant pulsing sensation in her left temple and her heart kept beating faster. "What about Tarrant?"

Fiona stepped forwards. "He's probably laughing his head off somewhere. You know he wanted you to live a full life after he died."

Sam wrapped her arms around herself as grief cascaded through her, cold and painful. "He said that, but I know he didn't really mean it. I promised him that he'd be the last." She tried to keep her breathing steady, to remain standing as her legs grew shaky.

"And he told me to make sure he wasn't." Fiona winked. "If I know my dad, he'd be on the phone trying to hook up an exclusive deal to sell the story for a million bucks." She glanced at Dominic.

"Don't look at me." Dominic narrowed his eyes. "I took over his role in the company, but I didn't turn into him."

Fiona bit her lip. "What about Sam's charities? We could sell the story to raise money for Save the Children or something."

"Hey, that's not a bad idea." Louis half smiled.

Sam's ears rang with all these lunatic suggestions. The hallway had started to pulse and throb with color. The floor had grown wobbly and unsteady under her and she wasn't sure she could keep standing much longer.

Her train was going off the tracks.

"You're standing here talking about my personal life like I don't even exist." Her high-pitched wail rang through the hallway.

She gasped for air, a sob rising dangerously in her throat. She stared right at Louis. "I'm a grown-up. I can make up my own mind. I don't need anyone to tell me what to do." Even as she tried to convince them that she was rational, her mind seemed to be shattering, thoughts and sensations clashing and colliding into a kaleidoscopic nightmare.

She needed to get away. "Please, don't follow me."

As tears clouded her eyes, she ran for the stairs.

"Sam." Louis's voice vaguely penetrated the roar of blood in her ears as a wave of hurt and anger crashed over her. Now she was crying in front of Dom and Amado and Fiona and all the staff. She'd wanted so badly to be a reassuring mother figure to them all, nurturing them and supporting them, instead she was a hysterical wreck. A source of scandal and humiliation.

She flew up five flights of stairs, right to the top of the house. She paused for breath, hands gripping the polished baluster.

No one followed. Good. At least they had some sense of decency not to hound her in the supposed privacy of her own home.

She unlatched the door to the roof deck, flung it open and plunged outside into the bright sunlight. The sky crouched over her, bright and clear. She gulped air, trying to stop the horrible sobbing sounds racking her body and escaping through her trembling lips.

One minute everything was okay. Fine. Wonderful even. The next minute the world was crashing in. She didn't seem to have any control over her own body, or even her own thoughts. *She couldn't live like this.*

She wouldn't live like this.

If she continued on this course, the tabloids were quite capable of hounding them for years, of disrupting all their lives and damaging the company's reputation.

It hadn't been easy to transform herself into Samantha Hardcastle, wife of one of the most powerful men in the world. She'd achieved considerable success, raising money for charities, cultivating friendships with people who were important to the company, helping to promote Hardcastle Enterprises and enhance its reputation in everything she did.

And most importantly, she'd worked hard to build the Hardcastle family and sustain it now that Tarrant was gone.

Her selfish, personal desires could not be allowed to draw hostile attention and ugly innuendo to her private circle.

Sam dragged in a long, shuddering breath of air. Her pulse rate slowed and the jagged edge of tears started to subside.

Good.

She'd made her decision, and this time she was sticking with it.

Louis pushed open the door to the roof. Sunlight blinded him and he raised a hand to shield his eyes. Sam stood, a frail figure in her skinny jeans and dark shirt, silhouetted against the bright sky.

Of course she was upset. He understood. Once he held her, she'd…

"It's over between us." She hurled the words at him like a handful of stones.

"Relax, Sam. You're just upset because of the press."

She held his gaze, her blue eyes bright. "I'm not upset, or overwrought or hysterical. I'm perfectly rational, and I've made the right decision."

Irritation rippled through him. "For who?"

"For *me*. And despite what you and all the other men in my past might think, I'm quite capable of making decisions for myself." She crossed her hands over her chest, defensive. "Or do you disagree?"

She'd issued a challenge. If he did disagree, he was no better than the other men in her life who'd tried to tell her what to do.

He spoke softly. "I think you should take some time to reflect. We could go to Europe for a while, Barcelona, perhaps. I have business to do there and we could…"

Sam squeezed her eyes shut. "No! I'm not running away.

I don't want to go to Europe or anywhere else. I just want to stop this crazy affair that's going to derail all of our lives if we let it."

How could he make her see without proving that he didn't respect her? For once words seemed to have deserted him, so he simply took a step toward her.

"Stop! Don't push me, Louis. I've made up my mind and all I ask is that you respect my decision."

Her delicate features now formed a mask of determination that echoed in her stern voice.

She was shutting him out and bolting the door.

A wave of desperation unleashed a tide of anger. "There are two of us in this relationship." His voice emerged as a growl.

"No. There is no relationship." Her expression didn't alter. She'd morphed into the polished society matron smiling from the party pages in the magazines. "It's all over. Now I'd appreciate you leaving me in peace."

He stared at her, his mind reeling. *He'd offered her his heart...his whole life.*

He planned to raise a family with her, something he'd never imagined doing, but that he now wanted with a painful and unfamiliar urgency.

He'd offered her *everything he had,* and now she replied with a haughty dismissal.

A steel band of emotion tightened around his chest and his muscles ached and throbbed.

But he wasn't going to beg.

Without another word, he turned and strode for the door.

Ten

"Samantha, darling, you've outdone yourself! Everyone—simply everyone—has been talking about this party for days. Who did the flowers? Marcel? He's such a talent, such an artist…"

Sam kept her smile in place while Cecilia Dawson-Crane exclaimed over the lilies. She should be glad. She put a lot of effort into getting those damn lilies just right.

So why did she feel like such a fraud standing here? The grand ballroom was abuzz with chat and laughter. She was surrounded by two thousand of her closest friends, all of whom had paid hundreds of dollars for the privilege of joining her for an intimate gourmet dinner.

She'd already raised over a million dollars, not including the raffle, for the World Refugee Fund. She should be ecstatic.

Instead she felt…desperate.

"Samantha, sweetheart!" She swung around to kiss another powdered cheek, this one belonging to her friend, Kitty. "Congratulations on snagging an art show."

Sam blushed. "It's just the church hall."

"It's not any old church hall, it's on Madison Avenue and I'm bringing all my art world friends."

"You're sweet. I just started experimenting with oils and I'm not sure I'm ready, but Margo insisted. And if anyone's foolish enough to buy one, it'll help pay for the church's new roof."

"Everyone will want one. Mark my words. I'm not the number-one selling agent for Darcy and Maclaine for no reason. Who knew you had so much talent hidden under that well-sculpted exterior?"

Not me, that's for sure. A few lessons with Louis's friend Margo had unlocked something inside Sam that had her up in her new studio day and night, diving into a turpentine-scented world of light and color.

"I do enjoy painting so much."

"Trust me, we can tell by looking at your work. That big one of the Louisiana bayou at dusk…" Kitty shook her head, which had no effect whatsoever on her spiky blond tresses. "It's magic."

Sam gulped. She'd been reluctant to include that in the show, given all the potboiler publicity over her affair with Louis. But Margo insisted that was all forgotten. And she was pretty much right. Since Sam never responded to the accusations and Louis had left for Europe, people assumed it was just more lies.

So she'd agreed to include the painting of Louis's special place. "That was my first painting."

"You're kidding?" Kitty's hazel eyes widened.

"No, it formed in my mind one morning and I couldn't put down the brush until it was done. It took me three days and nights. Anna brought me meals in my studio." She touched Kitty's forearm. "Lucky thing I'm a lady of leisure, huh?"

Kitty stared. "First of all, I've never met anyone in my life who works harder than you. Second of all…wow. I'm going to be keeping an eye on you as an investment, as well as a friend."

Sam flushed with pride. It seemed she actually was good at painting. Louis had been right about that.

Ugh, why did he keep sneaking into her mind when she least expected? Even painting and lunching and making phone calls around the clock didn't squeeze him out of her consciousness.

Especially at night. When she was in bed. Alone.

She excused herself from Kitty and hurried to the green room to see how the speakers were doing, then checked with the caterers on whether the take-home gifts were ready.

Everything in place. All going smoothly.

"Sam-mee!"

Sam tried not to roll her eyes at the annoying name only one person called her. "Hi, Bethanne," she said and kissed her on both cheeks. "How's the house in Amagansett coming?"

"Appallingly slow, but what do you expect? Apparently the marble shipment from Italy got impounded by customs or some such nonsense. But never mind that, where are those dangerously handsome young men you rounded up to be your lifelong consorts?"

Sam blinked. "Oh, you mean Dominic and Amado and…" Her throat closed as she tried to say Louis's name.

"Of course I do. What a marvelous idea to have sturdy young knights at your disposal and you don't even have to sleep with them. Honestly, some aspects of marriage are better left unexplored after a certain age." She winked a heavily mascaraed eyelash. "I don't imagine you'll remarry, dear, will you? Too much trouble defending your fortune from young turks, what with prenups being overturned in the courts every day. No, I wouldn't, either, in your shoes."

Bethanne Demarist leaned in, until her horrid scent threatened to choke Sam, "But just between you and me, I could quite understand enjoying the talents of those adorable young men."

"Dominic and Amado are both married," stammered Sam.

"That's not who I was talking about," replied Bethanne, with a knowing look.

"I...I...I must see if the hors d'oeuvres are being circulated."

"Come on, Sammy. I saw that picture in the paper."

"We weren't kissing. It was a trick of the light."

Bethanne narrowed her eyes. "A trick of the light, huh?"

"Yes, and you'd be amazed what they can do with digital photography these days." *And how easily I can tell a bold-faced fib on this topic.*

She really should be ashamed to outright lie about it. But it was in self-defense. And people got off even for murder when it was in self-defense, right?

"Ah, well," Bethanne's expression slipped into a smirk. "I have seen him pictured with a lot of beautiful women since then."

Sam blanched. She had, too. Over the winter he'd opened another restaurant, come second in a prestigious yacht race and judged a big film festival. The pictures of Louis entwined with a succession of gorgeous starlet types had tied her stomach in knots for days on end.

Which was ridiculous. She should be glad to see him enjoying himself.

"Exactly," Sam stammered. "He's got a busy life. That's why he's not here tonight."

"Trick of the light. I'll have to remember that one." With a wink, Bethanne melted into the crowd.

Sometimes she could barely remember the feel of his hands on her skin. Then, all at once, her skin would hum with sensation and she'd feel like he was right there.

Which he wasn't. *Trick of the senses.*

Everything in her life was going better than she could have dreamed. She'd visited Argentina for Christmas and Amado and Susannah had shared that they were expecting their first child. She'd already spent many happy hours fondling toy catalogs and she was secretly making a quilt.

Dominic had taken the retail sector of Hardcastle Enterprises to a whole new level by combining it with his own chain of stores, and his genius wife, Bella, had come up with a revolutionary sunblock that protected the skin from harmful rays, but allowed valuable vitamin D production.

She should be over the moon to be part of—even a catalyst behind—all the wonderful things going on around her.

Instead she felt hollow and empty inside. Even the joy of creating new worlds on canvas didn't fill the hole that seemed to gape a little wider each day.

She missed Louis.

Maybe she should just call to say hi. This long silence be-tween them was awkward. Unsettling. It undermined every-thing she'd hoped for about drawing the Hardcastle family closer.

They could chat and everything would be more...normal. Right?

"Wrong." Sam's heart sank as she looked up at Fiona. They sat curled up on the sofa in the Plum Room at the mansion. "The number, that is. Not in service."

"Maybe Louis got a new cell?"

"Could be. I tried the house first, and I keep getting the machine. I don't want to leave a message. You never know who could hear it and start trouble. He must have staff coming in and out since he's out of town so much."

"You're just going to have to go down there and find him." Fiona scrolled through her iPod playlist, as if she could care less either way.

"How would I even know if he's in town?"

"He's in town." Fiona grabbed her PDA off the floor, pressed a few keys and handed it to Sam. "Party at his restau-rant in the Quarter last night. Big jazz honchos all there."

Sam peered at the image on the tiny screen. Sure enough, there on a Web site called "Glitterati" was Louis, surrounded by smiling people she didn't recognize.

Her pulse picked up. So, he was down in New Orleans, right now.

"You could be at LaGuardia in forty-five minutes," mur-mured Fiona without looking up.

"Mmm-hmm." Sam bit her lip. "I really should go, don't you think? For the good of the family?"

A sly smile crept around Fiona's mouth. "Absolutely."

* * *

A light mist of rain fell through the dark as Sam rang Louis's doorbell. Her heart thudded and her palms were damp, but a sense of resolve and determination straightened her back. She had nothing to be ashamed of. She was human, and so was Louis. Life was short and meant to be lived.

And she wanted to live hers with Louis.

A light shone from the back of the house, and she could imagine Louis sitting upstairs in his office, or maybe eating a late dinner in the elegant dining room she could imagine, overlooking a garden.

She peered through the small squares of glass behind the scrolled wrought iron on the door, and saw a shadowy figure moving along the hallway. The door swung open to reveal an elegant older woman with her hair swept up into a white bun on top of her head.

"Yes?" The woman looked her up and down, which made Sam self-conscious. Her dress was wrinkled from travel and already damp from the rain.

"Is Louis here?" Sam tried to stop her voice from shaking.

"He's not expected back until morning." The woman raised a brow. "Can I take a message?" She had an air of wariness, like she's spent all night taking messages from forlorn women.

Which maybe she had.

"Um, do you know where he is?"

The woman's lips pursed. "I'm not at liberty to say."

Gone until morning. Which meant he was staying the night somewhere else. And why would he do that if there wasn't a woman involved?

Sam's heart clenched like a fist. She'd come too late. She'd seen those pictures of him with other women, but somewhere, deep inside, she'd assumed they were just pictures. Standing there, with rain dripping off the balcony behind her, she realized that all along she'd imagined Louis waiting patiently for her to come to her senses.

But now that she had, he was gone.

"Could you tell me the address of his fishing cabin? I'd like to visit it again before I go and I can't remember the way." Her lip quivered. At least of she was going back to New York alone she could get one more look at the bayou that had inspired her to start painting.

But the woman crossed her arms over her ample chest. "I'm afraid that address is strictly private. Would you like to leave a message for Mr. DuLac?"

Clearly she wanted to sweep Sam off her doorstep and get back to her quiet evening inside. But what message could Sam leave? It would only be awkward if Louis knew she'd come looking for him and had learned he was out all night with another woman.

"No message, thanks. Sorry to bother you."

"No problem, good night." With a forced smile, the woman closed the door, leaving Sam alone in the damp, dark street. She let out a shuddering sigh as disappointment soaked through her like rain.

As she wrapped her fingers around the handle of her rental car, ready to head back to the airport, she resolved to at least drive to the bayou to say goodbye. Even if she couldn't find the spot where Louis lived, she could sit there for a while and listen to the rain. Maybe even wait for the sunrise. If nothing else, another painting might come to her. The ability to create a private place and make it come alive on canvas was a surprising comfort in an unpredictable world, and her world was nothing if not unpredictable.

* * *

Louis swerved to avoid a large box turtle on the road. The tires skidded a little on the rain-soaked asphalt and he struggled to stay on the pavement.

Damn! Katie said she'd left hours ago. She hadn't even intended for him to find out she'd come. But when Katie described a tall, skinny woman with big blue eyes in a crazy-looking dress and high heels, he could only picture one person.

In all likelihood, Sam was on a plane back to New York right now, but instinct drove him deeper into the bayou country. Katie said she'd asked for the address of his cabin. Fiona had told him about the painting Sam did—the swamp afire with light—and that everyone was raving about her talent and begging for more of the same. Would she seek the scene of her inspiration in hope of finding more?

Maybe that was why she'd come down here in the first place.

He shouldn't delude himself that she'd come down here looking for *him*. Lord knew he'd done his best to get her out of his mind, opening the new café in Nice, keeping busy with friends.

With women.

A thick rope of sensation tugged at his chest. Nothing had helped. He only wanted one woman, and she'd shoved him out of her life like yesterday's garbage.

As a member of New York's high society she must be used to doing that. Probably changed her friends as often as she updated her expensive wardrobe.

Louis stuck his arm out the window of the car into the mist of rain hovering over the bayou. The drops felt cool and peaceful on his sweaty skin.

He'd told himself he'd get over her.

Eventually.

But so far it hadn't happened, and if tonight's high-speed chase along rain-streaked bayou roads was anything to go by, he was a long, long way from over her.

He turned onto the side road that led to the cabin just as the first silvery streaks of dawn rose above the swamp. For some reason he already felt closer to her. Which was ridiculous. There was nothing for miles but swaying grass and overgrown trees on a blue-gray haze of rain.

But he'd never really managed to banish memories of her bright smile, her hopeful gaze, the warmth that emanated from her like the steam rising from his car engine.

Even now, longing crept through his muscles and made his nerves kick with desire.

He pulled up by the boathouse. Was that a gleam of something in the dark? He jumped out of the car and strode toward the wood structure that stood silent and invisible in the damp darkness. Rain soaked through his shirt and cooled his skin, but it didn't ease the dull ache in his chest. The constant sense of yearning for the one thing he wanted and couldn't have.

"Sam."

His voice echoed around the empty swamp. He must be delusional to come here looking for her. Still, as he walked around the boathouse, he could almost feel her. He could swear he smelled her expensive scent hovering in the air like the haints the old people whispered about.

His hand brushed against something hard and cool—metal. He struggled to adjust his eyes to the thick darkness while his hands spread over the hood of a car. Cool already, its engine must have been off for a while.

"Sam?" Was she out there in the swamp alone? It was a dangerous place, with alligators and quicksand and sudden patches of deep water that could take you by surprise. "Sam!"

Panic ratcheted through his system, stoked by desire and painful longing. "Where are you?" He stood still, listening.

Patterns of sound played around him, rain on the leaves and grasses, and the hum of insects.

Louis.

His skin prickled with goose bumps. He could almost swear he heard someone call his name. He didn't actually hear it with his ears. He *felt* it.

Louis.

"I'm coming, Sam. Call out to me!" Urgency rang in his voice as he splashed around the boathouse and pulled the doors open. "Call for me, Sam. I'll find you."

Louis.

Again, he didn't hear her voice so much as feel it vibrate through him. "I'm coming for you, Sam. Keep calling." He didn't start the engine because it would drown out all sound. Instead he picked up the wooden paddle from the floor of the boat and started to row in the direction his instincts told him.

His muscles strained against the heavy, still water. He pushed the prow of the boat through the grasses thickening the dark, glistening surface as his whole being yearned and struggled toward Sam.

"Louis, I'm over here." At last her voice rose over the sound of raindrops. It was edged with desperation. He could hear her clear as a birdcall, about a hundred yards to his left.

In a split second he started the engine and chugged toward her. Moonlight picked out a slender female form, standing waist-high in tall grasses.

His heart leaped like a flying fish.

He cut the engine and paddled the last few yards, then reached out into the rain to grasp her hand in his. Powerful sensations surged through him as her fingers threaded through his, small and slippery with rain.

Her hair clung to her scalp and her flowered dress molded

to her slender body. A fierce wave of emotion crashed over him at the sight of her.

In a single, swift motion he seized her around the waist and tugged her into the boat, then found that he couldn't unlock his arms from around her, but kept clutching her closer and closer to his chest, although he had no idea why he was even here.

He didn't care why, as long as she *was* here.

Sobs racked her small frame. "Oh, Louis. I had to see you. I tried, I really did. I've been painting and everything, but nothing could stop me from…" Her voice rose to a high whine that cascaded into a shuddering sob.

"Shh." He put a finger to her quivering lips. "I've felt just the same. I can't get you out of my mind and it's driving me crazy." He pressed his cheek against her cool, wet one as feelings beyond words churned through him.

"Sorry."

Her wavering apology sent his chuckle rippling through both of them. "You should be. Driving us both half-mad when you knew all along that we're meant to be together."

Sam's eyes opened wide and stared into his. Rain and tears wet her lashes. "We are, aren't we? Meant to be together."

Fresh joy burst through him, so rich and sweet he couldn't help sassing her. "I could have told you that from day one. In fact, I think I did." He cocked his head. "But some people just won't listen to sense."

"And what you said, about having kids…" Her voice shook. "I might not be able to. I did try for three years with Larry and even though the tests didn't find anything, it's quite possible that—"

Louis crushed her to his chest. He couldn't stand to hear her doubt and fear, all of it so unnecessary.

"Then we'll adopt," he growled. "I'd love to welcome a child into our lives any way one is able to come. And you've already proved you can create a beautiful family from a group of confused and even angry strangers." He drew in a shuddering breath. "You're something else, Sam. You're really special and I'd be so honored and privileged to spend my life with you. Any child of yours will be the luckiest kid on earth."

Sam stared at him for a moment, water dripping from her nose and chin, then she let out a wail, something you might hear on an *I Love Lucy* episode when Ricky caught Lucy sneaking an expensive new hat into the house.

Louis burst into heartfelt laughter.

"But where will we live?" Panic flickered across her features. "You need to be in New Orleans, and to visit all your restaurants, but I need to be in New York most of the time to run the foundation. It isn't just a job I can pick up and leave. It's a huge responsibility that I take very seriously."

Louis struggled not to smile. She looked so very unprofessional with water soaking through her flowered dress and caressing the outlines of a flimsy-looking bra.

His voice emerged huskier than he intended. "We'll live like nomads, then."

"But what about the kids' schooling?" She swallowed. "I know it's a bit premature, but…"

"We'll homeschool them. My mom did that for me a lot of the time and I turned out okay. It'll be fun. They'll be at home wherever we go. Don't worry about trying to be 'normal' and to fit in with other people and their expectations. It's much more fun to just be *you*."

"You're right, of course." She inhaled and tucked a soggy strand of hair sheepishly behind her ears. "I've been painting."

"I know. Margo told me you're blowing people's minds

right, left and center. She thinks you're one of the major talents of the twenty-first century."

Sam blushed, even in the rain, and tried to wave her hand. "That ridiculous! They're just paintings. Representational. Totally unfashionable."

Louis just held her tighter, inhaling the rich, glorious scent of her and feeling for her warmth through her wet clothes. "Fashion means nothing when it comes to true beauty, Sam. That's what you have and what you create in the world around you. You've gotten lost a couple of times, and so have I…"

He drew in a breath as emotion threatened to choke him. "But I love you, Sam. And I know that as long as you and I stick together, we'll find our way somewhere wonderful."

Sam blinked at him, eyes glistening with hope and fear and so much more. "I love you, too, Louis. I tried not to, or at least not to love you in this way, but I couldn't help it."

She paused, and a smile flickered across her mouth. "And now I choose the road that leads into bed with you every night."

"We'd better make sure that bed has a roof over it, tonight." He looked up at the sky, dark with clouds spitting rain over the whole watery world. "I've got dry clothes at the cabin."

Mischief flickered in Sam's eyes. "I don't think we'll be needing those."

A jolt of lust shot straight to his groin. "I like the way you think."

He turned and tugged at the cord on the outboard motor and the engine grumbled to life. With one arm around Sam, Louis guided the boat through the familiar yet ever-changing waters.

To his favorite place, with his favorite person in the whole world.

* * * * *

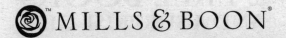

2 FREE BOOKS
AND A SURPRISE GIFT

We would like to take this opportunity to thank you for reading this Mills & Boon® book by offering you the chance to take TWO more specially selected books from the Desire™ 2-in-1 series absolutely FREE! We're also making this offer to introduce you to the benefits of the Mills & Boon® Book Club™—

- **FREE home delivery**
- **FREE gifts and competitions**
- **FREE monthly Newsletter**
- **Exclusive Mills & Boon Book Club offers**
- **Books available before they're in the shops**

Accepting these FREE books and gift places you under no obligation to buy, you may cancel at any time, even after receiving your free books. Simply complete your details below and return the entire page to the address below. You don't even need a stamp!

YES Please send me 2 free Desire stories in a 2-in-1 volume and a surprise gift. I understand that unless you hear from me, I will receive 2 superb new 2-in-1 books every month for just £5.25 each, postage and packing free. I am under no obligation to purchase any books and may cancel my subscription at any time. The free books and gift will be mine to keep in any case.

Ms/Mrs/Miss/Mr _____ Initials _____

Surname _____

Address _____

_____ Postcode _____

E-mail_____

Send this whole page to: Mills & Boon Book Club, Free Book Offer, FREEPOST NAT 10298, Richmond, TW9 1BR